I guess I should explain. I'm not exactly your typical sixteen-year-old girl.

Oh, I *seem* normal enough, I guess. I don't do drugs, or drink, or smoke—well, okay, except for that one time when my stepbrother caught me. I don't have anything pierced, except my ears, and only once on each earlobe. I don't have any tattoos. I've never dyed my hair. Except for my boots and leather jacket, I don't wear an excessive amount of black. I don't even wear dark fingernail polish. All in all, I am a pretty normal, everyday, American teenage girl.

Except, of course, for the fact that I can talk to the dead.

Books by
MEG CABOT

SAFE HOUSE

SANCTUARY

MISSING YOU

THE PRINCESS DIARIES

THE PRINCESS DIARIES, VOLUME II:
PRINCESS IN THE SPOTLIGHT

THE PRINCESS DIARIES, VOLUME III:
PRINCESS IN LOVE

THE PRINCESS DIARIES, VOLUME IV:
PRINCESS IN WAITING

VALENTINE PRINCESS: A PRINCESS DIARIES BOOK
(VOLUME IV AND A QUARTER)

THE PRINCESS DIARIES, VOLUME IV AND A HALF:
PROJECT PRINCESS

THE PRINCESS DIARIES, VOLUME V:
PRINCESS IN PINK

THE PRINCESS DIARIES, VOLUME VI:
PRINCESS IN TRAINING

THE PRINCESS PRESENT: A PRINCESS DIARIES BOOK
(VOLUME VI AND A HALF)

THE PRINCESS DIARIES, VOLUME VII:
PARTY PRINCESS

SWEET SIXTEEN PRINCESS: A PRINCESS DIARIES BOOK
(VOLUME VII AND A HALF)

THE PRINCESS DIARIES, VOLUME VIII:
PRINCESS ON THE BRINK

THE PRINCESS DIARIES, VOLUME IX:
PRINCESS MIA

THE PRINCESS DIARIES, VOLUME X:
FOREVER PRINCESS

Illustrated by Chesley McLaren:

PRINCESS LESSONS: A PRINCESS DIARIES BOOK

PERFECT PRINCESS: A PRINCESS DIARIES BOOK

HOLIDAY PRINCESS: A PRINCESS DIARIES BOOK

THE BOY NEXT DOOR

BOY MEETS GIRL

EVERY BOY'S GOT ONE

SIZE 12 IS NOT FAT

SIZE 14 IS NOT FAT EITHER

BIG BONED

QUEEN OF BABBLE

QUEEN OF BABBLE IN THE BIG CITY

QUEEN OF BABBLE GETS HITCHED

SHE WENT ALL THE WAY

RANSOM MY HEART

INSATIABLE

megcabot

the mediator

Shadowland · Ninth Key

HARPER TEEN
An Imprint of HarperCollinsPublishers

HarperTeen is an imprint of HarperCollins Publishers.

The Mediator: Volumes 1 and 2
Shadowland copyright © 2000 by Meggin Cabot
Originally published in 2000 by Simon Pulse,
an imprint of Simon & Schuster, Inc.
Ninth Key copyright © 2001 by Meggin Cabot
Originally published in 2001 by Pocket Books,
an imprint of Simon & Schuster, Inc.

Library of Congress catalog card number: 2010938213
ISBN 978-0-06-204020-6

11 12 13 14 15   CG/BV   10 9 8 7 6 5 4 3 2 1
❖
Revised paperback edition, 2011

CONTENTS

Shadowland

In memory of A. Victor Cabot,
and his brother, Jack "France" Cabot

CHAPTER 1

They told me there'd be palm trees.

I didn't believe them, but that's what they told me. They told me I'd be able to see them from the plane.

Oh, I know they have palm trees in southern California. I mean, I'm not a complete moron. I've watched *90210*, and everything. But I was moving to northern California. I didn't expect to see palm trees in northern California. Not after my mom told me not to give away all my sweaters.

"Oh, no," my mom had said. "You'll need them. Your coats, too. It can get cold there. Not as cold as New York, maybe, but pretty chilly."

Which was why I wore my black leather motorcycle jacket on the plane. I could have shipped it, I guess, with the rest of my stuff, but it kind of made me feel better to wear it.

So there I was, sitting on the plane in a black leather motorcycle jacket, seeing these palm trees through the window as we landed. And I thought, Great. Black leather and palm trees. Already I'm fitting in, just like I knew I would. . . .

. . . *Not.*

My mom isn't particularly fond of my leather jacket, but I swear I didn't wear it to make her mad, or anything. I'm not resentful of the fact that she decided to marry a guy who lives three thousand miles away, forcing me to leave school in the middle of my sophomore year; abandon the best—and pretty much only—friend I've had since kindergarten; leave the city I've been living in for all of my sixteen years.

Oh, no. I'm not a bit resentful.

The thing is, I really do like Andy, my new stepdad. He's good for my mom. He makes her happy. And he's very nice to me.

It's just this moving-to-California thing that bugs me.

Oh, and did I mention Andy's three other kids?

They were all there to greet me when I got off the plane. My mom, Andy, and Andy's three sons. Sleepy, Dopey, and Doc, I call them. They're my new step-brothers.

"Susie!" Even if I hadn't heard my mom squealing my name as I walked through the gate, I wouldn't have missed them—my new family. Andy was making his two youngest boys hold up this big sign that said WELCOME HOME, SUSANNAH! Everybody getting off my flight was walking by it, going, "Aw, look how cute," to their travel companions, and smiling at me in this sickening way.

Oh, yeah. I'm fitting in. I'm fitting in just great.

"Okay," I said, walking up to my new family fast. "You can put the sign down now."

But my mom was too busy hugging me to pay any attention. "Oh, Susie!" she kept saying. I hate when anybody but my mom calls me Susie, so I shot the boys this mean look over her shoulder, just in case they were getting any big ideas. They just kept grinning at me from over the stupid sign, Dopey because he's too dumb to know any better, Doc because—well, I guess because he might have been glad to see me. Doc's weird that way. Sleepy, the oldest, just stood there, looking . . . well, sleepy.

"How was your flight, kiddo?" Andy took my bag off my shoulder, and put it on his own. He seemed surprised by how heavy it was, and went, "Whoa, what've you got in here, anyway? You know it's a felony to smuggle New York City fire hydrants across state lines."

I smiled at him. Andy's this really big goof, but he's a nice big goof. He wouldn't have the slightest idea what constitutes a felony in the state of New York since he's only been there, like, five times. Which was, incidentally, exactly how many visits it took him to convince my mother to marry him.

"It's not a fire hydrant," I said. "It's a parking meter. And I have four more bags."

"Four?" Andy pretended he was shocked. "What do you think you're doing, moving in or something?"

Did I mention that Andy thinks he's a comedian? He's not. He's a carpenter.

"Suze," Doc said, all enthusiastically. "Suze, did you notice that as you were landing, the tail of the plane kicked up a little? That was from an updraft. It's caused when a mass moving at a considerable rate of speed encounters a counter-blowing wind velocity of equal or greater strength."

Doc, Andy's youngest kid, is twelve, but he's going on about forty. He spent almost the entire wedding reception telling me about alien cattle mutilation, and how Area 51 is just this big cover-up by the American government, which doesn't want us to know that We Are Not Alone.

"Oh, Susie," my mom kept saying. "I'm so glad you're here. You're just going to love the house. It just didn't feel like home at first, but now that you're here . . . Oh, and wait until you've seen your room. Andy's fixed it up so nice. . . ."

Andy and my mom spent weeks before they got married looking for a house big enough for all four kids to have their own rooms. They finally settled on this huge house in the hills of Carmel, which they'd only been able to afford because they'd bought it in this completely wretched state, and this construction company Andy does a lot of work for fixed it up at this big discount rate. My mom has been going on for days about my room, which she keeps swearing is the nicest one in the house.

"The view!" she kept saying. "An ocean view from the big bay window in your room! Oh, Suze, you're going to love it."

I was sure I was going to love it. About as much as I was going to love giving up bagels for alfalfa sprouts, and the subway for surfing, and all that sort of stuff.

For some reason, Dopey opened his mouth, and went, "Do you like the sign?" in that stupid voice of his. I can't believe he's my age. He's on the school wrestling team, though, so what can you expect? All he ever thinks about, from what I could tell when I had to sit next to him at the wedding reception—I had to sit between him and Doc, so you can imagine how the conversation just flowed—is choke holds and body-building protein shakes.

"Yeah, great sign," I said, yanking it out of his meaty hands, and holding it so that the lettering faced the floor. "Can we go? I wanna pick up my bags before someone else does."

"Oh, right," my mom said. She gave me one last hug.

"Oh, I'm just so glad to see you! You look so great. . . ." And then, even though you could tell she didn't want to say it, she went ahead and said it anyway, in a low voice, so no one else could hear: "Thought I've talked to you before about that jacket, Suze. And I thought you were throwing those jeans away."

I was wearing my oldest jeans, the ones with the holes in the knees. They went really well with my black silk T and my zip-up ankle boots. The jeans and boots, coupled with my black leather motorcycle jacket and my Army-Navy surplus shoulder bag, made me look like a teen runaway in a made-for-TV movie.

But hey, when you're flying for eight hours across the country, you want to be comfortable.

I said that, and my mom just rolled her eyes and dropped it. That's the good thing about my mom. She doesn't harp, like other moms do. Sleepy, Dopey, and Doc have no idea how lucky they are.

"All right," she said, instead. "Let's get your bags." Then, raising her voice, she called, "Jake, come on. We're going to get Suze's bags."

She had to call Sleepy by name, since he looked as if he had fallen asleep standing up. I asked my mother once if Jake, who is a senior in high school, has narcolepsy, or possibly a drug habit, and she was like, "No, why would you say that?" Like the guy doesn't just stand there blinking all the time, never saying a word to anyone.

Wait, that's not true. He did say something to me, once. Once he said, "Hey, are you in a gang?" He asked me that at the wedding, when he caught me standing outside with my leather jacket on over my maid of honor's dress, sneaking a cigarette.

Give me a break, all right? It was my first and only cigarette ever. I was under a lot of stress at the time. I was worried my mom was going to marry this guy and move to California and forget all about me. I swear I haven't smoked a single cigarette since.

And don't get me wrong about Jake. At six foot one, with the same shaggy blond hair and twinkly blue eyes as his dad, he's what my best friend Gina would call a hottie. But he's not the shiniest rock in the rock garden, if you know what I mean.

Doc was still going on about wind velocity. He was explaining the speed with which it is necessary to travel in order to break through the earth's gravitational force. This speed is called escape velocity. I decided Doc might be useful to have around, homework-wise, even if I am three grades ahead of him.

While Doc talked, I looked around. This was my first trip ever to California, and let me tell you, even though we were still only in the airport—and it was the San Jose International Airport—you could tell we weren't in New York anymore. I mean, first off, everything was clean. No dirt, no litter, no graffiti anywhere. The concourse was all done up in pastels, too, and you know how light colors show the dirt. Why do you think New Yorkers wear black all the time? Not to be cool. Nuh-uh. So we don't have to haul all our clothes down to the Laundromat every single time we wear them.

But that didn't appear to be a problem in sunny CA. From what I could tell, pastels were in. This one woman walked by us, and she had on pink leggings and a white Spandex sports bra. And that's all. If this is an example of what's *de rigueur* in California, I could tell I was in for some major culture shock.

And you know what else was strange? Nobody was fighting. There were passengers lined up here and there, but they weren't raising their voices at the people behind the ticket counter. In New York, if you're a customer, you fight with the people behind the counter, no matter where you are—airport, Bloomingdale's, hot dog stand. Wherever.

Not here. Everybody here was just way calm.

And I guess I could see why. I mean, it didn't look to me like there was anything to get upset about. Outside, the sun was beating down on those palm trees I'd seen from the sky. There were seagulls—not pigeons, but actual big white-and-gray seagulls—scratching around in the parking lot. And when we went to get my bags, nobody even checked to see if the stickers on them matched my ticket stubs. No, everybody was just like, "Buh-bye! Have a nice day!"

Unreal.

Gina—she was my best friend back in Brooklyn; well, okay, my *only* friend, really—told me before I left that I'd find there were advantages to having three stepbrothers. She should know since she's got four—not steps, but real brothers. Anyway, I didn't believe her any more than I'd believed people about the palm trees. But when Sleepy picked up two of my bags, and Dopey grabbed the other two, leaving me with exactly nothing to carry, since Andy had my shoulder bag, I finally realized what she was talking about: Brothers can be useful. They can carry really heavy stuff, and not even look like it's bothering them.

Hey, I packed those bags. I knew what was in them. They were not light. But Sleepy and Dopey were like, No problem here. Let's get moving.

My bags secure, we headed out into the parking lot. As the automatic doors opened, everyone—including my mom—reached into a pocket and pulled out a pair of sunglasses. Apparently, they all knew something I didn't know. And as I stepped outside, I realized what it was.

It's *sunny* here.

Not just sunny, either, but bright—so bright and colorful, it hurts your eyes. I had sunglasses, too, somewhere, but since it had been about forty degrees and sleeting when I left New York, I hadn't thought to put them anywhere easily accessible. When my mother had first told me we'd be moving—she and Andy decided it was easier for her, with one kid and a job as a TV news reporter, to relocate than it would be for Andy and his three kids to do it, especially considering that Andy owns his own business—she'd explained to me that I'd love northern California. "It's where they filmed all those Goldie Hawn, Chevy Chase movies!" she told me.

I like Goldie Hawn, and I like Chevy Chase, but I never knew they made a movie together.

"It's where all those Steinbeck stories you had to read in school took place," she said. "You know, *The Red Pony.*"

Well, I wasn't very impressed. I mean, all I remembered from *The Red Pony* was that there weren't any girls in it, although there were a lot of hills. And as I stood in the parking lot, squinting at the hills surrounding the San Jose International Airport, I saw that there were a lot of hills, and the grass on them was dry and brown.

But dotting the hills were these trees, trees not like any I'd ever seen before. They were squashed on top as if a giant fist had come down from the sky and given them a thump. I found out later these were called cypress trees.

And all around the parking lot, where there was evidently a watering system, there were these fat bushes with these giant red flowers on them, mostly squatting down at the bottom of these impossibly tall, surprisingly thick palm trees. The flowers, I found out, when I looked them up later, were hibiscus. And the strange-looking bugs that I saw hovering around them, making a *brrr*-ing noise, weren't bugs at all. They were hummingbirds.

"Oh," my mom said when I pointed this out. "They're everywhere. We have feeders for them up at the house. You can hang one from your window if you want."

Hummingbirds that come right up to your window? The only birds that ever came up to my window back in Brooklyn were pigeons. My mom never exactly encouraged me to feed them.

My moment of joy about the hummingbirds was shattered when Dopey announced suddenly, "I'll drive," and started for the driver's seat of this huge utility vehicle we were approaching.

"*I* will drive," Andy said firmly.

"Aw, Dad," Dopey said. "How'm I ever going to pass the test if you never let me practice?"

"You can practice in the Rambler," Andy said. He opened up the back of his Land Rover, and started putting my bags into it. "That goes for you, too, Suze."

This startled me. "What goes for me, too?"

"You can practice driving in the Rambler." He wagged a finger jokingly in my direction. "But only if there's someone with a valid license in the passenger seat."

I just blinked up at him. "I can't drive," I said.

Dopey let out this big horse laugh. "You can't drive?" He elbowed Sleepy, who was leaning against the side of the truck, his face turned toward the sun. "Hey, Jake, she can't drive!"

"It isn't at all uncommon, Brad," Doc said, "for a native New Yorker to lack a driver's license. Don't you know that New York City boasts the largest mass transit system in North America, serving a population of thirteen point two million people in a four-thousand-square-mile radius fanning out from New York City through Long Island all the way to Connecticut? And that one point seven billion riders take advantage of their extensive fleet of subways, buses, and railroads every year?"

Everybody looked at Doc. Then my mother said carefully, "I never kept a car in the city."

Andy closed the doors to the back of the Land Rover. "Don't worry, Suze," he said. "We'll get you enrolled in a driver's ed course right away. You can take it and catch up to Brad in no time."

I looked at Dopey. Never in a million years had I ever expected that someone would suggest that I needed to catch up to *Brad* in any capacity whatsoever.

But I could see I was in for a lot of surprises. The palm trees had only been the beginning. As we drove to the house, which was a good hour away from the airport—and not a quick hour, either, with me wedged in between Sleepy and Dopey, with Doc in the "way back," perched on top of my luggage, still expounding on the glories of the New York City transportation authority—I began to realize that things were going to be different—very, very different—than I had anticipated, and certainly different from what I was used to.

And not just because I was living on the opposite side of the continent. Not just because everywhere I looked, I saw things I'd never have seen back in New York: roadside stands advertising artichokes or pomegranates, twelve for a dollar; field after field of grapevines, twisting and twisting around wooden arbors; groves of lemon and avocado trees; lush green vegetation I couldn't even identify. And arcing above it all, a sky so blue, so vast, that the hot-air balloon I saw floating through it looked impossibly small—like a button at the bottom of an Olympic-sized swimming pool.

There was the ocean, too, bursting so suddenly into view that at first I didn't recognize it, thinking it was just another field. But then I noticed that this field was sparkling, reflecting the sun, flashing little Morse code SOSs at me. The light was so bright, it was hard to look at without sunglasses. But there it was, the Pacific Ocean . . . huge, stretching almost as wide as the sky, a living, writhing thing, pushing up against a comma-shaped strip of white beach.

Being from New York, my glimpses of ocean—at

least the kind with a beach—had been few and far between. I couldn't help gasping when I saw it. And when I gasped, everybody stopped talking—except for Sleepy, who was, of course, asleep.

"What?" my mother asked, alarmed. "What is it?"

"Nothing," I said. I was embarrassed. Obviously, these people were used to seeing the ocean. They were going to think I was some kind of freak that I was getting so excited about it. "Just the ocean."

"Oh," said my mother. "Yes, isn't it beautiful?"

Dopey went, "Good curl on those waves. Might have to hit the beach before dinner."

"Not," his father said, "until you've finished that term paper."

"Aw, Dad!"

This prompted my mother to launch into a long and detailed account of the school to which I was being sent, the same one Sleepy, Dopey, and Doc attended. The school, named after Junipero Serra, some Spanish guy who came over in the 1700s and forced the Native Americans already living here to practice Christianity instead of their own religion, was actually a huge adobe mission that attracted twenty thousand tourists a year, or something.

I wasn't really listening to my mother. My interest in school has always been pretty much zero. The whole reason I hadn't been able to move out here before Christmas was that there had been no space for me at the Mission School, and I'd been forced to wait until second semester started before something opened up. I hadn't minded—I'd gotten to live with my grandmother for a few months, which hadn't been at all bad. My grandmother, besides being a really excellent criminal attorney, is an awesome cook.

I was still sort of distracted by the ocean, which had disappeared behind some hills. I was craning my neck, hoping for another glimpse, when it hit me. I went, "Wait a minute. When was this school built?"

"The eighteenth century," Doc replied. "The mission system, implemented by the Franciscans under the guidelines of the Catholic Church and the Spanish government, was set up not only to Christianize the Native Americans, but also to train them to become successful tradespeople in the new Spanish society. Originally, the mission served as a—"

"Eighteenth century?" I said, leaning forward. I was wedged between Sleepy—whose head had slumped forward until it was resting on my shoulder, enabling me to tell, just by sniffing, that he used Finesse shampoo—and Dopey. Let me tell you, Gina hadn't mentioned a thing about how much room boys take up, which, when they're both nearly six feet tall, and in the two-hundred-pound vicinity, is a lot. "Eighteenth century?"

My mother must have heard the panic in my voice, since she turned in her seat and said soothingly, "Now,

Suze, we discussed this. I told you there's a year's waiting list at Robert Louis Stevenson, and you told me you didn't want to go to an all-girls school, so Sacred Heart is out, and Andy's heard some awful stories about drug abuse and gang violence in the public schools around here—"

"Eighteenth century?" I could feel my heart starting to pound hard, as if I'd been running. "That's like *three hundred years old!*"

"I don't get it." We were driving through the town of Carmel-by-the-Sea now, all picturesque cottages—some with thatched roofs, even—and beautiful little restaurants and art galleries. Andy had to drive carefully because the traffic was thick with people in cars with out-of-state licenses, and there weren't any stoplights, something that, for some reason, the natives took pride in. "What's so bad," he wanted to know, "about the eighteenth century?"

My mother said, without any inflection in her voice whatsoever—what I call her bad-news voice, the one she uses on TV to report plane crashes and child murders, "Suze has never been very wild about old buildings."

"Oh," Andy said. "Then I guess she isn't going to like the house."

I gripped the back of his headrest. "Why?" I demanded in a tight voice. "Why am I not going to like the house?"

I saw why, of course, as soon as we pulled in. The house was huge, and impossibly pretty, with Victorian-style turrets and a widow's walk—the whole works. My mom had had it painted blue and white and cream, and it was surrounded by big, shady pine trees, and sprawling, flowering shrubs. Three stories high, constructed entirely from wood, and not the horrible glass-and-steel or terra-cotta stuff the houses around it were made of, it was the loveliest, most tasteful house in the neighborhood.

And I didn't want to set foot in it.

I knew when I'd agreed to move with my mom to California that I'd be in for lots of changes. The roadside artichokes, the lemon groves, the ocean . . . they were nothing, really. The fact was, the biggest change was going to be sharing my mom with other people. In the decade since my father had died, it had been just the two of us. And I have to admit, I sort of liked it like that. In fact, if it hadn't been for the fact that Andy made my mom so obviously happy, I would have put my foot down and said no way to the whole moving thing.

But you couldn't even look at them together—Andy and my mom—and not be able to tell right away that they were completely gaga over each other. And what kind of daughter would I have been if I said no way to that? So I accepted Andy, and I accepted his three sons, and I accepted the fact that I was going to have to leave behind everything I had ever known and loved—my best friend, my grandmother, bagels, SoHo—in order to give my mom the happiness she deserved.

But I hadn't really considered the fact that, for the first time in my life, I was going to have to live in a *house*.

And not just any house, either, but, as Andy proudly told me as he was taking my bags from the car, and thrusting them into his sons' arms, a *nineteenth-century* converted boardinghouse. Built in 1849, it had apparently had quite a little reputation in its day. Gunfights over card games and women had taken place in the front parlor. You could still see the bullet holes. In fact, Andy had framed one rather than filling it in. It was a bit morbid, he admitted, but interesting, too. He bet we were living in the only house in the Carmel hills that had a nineteenth-century bullet hole in it.

"Huh," I said. I bet that was true.

My mother kept glancing in my direction as we climbed the many steps to the front porch. I knew she was nervous about what I was going to think. I was kind of irked at her, really, for not warning me. I guess I could understand why she hadn't, though. If she'd told me she had bought a house that was more than a hundred years old, I wouldn't have moved out here. I would have stayed with Grandma until it came time for me to leave for college.

Because my mom's right: I don't like old buildings.

Although I saw, as old buildings went, this one was really something. When you stood on the front porch, you could see all of Carmel beneath you, the village, the valley, the beach, the sea. It was a breathtaking view, one that people would—and had, judging from the fanciness of the houses around ours—pay millions for; one that I shouldn't have resented, not in the least.

And yet, when my mom said, "Come on, Suze. Come see your room," I couldn't help shuddering a little.

The house was as beautiful inside as it was outside. All shiny maple and cheerful blues and yellows. I recognized my mom's things, and that made me feel a little better. There was the pie-safe she and I had bought once on a weekend trip to Vermont. There were my baby pictures, hanging on the wall in the living room, right alongside Sleepy's, Dopey's, and Doc's. There were my mother's books in the built-in shelves in the den. Her plants, which she'd paid so exorbitant a price to have shipped because she'd been unable to bear parting with them, were everywhere, on wooden stands, hanging in front of the stained-glass windows, perched on top of the newel post at the end of the stairs.

But there were also things I didn't recognize: a sleek white computer sitting on the desk where my mother used to write out checks to pay the bills; a wide-screen

TV incongruously tucked into a fireplace in the den, to which shift-sticks were wired for some sort of video game; surfboards leaning up against the wall by the door to the garage; a huge, slobbery dog, who seemed to think I was harboring food in my pockets since he kept thrusting his big wet nose into them.

These all seemed like obtrusively masculine things, foreign things in the life my mother and I had carved out for ourselves. They were going to take some getting used to.

My room was upstairs, just above the roof of the front porch. My mother had been going on nervously for almost the entire trip from the airport about the window seat Andy had installed in the bay window. The bay windows looked out over the same view as the porch, that sweeping vista that incorporated all of the peninsula. It was sweet of them, really, to give me such a nice room, the room with the best view in the whole house.

And when I saw how much trouble they'd gone to, to make the room feel like home to me—or at least to some excessively feminine, phantom girl . . . not *me*. *I* had never been the glass-topped dressing table, princess phone type—how Andy had put cream-colored wallpaper, dotted with blue forget-me-nots, all along the top of the intricate white wainscoting that lined the walls; how the same wallpaper covered the walls of my own personal adjoining bathroom; how they'd bought me a new bed—a four-poster with a lace canopy, the kind my mother had always wanted for me and had evidently been unable to resist—I felt bad about how I'd acted in the car. I really did. I thought to myself as I walked around the room, *Okay, this isn't so bad. So far you're in the clear. Maybe it'll be all right, maybe no one was ever unhappy in this house, maybe all those people who got shot deserved it.* . . .

Until I turned toward the bay window, and saw that someone was already sitting on the window seat Andy had so lovingly made for me.

Someone who was not related to me, or to Sleepy, Dopey, or Doc.

I turned toward Andy, to see if he'd noticed the intruder. He hadn't, even though he was right there, right in front of his face.

My mother hadn't seen him, either. All she saw was my face. I guess my expression must not have been the most pleasant, since her own fell, and she said with a sad sigh, "Oh, Suze. Not again."

CHAPTER 2

I guess I should explain. I'm not exactly your typical sixteen-year-old girl.

Oh, I *seem* normal enough, I guess. I don't do drugs, or drink, or smoke—well, okay, except for that one time when Sleepy caught me. I don't have anything pierced, except my ears, and only once on each earlobe. I don't have any tattoos. I've never dyed my hair. Except for my boots and leather jacket, I don't wear an excessive amount of black. I don't even wear dark fingernail polish. All in all, I am a pretty normal, everyday, American teenage girl.

Except, of course, for the fact that I can talk to the dead.

I probably shouldn't put it that way. I should probably say that the dead talk to me. I mean, I don't go around initiating these conversations. In fact, I try to avoid the whole thing as much as possible.

It's just that sometimes they won't let me.

The ghosts, I mean.

I don't think I'm crazy. At least, not any crazier than your average sixteen-year-old. I guess I might *seem* crazy to some people. Certainly the majority of kids in my old neighborhood thought I was. Nuts, I mean. I've had the school counselors sicced on me more than once. Sometimes I even think it might be simpler just to *let* them lock me up.

But even on the ninth floor of Bellevue—which is where they lock up the crazy people in New York—I probably wouldn't be safe from the ghosts. They'd find me.

They always do.

I remember my first. I remember it as clearly as any of my other memories of that time, which is to say, not very well, since I was about two years old. I guess I remember it about as well as I remember taking a mouse away from our cat and cradling it in my arms until my horrified mother took it away.

Hey, I was two, okay? I didn't know then that mice were something to be afraid of. Ghosts, either, for that matter. That's why, fourteen years later, neither of them frighten me. Startle me, maybe, sometimes. Annoy me, a lot. But frighten me?

Never.

The ghost, like the mouse, was little, gray, and help-less. To this day, I don't know who she was. I spoke to her, some baby gibberish that she didn't understand. Ghosts can't understand two-year-olds any better than anybody else. She just looked at me sadly from the top of the stairs of our apartment building. I guess I felt sorry for her, the way I had for the mouse, and wanted to help her. Only I didn't know how. So I did what any uncertain two-year-old would do. I ran for my mother.

That was when I learned my first lesson concern-ing ghosts: only I can see them.

Well, obviously, other people *can* see them. How else would we have haunted houses and ghost stories and *Unsolved Mysteries* and all of that? But there's a difference. Most people who see ghosts only see *one*. I see *all* ghosts.

All of them. Anybody. Anybody who has died and for whatever reason is hanging around on Earth instead of going wherever it is he or she is supposed to go, I can see.

And let me tell you, that is *a lot* of ghosts.

I found out the same day that I saw my first ghost that most people—even my own mother—can't see them at all. Neither can anyone else I have ever met. At least, no one who'll admit it.

Which brings us to the second thing I learned about ghosts that day fourteen years ago: It's really better, in the long run, not to mention that you've seen one. Or, as in my case, any.

I'm not saying my mother figured out that it was a ghost I was pointing to and gibbering about that afternoon when I was two. I doubt she knew it. She probably thought I was trying to tell her something about the mouse, which she had confiscated from me earlier that morning. But she looked gamely up the stairs and nodded and said, "Uh-huh. Listen, Suze. What do you want for lunch today? Grilled cheese? Or tuna fish?"

I hadn't exactly expected a reaction similar to the one the mouse had gotten—my mother, who'd been cradling a neighbor's newborn at the time, had let out a glorious shriek at the sight of the mouse in my arms, and had screamed even harder at my proud announcement, "Look, Mommy. Now I've got a baby, too," which I realize now she couldn't have understood, since she didn't get it about the ghost.

But I had expected at least an *acknowledgment* of the thing floating at the top of the stairs. I was given explanations for virtually everything else I encountered on a daily basis, from fire hydrants to electrical outlets. Why not the thing at the top of the stairs?

But as I sat munching my grilled cheese a little later, I realized that the reason my mother had offered no explanation for the gray thing was that she hadn't been able to see it. To her, it wasn't there.

At two years old, this didn't seem unreasonable to me. It just seemed, at the time, like another thing that separated children from adults: Children had to eat all their vegetables. Adults did not. Children could ride the merry-go-round in the park. Adults could not. Children could see the gray things. Adults could not.

And even though I was only two years old, I understood that the little gray thing at the top of the stairs was not something to be discussed. Not with anybody. Not ever.

And I never did. I never told anyone about my first ghost, nor did I ever discuss with anyone the hundreds of other ghosts I encountered over the course of the next few years. What was there to discuss, really? I saw them. They spoke to me. For the most part, I didn't understand what they were saying, what they wanted, and they usually went away. End of story.

It probably would have gone on like that indefinitely if my father hadn't suddenly up and died.

Really. Just like that. One minute he was there, cooking and making jokes in the kitchen like he'd always done, and the next day he was gone.

And, people kept assuring me all through the week following his death—which I spent on the stoop in front of our building, waiting for my dad to come home—he was never coming back.

I, of course, didn't believe their assurances. Why should I? My dad, not coming back? Were they nuts?

Sure, he might have been dead. I got that part. But he was definitely coming back. Who was going to help me with my math homework? Who was going to wake up early with me on Saturday mornings, and make French toast and watch cartoons? Who was going to teach me to drive, like he'd promised, when I turned sixteen? My dad might have been dead, but I was definitely going to see him again. I saw lots of dead people on a daily basis. Why shouldn't I see my dad?

It turned out I was right. Oh, my dad was dead. No doubt about that. He'd died of a massive coronary. My mom had his body cremated, and she put his ashes in an antique German beer tankard. You know, that kind with a lid. My dad had always really liked beer. She put the tankard on a shelf, high up, where the cat couldn't knock it over, and sometimes, when she didn't think I was around, I caught her talking to it.

This made me feel really sad. I mean, I guess I couldn't blame her, really. If I didn't know any better, I'd probably have talked to that tankard, too.

But that, you see, was what all those people on my block had been wrong about. My dad was dead, yeah. But I *did* see him again.

In fact, I probably see him more now than I did when he was alive. When he was alive, he had to go to work most days. Now that he's dead, he doesn't have all that much to do. So I see him a lot. Almost too much, in fact. His favorite thing to do is suddenly materialize when I least expect it. It's kind of annoying.

My dad was the one who finally explained it to me. So I guess, in a way, it's a good thing he did die, since I might never have known, otherwise.

Actually, that isn't true. There was a tarot card reader who said something about it once. It was at a school carnival. I only went because Gina didn't want to go alone. I pretty much thought it was a crock, but I went along because that's what best friends do for one another. The woman—Madame Zara, Psychic Medium—read Gina's cards, telling her exactly what she wanted to hear: Oh, you're going to be very successful, you'll be a brain surgeon, you'll marry at thirty, and have three kids, blah, blah, blah. When she was done, I got up to go, but Gina insisted Madame Zara do a reading for me, too.

You can guess what happened. Madame Zara read the cards once, looked confused, and shuffled them up and read them again. Then she looked at me.

"You," she said, "talk to the dead."

This excited Gina. She went, "Oh my God! Oh my God! Really? Suze, did you hear that? You can talk to the dead! You're a psychic medium, too!"

"Not a medium," Madame Zara said. "A *mediator.*"

Gina looked crushed. "A what? What's *that*?"

But I knew. I'd never known what it was called, but I knew what it was. My dad hadn't put it quite that way when he'd explained things, but I got the gist of it, anyway: I am pretty much the contact person for just about anybody who croaks leaving things . . . well, untidy. Then, if I can, I clean up the mess.

That's the only way I can think to explain it. I don't know how I got so lucky—I mean, I am normal in every other respect. Well, almost, anyway. I just have this unfortunate ability to communicate with the dead.

Not *any* dead, either. Only the unhappy dead.

So you can see that my life has really been just a bowl of cherries these past sixteen years.

Imagine, being haunted—literally haunted—by the dead, every single minute of every single day of your life. It is not pleasant. You go down to the deli to get a soda—oops, dead guy on the corner. Somebody shot him. And if you could just make sure the cops get the guy who did it, he can finally rest in peace.

And all you wanted was a soda.

Or you go to the library to check out a book—oops, the ghost of some librarian comes up to you and wants you to tell her nephew how mad she is about what he did with her cats after she kicked the bucket.

And those are just the folks who *know* why they're still sticking around. Half of them don't have any idea why they haven't slipped off into the afterlife like they're supposed to.

Which is irritating because, of course, I'm the schmuck who's supposed to help them get there.

I'm the mediator.

I tell you, it is not a fate I would wish on anybody.

There isn't a whole lot of payoff in the mediation field. It isn't like anyone's ever offered me a salary or anything. Not even *hourly* compensation. Just the occasional warm fuzzies you get when you do a good turn for somebody. Like telling some girl who didn't get to say good-bye to her grandfather before he passed away that he really loves her, and he forgives her for that time she trashed his El Dorado. That kind of thing can warm the heart, it really can.

But for the most part, it's cold pricklies all the way. Besides the hassle—constantly being pestered by folks nobody but you can see—there's the fact that a lot of ghosts are really rude. I mean it. They are royal pains to deal with. These are generally the ones who actually *want* to hang around in this world instead of taking off for the next one. They probably know that based on their behavior in their most recent life, they aren't in for much of a treat in the one they've got coming up. So they just stay here and bug people, slamming doors, knocking over things, making cold spots, groaning. You know what I mean. Your basic poltergeists.

Sometimes, though, they can get rough. I mean, they try to hurt people. On *purpose*. That's when I usually get mad. That's when I usually feel compelled to kick a little ghost butt.

Which was what my mom meant when she said, "Oh, Suze. Not again." When I kick ghost butt, things have a tendency to get a little . . . messy.

Not that I had any intention of messing up my new room. Which is why I turned my back on the ghost sitting on my window seat and said, "Never mind, Mom. Everything's fine. The room is great. Thanks so much."

I could tell she didn't believe me. It's hard to fake out my mom. I know she suspects there's something up with me. She just can't figure out what it is. Which is probably a good thing because it would shake up the world as she knows it in too major a way. I mean, she's a television news reporter. She only believes what she can see. And she can't see ghosts.

I can't tell you how much I wish I could be like her.

"Well," she said, "I'm glad you like it. I was sort of worried. I mean, I know how you get about . . . well, old places."

Old places are the worst for me because the older a building is, the more chance there is that someone has died in it, and that he or she is still hanging around there looking for justice or waiting to deliver some final message to someone. Let me tell you, this led to some pretty interesting results back when my mom and I used to go apartment hunting in the city. We would walk into these seemingly perfect apartments, and I'd be like, "Nuh-uh. No way," for no reason that I could actually explain. It's really a wonder my mom never just packed me off to boarding school.

"Really, Mom," I said. "It's great. I love it."

Andy, hearing this, hustled around the room all excitedly, showing me the clap-on, clap-off lights (oh, boy) and various other gadgets he'd installed. I followed him around, expressing my delight, being careful not to look in the ghost's direction. It really was sweet, how much Andy wanted me to be happy. And I was determined, because he wanted it so much, to *be* happy. At least as happy as it's possible for someone like me to be.

After a while, Andy ran out of stuff to show me, and went away to start the barbecue, since in honor of my arrival, we were having surf and turf for dinner. Sleepy and Dopey took off to "hit some waves" before we ate, and Doc, muttering mysteriously about an "experiment" he'd been working on, drifted off to another part of the house, leaving me alone with my mother . . . well, sort of.

"Is it *really* all right, Suze?" my mom wanted to know. "I know it's a big change. I know it's asking a lot of you—"

I took off my leather jacket. I don't know if I've mentioned this, but it was pretty hot out for January. Like seventy. I'd nearly roasted in the car. "It's fine, Mom," I said. "Really."

"I mean, asking you to leave Grandma, and Gina, and New York. It's selfish of me, I know. I know things haven't been . . . well, easy for you. Especially since Daddy died."

My mother likes to think that the reason I'm not like the traditional teenage girl she was when she was my age—she was a cheerleader, and homecoming queen, and had lots of boyfriends and stuff—is that I lost my father at such an early age. She blames his death for everything, from the fact that I have no friends—with the exception of Gina—to the fact that I sometimes engage in extremely weird behavior.

And I suppose some of the stuff I've done in the past would seem pretty weird to someone who didn't know why I was doing it, or couldn't see who I was doing it for. I have certainly been caught any number of times in places I wasn't supposed to be. I've been brought home by the police a few times, accused of trespassing or vandalism or breaking and entering.

And while I've never actually been convicted of anything, I've spent any number of hours in my mother's therapist's office, being assured that this tendency I have to talk to myself is perfectly normal, but that my propensity to talk to people *who aren't there* probably isn't.

Ditto my dislike of any building not constructed in the past five years.

Ditto the amount of time I spend in graveyards, churches, temples, mosques, other people's (locked) apartments or houses, and school grounds after hours.

I suppose Andy's boys must have overheard something about this, and that's where the whole gang thing came from. But like I said, I've never actually served time for anything I've done.

And that two-week suspension in the eighth grade isn't even reflected on my permanent record.

So maybe it wasn't so unusual for my mother to be sitting there on my bed, talking about "fresh starts" and all of that. It was kind of weird that she was doing it while this ghost was sitting a few feet away, watching us. But whatever. She seemed to have a need to talk about how things were going to be much better for me out here on the West Coast.

And if that's what she wanted, I was going to do my best to make sure she got it. I had already resolved not to do anything out here that was going to end up getting me arrested, so that was a start, anyway.

"Well," my mom said, running out of steam after her you-won't-make-friends-unless-you-project-a-friendly-demeanor speech. "I guess if you don't want help unpacking, I'll go see how Andy is doing with dinner."

Andy, in addition to being able to build just about anything, was also an excellent cook, something my mother most definitely was not.

I said, "Yeah, Mom, you go do that. I'll just get settled in here, and I'll be down in a minute."

My mom nodded and got up—but she wasn't about to let me escape that easily. Just as she was about to go out the door, she turned around and said, her blue eyes all filled with tears, "I just want you to be happy,

Susie. That's all I've ever wanted. Do you think you can be happy here?"

I gave her a hug. I'm as tall as she is, in my ankle boots. "Sure, Mom," I said. "Sure, I'll be happy here. I feel at home already."

"Really?" My mom was sniffling. "You swear?"

"I do." And I wasn't lying, either. I mean, there'd been ghosts in my bedroom back in Brooklyn all the time, too.

She went away, and I shut the door quietly behind her. I waited until I couldn't hear her heels on the stairs anymore, and then I turned around.

"All right," I said, to the presence on the window seat. "Who the hell are you?"

CHAPTER 3

To say that the guy looked *surprised* to be addressed in this manner would have been a massive understatement. He didn't just look surprised. He actually looked over his shoulder, to see if it was really him I was talking to.

But of course, the only thing behind him was the window, and through it, that incredible view of Carmel Bay. So then he turned back to look at me, and must have seen that my gaze was fastened directly on his face, since he breathed, *"Nombre de Dios,"* in a manner that would have had Gina, who has a thing for Latino guys, swooning.

"It's no use calling on your higher power," I informed him, as I swung the pink-tasseled chair to my new dressing table around, and straddled it. "In case you haven't noticed, He isn't paying a whole lot of attention to you. Otherwise, He wouldn't have left you here to fester for—" I took in his outfit, which looked a lot like something they'd have worn on *The Wild, Wild West*. "What is it, a hundred and fifty years? Has it really been that long since you croaked?"

He stared at me with eyes that were as black and liquid as ink. "What is . . . croaked?" he asked, in a voice that sounded rusty from disuse.

I rolled my eyes. "Kicked the bucket," I translated. "Checked out. Popped off. Bit the dust." When I saw from his perplexed expression that he still didn't understand, I said, with some exasperation, *"Died."*

"Oh," he said. "Died." But instead of answering my question, he shook his head. "I don't understand," he said, in tones of wonder. "I don't understand how it is that you can see me. All these years, no one has ever—"

"Yeah," I said, cutting him off. I hear this kind of thing a lot, you understand. "Well, listen, the times, you know, they are a-changin'. So what's your glitch?"

He blinked at me with those big dark eyes. His eyelashes were longer than mine. It isn't often I run into a ghost who also happens to be a hottie, but this guy . . . boy, he must have been something back when he was alive because here he was dead and I was already trying to catch a peek at what was going on beneath the white shirt he was wearing very much open at the throat, exposing quite a bit of his chest, and some of his stomach, too. Do ghosts have six-packs? This was not something I had ever had occasion—or a desire—to explore before.

Not that I was about to let myself get distracted by that kind of thing now. I'm a professional, after all.

"Glitch?" he echoed. Even his voice was liquid, his English as flat and unaccented as I fancied my own was, slight Brooklyn blurring of my t's aside. He clearly had some Spaniard in him, as his *Dios* and his coloring indicated, but he was as American as I was—or as American as someone who was born before California became a state *could* be.

"Yeah." I cleared my throat. He had turned a little and put a boot up onto the pale blue cushion that covered the window seat, and I had seen definitive proof that yes, ghosts could indeed have six-packs. His abdominal muscles were deeply ridged, and covered with a light dusting of silky black hair.

I swallowed. Hard.

"Glitch," I said. "Problem. Why are you still here?" He looked at me, his expression blank, but interested. I elaborated. *"Why haven't you gone to the other side?"*

He shook his head. Have I mentioned that his hair was short and dark and sort of crisp-looking, like if you touched it, it would be really, really thick? "I don't know what you mean."

I was getting sort of warm, but I had already taken

off my leather jacket, so I didn't know what to do about it. I couldn't very well take off anything else with him sitting there watching me. This realization might have contributed to my suddenly very foul mood.

"What do you mean, you don't know what I mean?" I snapped, pushing some hair away from my eyes. "You're *dead*. You don't belong here. You're supposed to be off doing whatever it is that happens to people after they're dead. Rejoicing in heaven, or burning in hell, or being reincarnated, or ascending another plane of consciousness, or whatever. You're not supposed to be just . . . well, just *hanging around*."

He looked at me thoughtfully, balancing his elbow on his uplifted knee, his arm sort of dangling. "And what if I happen to like just *hanging around*?" he wanted to know.

I wasn't sure, but I had a feeling he was making fun of me. And I don't like being made fun of. I really don't. People back in Brooklyn used to do it all the time—well, until I learned how effectively a fist connecting with their nose could shut them up.

I wasn't ready to hit this guy—not yet. But I was close. I mean, I'd just traveled a gazillion miles for what seemed like days in order to live with a bunch of stupid boys; I still had to unpack; I had already practically made my mother cry; and then I find a ghost in my bedroom. Can you blame me for being . . . well, short with him?

"Look," I said, standing up fast, and swinging my leg around the back of the chair. "You can do all the hanging around you want, *amigo*. Slack away. I don't really care. But you can't do it here."

"Jesse," he said, not moving.

"What?"

"You called me *amigo*. I thought you might like to know I have a name. It's Jesse."

I nodded. "Right. That figures. Well, fine. Jesse, then. You can't stay here, Jesse."

"And you?" Jesse was smiling at me now. He had a nice face. A good face. The kind of face that, back in my old high school, would have gotten him elected prom king in no time flat. The kind of face Gina would have cut out of a magazine and taped to her bedroom wall.

Not that he was pretty. Not at all. Dangerous was how he looked. Mighty dangerous.

"And me, what?" I knew I was being rude. I didn't care.

"What is your name?"

I glared at him. "Look. Just tell me what you want, and get out. I'm hot, and I want to change clothes. I don't have time for—"

He interrupted, as amiably as if he hadn't heard me talking at all, "That woman—your mother—called you Susie." His black eyes were bright on me. "Short for Susan?"

"Susannah," I said, correcting him automatically. "As in, 'Don't you cry for me.'"

He smiled. "I know the song."

"Yeah. It was probably in the top forty the year you were born, huh?"

He just kept on smiling. "So this is your room now, is it, Susannah?"

"Yeah," I said. "Yeah, this is my room now. So you're going to have clear out."

"*I'm* going to have to clear out?" He raised one black eyebrow. "This has been my home for a century and a half. Why do *I* have to leave it?"

"Because." I was getting really mad. Mostly because I was so hot, and I wanted to open a window, but the windows were behind him, and I didn't want to get that close to him. "This is *my* room. I'm not sharing it with some dead cowboy."

That got to him. He slammed his foot back down on the floor—hard—and stood up. I instantly wished I hadn't said anything. He was tall, way taller than me, and in my ankle boots I'm five eight.

"I am *not* a cowboy," he informed me angrily. He added something in Spanish in an undertone, but since I had always taken French, I had no idea what he was saying. At the same time, the antique mirror hanging over my new dressing table started to wobble dangerously on the hook that held it to the wall. This was not due, I knew, to a California earthquake, but to the agitation of the ghost in front of me, whose psychic abilities were obviously of a kinetic bent.

That's the thing about ghosts: They're so touchy! The slightest thing can set them off.

"Whoa," I said, holding up both my hands, palms outward. "Down. Down, boy."

"My family," Jesse raged, wagging a finger in my face, "worked like slaves to make something of themselves in this country, but never, never as a *vaquero*—"

"Hey," I said. And that's when I made my big mistake. I reached out, not liking the finger he was jabbing at me, and grabbed it, hard, yanking on his hand and pulling him toward me so I could be sure he heard me as I hissed, "Stop with the mirror already. And stop shoving your finger in my face. Do it again, and I'll break it."

I flung his hand away, and saw, with satisfaction, that the mirror had stopped shaking. But then I happened to glance at his face.

Ghosts don't have blood. How can they? They aren't alive. But I swear, at that moment, all the color drained from Jesse's face, as if every ounce of blood that had once been there had evaporated just at that moment.

Not being alive, and not possessing blood, it follows that ghosts aren't made of matter, either. So it didn't make sense that I had been able to grab his finger. My hand should have passed right through him. Right?

Wrong. That's how it works for most people. But not for people like me. Not for the mediators. We can see ghosts, we can talk to ghosts, and, if necessary, we can kick a ghost's butt.

But this isn't something I like to go around advertising. I try to avoid touching them—touching anybody, really—as much as possible. If all attempts at mediation have failed, and I have to use a little physical coercion on a recalcitrant spirit, I generally prefer him or her not to know beforehand that I am capable of doing so. Sneak attacks are always advisable when dealing with members of the underworld, who are notoriously dirty fighters.

Jesse, looking down at his finger as if I'd burned a hole through it, seemed perfectly incapable of saying anything. It was probably the first time he'd been touched by anyone in a century and a half. That kind of thing can blow a guy's mind. Especially a dead guy.

I took advantage of his astonishment, and said, in my sternest, most no-nonsense tone, "Now, look, Jesse. This is my room, understand? You can't stay here. You've either got to let me help you get to where you're supposed to go, or you're going to have to find some other house to haunt. I'm sorry, but that's the way it is."

Jesse looked up from his finger, his expression still one of utter disbelief. "Who *are* you?" he asked softly. "What kind of . . . girl are you?"

He hesitated so long before he said the word *girl* that it was clear he wasn't at all certain it was appropriate in my case. This kind of bugged me. I mean, I may not have been the most popular girl in school, but no one ever denied I was an actual girl. Truck drivers honk at me at crosswalks now and then, and not because they want me to get out of the way. Construction workers sometimes holler rude things at me, especially when I wear my leather miniskirt. I am not unattractive, or mannish in any way. Sure, I'd just threatened to break his finger off, but that didn't mean I wasn't a *girl*, for God's sake!

"I'll tell you what kind of girl I'm not," I said crankily. "I am *not* the kind of girl who's looking to share her room with a member of the opposite sex. Understand me? So either you move out, or I force you out. It's entirely up to you. I'll give you some time to think about it. But when I get back here, Jesse, I want you gone."

I turned around and left.

I had to. I don't usually lose arguments with ghosts, but I had a feeling I was losing that one, and badly. I shouldn't have been so short with him, and I shouldn't have been rude. I don't know what came over me, I really don't. I just . . .

I guess I just wasn't expecting to find the ghost of such a cute guy in my bedroom, is all.

God, I thought, as I stormed down the hall. *What*

am I going to do if he doesn't leave? I won't be able to change clothes in my own room!

Give him a little time, a voice inside my head went. It was a voice I'd very carefully avoided telling my mom's therapist about.

Give him a little time. He'll come around. They always do.

Well, most of the time, anyway.

CHAPTER 4

Dinner at the Ackerman household was pretty much like dinner in any other large household I had ever known: Everybody talked at once—except of course for Sleepy, who only spoke when asked a direct question—and nobody wanted to clear the table afterward. I made a mental note to call Gina and tell her she'd been wrong. There really was no advantage, that I could see, in having brothers: They chewed with their mouths open, and ate every single Poppin' Fresh bread roll before I'd even had one.

After dinner, I decided it would be wise to avoid my room, and give Jesse plenty of time to make up his mind about whether he was leaving with or without his teeth. I'm not a big fan of violence, but it's an unfortunate by-product of my profession. Sometimes, the only way you can make someone listen is with your fist. This is not a technique espoused, I know, by the diagnostic manuals on most therapists' shelves.

Then again, nobody ever said I was a therapist.

The problem with my plan, of course, was that it was Saturday night. I'd forgotten what day it was in all the stress of the move. Back home on a Saturday night, I'd probably have gone out with Gina, taken the subway to the Village and gone to see a movie, or just hung around Joe's Pizza watching people walk by. Hey, I may be a big-city girl, but that doesn't mean my life there was glamorous by any means. I have never even been asked out by a boy, unless you count that time in the fifth grade when Daniel Bogue asked me to skate with him during a couples-only song at Rockefeller Center's ice rink.

And then I'd embarrassed myself by falling flat on my face.

My mom, however, was all anxious for me to throw myself into the social scene of Carmel. As soon as the dishwasher was loaded, she was like, "Brad, what are you doing tonight? Are there any parties, or anything? Maybe you could take Suze and introduce her to some people."

Dopey, who was mixing himself a protein shake—apparently, the two dozen jumbo shrimps and massive shell steak he'd consumed at dinner hadn't been filling enough—went, "Yeah, maybe I could, if Jake wasn't working tonight."

Sleepy, roused by the mention of his name, squinted down at his watch and said, "Damn," picked up his jean jacket, and left the house.

Doc looked at the clock and made a *tsk-tsk*ing noise. "Late again. He's going to get himself fired if he doesn't watch it."

Sleepy had a job? This was news to me, so I asked, "Where's he work?"

"Peninsula Pizza." Doc was performing some sort of bizarre experiment that involved the dog and my mother's treadmill. The dog, who was huge—a cross between a St. Bernard and a bear, I think—was sitting very patiently on the floor while Doc attached electrodes to small patches of the dog's skin he'd shaved free of fur. The strangest thing was that nobody seemed to mind this, least of all the dog.

"Slee—I mean, Jake works in a pizza place?"

Andy, scouring a baking dish in the sink, said, "He delivers for them. Brings home a bundle in tips."

"He's saving up," Dopey informed me, a thick white milkshake mustache on his upper lip, "for a Camaro."

"Huh," I said.

"You guys want me to drop you anywhere," Andy offered generously, "I'd be happy to. Whaddya say, Brad? Want to show Suze the action down at the mall?"

"Nah," Dopey said, wiping his mouth with the

sleeve of his sweatshirt. "Everybody's still up in Tahoe for the break. Next weekend, maybe."

I nearly collapsed with relief. The word *mall* always filled me with a sort of horror, a horror that had nothing to do with the undead. They don't have malls in New York City, but Gina used to love to take the PATH train to this one in New Jersey. Usually after about an hour, I'd develop sensory overload, and have to sit down in the This Can't Be Yogurt and sip an herbal tea until I calmed down.

And I have to admit, I wasn't that thrilled with the idea of anybody "dropping" me somewhere. My God, what was *wrong* with this place? I could see how, given the San Andreas fault, subways might not be such a great idea, but why hadn't anybody established a decent bus system?

"I know," Dopey said, slamming his empty glass down. "I'll play you a few games of Cool Boarders, Suze."

I blinked at him. "You'll what?"

"I'll play you in Cool Boarders." When my expression remained blank, Dopey said, "You never heard of Cool Boarders? Come on."

He led me toward the wide-screen TV in the den. Cool Boarders, it turned out, was a video game. Each player got assigned a snowboarder, and then you raced each other down various slopes using a joystick to control how fast your boarder went and what kind of fancy moves she might make.

I beat Dopey at it eight times before he finally said, "Let's watch a movie instead."

Sensing that I had probably erred in some way—I guess I should have let the poor boy win at least once—I tried to make amends by volunteering to supply the popcorn, and went into the kitchen.

It was only then that a wave of tiredness hit me. There is a three-hour time difference between New York and California, so even though it was only nine o'clock, I was as tired as if it were midnight. Andy and my mom had retired to the massive master bedroom, but they had left the door to it wide open, I guess so that we wouldn't get any wrong ideas about what they were doing in there. Andy was reading a spy novel, and my mother was watching a made-for-TV movie.

This, I was sure, was strictly for the benefit of us kids; most other Saturday nights I bet they'd have closed that door, or at least have gone out with Andy's friends or my mom's new colleagues at the TV station in Monterey where she'd been hired. They were obviously trying to establish some sort of domestic pattern to make us kids feel secure. You had to give them snaps for doing their best.

I wondered, as I stood there, waiting for the popcorn to pop, what my dad thought of all this. He hadn't been too enthused about Mom's remarrying, even though, as I've said, Andy is a pretty great guy. He'd been even less enthused about my moving out to the West Coast.

"How," he'd wanted to know, when I told him, "am I going to pop in on you when you're living three thousand miles away?"

"The point, Dad," I'd said to him, "is that you aren't supposed to be popping in on me. You're supposed to be dead, remember? You're supposed to be doing whatever it is dead people do, not spying on me and Mom."

He'd looked sort of hurt by that. "I'm not spying," he'd said. "I'm just checking up. To make sure you're happy, and all of that."

"Well, I am," I'd assured him. "I'm very happy, and so is Mom."

I'd been lying, of course. Not about Mom, but about me. I'd been a nervous wreck at the prospect of moving. Even now, I wasn't really sure it was going to work out. This thing with Jesse . . . I mean, where was my dad, anyway? Why wasn't he upstairs kicking that guy's butt? Jesse was, after all, a boy, and he was in my bedroom, and fathers are supposed to hate that kind of thing. . . .

But that's the thing about ghosts. They are never around when you actually need them. Even if they happen to be your dad.

I guess I must have zoned out for a little while because next thing I knew, the microwave was dinging. I took the popcorn out and opened the bag. I was pouring it into a big wooden bowl when my mom came into the kitchen and switched on the overhead light.

"Hi, honey," she said. Then she looked at me. "Are you all right, Susie?"

"Sure, Mom," I said. I shoveled some popcorn into my mouth. "Dope—I mean, *Brad* and I are gonna watch a movie."

"Are you sure?" My mother was peering at me curiously. "Are you sure you're all right?"

"Yeah, I'm fine. Just tired, is all."

She looked relieved. "Oh, yes. Well, I expected you'd have a bit of jet lag. But . . . well, it's just that you looked so upset when you first walked into your room upstairs. I know the canopy bed was a bit much, but I couldn't resist."

I chewed. I was totally used to this kind of thing. "The bed's fine, Mom," I said. "The room's fine, too."

"I'm so glad," my mom said, pushing a strand of hair from my eyes. "I'm so glad you like it, Suze."

My mother looked so relieved, I sort of felt sorry for her, in a way. I mean, she's a nice lady and doesn't deserve to have a mediator for a daughter. I know I've always been a bit of a disappointment to her. When I turned fourteen, she got me my own phone line, thinking so many boys would be calling me, her friends would never be able to get through. You can imagine how disappointed she was when nobody except Gina ever called me on my private line, and then it was usually only to tell me about the dates *she'd* been on. Like I said, the boys in my neighborhood were never much interested in asking *me* out.

My poor mom. She always wanted a nice, normal teenage daughter. Instead, she got me.

"Honey," she said. "Don't you want to change? You've been wearing those same clothes since six o'clock this morning, haven't you?"

She asked me this right as Doc was coming in to get more glue for his electrodes. Not that I was going to say anything like, *Well, to tell you the truth, Mom, I'd like to change, but I'm not real excited about doing it in front of the ghost of the dead cowboy that's living in my room.*

Instead, I shrugged and said with elaborate casualness, "Yeah, well, I'm gonna change in a bit."

"Are you sure you don't want help unpacking? I feel terrible. I should have—"

"No, I don't need any help. I'll unpack in a bit." I watched Doc forage through a drawer. "I better go," I said. "I don't want to miss the beginning of the movie."

Of course, in the end, I missed the beginning, middle, and end of the movie. I fell asleep on the couch, and didn't wake up until Andy shook my shoulder a little after eleven.

"Up and at 'em, kiddo," he said. "I think it's time to admit you've gone down for the count. Don't worry. Brad won't tell anybody."

I got up groggily, and made my way up to my room. I headed straight for the windows, which I yanked open. To my relief there was no Jesse to block the way. *Yes.* I've still got it.

I grabbed my duffel bag and went into the bathroom where I showered and, just to be on the safe side—I didn't know for sure whether or not Jesse had gotten the message and vamoosed—changed into my pajamas. When I came out of the bathroom, I was a little more awake. I looked around, feeling the cool breeze seeping in, smelling the salt in the air. Unlike back in Brooklyn, where our ears were under constant assault by sirens and car alarms, it was quiet in the hills, the only sound the occasional hoot of an owl.

I found, rather to my surprise, that I was alone. Really alone. A ghost-free zone. Exactly what I'd always wanted.

I got into bed and clapped my hands, dousing the lights. Then I snuggled deep beneath my crisp new sheets.

Just before I fell asleep again, I thought I heard something besides the owl. It sounded like someone singing the words *Oh, Susannah, now don't you cry for me, 'cause I come from Alabama with this banjo on my knee.*

But that, I'm sure, was just my imagination.

CHAPTER 5

The Junipero Serra Catholic Academy, grades K–12, had been made coeducational in the 1980s, and had, much to my relief, recently dropped its strict uniform policy. The uniforms had been royal blue and white, not my best colors. Fortunately, the uniforms had been so unpopular that they, like the boys-only rule, had been abandoned, and though the pupils still couldn't wear jeans, they could wear just about anything else they wanted. Since all I wanted was to wear my extensive collection of designer clothing—purchased at various outlet stores in New Jersey with Gina as my fashion coordinator—this suited me fine.

The Catholic thing, though, was going to be a

problem. Not really a problem so much as an inconvenience. You see, my mother never really bothered to raise me in any particular religion. My father was a nonpracticing Jew, my mother Christian. Religion had never played an important part in either of my parents' lives, and, needless to say, it had only served to confuse me. I mean, you would think I'd have a better grasp on religion than anybody, but the truth is, I haven't the slightest idea what happens to the ghosts I send off to wherever it is they're supposed to go after they die. All I know is, once I send them there, they do not come back. Not ever. The end.

So when my mother and I showed up at the Mission School's administrative office the Monday after my arrival in sunny California, I was more than a little taken aback to be confronted with a six-foot Jesus hanging on a crucifix behind the secretary's desk.

I shouldn't have been surprised, though. My mom had pointed out the school from my room on Sunday morning as she helped me to unpack. "See that big red dome?" she'd said. "That's the Mission. The dome covers the chapel."

Doc happened to be hanging around—I'd noticed he did that a lot—and he launched into another one of his descriptions, this time of the Franciscans, who were members of a Roman Catholic religious order that followed the rule of St. Francis, approved in 1209. Father Junipero Serra, a Franciscan monk, was, according to Doc, a tragically misunderstood historical figure. A controversial hero in the Catholic church, he had been considered for sainthood at one time, but, Doc explained, Native Americans questioned this move as "a general endorsement of the exploitative colonization tactics of the Spanish. Though Junipero Serra was known to have argued on behalf of the property rights and economic entitlement of converted Native Americans, he consistently advocated against their right to self-governance, and was a staunch supporter of corporal punishment, appealing to the Spanish government for the right to flog Indians."

When Doc had finished this particular lecture, I just looked at him and went, "Photographic memory much?"

He looked embarrassed. "Well," he said. "It's good to know the history of the place where you're living."

I filed this away for future reference. Doc might be just the person I needed if Jesse showed up again.

Now, standing in the cool office of the ancient building Junipero Serra had constructed for the betterment of the natives in the area, I wondered how many ghosts I was going to encounter. That Serra guy had to have a bunch of Native Americans mad at him—particularly considering that corporal punishment thing—and I hadn't any doubt I was going to encounter all of them.

And yet, when my mom and I walked through

the school's wide front archway into the courtyard around which the Mission had been constructed, I didn't see a single person who looked as if he or she didn't belong there. There were a few tourists snapping pictures of the impressive fountain, a gardener working diligently at the base of a palm tree—even at my new school there were palm trees—a priest walking in silent contemplation down the airy breezeway. It was a beautiful, restful place—especially for a building that was so old and had to have seen so much death.

I couldn't understand it. Where were all the ghosts?

Maybe they were afraid to hang around the place. *I* was a little afraid, looking up at that crucifix. I mean, I've got nothing against religious art, but was it really necessary to portray the crucifixion so realistically, with so many scabs and all?

Apparently, I was not alone in thinking so, since a boy who was slumped on a couch across from the one where my mom and I had been instructed to wait noticed the direction of my gaze and said, "He's supposed to weep tears of blood if any girl ever graduates from here a virgin."

I couldn't help letting out a little bark of laughter. My mother glared at me. The secretary, a plump middle-aged woman who looked as if something like that ought to have offended her deeply, only rolled her eyes, and said tiredly, "Oh, Adam."

Adam, a good-looking boy about my age, looked at me with a perfectly serious face. "It's true," he said gravely. "It happened last year. My sister." He dropped his voice conspiratorially. "She's adopted."

I laughed again, and my mother frowned at me. She had spent most of yesterday explaining to me that it had been really, really hard to convince the school to take me, especially since she couldn't produce any proof that I'd ever been baptized. In the end, they'd only let me in because of Andy, since all three of his boys went there. I imagine a sizable donation had also played a part in my admittance, but my mother wouldn't tell me that. All she said was that I had better behave myself, and not hurl anything out of any windows—even though I reminded her that that particular incident hadn't been my fault. I'd been fighting with a particularly violent young ghost who'd refused to quit haunting the girls' locker room at my old school. Throwing him through that window had certainly gotten his attention, and convinced him to trod the path of righteousness ever after.

Of course, I'd told my mother that I'd been practicing my tennis swing indoors, and the racket had slipped from my hands—an especially unbelievable story, since a racket was never found.

It was as I was reliving this painful memory that a heavy wooden door opened, and a priest came out and said, "Mrs. Ackerman, what a pleasure to see you again.

And this must be Susannah Simon. Come in, won't you?" He ushered us into his office, then paused, and said to the boy on the couch, "Oh, no, Mr. McTavish. Not on the first day of a brand-new semester."

Adam shrugged. "What can I say? The broad hates me."

"Kindly do not refer to Sister Ernestine as a broad, Mr. McTavish. I will see to you in a moment, after I have spoken with these ladies."

We went in, and the principal, Father Dominic—that was his name—sat and chatted with us for a while, asking me how I liked California so far. I said I liked it fine, especially the ocean. We had spent most of the day before at the beach, after I'd finished unpacking. I had found my sunglasses, and even though it was too cold to swim, I had a great time just lying on a blanket on the beach, watching the waves. They were huge, bigger than on *Baywatch*, and Doc spent most of the afternoon explaining to me why that was. I forget now, since I was so drugged by the sun, I was hardly even listening. I found that I loved the beach, the smell of it, the seaweed that washed up on shore, the feel of the cool sand between my toes, the taste of salt on my skin when I got home. Carmel might not have had a Bagel Bob's, but Manhattan sure didn't have no beach.

Father Dominic expressed his sincere hope that I'd be happy at the Mission Academy, and went on to explain that even though I wasn't Catholic, I shouldn't feel unwelcome at Mass. There were, of course, Holy Days of Obligation, when the Catholic students would be required to leave their lessons behind and go to church. I could either join them, or stay behind in the empty classroom, whatever I chose.

I thought this was kind of funny, for some reason, but I managed to keep from laughing. Father Dominic was old, but what you'd probably call spry, and he struck me as sort of handsome in his white collar and black robes—I mean, handsome for a sixty-year-old. He had white hair, and very blue eyes, and well-maintained fingernails. I don't know many priests, but I thought this one might be all right—especially since he hadn't come down hard on the boy in the outer office who'd called that nun a broad.

After Father Dominic had described the various offenses I could get expelled for—skipping class too many times, dealing drugs on campus, the usual stuff— he asked me if I had any questions. I didn't. Then he asked my mother if she had any questions. She didn't. So then Father Dominic stood up and said, "Fine then. I'll say good-bye to you, Mrs. Ackerman, and walk Susannah to her first class. All right, Susannah?"

I thought it was kind of weird that the principal, who probably had a lot to do, was taking time out to walk me to my first class, but I didn't say anything about it. I just picked up my coat—a black wool trench by Esprit, *très chic* (my mom wouldn't let me wear leather my first day of school)—and waited while he and my mother shook hands. My mom kissed me good-bye, and reminded me to find Sleepy at 3:00, since he was in charge of driving me home—only she didn't call him Sleepy. Once again, a woeful lack of public transportation meant that I had to bum rides to and from school with my stepbrothers.

Then she was gone, and Father Dominic was walking me across the courtyard after having instructed Adam to wait for him.

"No prob, *padre*," was Adam's response. He leered at me behind the father's back. It isn't often I get leered at by boys my own age. I hoped he was in my class. My mother's wishes for my social life just might be realized at last.

As we walked, Father Dominic explained a little about the building—or buildings, I should say, since that's what they were. A series of thick-walled adobe structures were connected by low-ceilinged breezeways, in the middle of which existed the beautiful courtyard that came complete with palm trees, bubbling fountain, and a bronze statue of Father Serra with these women—your stereotypical Indian squaws, complete with papooses strapped to their backs—kneeling at his feet. On the other side of the breezeway were stone benches for people to sit on while they enjoyed solitary contemplation of the courtyard's splendor, the doors to the classrooms and steel lockers were built right into the adobe wall. One of those lockers, Father Dominic explained to me, was mine. He had the combination with him. Did I want to put away my coat?

I had been surprised when I'd wakened Sunday morning to find myself shivering in my bed. I'd had to stumble out from beneath the sheets and slam my windows shut. A thick fog, I saw with dismay, had enshrouded the valley, obscuring my view of the bay. I thought for sure some horrible tropical storm had rolled in, but Doc had explained to me, quite patiently, that morning fog was typical in the Northwest, and that the *Pacífico*—Spanish for passive—was so named because of its relative lack of storms. The fog, Doc had assured me, would burn off by noon, and it would then be just as hot as it had been the day before.

And he'd been right. By the time I returned home from the beach, sunburned and happy, my room had become an oven again, and I'd pried the windows back open—only to find that they'd been gently shut again when I woke up this morning, which I thought was sweet of my mom, looking out for me like that.

At least, I *hope* it was my mom. Now that I think about it . . . but no, I hadn't seen Jesse since that first day I'd moved in. It had definitely been my mom who'd shut my windows.

Anyway, when I'd walked outside to get into Mom's

car, I'd found that it was freezing out again, and that was why I was wearing the wool coat.

Father Dominic told me that my locker was number 273, and he seemed content to let me find it myself, strolling behind me with his eyes on the breezeway's rafters, in which, much to his professed delight, families of swallows nested every year. He was apparently quite fond of birds—of all animals, actually, since one of the questions he'd asked me was how was I getting along with Max, the Ackermans' dog—and openly scoffed at Andy's repeated assurances that the timber in the breezeways was going to have to be replaced thanks to the swallows and their refuse.

268, 269, 270. I strolled down the open corridor, watching the numbers on the beige locker doors. Unlike the ones in my school back in Brooklyn, these lockers were not graffitied, or dented, or plastered with stickers from heavy metal bands. I guess students on the West Coast took more pride in their school's appearance than us Yankees.

271, 272. I stumbled to a halt.

In front of locker number 273 stood a ghost.

It wasn't Jesse, either. It was a girl, dressed very much like I was, only with long blonde hair, instead of brown, like mine. She also had an extremely unpleasant look on her face.

"What," she said to me, "are *you* looking at?" Then, speaking to someone behind me, she demanded, "*This* is who they let in to take my place? I am so sure."

Okay, I admit it. I freaked out. I spun around, and found myself gaping up at Father Dominic, who was squinting down at me curiously.

"Ah," he said, when he saw my face. "I thought so."

CHAPTER 6

I looked from Father Dominic to the ghost girl, and back again. Finally, I managed to blurt out, "You can *see* her?"

He nodded. "Yes. I suspected when I first heard your mother speak about you—and your . . . *problems* at your old school—that you might be one of us, Susannah. But I couldn't be sure, of course, so I didn't say anything. Although the name Simon, I'm sure you're aware, is from the Hebrew word meaning "intent listener," which, as a fellow mediator, you of course would be. . . ."

I barely heard him. I couldn't get over the fact that finally, after all these years, I'd met another mediator.

"So *that's* why there aren't any Indian spirits around here!" I practically yelled. "*You* took care of them. Jeez, I was *wondering* what happened to them all. I expected to find hundreds—"

Father Dominic bowed his head modestly and said, "Well, there weren't hundreds, exactly, but when I first arrived, there were quite a few. But it was nothing, really. I was only doing my duty, after all, making use of the heavenly gift I received from God."

I made a face. "Is *that* who's responsible for it?"

"But of course ours is a gift from God." Father Dominic looked down at me with that special kind of pity the faithful always bestow upon us poor, pathetic creatures who have doubts. "Where else do you think it could come from?"

"I don't know. I've always kind of wanted to have a word with the guy in charge, you know? Because, given a choice, I'd much rather not have been blessed with this particular gift."

Father Dominic looked surprised. "But why ever not, Susannah?"

"All it does is get me into trouble. Do you have any idea how many hours I've spent in psychiatrists' offices? My mom's convinced I'm a complete schizo."

"Yes." Father Dominic nodded thoughtfully. "Yes, I could see how a miraculous gift like ours might be considered by a layperson as—well, unusual."

"Unusual? Are you *kidding* me?"

"I suppose I have been rather sheltered here in the Mission," Father Dominic admitted. "It never occurred to me that it must be extremely difficult for those of you out in the, er, trenches, so to speak, with no real ecclesiastical support—"

"Those of us?" I raised my eyebrows. "You mean there's more than just you and me?"

He looked surprised. "Well, I just assumed . . . surely there must be. We can't be the last of our kind. No, no, surely there are others."

"Excuse me." The ghost looked at us very sarcastically. "But would you mind telling me what's going on here? Who is this bitch? Is she the one taking my place?"

"Hey! Watch your mouth." I shot her a dirty look. "This guy's a priest, you know."

She sneered at me. "Uh, duh. I *know* he's a priest. He's only been trying to get rid of me all week."

I glanced at Father Dominic in surprise, and he said, looking embarrassed, "Well, you see, Heather's being a bit obstinate—"

"If you think," Heather said, in her snotty little voice, "that I'm going to just stand back and let you assign my locker to this bitch—"

"Call me a bitch one more time, missy," I said, "and I'll make sure you spend the rest of eternity inside this locker of yours."

Heather looked at me without the slightest trace of fear. "Bitch," she said, stretching the word out so it contained multiple syllables.

I hit her so fast she never saw my fist coming. I hit her hard, hard enough to send her reeling into the line of lockers and leave a long, body-shaped dent in them. She landed hard, too, on the stone floor, but was on her feet again a second later. I expected her to strike back at me, but instead, Heather got up and, with a whimper, ran for all she was worth down the corridor.

"Huh," I said, mostly to myself. *"Chicken."*

She'd be back, of course. I'd only startled her. She'd be back. But hopefully when I saw her again, she'd have a slightly improved attitude.

Heather gone, I blew lightly on my knuckles. Ghosts have surprisingly bony jaws.

"So," I said. "What were you saying, Father?"

Father Dominic, still staring where Heather had been standing, remarked, pretty dryly for a priest, "Interesting mediation techniques they're teaching out east these days."

"Hey," I said. "Nobody calls me names and gets away with it. I don't care how tortured he was in his past life. Or hers."

"I think," Father Dominic said thoughtfully, "there are some things we need to discuss, you and I."

Then he brought a finger to his lips. To one side of us a door opened and a large man, his face heavily bearded, looked out into the breezeway, having heard the crash of Heather's astral body—funny how much the dead can weigh—hitting the row of lockers.

"Everything all right, Dom?" he asked, when he saw Father Dominic.

"Everything's fine, Carl," Father Dominic said. "Just fine. And look what I've brought you." Father Dominic placed a hand on my shoulder. "Your newest pupil, Susannah Simon. Susannah, meet your home-room teacher, Carl Walden."

I stuck out the hand I'd just knocked Heather senseless with. "How do you do, Mr. Walden?"

"Just fine, Miss Simon. Just fine." Mr. Walden's enormous hand engulfed mine. He didn't look much like a teacher to me. He looked more like a lumberjack. In fact, he practically had to flatten himself against the wall to give me room to slip past him into his class-room. "Nice to have you with us," he said in his big, booming voice. "Thanks, Dom, for bringing her over."

"Not a problem," Father Dominic said. "We were just having a little difficulty with her locker. You prob-ably heard it. Didn't mean to disturb you. I'll have the custodian look into it. In the meantime, Susannah, I'll expect you back in my office at three, to, um, fill out the rest of those forms."

I smiled at him sweetly. "Oh, no can do, Father. My ride leaves at three."

Father Dominic scowled at me. "Then I'll send you a pass. Expect one around two."

"Okay," I said, and waggled my fingers at him. "Buh-bye."

I guess on the West Coast you aren't supposed to say buh-bye to the principal, or waggle your fingers at him, since when I turned around to face my new classmates, they were all staring at me with their mouths hanging open.

Maybe it was my outfit. I had worn a little bit more black than usual, due to nerves. When in doubt, I always say, wear black. You can never go wrong with black.

Or maybe you can. Because as I looked around at the gaping faces, I didn't see a single black garment in the lot. A lot of white, a few browns, and a heck of a lot of khaki, but no black.

Oops.

Mr. Walden didn't seem to notice my discomfort. He introduced me to the class, and made me tell them where I came from. I told them, and they all stared at me blankly. I began to feel sweat pricking the back of my neck. I have to tell you, sometimes I prefer the company of the undead to the company of my peers. Sixteen-year-olds can be really scary.

But Mr. Walden was a good guy. He only made me stand there a minute, under all those stares, and then he told me to take a seat.

This sounds like a simple thing, right? Just go and take a seat. But you see, there were two seats. One was next to this really pretty tanned girl, with thick, curly, honey-blond hair. The other was way in the back, behind a girl with hair so white, and skin so pink, she could only be an albino.

No, I am not kidding. An *albino*.

Two things influenced my decision. One was that when I saw the seat in the back, I also happened to see that the windows, directly behind that seat, looked out across the school parking lot.

Okay, not such an inspiring view, you might say. But beyond the parking lot was the sea.

I am not kidding. This school, my new school, had a view of the Pacific that was even better than the one in my bedroom since the school was so much closer to the beach. You could actually see the waves from my homeroom's windows. I wanted to sit as close to the window as possible.

The second reason I sat there was simple: I didn't want to take the seat by the tan girl and have the albino girl think I'd done it because I didn't want to sit near anyone as weird looking as she was. Stupid, right? Like she'd even care what I did. But I didn't even hesitate. I saw the sea, I saw the albino, and I went for it.

As soon as I sat down, of course, this girl a few seats away snickered and went, under her breath, but perfectly audibly, "God, sit by the freak, why don't you."

I looked at her. She had perfectly curled hair and perfectly made-up eyes. I said, not talking under my breath at all, "Excuse me, do you have Tourette's?"

Mr. Walden had turned around to write something

on the board, but the sound of my voice stopped him. Everybody turned around to look at me, including the girl who'd spoken. She blinked at me, startled. "What?"

"Tourette's Syndrome," I said. "It's a neurological disorder that causes people to say things they don't really mean. Do you have it?"

The girl's cheeks had slowly started turning scarlet. "No."

"Oh," I said. "So you were being purposefully rude."

"I wasn't calling *you* a freak," the girl said quickly.

"I'm aware of that," I said. "That's why I'm only going to break *one* of your fingers after school, instead of *all* of them."

She spun around real fast to face the front of the classroom. I settled back into my chair. I don't know what everybody started buzzing about after that, but I did see the albino's scalp—which was plainly visible beneath the white of her hair—turn a deep magenta with embarrassment. Mr. Walden had to call everyone to order, and when people ignored him, he slammed his fist down on his desk and told us that if we had so damned much to say, we could say it in a thousand-word essay on the battle at Bladensburg during the War of 1812, double-spaced, and due on his desk first thing tomorrow morning.

Oh well. Good thing I wasn't in school to make friends.

CHAPTER 7

And yet I did. Make friends, I mean.

I didn't try to. I didn't even really want to. I mean, I have enough friends back in Brooklyn. I have Gina, the best friend anybody could have. I didn't need any more friends than that.

And I really didn't think anybody here was going to like me—not after having been assigned a thousand-word essay because of what happened when I sat down. And especially not after what happened when we were informed that it was time for second period—there was no bell system at the Mission School, we changed class on the hour, and had five minutes to get to where we were going. No sooner had Mr. Walden dismissed us than the albino girl turned around in her seat and asked, her purple eyes glowing furiously behind the tinted lenses of her glasses, "Am I supposed to be grateful to you, or something, for what you said to Debbie?"

"You," I said, standing up, "aren't supposed to be anything, as far as I'm concerned."

She stood up, too. "But that's why you did it, right? Defended the albino? Because you felt sorry for me?"

"I did it," I said, folding my coat over my arm, "because Debbie is a troll."

I saw the corners of her lips twitch. Debbie had swept up her books and practically run for the door the minute Mr. Walden had dismissed us. She and a bunch of other girls, including the pretty tanned one who'd had the empty seat next to her, were whispering among themselves and casting me dirty looks over their Ralph Lauren sweater–draped shoulders.

I could tell the albino girl wanted to laugh at my calling Debbie a troll, but she wouldn't let herself. She said fiercely, "I can fight my own battles, you know. I don't need your help, New York."

I shrugged. "Fine with me, Carmel."

She couldn't help smiling then. When she did, she revealed a mouthful of braces that winked as brightly as the sea outside the window. "It's CeeCee," she said.

"What's CeeCee?"

"My name. I'm CeeCee." She stuck out a milky-white hand, the nails of which were painted a violent orange. "Welcome to the Mission Academy."

At 9:00, Mr. Walden had dismissed us. By 9:02, CeeCee had introduced me to twenty other people, most of whom trotted after me as we moved to our next class, wanting to know what it was like to have lived in New York City.

"Is it really," one horsey-looking girl asked wistfully, "as . . . as . . ." She struggled to think of the word she was looking for. "As . . . *metropolitan* as they all say?"

These girls, I probably don't have to add, were not the class lookers. They were not, I saw at once, on speaking terms with the pretty tanned girl and the one whose fingers I'd threatened to break after school, who were the ones so well-turned out in their sweater sets and khaki skirts. Oh, no. The girls who came up to me were a motley bunch, some acned, some overweight, or way way too skinny. I was horrified to see that one was wearing open-toe shoes with reinforced toe pantyhose. Beige pantyhose, too. And white shoes. In January!

I could see I was going to have my work cut out for me.

CeeCee appeared to be the leader of their little pack. Editor of the school paper, the *Mission News*, which she called "more of a literary review than an actual newspaper," CeeCee had been in earnest when she'd informed me she did not need me to fight her battles for her. She had plenty of ammunition of her own, including a pretty packed arsenal of verbal zingers and an extremely serious work ethic. Practically the first thing she asked me—after she got over being mad at me—was if I'd be interested in writing a piece for her paper.

"Nothing fancy," she said airily. "Maybe just an essay comparing East Coast and West Coast teen culture. I'm sure you must see a lot of differences between us and your friends back in New York. Whaddaya say? My readers would be plenty interested—especially girls like Kelly and Debbie. Maybe you could slip in something about how on the East Coast being tan is like a *faux pas*."

Then she laughed, not sounding evil exactly, but definitely not innocent, either. But that, I soon realized, was CeeCee, all bright smiles—made brighter by those wicked-looking braces—and bouncy good humor. She was as famous, apparently, for her wisecracking as for her big horse-laugh, which sometimes bubbled out of her when she couldn't control it, and rang out with unabashed joy, and was inevitably hushed by the prissy novices who acted as hall monitors, keeping us from bothering the tourists who came to snap pictures of Junipero Serra being fawned over by those poor bronze Indian women.

The Mission Academy was a small one. There were only seventy sophomores. I was thankful that Dopey and I had conflicting schedules, so that the only period we shared in common was lunch. Lunch, by the way, was conducted in the school yard, which was to one side of the parking lot, a huge grassy playground overlooking the sea, with seniors slumping on the same benches as second graders, and seagulls converging on anyone foolish enough to toss out a fry. I know because I tried it. Sister Ernestine—the one Adam, who was in my social studies class, it turned out, had called a broad—came up to me and told me never to do it again. As if I hadn't gotten the point the minute fifty giant squawking gulls came swooping down from the sky and surrounded me, the way the pigeons used to in Washington Square Park if you were foolish enough to throw out a bit of pretzel.

Anyway, Sleepy and Doc shared my lunch period, too. That was the only time I saw any of the Ackermans at school. It was interesting to observe them in their native environment. I was pleased to see that I had been correct in my estimation of their characters. Doc hung with a crowd of extremely nerdy-looking kids, most of whom wore glasses and actually balanced their laptop computers on their laps, something I'd never thought was actually done. Dopey hung with the jocks, around whom flocked—the way the seagulls had flocked around me—the pretty tanned girls in our class, including the one I'd eschewed sitting beside. Their conversation seemed to consist of what they'd gotten for Christmas, this being their first day back from winter break, and who'd broken the most limbs skiing in Tahoe.

Sleepy was perhaps the most interesting, however. Not that he woke up. Please. But he sat at one of the picnic tables with his eyes closed and his face turned to the sun. Since I can see this at home, this was not what interested me. No, what interested me was what was going on beside Sleepy. And that was an incredibly good-looking boy who did nothing but stare straight ahead of him with a look of abject sadness on his face. Occasionally, girls would walk by—as girls will when there is a good-looking boy nearby—and say hi to him, and he'd tear his eyes away from the sea—which was what he was staring at—and say, "Oh, hi," to them before turning his gaze back to those hypnotic waves.

It occurred to me that Sleepy and his friend might very well be potheads. It would explain a lot about Sleepy.

But when I asked CeeCee if she knew who the guy was, and whether or not he had a drug problem, she said, "Oh, that's Bryce Martinson. No, he's not on drugs. He's just sad, you know, 'cause his girlfriend died over the break."

"Really?" I chewed on my corn dog. The food service at the Mission Academy left a lot to be desired. I could see now why so many kids brought their own. Today's entree had been hot dogs. I am not kidding.

Hot dogs. "How'd she die?"

"Put a bullet in her brain." Adam, the kid from the principal's office, had joined us. He was eating Chee-tos from a giant bag he'd pulled from a leather backpack. A Louis Vuitton backpack, I might add. "Blew the back of her head away."

One of the horsey girls turned around, having overheard, and went, "God, Adam. How cold can you get?"

Adam shrugged. "Hey. I didn't like her when she was alive. I'm not gonna say I liked her now just because she's dead. In fact, if anything, I hate her more. I heard we're all going to have to do the Stations of the Cross for her on Wednesday."

"Right." CeeCee looked disgusted. "We have to pray for her immortal soul since she committed suicide and is destined to burn in hell for all eternity now."

Adam looked thoughtful. "Really? I thought suicides went to Purgatory."

"No, stupid. Why do you think Monsignor Constantine won't let Kelly have her dumb memorial service? Suicide is a mortal sin. Monsignor Constantine won't allow a suicide to be memorialized in his church. He won't even let her parents bury her in consecrated ground." CeeCee rolled her violet eyes. "I never liked Heather, but I *hate* Monsignor Constantine and his stupid rules even more. I'm thinking of doing an article about it, and calling it 'Father, Son, and the Holy Hypocrite.' "

The other girls tittered nervously. I waited until they were done and then I asked, "Why'd she kill herself?"

Adam looked bored. "Because of Bryce, of course. He broke up with her."

A pretty black girl named Bernadette, who towered over the rest of us at six feet, leaned down to whisper, "I heard he did it at the mall. Can you believe it?"

Another girl said, "Yeah, on Christmas Eve. They were Christmas shopping with each other, and she pointed to this diamond ring in the window at Bergdorf's, and was, like, 'I want that.' And I guess he freaked—you know, it was clearly an engagement ring—and broke up with her on the spot."

"And so she went home and shot herself?" I found this story extremely far-fetched. When I'd asked CeeCee where we were supposed to have lunch if, God forbid, it should happen to rain, she told me that everyone had to sit in their homeroom and eat, and the nuns brought out board games like Parcheesi for people to play. I was wondering if this story, like the one about rainyday lunches, was an invention. CeeCee was exactly the kind of girl who would get a kick out of lying to the new kid—not out of maliciousness, but just to amuse herself.

"Not then," CeeCee said. "She tried to get back together with him for a while. She called him like every ten minutes, until finally his mother told her not to call anymore. Then she started sending him letters, telling him what she was going to do—you know, kill herself if he didn't get back together with her. When he didn't respond, she got her dad's forty-four and drove to Bryce's house and rang the bell."

Adam took up the narrative at this point, so I knew gore was probably going to be involved. "Yeah," he said, standing up so that he could act it, using a Chee-to as the gun. "The Martinsons were having a New Year's party—it was New Year's Eve—so they were home and everything. They opened up the door, and there was this crazy girl on their porch, with a gun to her head. She said if they didn't get Bryce, she was going to pull the trigger. But they couldn't get Bryce, because they'd sent him to Antigua—"

"—Hoping a little sun and surf would soothe his frazzled nerves," CeeCee put in, "because, you know, he's got his college apps to worry about right now. He doesn't need to have the added pressure of a stalker."

Adam glared at her, and went on, holding the Chee-to to the side of his head. "Yeah, well, that was a gross error on the part of the Martinsons. As soon as she heard Bryce was out of the country, she pulled the trigger, and blew out the back of her skull, and bits of her brain and stuff stuck to the Christmas lights the Martinsons had strung up."

Everyone but me groaned at this particular detail. I had other things on my mind, however. "The empty

chair in homeroom. The one by what's-her-name—
Kelly. That was the dead girl's seat, wasn't it?"

Bernadette nodded. "Yeah. That's why we thought
it was so weird when you walked past it. It was like
you *knew* that that was where Heather had sat. We all
thought maybe you were psychic or something—"

I didn't bother telling them that the reason I hadn't
sat in Heather's seat had nothing whatsoever to do
with being psychic. I didn't say anything, actually. I
was thinking, *Gee, Mom, nice of you to tell me why
there was suddenly this space for me, when before the
school had been too crowded to let in another new student.*

I stared at Bryce. He was tanned from his trip to
Antigua. He sat on the picnic table with his feet on
the bench, his elbows on his knees, staring out at the
Pacific. A gentle wind tugged at some of his sandy-
blond hair.

He has no idea, I thought. *He has no idea at all. He
thinks his life is bad now? Just wait.*

Just wait.

CHAPTER 8

He didn't have to wait long. In fact, it was right after lunch that she came after him. Not that he ever knew it, of course. I spotted her immediately in the crowd as everybody headed toward their lockers. Ghosts have a sort of glow about them that sets them apart from the living—thank God, too, or half the time I might never have known the difference.

Anyway, there she was staring daggers at him like one of those blond kids out of *Village of the Damned*. People, not knowing she was there, kept walking straight through her. I sort of envied them. I wish ghosts were invisible to me like they were to everybody else. I know that would mean I wouldn't have been able to enjoy my dad's company these past few years, but, hey, it also would have meant I wouldn't be standing there knowing Heather was about to do something horrible.

Not that I knew what it was she planned on doing to him. Ghosts can get pretty rough sometimes. The trick Jesse had done with the mirror was nothing, really. I've had objects thrown at me with enough force that, if I hadn't ducked, I'd certainly be one with the spirit world as well. I've had concussions and broken bones galore. My mom just thinks I'm accident-prone. Yeah, Mom. That's right. I broke my wrist falling down the stairs. Oh, and the reason I fell down the stairs is that the ghost of a three-hundred-year-old conquistador pushed me.

The minute I saw Heather, though, I knew she was up to no good. I was not basing this assumption on my previous interaction with her. Oh, no. See, I followed the direction of Heather's gaze, and saw that it wasn't Bryce, exactly, that she was staring at. It was actually one of the rafters in the section of breezeway beneath which Bryce was walking that had attracted her attention. And, as I stood there, I saw the timber start to shake. Not the whole breezeway. Oh, no. Just one single, heavy piece. The piece directly over Bryce's head.

I acted without thought. I threw myself as hard as I could at Bryce. We both went flying. And good thing, too. Because we were still rolling when I heard an enormous explosion. I ducked my head to shield my eyes, so I didn't actually see the piece of timber explode. But I heard it. And I felt it, too. Those tiny splinters of wood *hurt* as they pelted me. Good thing I was wearing wool slacks, too.

Bryce lay so still beneath me that I thought maybe a chunk of wood had got him between the frontal lobes, or something. But when I lifted my face from his chest, I saw that he was okay—he was just staring, horrified, at the ten-inch-thick plank of wood, nearly two feet long, that lay a few feet away from us. All around us were scattered shards of wood that had broken off the main piece. I guess Bryce was realizing that if that plank had succeeded in splintering his cranium, there'd have been little pieces of Bryce scattered all around that stone floor, too.

"Excuse me. Excuse me—" I heard Father Dominic's strained voice, and saw him push through the crowd of stunned onlookers. He froze when he saw the chunk of wood, but when his gaze took in Bryce and me, he sprung into action again.

"Good God in heaven," he cried, hurrying toward us. "Are you children all right? Susannah, are you hurt? Bryce?"

I sat up slowly. I frequently have to check for broken bones, and have found, over the years, that the slower you get up, the more chance you have at discovering what's broken, and the less chance there is you'll put weight on it.

But in this particular case, nothing seemed broken. I got to my feet.

"Good gracious," Father Dom was saying. "Are you sure you're all right?"

"I'm fine," I said, brushing myself off. There were little pieces of wood all over me. And this was my best Donna Karan jacket. I looked around for Heather—really, if I'd have found her at that particular moment, I'd have killed her, I really would have . . . except, of course, that she's already dead. But she was gone.

"God," Bryce said, coming up to me. He didn't look hurt, just shaken up a little. Actually, it would have been hard to hurt a guy as big as he was. He was six feet tall and broad shouldered, a genuine Baldwin.

And he was talking to me. *Me!*

"God, are you okay?" he wanted to know. "Thank you. God. I think you must have saved my life."

"Oh," I said. "It was nothing, really." I couldn't resist reaching out and plucking a splinter of wood from his sweater vest. Cashmere. Just as I'd suspected.

"What is going on here?" A tall guy in a lot of robes with a red beanie on his head came pushing through the crowd. When he saw the wood on the ground, then looked up to take in the gaping hole where it was supposed to be, he turned on Father Dom and said, "See? See, Dominic? This is what comes of you letting your precious birds nest wherever they want! Mr. Ackerman warned us this might happen, and look! He was right!

Somebody might have been killed!"

So this, then, was Monsignor Constantine.

"I'm so sorry, Monsignor," Father Dom said. "I can't think how such a thing could have happened. Thank heavens no one was hurt." He turned to Bryce and me. "You two *are* all right? You know, I think Miss Simon looks a little pale. I'll just take her off to see the nurse, if that's all right with you, Susannah. The rest of you children get on to class now. Everyone is all right. It was just an accident. Run along, now."

Amazingly, people did as he said. Father Dominic had that kind of way about him. You just sort of had to do what he said. Thank God he used his powers for good instead of evil!

I wish the same could have been said of the monsignor. He stood in the suddenly empty corridor, staring down at the piece of wood. Anybody could tell just to look at it that it wasn't the least bit rotten. The wood wasn't new by any means, but it was perfectly dry.

"I'm having those bird nests removed, Dominic," the monsignor said bitterly. "All of them. We simply can't take these kinds of risks. Supposing one of the tourists had been standing here? Or, God forbid, the archbishop. He's coming next month, you know. What if Archbishop Rivera had been standing here and this beam had fallen? What then, Dominic?"

The nuns who'd come out, hearing all the ruckus,

cast looks of such reproof at poor Father Dominic that I nearly said something. I opened my mouth to do so, in fact, but Father Dom tightened his grip on my arm and started marching me away. "Of course," he called. "You're quite right. I'll get the custodial staff right on it, Monsignor. We couldn't have the archbishop injured. No, indeed."

"God, what a pus-head!" I said, as soon as we were safely behind the closed door to the principal's office. "Is he kidding, thinking a couple of birds could do that?"

Father Dominic had gone straight across the room to a small cabinet in which there were a number of trophies and plaques—teaching awards, I found out later. Before he'd been reassigned by the diocese to an administrative position, Father Dominic had been a popular and much-loved teacher of biology. He reached behind one of the awards and drew out a packet of cigarettes.

"I'm not sure it isn't a bit sacrilegious, Susannah," he said, looking down at the red-and-white pack, "to refer to a monsignor in the Catholic church as a pus-head."

"Good thing I'm not Catholic, then," I said. "And you can smoke one of those if you want to." I nodded at the cigarettes in his hand. "I won't tell."

He looked down longingly at the pack for a minute more, then heaved this big sigh, and put them back where he'd found them. "No," he said. "Thank you, but I'd better not."

Jeez. Maybe it was a good thing I'd never really gotten the hang of the smoking thing.

I thought I'd better change the subject, so I stooped to examine some of the teaching awards. "1964," I said. "You've been around a while."

"I have." Father Dom sat down behind his desk. "What, in heaven's name, happened out there, Susannah?"

"Oh," I shrugged. "That was just Heather. I guess we know now why she's sticking around. She wants to kill Bryce Martinson."

Father Dominic shook his head. "This is terrible. It really is. I've never seen such . . . such violence from a spirit. Never, not in all my years as a mediator."

"Really?" I looked out the window. The principal's office looked, not out to the sea, but toward the hills where I lived. "Hey," I said. "You can see my house from here!"

"And she was always such a sweet girl, too. We never had a disciplinary problem from Heather Chambers, not in all her years at the Mission Academy. What could be causing her to feel so much hatred for a young man she professed to love?"

I glanced at him over my shoulder. "Are you kidding me?"

"Yes, well, I know they broke up, but such extreme

emotions—this killing rage she's in. Surely that's quite unusual—"

I shook my head. "Excuse me, I know you took a vow of celibacy and all, but haven't you ever been in love? Don't you know what it's like? That guy hosed her. She thought they were going to get married. I know, that was stupid, especially since she's only what, sixteen? Still, he just hosed her. If that's not enough to inspire a killing rage in a girl, I don't know what is."

He studied me thoughtfully. "You're speaking from experience."

"Who me? Not quite. I mean, I've had crushes on guys and stuff, but I can't say any of them have ever returned the favor." Much to my chagrin. "Still, I can *imagine* how Heather must have felt when he broke up with her."

"Like killing herself, I suppose," Father Dominic said.

"Exactly. But killing herself didn't turn out to be enough. She won't be satisfied until she takes him down with her."

"This is dreadful," Father Dominic said. "Really, really dreadful. I've talked with her until I was blue in the face, and she won't listen. And now, the first day back, this happens. I'm going to have to advise that the young man stay home until we can get this resolved."

I laughed. "How are you going to do that? Tell him his dead girlfriend's trying to kill him? Oh, yeah, that'll go over well with the monsignor."

"Not at all." Father Dom opened a drawer, and started rifling through it. "With a little ingenuity, I can see that Mr. Martinson is out for a solid week or two."

"Oh, no way!" I felt myself go pale. "You're going to poison him? I thought you were a priest! Isn't there a rule against that sort of thing?"

"Poison? No, no, Susannah. I was thinking of giving him head lice. The nurse checks for them once a semester. I'll just see that young Mr. Martinson comes down with a bad case of them—"

"Oh my God!" I shrieked. "That's disgusting! You can't put lice in that guy's hair!"

Father Dominic looked up from his drawer. "Why ever not? It will serve our purposes exactly. Keep him out of harm's way long enough for you and I to talk some sense into Miss Chambers, and—"

"You can't put lice in that guy's hair," I said again, more vehemently than was, perhaps, necessary. I don't know why I was so against the idea, except that . . . well, he had such nice hair. I'd gotten a pretty close look at it when we'd been sprawled on the ground together. It was curly, soft-looking hair, the kind of hair I could picture myself running my fingers through. The thought of bugs crawling around in it turned my stomach. How did that kid's rhyme go?

You gazed into my eyes
What could I do but linger?
I ran my hands all through your hair
And a cootie bit my finger.

"Aw, jeez," I said, sitting down on top of the desk. "Hold the lice, will you? Let me deal with Heather. You say you've been talking to her for how long now? A week?"

"Since the New Year," Father Dominic said. "Yes. That's when she first showed up here. I can see now she's just been waiting for Bryce."

"Right. Well, let me take care of it. Maybe she just needs a little dose of girl talk."

"I don't know." Father Dominic regarded me a little dubiously. "I really feel that you have a bit of a propensity toward . . . well, toward the physical. The role of a mediator is supposed to be a nonviolent one, Susannah. You are supposed to be someone who *helps* troubled spirits, not *hurts* them."

"Hello? Were you out there just now? You think I was just supposed to stand there and *talk* that beam into not crushing that guy's skull?"

"Of course not. I'm just saying that if you tried a little compassion—"

"Hey. I have plenty of compassion, Father. My heart bleeds for this girl, it really does. But this is *my* school. Got it? Mine. Not hers, not anymore. She made her decision, and now she's got to stick with it. And I'm not letting her take Bryce—or anyone else—down with her."

"Well." Father Dominic looked skeptical. "Well, if you're sure . . ."

"Oh, I'm sure." I hopped off his desk. "Just leave it to me, all right?"

Father Dominic said, "All right." But he said it kind of faintly, I noticed. I had to get him to write me a hall pass so I could get back to class without getting busted by one of the nuns. I was waiting for one of them— a pinch-faced novice—to finish scrutinizing this pass before she'd let me go on down the corridor when a side door marked NURSE opened, and out stepped Bryce with a hall pass of his own.

"Hey," I couldn't help blurting out. "What happened? Did she—I mean, did something else happen? Are you hurt?"

He grinned a bit sheepishly. "No. Well, unless you count this wicked splinter I got under my thumbnail. I was trying to brush all those little pieces of wood off my pants, you know, and one of them got under there, and—" He held up his right hand. A large bandage had been wrapped around his thumb.

"Yikes," I said.

"I know." He looked mournful. "She used Mercurochrome, too. I *hate* that stuff."

"Man," I said. "You have had a rotten day."

"Not really," he said, putting his thumb down. "At least, not as bad as it would have been if you hadn't been here. If it weren't for you, I'd be dead." He noticed that I'd come through the door marked PRINCIPAL and asked, "Did you get in trouble or something?"

"No," I said. "Father Dominic just wanted me to fill out some forms. I'm new, you know."

"And as a new student," the novice said severely, "you ought to be made aware that loitering in the halls is not allowed. Both of you had better get to your classes."

I apologized and took back my pass. Bryce very chivalrously offered to show me where my next class was, and the novice went away, seemingly satisfied. As soon as she was out of earshot, Bryce said, "You're Suze, right? Jake told me about you. You're his new stepsister from New York."

"That's me," I said. "And you're Bryce Martinson."

"Oh, Jake's mentioned me?"

I almost laughed out loud at the idea of Sleepy mentioning much of anything. I said, "No, it wasn't Jake."

He said, "Oh," in such a sad voice that I almost felt sorry for him. "I guess people must be talking about me, huh?"

"A little." I took the plunge. "I'm sorry about what happened with your girlfriend."

"So am I, believe me." If he was mad that I'd brought the subject up, you couldn't tell. "I didn't even want to come back here after . . . you know. I tried to transfer to RLS, but they're full. Even the public school didn't want me. It's tough to transfer with only one semester to go. I wouldn't have come back at all except that . . . well, you know. Colleges generally want you to have graduated from high school before they'll let you in."

I laughed. "I've heard that."

"Anyway." Bryce noticed I was holding my coat—I'd been dragging it around all day since I couldn't use my locker, the door having been dented permanently shut when I'd knocked Heather into it—and said, "Want me to carry that for you?"

I was so shocked by this civility that without even thinking, I said, "Sure," and passed it over to him. He folded it over one arm, and said, "So, I guess everybody must be blaming me for what happened. To Heather, I mean."

"I don't think so," I said. "If anything, people are blaming Heather for what happened to Heather."

"Yeah," Bryce said, "but I mean, I drove her to it, you know? That's the thing. If I just hadn't broken up with her—"

"You have a pretty high opinion of yourself, don't you?"

He looked taken aback. "What?"

"Well, your assumption that she killed herself because you broke up with her. I don't think that's why she killed herself at all. She killed herself because she was sick. You had nothing to do with making her that way. Your breaking up with her may have acted as a sort of catalyst for her final breakdown, but it could just have easily been some other crisis in her life—her parents getting divorced, her not making the cheerleader squad, her cat dying. Anything. So try not to be so hard on yourself." We were at the door to my classroom—geometry, I think it was, with Sister Mary Catherine. I turned to him and took my coat back. "Well, this is my stop. Thanks for the lift."

He held onto one sleeve of my coat. "Hey," he said, looking down at me. It was hard to see his eyes—it was pretty dark beneath the breezeway, shadowed as it was from the sun. But I remembered from when we'd fallen down together that his eyes were blue. A really nice blue. "Hey, listen," he said. "Let me take you out tonight. To thank you for saving my life and everything."

"Thanks," I said, giving my coat a tug. "But I already have plans." I didn't add that my plans involved him in a most intimate manner.

"Tomorrow night, then," he said, still not relinquishing my coat.

"Look," I said, "I'm not allowed to go out on school nights."

This was patently untrue. Except for the fact that the police have brought me home a few times, my mother trusted me implicitly. If I wanted to go out with a boy on a school night, she'd have let me. The thing is, the subject had never really come up, no boy ever having offered to take me out on a school night, or any other for that matter.

Not that I'm a dog or anything. I mean, I'm no Cindy Crawford, but I'm not exactly busted, either. I guess the truth of the matter is, I was always considered something of a weirdo in my old school. Girls who spend a lot of time talking to themselves and getting in trouble with the police generally are.

Don't get me wrong. Occasionally new guys would show up at school, and they'd express some interest in me . . . but only until someone who knew me filled them in. Then they'd avoid me like I had the plague or something.

East Coast boys. What did *they* know?

But now I had a chance to start all over, with a new population of boys who had no idea about my past— well, except for Sleepy and Dopey, and I doubted they would tell since neither of them are what you'd call . . . well, verbal.

Neither of them had evidently gotten to Bryce, anyway, since the next words out of his mouth were, "This weekend, then. What are you doing Saturday night?"

I wasn't sure it was such a good idea to get involved with a guy whose dead girlfriend was trying to kill him. I mean, what if she found out and resented me for it? I was sure Father Dominic wouldn't think it was very cool, me going out with Bryce.

Then again, how often did a girl like me get asked out by a totally hot guy like Bryce Martinson?

"Okay," I said. "Saturday it is. Pick me up at seven?"

He grinned. He had very nice teeth, white and even. "Seven," he said, letting go of my coat. "See you then. If not before."

"See you then." I stood with my hand on the door to Sister Mary Catherine's geometry class. "Oh, and Bryce."

He had started down the breezeway, toward his own classroom. "Yeah?"

"Watch your back."

I think he winked at me, but it was kind of hard to tell in the shade.

CHAPTER 9

When I climbed into the Rambler at the end of the day, Doc was all over me. "Everybody's talking about it!" he cried, bouncing up and down on the seat. "Everybody saw it! You saved that guy's life! You saved Bryce Martinson's life!"

"I didn't save his life," I said, calmly twisting the rearview mirror so I could see how my hair looked. Perfect. Salt air definitely agrees with me.

"You did so. I saw that big chunk of wood. If that'd landed on his head, it would've killed him! You saved him, Suze. You really did."

"Well." I rubbed a little gloss into my lips. "Maybe."

"God, you've only been at the Mission one day, and already you're the most popular girl in school!"

Doc was completely unable to contain himself. Sometimes I wondered whether Ritalin might have been the answer. Not that I didn't like the kid. In fact, I liked him best out of all of Andy's boys—which I realize is not saying much, but it's all I've got. It had been Doc who, just the night before, had come to me while I'd been trying to decide what to wear my first day at school and asked me, his face very pale, if I was sure I didn't want to trade bedrooms with him.

I'd looked at him like he was nuts. Doc had a nice room, and everything, but please. Give up my private bath and sea view? No way. Not even if it meant ridding myself of my unwanted roommate, Jesse, whom I hadn't actually heard from since I'd told him to get the hell out.

"What on earth makes you think I'd want to give up my room?" I asked him.

Doc shrugged. "Just that . . . well, this room's kinda creepy, don't you think?"

I stared at him. You should have seen my room just then. With the bedside lamp on, casting a cheerful pink glow over everything, and my CD player belting out Janet Jackson—loud enough that my mother had shouted twice for me to turn it down—creepy was the last thing anyone would have called my room. "Creepy?" I echoed, looking around. No sign of Jesse. No sign of anything at all undead. We were quite firmly in the realm of the living. "What's creepy about it?"

Doc pursed his lips. "Don't tell my dad," he said, "but I've been doing a lot of research into this house, and I've come to the conclusion—quite a definitive one—that it's haunted."

I blinked at his freckled little face, and saw that he was serious. *Quite* serious, as his next remark proved.

"Although modern scientists have, for the most part, debunked the majority of claims of paranormal activity in this country, there is still ample evidence that unexplained spectral phenomena exist in our world. My own personal investigation of this house was unsatisfactory insofar as traditional indications of a spiritual presence, such as the so-called cold spot. But there was nevertheless a very definite fluctuation of temperature in this room, Suze, leading me to believe that it was probably the scene of at least one incidence of great violence—perhaps even a murder—and that some remnant of the victim—call it the soul, if you will—still lurks here, perhaps in the vain hope of gaining justice for his untimely death."

I leaned against one of the posts of my bedframe. I had to, or I might have fallen down. "Gee," I said, keeping my voice steady with an effort. "Way to make a girl feel welcome."

Doc looked embarrassed. "I'm sorry," he said, the tips of his sticky-outy ears turning red. "I shouldn't have said anything. I did mention it to Jake and Brad, and they told me I was nuts. I probably am." He swallowed bravely. "But I feel it's my duty, as a man, to offer to trade rooms with you. You see, I'm not afraid."

I smiled at him, my shock forgotten in a sudden rush of affection for him. I was really touched. You could see the offer had taken all the guts the little guy had. He really and truly believed my room was haunted, in spite of everything that science told him, and yet he'd been willing to sacrifice himself for my sake, out of some sort of inborn chivalry. You had to like the little guy. You really did.

"That's okay, Doc," I said, forgetting myself in a sudden burst of sentimentality and calling him by my own private nickname for him. "I think I can pretty much handle any paranormal phenomena that might occur around here."

He didn't seem to mind the new nickname, though. He said, obviously relieved, "Well, if you really don't mind—"

"No, it's okay. But let me ask you something." I lowered my voice, just in case Jesse was lurking around somewhere. "In all of your extensive research, did you ever come across the name of this poor slob whose soul is inhabiting my room?"

Doc shook his head. "Actually, I'm sure I could get it for you, if you really want it. I can look it up down at the library. They have all the newspapers ever printed in the area since the first press started running, shortly before this house was built. It's on microfiche, but I'm sure if I spend enough time looking—"

It seemed kind of wacky to me, some kid spending all his time in a dark library basement looking at microfiche, when a block or two away was this beautiful beach. But hey, to each his own, right?

"Cool," was all I said, however.

Now I could see that Doc's little crush on me was threatening to get blown all out of proportion. First I'd willingly volunteered to abide in a room rumored to be haunted, and then I'd gone and saved Bryce Martinson's life. What was I going to do next? Run a three-minute mile?

"Look," I said, as Sleepy struggled with the ignition, which apparently had a tendency not to work on the first try. "I just did what any of you would have done if you'd been standing nearby."

"Brad *was* standing nearby," Doc said, "and he didn't do anything."

Dopey said, "Jesus Christ, I didn't *see* the stupid beam, okay? If I'd seen it, I'd have pushed him out of the way, too. Christ!"

"Yeah, but you didn't see it. You were probably too busy looking at Kelly Prescott."

This earned Doc a hard slug on the arm. "Shuddup, David," Dopey said. "You don't know anything about it."

"*All* of you shut up," Sleepy said with uncharacteristic grumpiness. "I'll never get this damned car started if you all don't keep distracting me. Brad, stop hitting David, David stop yelling in my ear, and Suze, if you don't move your big head out of the mirror I'll never be able to see where the hell we're going. Damn, I can't *wait* till I get that Camaro!"

The phone call came after dinner. My mother had to scream up the stairs at me because I had my headphones on. Even though it was only the first day of the new semester, I had a lot of homework to do, especially in geometry. We'd only been on Chapter Seven back in my old school. The Mission Academy sophomores were already on Chapter Twelve. I knew I was pretty much dead meat if I didn't start trying to catch up.

When I came downstairs to pick up the phone, my mom was already so mad at me for making her scream—she has to watch her vocal cords for her job and everything—that she wouldn't tell me who it was. I picked up the receiver and went, "Hello?"

There was a pause, and then Father Dominic's voice came on. "Hello? Susannah? Is that you? Look, I'm sorry to bother you at home, but I've been giving this some thought and I really think—yes, I really do think we need to do something right away. I can't stop thinking about what might have happened to poor Bryce if you hadn't been there."

I looked over my shoulder. Dopey was playing Cool Boarders—with his dad, the only person in the house who let him win—my mom was working on her computer, Sleepy was out subbing for some pizza deliverer who'd called in sick, and Doc was sitting at the dining room table working on a science project that wasn't due until April.

"Uh," I said. "Look. I can't really talk right now."

"I realize that," Father Dom said. "And don't worry—I had one of the novices ask for you. Your mother thinks it's just some new little friend you've made at school. But the thing of it is, Susannah, we've got to do something, and I think it had better be tonight—"

"Look," I said. "Don't worry about it. I've got it under control."

Father Dom sounded surprised. "You do? You *do*? *How? How* have you got it under control?"

"Never mind. But I've done this before. Everything will be fine. I promise."

"Yes, well, it's all very well to promise everything will be fine, but I've seen you at work, Susannah, and I can't say I've been very impressed with your technique. We've got the archbishop visiting in a month, and I can't very well—"

The call-waiting went off. I said, "Oh, hang on a sec. I've got another call." I hit the hook and went, "Ackerman-Simon residence."

"Suze?" A boy's voice, unrecognizable to me.

"Yes. . . ."

"Oh, hi. It's Bryce. So. What's going on?"

I looked at my mother. She was scowling into the

story she was working on. "Um," I said. "Nothing much. Can you hold on a second, Bryce? I've got someone on the other line."

"Sure," Bryce said.

I switched back to Father Dominic. "Uh, hi," I said, careful not to say his name. "I gotta go. My mother has a very important caller on the other line. A senator. State senator." I was probably going to go to hell for it—if there was such a place—but I couldn't very well tell Father Dominic the truth: that I was dating the ghost's ex-boyfriend.

"Oh, of course," Father Dominic said. "I—well, if you have a plan."

"I do. Don't worry. Nothing will ruin the archbishop's visit. I promise. Bye." I hung up and got back to Bryce. "Uh, hi. Sorry about that. What's up?"

"Oh, nothing. I was just thinking about you. What do you want to do on Saturday? I mean, do you want to go to dinner, or to a movie, or both, maybe?"

The other line went off. I said, "Bryce, I'm really sorry, it's a zoo here, could you hang on a minute? Thanks. Hello?"

A girl's voice I'd never heard before said, "Oh, hi, is this Suze?"

"Speaking," I said.

"Oh, hi, Susie. It's Kelly. Kelly Prescott, from your homeroom? Listen, I just wanted to let you know—what you did today for Bryce—that was so righteous. I mean, I have never in my life seen any- thing so brave. They should totally put you on the news or something. Anyway, I'm having a little get- together at my place this Saturday—nothing much, just a pool party, my folks'll be out of town, and our pool's heated, of course—so I thought, if you wanted, maybe you could stop by."

I stood there, holding the phone, totally stunned. Kelly Prescott, the richest, most beautiful girl in the entire sophomore class, was inviting me to a pool party on the same night I was going out on a date with the sexiest boy in school. Who happened to be on the other line.

"Yeah, sure, Kelly," I said. "I'd love to. Does Brad know where it is?"

"Brad?" Kelly said. Then, "Oh, *Brad*. That's right, he's your half brother or something, right? Oh, yeah, bring him. Listen—"

"I'd love to chat, Kelly, but I got somebody on the other line. Can I talk to you about it tomorrow in school?"

"Oh, totally. Bye."

I clicked back to Bryce, asked him to hold on another second, put my hand over the mouthpiece and yelled, "Brad, pool party at Kelly Prescott's this Saturday. Be there or be square."

Dopey dropped his joystick. "No way!" he yelled joyfully. "No freakin' way!"

"Hey!" Andy rapped him on the head. "Watch the language."

I got back on with Bryce. "Dinner would be great," I said. "Anything but health food."

Bryce went, "Great! Yeah, I hate health food, too. There's nothing like a really good piece of meat, you know, with some fries on the side, and some gravy—"

"Uh, yeah, right, Bryce. Listen, that's my call-waiting again, I'm really sorry, but I have to go, okay? I'll talk to you tomorrow in school."

"Oh. Okay." Bryce sounded taken aback. I guess I was the first girl who'd ever answered her call-waiting when he was on the line. "Bye, Suze. And, uh, thanks again."

"No problem. Anytime." I hit the receiver. "Hello?"

"Suze! It's CeeCee!"

In the background, I heard Adam yell, "And me, too!"

"Hey, girlfriend," CeeCee said, "we're heading down to the Clutch. Want us to pick you up? Adam just got his license."

"I'm legal!" Adam shouted into the phone.

"The Clutch?"

"Yeah, the Coffee Clutch, downtown. You drink coffee, don't you? I mean, aren't you, like, from New York?"

I had to think about that one. "Uh, yeah. The thing is—I sort of have something I have to do."

"Oh, come *on*. What do you have to do? Wash your cape? I mean, I know you're a big hero and all of that, and probably don't have time for us little people, but—"

"I haven't finished my thousand-word essay on the battle of Bladensburg for Mr. Walden," I said. "And I've got a lot of geometry to do if I'm going to catch up to you geniuses."

"Oh, gawd," CeeCee said. "All *right*. But you have to promise to sit by us at lunch tomorrow. We want to hear all about how you pressed your body up against Bryce's and what it felt like and all that stuff."

"*I* don't," Adam declared, sounding horrified.

"Okay," CeeCee said. "So *I* want to hear all about it."

I assured her I'd spare no detail and hung up. Then I looked down at the phone. To my relief, it did not ring again. I couldn't quite believe it. Never in my life had I been so popular. It was *weird*.

I had lied about my homework, of course. The essay was done, and I had worked through two chapters of geometry—about all I could handle in one night. The truth, of course, was that I had an errand to run, and I had a bit of preparation to do for it.

You don't need a whole lot of tools to do a mediation. I mean, all that stuff about crosses and holy water, I guess you need those things to kill a vampire—and I can tell you right now that I have never in my life met a vampire, and I've spent a *lot* of time in graveyards—

but for ghosts, well, you sort of have to wing it.

Sometimes, though, to get the job done right, you have to do a little breaking and entering. For that you need some tools. I highly recommend just using stuff you find on site because then you don't have a lot to carry. But I do have a tool belt with a flashlight and some screwdrivers and pliers and stuff, which I wear over a pair of black leggings. I was fastening this on at around midnight, satisfied that everyone else in the house was asleep—including Sleepy, who was back from his pizza round by then—and had just shrugged into my motorcycle jacket when I got a visit from good old you-know-who.

"Jeez," I said, when I caught a glimpse of his reflection behind mine in the mirror into which I was primping. I swear, I've been seeing ghosts for years, but it still freaks me out every time one of them materializes in front of me. I spun around, angry not so much that he was there, but because he'd managed to catch me so unaware. "Why are you still hanging around? I thought I told you to get lost."

Jesse was leaning very casually against one of the posts to my bed. His dark-eyed gaze roved from the top of my hooded head to the toes of my black high-tops. "It's a little late to be going out, don't you think, Susannah?" he asked as conversationally as if we'd been in the middle of a discussion about, oh, I don't know, the second Fugitive Slave Act, which I believe had been enacted at or around the time he'd died.

"Uh," I said, pulling the hood back. "Look, no offense, Jesse, but this is my room. How about you try getting out of it? And my business, too, please?"

Jesse didn't move. "Your mother won't like your going out so late at night."

"My mother." I glared at him. Up at him, I should say. He was really disconcertingly tall for someone who was dead. "What would *you* know about my mother?"

"I like your mother very much," Jesse said calmly. "She is a good woman. You are very lucky to have a mother who loves you so very much. It would upset her, I think, to see you putting yourself in the path of danger."

The path of danger. Right! "Yeah, well, news flash, Jesse. I've been sneaking out at night for a long time, and my mom's never said boo about it before. She knows I can take care of myself."

Okay, a lie, but hey, how was he to know?

"Can you?" Jesse lifted a black eyebrow dubiously. I couldn't help noticing that there was a raised scar sliced through the middle of that eyebrow, like someone had taken a swipe at Jesse's face once with a knife. I sort of understood the feeling. Especially when he let out a chuckle, and said, "I don't think so, *querida*. Not in this case."

I held up both my hands. "Okay. Number one, don't

call me stuff in Spanish. Number two, you don't even know where I'm going, so I suggest you just get off my back."

"But I do know where you're going, Susannah. You are going down to the school to talk to the girl who is trying to kill that boy, that boy you seem . . . fond of. But I'm telling you, *querida*, she is too much for you to handle alone. If you must go, you ought to have the priest with you."

I stared at him. I had a feeling my eyes were probably bugging out, but I really couldn't believe it. "What?" I sputtered. "How could you know all that? Are you . . . are you *stalking* me?"

He must have realized from my expression that he'd said the wrong thing, since he straightened up and said, "I don't know what that word means, *stalking*. All I know is that you are walking into harm's way."

"You've been following me," I said, stabbing a finger at him accusingly. "Haven't you? God, Jesse, I already have an older brother, thank you very much. I don't need you going around spying—"

"Oh, yes," Jesse said, very sarcastically. "This brother cares for you very much. Almost as much as he cares about his sleep."

"Hey!" I said, coming, against all odds, to Sleepy's defense. "He works nights, okay? He's saving up for a Camaro!"

Jesse made what I'm quite sure was a rude gesture—back in 1850. "You," he said, "aren't going anywhere."

"Oh, yeah?" I turned heel and stormed toward the door. "Try and stop me, cadaver breath."

He did a good job. My hand was on the doorknob when the deadbolt slid into place. I hadn't even realized before that there was a deadbolt on my door—it must have been an ancient one. The handle to it was gone, and God only knew, the key must have long since been lost.

I stood there for half a minute, staring down at my hand in wonder as it pulled futilely on the knob. Then I took a deep cleansing breath, the way my mom's therapist had suggested. She hadn't meant I should do this when dealing with a stalker ghost. She just meant to do it in general, whenever I was feeling stressed.

But it helped. It helped a lot.

"Okay," I said, turning around. "Jesse. This is way uncool."

Jesse looked pretty uncomfortable. I could tell as soon as I looked at him that he wasn't very happy with what he'd done. Whatever had gotten him killed in his previous life, it wasn't because he was innately cruel, or enjoyed hurting people. He was a good guy. Or at least, he was trying to be.

"I can't," he said. "Susannah. Don't go. This woman—this girl, Heather. She isn't like other spirits you might have known in the past. She's filled with hate. She'll kill you if she can."

I smiled at him encouragingly. "Then it's up to me to get rid of her, right? Come on. Unlock the door now."

He hesitated. For a second, I thought he was going to do it. But he didn't, in the end. He just stood there, looking uncomfortable . . . but firm.

"Suit yourself," I said, and walked around him, straight across the room to the bay window. I put a foot onto the seat Andy had made, and easily lifted the screen in the middle window. I had one leg over the sill when I felt his hand go around my wrist.

I turned to look at him. I couldn't see his face since the light from my bedside lamp was behind him, but I could hear his voice well enough and the soft pleading in it.

"Susannah," he said.

And that was all. Just my name.

I didn't say anything. I couldn't, sort of. I mean, I could—it wasn't like there was a lump in my throat, or anything. I just . . . I don't know.

Instead, I looked down at his hand, which was really big and kind of brown, even against the black leather of my jacket. He had a heck of a grip for a dead guy. Even for a live guy. He saw my gaze drop, and looked where I was looking, and saw his hand holding tight around my wrist.

He let go of me as if my skin had suddenly started to blister or something. I finished climbing out the window. When I had successfully maneuvered my way across the porch roof and down to the ground, I turned to look up at my bedroom window.

But he was gone of course.

CHAPTER 10

It was a cool, clear night. The moon was full. Standing in my front yard, I could see it hanging over the sea like a lightbulb—not a hundred watter, like the sun, but maybe one of those twenty-five dealies you put in those swivel-neck desk lamps. The Pacific, looking smooth as glass from this distance, was black, except for a narrow band of reflected light from the moon, which was white as paper.

I could see in the moonlight the red dome of the Mission's church. But just because I could see the Mission, didn't mean the Mission was nearby. It was a good two miles away. In my pocket were the keys to the Rambler, which I'd snatched a half hour earlier. The metal was warm from the heat of my body. The

Rambler, which was turquoise in daylight, looked gray as it sat in the shadow of the driveway.

Hey, I *know* I don't have a license. But if Dopey can do it . . .

Okay. So I chickened out. Look, isn't it better I chose not to drive? I mean, not knowing how and all. Not that I don't know how. Of course I know how to drive. I just haven't had a whole lot of practice, having lived all my life in the public transportation capital of the world. . . .

Oh, never mind. I turned around and started heading for the garage. There had to be a bike around somewhere. Three boys, right? There had to be at least one bike.

I found one. It was a boy's bike, of course, with that stupid bar, and a *really* hard, really skinny seat. But it seemed to work all right. At least the tires weren't flat.

Then I thought, *Okay, girl dressed in black, riding a bike on the streets after midnight, what do I need?*

I didn't think I was going to find any reflective tape, but I thought maybe a bike helmet might do the trick. There was one hanging on a peg on the side of the garage. I put down the hood of my sweatshirt, and fastened the thing on. Oh, yeah. Stylish and safety conscious, that's me.

And then I was off, rolling down the driveway—okay, gravel is not the easiest stuff to ride a bike on, especially going downhill. And the whole way turned out to be downhill since the house, looking out over the bay, was perched on the side of this mountainy kind of thing. Going downhill was certainly better than going uphill—there was no way I was ever going to be able to ride back up this thing; I had a pretty good idea I'd be doing some pushing on my way home—but going downhill was pretty harrowing. I mean, the hill was so steep, the way so twisty, and the night air so cold, that I rode with my heart in my throat practically the whole time, tears streaming down the sides of my cheeks because of the wind. And those potholes—

God! Did that stupid seat hurt when I hit a pothole.

But the hill wasn't the worst of it. When I got down the hill I hit an intersection. This was much scarier than the hill because even though it was after midnight, there were cars there. One of them honked at me. But it wasn't my fault. I was going so fast, because of the hill and all, that if I'd stopped I'd probably have gone right over the handlebars. So I kept on going, narrowly avoiding getting hit by a pickup, and then, I don't know how, I was pulling into the school parking lot.

The Mission looked a lot different at night than it did during the day. For one thing, during the day the parking lot was always full, packed with cars belonging to teachers, students, and tourists visiting the church. The lot was empty now, not a single car, and so quiet that you could hear, way off in the distance, the sound of waves hitting Carmel Beach.

The other thing was that, for tourist reasons, I guess, they had set up these spotlights to shine on certain parts of the building, like the dome—it was all lit up—and the front of the church, with its huge arched entranceway. The back of the building, where I pulled up, was pretty dark. Which suited me fine, actually. I hid the bike behind a Dumpster, leaving the helmet dangling from one of the handles, and went up to a window. The Mission was built like a bazillion years ago, back when they didn't have air-conditioning or central heating, so to keep cool in summer and warm in winter, people built their houses really thick. That meant that all the windows in the Mission were set back about a foot into the adobe, with another foot sticking out into the room behind them.

I climbed up onto one of these built-in window seats, looking around first to make sure no one saw me. But there wasn't anybody around except a couple of raccoons that were rooting around the Dumpster for some of the lunch leftovers. Then I cupped my hands over my face, to cut out the light of the moon, and peered inside.

It was Mr. Walden's classroom. With the moonlight flooding into it, I could see his handwriting on the chalkboard, and the big poster of Bob Dylan, his favorite poet, on the wall.

It only took me a second to punch out the glass

in one of the old-fashioned iron panes, reach in, and unlatch the window. The hard part about breaking a window isn't the breaking part, or even the reaching in part. It's getting your hand out again that always causes cuts. I had on my best ghost-busting gloves, thick black ones with rubbery stuff on the knuckles, but I've had my sleeve get caught before, and gotten my arm all scratched up.

That didn't happen this time. Plus, the window opened out, instead of up, swinging forward just enough to let a girl like me inside. Occasionally, I've broken in to places that turned out to have alarms—resulting in an uncomfortable ride for me in the back of a car belonging to one of New York's finest—but the Mission hadn't gotten that high-tech with their security system yet. In fact, their security system seemed to consist of locking the doors and windows, and hoping for the best.

Which certainly suited me fine.

Once I was inside Mr. Walden's room, I closed the window behind me. No sense alerting anybody who might happen to be manning the perimeter—as if. It was easy to maneuver between the desks, since the moon was so bright. And once I got the door open and stepped out into the breezeway, I found I didn't need my flashlight, either. The courtyard was flooded with light. I guess the Mission must stay open pretty late for the tourists because there were these big yellow floodlights hidden in the breezeway's eaves, and pointed at various objects of interest: the tallest of the palm trees, the one with the biggest hibiscus bush at its base; the fountain, which was on even though the place was closed; and of course the statue of Father Serra, with one light shining on his bronze head and another on the heads of the Native American women at his feet.

Geesh. It was a good thing Father Serra was good and dead. I had a feeling that statue would have completely embarrassed him.

The breezeway was empty, as was the courtyard. No one was around. All I could hear was the gentle splash of the water in the fountain and the chirping of crickets hidden in the garden. It was a sort of restful place, actually, which was surprising. I mean, none of my other schools had ever struck me as restful. At least, this one did, until this hard voice behind me went, "What are *you* doing here?"

I spun around, and there she was. Just leaning up against her locker—excuse me, *my* locker—and glaring at me, her arms folded across her chest. She was wearing a pair of charcoal-colored slacks—nice ones—and a gray cashmere sweater set. She had an add-a-pearl necklace around her neck, one pearl for every Christmas and birthday she'd been alive, given to her, no doubt, by a set of doting grandparents. On her feet were a pair of shiny black loafers. Her hair, as shiny as her shoes in the yellow light from the flood-lamps, looked smooth and golden. She really was a beautiful girl.

Too bad she had blown her head off.

"Heather," I said, pushing the hood of my sweat-shirt down. "Hi. I'm sorry to bother you"— it always helps at least to start out polite—"but I really think we need to talk, you and I."

Heather didn't move. Well, that's not true. Her eyes narrowed. They were pale eyes, gray, I think, though it was hard to tell, in spite of the floodlamps. The long eyelashes—dark with mascara—were tastefully ringed in charcoal liner.

"Talk?" Heather echoed. "Oh, yeah. Like I really want to talk to *you*. I know about you, *Susie*."

I winced. I couldn't help it. "It's Suze," I said.

"Whatever. I know what you're doing here."

"Well, good," I said. "Then I don't have to explain. You want to go sit down, so we can talk?"

"Talk? Why would I want to talk to *you*? What do you think I am, stupid? God, you think you're so sly. You think you can just move right in, don't you?"

I blinked at her. "I beg your pardon?"

"Into my place." She straightened and stepped away from the locker, and walked toward the court-yard as if she were admiring the fountain. "You," she said, tossing me a look over her shoulder. "The new girl. The new girl who thinks she can just slip right into the place I left behind. You've already got my locker. You're on your way to stealing my best friend. I know Kelly called you and asked you to her stupid party. And now you think you can steal my boyfriend."

I put my hands on my hips. "He's not your boyfriend, Heather, remember? He broke up with you. That's why you're dead. You blew your brains out in front of his mother."

Heather's eyes widened. "Shut up," she said.

"You blew your brains out in front of his mother because you were too stupid to realize that no boy— not even Bryce Martinson—is worth dying for." I strolled past her, out onto one of the gravel pathways between the garden beds. I didn't want to admit it, not even to myself, but it was making me a little nervous, standing under the breezeway after what had happened to Bryce. "Boy, you must have been mad when you realized what you'd done. Killed yourself. And over something so stupid. Because of a guy."

"Shut up!" This time she didn't just say it. She screamed it, so loud that she had to ball her hands up into fists at her sides, close her eyes, and hunch up her shoulders to do it. The scream was so loud, my ears were ringing afterward. But no one came running from the rectory, where I saw a few lights on. The mourning doves that I'd heard cooing in the eaves of the breezeway hadn't uttered a peep since Heather had shown up, and the crickets had cut short their mid-night serenade.

People can't hear ghosts—well, most people, any-way—but the same can't be said for animals and even insects. They are hyperalert to the presence of the paranormal. Max, the Ackermans' dog, won't go near my room thanks to Jesse.

"It's no use your screaming like that," I said. "No one but me can hear it."

"I'll scream all I want," she shrieked. And then she proceeded to do so.

Yawning, I went and sat down on one of the wooden benches by Father Serra's statue. There was a plaque, I noticed, at the statue's base. I could read it easily with the help of the floodlamps and the moon.

THE VENERABLE FATHER JUNIPERO SERRA, the plaque read, 1713–1784. HIS RIGHTEOUS WAYS AND SELF-ABNEGATION WERE A LESSON TO ALL WHO KNEW HIM AND RECEIVED HIS TEACHINGS.

Huh. I was going to have to look up self-abnegation in the dictionary when I got home. I wondered if it was the same as self-flagellation, something for which Serra had also been known.

"Are you listening to me?" Heather screamed.

I looked at her. "Do you know what the word *abne-gation* means?" I asked.

She stopped screaming and just stared at me. Then she strode forward, her face a mask of livid rage.

"Listen to me, you bitch," she said, stopping when she stood a foot away from me. "I want you gone, do you understand? I want you out of this school. That is *my* locker. Kelly Prescott is *my* best friend. And Bryce Martinson is *my* boyfriend! You get out, you go back to where you came from. Everything was just fine before you got here—"

I had to interrupt. "I'm sorry, Heather, but everything was *not* just fine before I got here. You know how I know that? Because you're dead. Okay? *You are dead.* Dead people don't have lockers, or best friends, or boyfriends. You know why? Because they're dead."

Heather looked as if she was about to start screaming again, but I headed her off at the pass. I said, smoothly and evenly, "Now, I know you made a mistake. You made a horrible, terrible mistake—"

"I'm not the one who made the mistake," Heather said flatly. "Bryce made the mistake. Bryce is the one who broke up with me."

I said, "Yeah, well, that wasn't the mistake I was talking about. I was talking about you shooting yourself because a stupid boy broke up with—"

"If you think he's so stupid," Heather said with a sneer, "why are you going out with him on Saturday? That's right. I heard him ask you out. The rat. He probably wasn't faithful a day the whole time we were going out."

"Oh," I said. "Well, that's just great. All the more

reason for you to kill yourself over him."

There were tears, sparkling like those rhinestones you buy and glue to your fingernails, gathered beneath her lashes. "I loved him," she breathed. "If I couldn't have him, I didn't want to live."

"And now that you're dead," I said tiredly, "you figure he ought to join you, right?"

"I don't like it here," she said softly. "No one can see me. Just you and F-Father Dominic. I get so lonely. . . ."

"Right. That's understandable. But Heather, even if you do manage to kill him, he probably isn't going to like you for it much."

"I can make him like me," Heather said confidently. "After all, it'll just be me and him. He'll have to like me."

I shook my head. "No, Heather. It doesn't work that way."

She stared at me. "What do you mean?"

"If you kill Bryce, there's no guarantee he'll end up here with you. What happens to people after they die—well, I'm not sure, but I think it's different for everyone. If you kill Bryce, he'll go to wherever it is he's supposed to go. Heaven, hell, his next life—I don't know for sure. But I do know he won't end up here with you. It doesn't work that way."

"But—" Heather looked furious. "But that isn't fair!"

"Lots of things aren't fair, Heather. It isn't fair, for

example, that you have to suffer for all eternity for a mistake that you made in the heat of a moment. I'm sure if you'd known what it was like to be dead, you never would have killed yourself. But, Heather, it doesn't have to be this way."

She stared down at me. The tears were frozen there, like little tiny shards of ice. "It doesn't?"

"No. It doesn't."

"You mean . . . you mean I can go back?"

I nodded. "You can. You can start over."

She sniffled. "How?"

I said, "All you have to do is make up your mind to do it."

A scowl passed over her pretty face. "But I already made up my mind that that's what I want. All I've wanted since it . . . since it happened . . . was to get my life back."

I shook my head. "No, Heather," I said. "You misunderstand me. You can never have your life—your *old* life—back. But you can start a new one. That's got to be better than this, than being here all by yourself forever, storming around in a rage, hurting people—"

She shouted, "You said I could get my life back!"

I realized, all in a flash, that I'd lost her. "I didn't mean your old life. I just meant *a* life—"

But it was too late. She was freaking.

I understood now why Bryce's parents had sent him to Antigua. I wished I were there—anywhere, really, if it would get me out of the way of this girl's wrath.

"You told me," Heather screamed, "you told me I could get my life back! You lied to me!"

"Heather, I didn't lie. I just meant that your life—well, your life is over. Heather, you ended it yourself. I know that sucks, but hey, you should have thought of that—"

She cut me off with an unearthly—well, of course—wail. "I won't let you," she shrieked. "I won't let you take over my life!"

"Heather, I told you, I'm not trying to. I have my own life. I don't need yours—"

With the crickets and the birds silent, the sound of the water burbling in the fountain a few yards away had been the only noise in the courtyard—with the exception of Heather's screaming, that is. But the water sounded strange, suddenly. It was making a funny popping noise. I looked toward it, and saw that steam was rising from its surface. I wouldn't have thought that was so strange—it was cold out, and the water temperature might have been warmer than the air around it—if I hadn't seen a great big bubble burst suddenly on the water's surface.

That's when it hit me. She was making the water boil. She was making the water boil with the force of her rage.

"Heather," I said, from my bench. "Heather, listen to me. You've got to calm down. We can't talk when you're—"

"You . . . said . . ." Heather's eyes, I was alarmed to see, had rolled back into her head. "I . . . could . . . start . . . over!"

Okay. It was time to do something. I didn't need the bench beneath me to start shaking so violently that I was nearly thrown from it. I knew it was time to get up.

I did so, fast. Fast so that I wouldn't get hit by the bench. Fast so that I could reach Heather before she noticed, and deck her as hard as I could with a right beneath the chin.

Only to my astonishment, she didn't even seem to feel it. She was too far gone. Way too far gone. Hitting her had no effect whatsoever—except that it really hurt my knuckles. And, of course, it seemed to make her even madder, always a plus when dealing with a severely disturbed individual.

"You," Heather said in a deep voice that was nothing like her normal cheerleader chirp, "are going to be sorry now."

The water in the fountain suddenly reached boiling point. Giant waves of it began sloshing over the side of the basin. The jets, which normally bubbled a mere four feet into the air, suddenly shot up to ten, twenty feet, cascading back down into a bubbling, steaming cauldron. The birds in the treetops took off as one, their wings momentarily blocking out the light from the moon.

I had a funny feeling Heather was serious. What's more, I had a feeling she could do it, too. Without even lifting a finger.

And I had confirmation of that fact when suddenly, Junipero Serra's head was whipped from his statue's body. That's right. It just snapped off as easily as if the solid bronze it was made out of was actually spun candy. Noiselessly, too, she broke it off. The head hung in the air for a moment, its look of sympathetic compassion transformed from the bizarre angle at which it hung over my face into a demonic sneer. Then, as I stood there, transfixed, staring at the way the floodlights winked against the metal ball, I saw it dip suddenly . . .

Then plunge toward me, hurtling so fast it was only a blur in the night sky, like a comet, or a—

I didn't get a chance to think what else it reminded me of because a split second later something heavy hit me in the stomach and sent me sprawling to the dirt, where I lay, looking up at the starry sky. It was so pretty. The night was so black, and the stars so cold and far off and twinkly—

"Get up!" A man's voice sounded harshly in my ear. "I thought you were supposed to be good at this!"

Something exploded in the dirt just an inch from my cheek. I turned my head and saw Junipero Serra's head grinning obscenely at me.

Then Jesse was yanking me to my feet and pulling me toward the breezeway.

CHAPTER 11

We made it back into Mr. Walden's classroom. I don't know how, but we did it, the statue's head hurtling after us the whole way, the velocity with which it was traveling causing it to whistle eerily, as if Father Serra were screaming. The head collided with all the force of a cannonball against the heavy wooden door just as we slammed it closed behind us.

"*Jesucristo,*" Jesse sputtered, as we leaned, panting, with our backs pressed up against the door as if with our sheer weight, we could keep her out—Heather, who could walk through walls if she wanted to. "'I can take care of myself,' you said. 'I'll just have to get rid of her first,' you told me. Right!"

I was trying to catch my breath, think what to do.

I had never seen anything like that. Never. "Shut up," I said.

"Cadaver breath." Jesse turned his head to look down at me. His chest was rising and falling. "Do you realize that's what you called me? That hurt, you know, *querida*. It really hurt."

"I told you—" Something heavy was buffeting against the door. I could feel it knocking against my spine. It didn't take a genius to guess it was the founder of a certain mission's head. "—not to call me that."

"Well, I would appreciate if you didn't make disparaging remarks about my—"

"Look," I said. "This door isn't going to hold up forever."

"No," he agreed, just as the metal head managed to smash its way partly through a spot it had weakened in the wood. "May I make a suggestion?"

I was staring, horrified, down at the head, which had turned, halfway in and halfway out of the door, to look up at me with cold, bronze eyes. It's crazy, but I could have sworn it was smiling at me. "Sure," I said.

"Run."

I wasted no time in taking his advice. I ran for the windowsill and, heedless of the shards of broken glass, swung myself up onto it. It only took a few seconds to open the window again, but that was long enough for Jesse, still pushing against what had begun to sound like a hurricane with all the banging and wailing, to say, "Uh, hurry, please?"

I jumped down into the parking lot. It was kind of funny how, outside the thick adobe walls of the Mission, you couldn't tell at all that there was a severe paranormal disturbance going on inside. The parking lot was still empty, and still quiet, except for the gentle, rhythmic sound of ocean waves. It's just amazing what can be going on beneath people's noses, and they have no idea . . . no idea at all.

"Jesse!" I hissed through the window. "Come on!" I had no idea if Heather might decide to take out her rage with me on an innocent party—or, if she did, whether Jesse had any cool tricks, like the one she'd pulled with the statue's head, of his own. All I knew was that the sooner the both of us got out of her range, the better.

Okay, let me state right now that I am not a coward. I'm really not. But I'm not a fool, either. I think if you recognize that you are up against a force greater than your own, it is perfectly okay to run.

It's not okay to leave others behind, though.

"Jesse!" I screamed through the window.

"I thought I told you," said a very irritated voice from behind me, "to run."

I gasped and spun around. Jesse stood there on the asphalt of the parking lot, the moon at his back, casting his face into shadow.

"Oh my God." My heart was beating so fast, I

thought it was going to explode. I had never been so scared in all my life. Never.

Maybe that's why I did what I did next, which was reach out and grab the front of Jesse's shirt in both my hands. "Oh my God," I said again. "Jesse, are you all right?"

"Of course I'm all right." He sounded surprised I'd even bother to ask. And I guess it *was* stupid. What could Heather do to Jesse, after all? She couldn't exactly kill him. "Are *you* all right?"

"Me? I'm fine." I turned my head to search the darkened windows of Mr. Walden's classroom. "Do you think she's . . . done?"

"For now," Jesse said.

"How do you know?" I was shocked to find that I was shaking—really shaking—all over. "How do you know she won't come bursting through that wall there and start uprooting all those trees and hurling them at us?"

Jesse shook his head, and I could see that he was smiling. You know, for a guy who died before they invented orthodontia, he had pretty nice teeth. Almost as nice as Bryce's. "She won't."

"How do you *know*?"

"Because she won't. She doesn't know she can. She's too new at all this, Susannah. She doesn't know yet all that she can do."

If that was supposed to make me feel better, it

didn't work. The fact that he admitted she *could* uproot trees and start hurling them at me—she was *that* powerful—and only hadn't due to lack of experience, was enough to stop my shaking cold, and drop the handfuls of shirt I held. Not that I didn't think Heather could have followed me if she wanted to. She could, the same way Jesse had followed me down to the Mission. But the thing of it was, Jesse knew he could. He'd been a ghost a lot longer than Heather. She was only just beginning to explore her new powers.

That was the scariest part. She was so new at all of this . . . and already that powerful.

I started pacing around the parking lot like a crazy woman.

"We've got to do something," I said. "We've got to warn Father Dominic—and Bryce. My God, we've got to warn Bryce not to come to school tomorrow. She'll kill him the minute he sets foot on campus—"

"Susannah," Jesse said.

"I guess we could call him. It's one in the morning, but we could call him, and tell him—I don't know what we could tell him. We could tell him there's been a death threat on him or something. That might work. Or—we could *leave* a death threat. Yeah, that's what we could do! We could call his house and I could disguise my voice, and I could be like 'Don't come to school tomorrow, or you'll die.' Maybe he'd listen. Maybe he'd—"

"Susannah," Jesse said again.

"Or we could have Father Dom do it! We could have Father Dom call Bryce and tell him not to come to school, that there's been some kind of accident or something—"

"Susannah." Jesse stepped in front of me just as I turned around to retread the same five feet I'd been pacing for the past few minutes. I came up short, startled by his sudden proximity, my nose practically banging into the place where his shirt collar was open. Jesse seized both my arms quickly, to steady me.

This was not a good thing. I mean, I know a minute ago I had grabbed him—well, not really him, but his shirt. But I don't like being touched under normal circumstances, and I especially don't like being touched by ghosts. And I *especially* don't like being touched by ghosts who have hands as big and as tendony and strong-looking as Jesse's.

"Susannah," he said again, before I could tell him to get his big tendony hands off me. "It's all right. It's not your fault. There was nothing you could do."

I sort of forgot about being mad about his hands. "Nothing I could do? Are you kidding me? I should have kicked that girl back into her grave!"

"No." Jesse shook his head. "She'd have killed you."

"Bull! I totally could have taken her. If she hadn't done that thing with that guy's head—"

"Susannah."

"I mean it, Jesse, I could totally have handled her if she hadn't gotten so mad. I bet if I just wait a little while until she's calmed down and go back in there, I can talk her into—"

"No." He let go of my arms, but only so he could wrap one of his own around my shoulders and start steering me away from the school and toward the Dumpster where I'd parked my bike. "Come on. Let's go home."

"But what about—"

The grip on my shoulders tightened. "No."

"Jesse, you don't understand. This is my *job*. I have to—"

"It's Father Dominic's job, too, no? Let him take it from here. There's no reason why you have to be burdened with all the responsibility yourself."

"Well, yes, there is. I'm the one who screwed up."

"You put the gun to her head and pulled the trigger?"

"Of course not. But I'm the one who got her so mad. Father Dom didn't. I can't ask Father Dom to clean up my messes. That is totally unfair."

"What is totally unfair," Jesse explained—patiently, I guess, for him, "is for anyone to expect a young girl like yourself to do battle with a demon from hell like—"

"She isn't a demon from hell. She's just mad. She's mad because the one guy she thought she could trust turned out to be a—"

"Susannah." Jesse stopped walking suddenly. The only reason I didn't lurch forward and fall flat on my face was that he still kept hold of my shoulder.

For a minute—just a minute—I really thought . . . well, I thought he was going to kiss me. I'd never been kissed before, but it seemed as if all the necessities for a kiss to happen were there: You know, his arm was around me, there was moonlight, our hearts were racing—oh, yeah, and we'd both just narrowly escaped being killed by a really pissed-off ghost.

Of course, I didn't know how I felt about my first kiss coming from one of the undead, but hey, beggars can't be choosers, and let me tell you something, Jesse was way cuter than any live guy I'd met lately. I'd never seen such a nice-looking ghost. He couldn't, I thought, have been more than twenty when he died. I wondered what had killed him. It's usually hard to tell with ghosts, since their spirits tend to take on the shape their body was in just before they stopped functioning. My dad, for instance, doesn't look any different when he appears to me now than he did the day before he went out for that fatal jog around Prospect Park ten years ago.

I could only assume Jesse had died at someone else's hands since he looked pretty damned healthy to me. Chances were he'd been a victim of one of those bullet holes downstairs. Nice of Andy to frame it for posterity's sake.

And now this extremely nice-looking ghost looked as if he were going to kiss me. Well, who was I to stop him?

So I sort of leaned my head back and looked out at him from underneath my eyelids, and sort of let my mouth get all relaxed, you know? And that's when I noticed his attention wasn't focused anywhere near my lips, but way below them. And not my chest, either, which would have been an okay second.

"You're bleeding," he said.

Well, that pretty much spoiled the moment. My eyes popped wide open at *that* remark.

"I am not," I said automatically since I didn't feel any pain. Then I looked down. There were smallish stains flowering on the pavement below my feet. You couldn't tell what color they were because it was so dark. In the moonlight, they looked black. There were similar dark stains, I saw with horror, on the front of Jesse's shirt.

But they were definitely coming from me. I checked myself out, and found that I'd managed to open what was probably one of the smaller, but still fairly important, veins in my wrist. I'd peeled off my gloves and stuffed them in my pockets while I'd been talking to Heather, and in my haste to escape during her fit of rage, I'd forgotten to put them back on. I'd probably sliced myself on the broken glass still littering the windowsill in Mr. Walden's classroom when I'd vaulted up onto it during my escape. Which just proved my theory that it's always on the way out that you get stuck.

"Oh," I said, watching the blood ooze out. I couldn't think of anything else to say but, "What a mess. I'm sorry about your shirt."

"It's nothing." Jesse reached into one of the pockets of his dark, narrow-fitting trousers and pulled out something white and soft that he wrapped around my wrist a few times, then tied into place like a tourniquet, only not as tight. He didn't say anything as he did this, concentrating on what he was doing. I have to say this was the first time a ghost had ever performed first aid on me. Not quite as interesting as a kiss would have been, but not entirely boring, either.

"There," he said when he was finished. "Does that hurt?"

"No," I said, since it didn't. It wouldn't start hurting, I knew from experience, for a few hours. I cleared my throat. "Thanks."

"It's nothing," he said.

"No," I said. Suddenly, ridiculously, I felt like crying. Really. And I never cry. "I mean it. Thanks. Thanks for coming out here to help me. You shouldn't have done it. I mean, I'm glad you did. And . . . well, thanks. That's all."

He looked embarrassed. Well, I suppose that was natural, me going all mushy on him the way I had just then. But I couldn't help it. I mean, I still couldn't really believe it. No ghost had ever been so nice to me. Oh, my dad tried, I guess. But he wasn't exactly what you'd call reliable about it. I could never really count on him, especially in a crisis.

But Jesse. Jesse had come through for me. And I hadn't even asked him to. In fact, I'd been pretty unpleasant to him, overall.

"Never mind," was all he said, though. And then he added, "Let's go home."

CHAPTER 12

Let's go home.

It had a very cozy feel to it, that "Let's go home."

Except, of course, that the house we shared didn't quite feel like home to me yet. How could it? I'd only lived there a few days.

And, of course, *he* shouldn't have been living there at all.

Still, ghost or not, he'd saved my life. There was no denying that. He'd probably only done it to get on my good side so I wouldn't kick him out of the house entirely.

But regardless of why he'd done it, it had still been pretty nice of him. Nobody had ever volunteered to help me before—mostly because, of course, nobody knew I needed help. Even Gina, who'd been there when Madame Zara had first pronounced me a mediator, never knew why it was I would show up to school so groggy-eyed, or where it was I went when I cut class—which I did all too frequently. And I couldn't exactly explain. Not that Gina would have thought I was crazy or anything, but she'd have told someone—you can't keep something like this secret unless it's happening to you—who'd have told someone else, and eventually, somewhere along the line, I knew someone would have told my mother.

And my mother would have freaked. That is, naturally, what mothers do, and mine is no exception. She'd already stuck me in therapy where I was forced to sit and invent elaborate lies in the hopes of explaining my antisocial behavior. I did not need to spend any time in a mental institution, which was undoubtedly where I'd have ended up if my mother had ever found out the truth.

So, yeah, I was grateful to have Jesse along, even though he sort of made me nervous. After the debacle at the Mission, he walked me home, which was gentlemanly and all. He even, in deference to my injury, insisted on pushing the bike. I suppose if anybody had looked out the window of any of the houses we were passing, they would have thought their eyes were playing tricks on them: They'd have seen me plodding along with this bike rolling effortlessly beside me—

only my hands weren't touching the bike.

Good thing people on the West Coast go to bed so early.

The whole way home, I obsessed over what I'd done wrong in my dealings with Heather. I didn't do it out loud—I figured I'd done enough of that; I didn't want to sound like a broken record or player piano, or whatever it was they had back in Jesse's day. But it was all I could think about. Never, not in all my years of mediating, had I ever encountered such a violent, irrational spirit. I simply did not know what to do. And I knew I had to figure it out, and quick; I only had a few hours before school started and Bryce walked straight into what was, for him, a deathtrap.

I don't know if Jesse figured out why I was so quiet, or if he was thinking about Heather, too, or what. All I know was that suddenly, he broke the silence we'd been walking in and went, "'Heav'n has no rage like love to hatred turn'd, nor hell a fury like a woman scorned.'"

I looked at him. "Are you speaking from experience?"

I saw him smile a little in the moonlight. "Actually," he said, "I am quoting William Congreve."

"Oh." I thought about that. "But you know, sometimes the woman scorned has every right to be mad."

"Are *you* speaking from experience?" he wanted to know.

I snorted. "Not hardly." A guy has to like you before he can scorn you. But I didn't say that out loud. No way would I ever say something like that out loud. I mean, not that I *cared* what Jesse thought about me. Why should I care what some dead cowboy thought of me?

But I wasn't about to admit to him that I'd never had a boyfriend. You just don't go around saying things like that to totally hot guys, even if they're dead.

"But we don't know what went on between Heather and Bryce—not really. I mean, she could have every right to feel resentful."

"Toward him, I suppose she does," Jesse said, though he sounded grudging about admitting it. "But not toward *you*. She had no right to try to hurt *you*."

He sounded so mad about it that I thought it was probably better to change the subject. I mean, I guess I should have been mad about Heather trying to kill me, but you know, I'm sort of used to dealing with irrational people. Well, okay, not quite as irrational as Heather, but you know what I mean. And one thing I've learned is, you can't take it personally. Yeah, she'd tried to kill me, but I wasn't really sure she knew any better. Who knew what kind of parents she had, after all? Maybe they went around murdering anybody who made them mad. . . .

Although somehow, after having seen that add-a-pearl necklace, I sort of doubted that.

Thinking about murder made me wonder what

had gotten Jesse so hot under the collar about it. Then I realized that he'd probably been murdered. Either that or he'd killed himself. But I didn't think he was really the suicide type. I supposed he could have died of some sort of wasting disease. . . .

It probably wasn't very tactful of me—but then, nobody's ever accused me of tact—but I went ahead and just asked him as we were climbing the long gravel driveway to the house, "Hey. How'd you die, anyway?"

Jesse didn't say anything right away. I'd probably offended him. Ghosts don't really like talking about how they died, I've noticed. Sometimes they can't even remember. Car crash victims usually haven't the slightest clue what happened to them. That's why I always see them wandering around looking for the other people who were in the car with them. I have to go up and explain to them what happened, and then try to figure out where the people are that they're look- ing for. This is a major pain, too, let me tell you. I have to go all the way to the precinct that took the accident report and pretend I'm doing a school report or what- ever and record the names of the victims, then follow up on what happened to them.

I tell you, sometimes I feel like my work never ends.

Anyway, Jesse was quiet for a while, and I figured he wasn't going to tell me. He was looking straight ahead, up at the house—the house where he'd died, the house he was destined to haunt until . . . well, until he resolved whatever it was that was holding him to this world.

The moon was still out, pretty high in the sky now, and I could see Jesse's face almost as if it were day. He didn't look a whole lot different than usual. His mouth, which was on the thin-but-wide side, was kind of frowning, which, as near as I could tell, was what it usually did. And underneath those glossy black eyebrows, his thickly lashed eyes revealed about as much as a mirror—that is, I could probably have seen my reflection in them, but I could read nothing about what he might be thinking.

"Um," I said. "You know what? Never mind. If you don't want to tell me, you don't have to—"

"No," he said. "It's all right."

"I was just kinda curious, that's all," I said. "But if it's too personal . . ."

"It isn't too personal." We had reached the house by then. He wheeled the bike to where it was supposed to go, and leaned it up against the carport wall. He was deep in the shadows when he said, "You know this house wasn't always a family home."

I went, "Oh, really?" Like this was the first I'd heard of it.

"Yes. It was once a hotel. Well, more like a boardinghouse, really, than a hotel."

I asked brightly, "And you were staying here as a guest?"

"Yes." He came out from the shade of the carport, but he wasn't looking at me when he spoke next. He was squinting out toward the sea.

"And . . ." I tried to prompt him. "Something happened while you were staying here?"

"Yes." He looked at me then. He looked at me for a long time. Then he said, "But it's a long story, and you must be very tired. Go to bed. In the morning we will decide what to do about Heather."

Talk about unfair!

"Wait a minute," I said. "I am not going anywhere until you finish that story."

He shook his head. "No. It's too late. I'll tell you some other time."

"Jeez!" I sounded like a little kid whose mom had told him to go to bed early, but I didn't care. I was mad. "You can't just start a story and then not finish it. You have to—"

Jesse was laughing at me now. "Go to bed, Susannah," he said, coming up and giving me a gentle push toward the front steps. "You have had enough scaring for one night."

"But you—"

"Some other time," he said. He had steered me in the direction of the porch, and now I stood on the lowest step, looking back at him as he laughed at me.

"Do you promise?"

I saw his teeth flash white in the moonlight. "I

promise. Good night, *querida*."

"I told you," I grumbled, stomping up the steps, "not to call me that."

It was nearly 3:00 in the morning, though, and I could only summon up token indignation. I was still on New York time, remember, three hours ahead. It had been hard enough getting up in time for school when I'd had a full eight hours of sleep. How hard was it going to be after only having had four?

I slipped into the house as quietly as I could. Fortunately, everybody except the dog was dead asleep. The dog looked up from the couch on which he was reclining and wagged his tail when he saw it was me. Some watchdog. Plus my mom didn't want him sleeping on her white couch. But I wasn't about to make an enemy out of Max by shooing him off. If allowing him to sleep on the couch was all that was necessary to keep him from alerting the household that I'd been out, then it was well worth it.

I slogged up the stairs, wondering the whole time what I was going to do about Heather. I guessed I was going to have to wake up early and call over to the school, and warn Father Dom to meet Bryce the minute he set foot on campus and send him home. Even, I decided, if we had to resort to head lice, I wouldn't object. All that mattered, in the long run, was that Heather was kept from her goal.

Still, the thought of waking up early to do anything—even save the life of my date for Saturday night—was not very appealing. Now that the adrenaline rush was gone, I realized I was dead tired. I staggered into the bathroom to change into my pj's—hey, I was pretty sure Jesse wasn't spying on me, but he still hadn't told me how he'd died, so I wasn't taking any chances. He could have been hanged, you know, for Peeping Tomism, which I believed happened occasionally a hundred and fifty years ago.

It wasn't until I was changing the bandage on the cut on my wrist that I happened to take a look at the thing he'd wrapped around it.

It was a handkerchief. Everybody carried one in the olden days because there was no such thing as Kleenex. People were pretty fussy about them, too, sewing their initials onto them so they didn't get mixed up in the wash with other people's hankies.

Only Jesse's handkerchief didn't have his initials on it, I noticed after I'd rinsed it in the sink then wrung out my blood as best I could. It was a big linen square, white—well, kind of pink now—with an edging all around it of this delicate white lace. Kind of femme for a guy. I might have been a little concerned about Jesse's sexual orientation if I hadn't noticed the initials sewn in one corner. The stitches were tiny, white thread on white material, but the letters themselves were huge, in flowery script: MDS. That was right. MDS. No J to be found.

Weird. Very weird.

I hung the cloth up to dry. I didn't have to worry about anybody seeing it. In the first place, nobody used my bathroom but me, and in the second place, nobody would be able to see it anymore than they could see Jesse. It would be there tomorrow. Maybe I wouldn't give it back to him without demanding some sort of explanation as to those letters. MDS.

It wasn't until I was falling asleep that I realized MDS must have been a girl. Why else would there have been all that lace? And that curlicue script? Had Jesse died not in a gunfight, as I'd originally assumed, but in some sort of lovers' quarrel?

I don't know why the thought disturbed me so much, but it did. It kept me awake for about three whole minutes. Then I rolled over, missed my old bed very briefly, and fell asleep.

CHAPTER 13

My intention, of course, had been to wake up early and call Father Dominic to warn him about Heather. But intentions are only as good as the people who hold them, and I guess I must be worthless because I didn't wake up until my mother shook me awake, and by then it was 7:30, and my ride was leaving without me.

Or so they thought. There was a huge delay when Sleepy discovered he'd lost the keys to the Rambler, so I was able to drag myself out of bed and into some kind of outfit—I had no idea what. I came staggering down the stairs, feeling like somebody had hit me on the head a few times with a bag of rocks just as Doc was telling everybody that Sister Ernestine had warned him if he missed another Assembly, he'd be held back a year.

That's when I remembered the keys to the Rambler were still in the pocket of my leather jacket where I'd left them the night before.

I slunk back up the stairs and pretended to find the keys on the landing. There was some jubilation over this, but mostly a lot of grumbling, since Sleepy swore he'd left them hanging on the key hook in the kitchen and couldn't figure out how they'd gotten to the landing. Dopey said, "It was probably Dave's ghost," and leered at Doc, who looked embarrassed.

Then we all piled into the car and took off.

We were late, of course. Assembly at the Junipero Serra Mission Academy begins promptly at 8:00. We got there at around two after. What happens at Assembly is, they make everybody stand outside in these lines separated by sex, boys on one side, girls on the other— like we're Quakers or something—for fifteen minutes before school officially starts, so they can take attendance and read announcements and stuff. By the time we got there, of course, Assembly had already started. I had intended to duck right past and head straight to Father Dominic's office, but of course, I never got the chance. Sister Ernestine caught us traipsing in late, and gave each of us the evil eye until we slunk into our various lines. I didn't much care what Sister Ernestine jotted down in her little black book about me, but I could see that getting to the principal's office was going to be impossible, due to the yellow caution tape strung up across every single archway that led to the courtyard—and, of course, all the cops.

I guess what had happened was, all the priests and nuns and stuff had gotten up for matins, which is what they call the first mass of the morning, and they'd all walked outside and seen the statue of their church's founder with his head cut off, and the fountain with hardly any water left in it, and the bench where I'd been sitting all twisted and tipped over, and the door to Mr. Walden's classroom in smithereens.

Understandably, I guess, they freaked out and called the cops. People in uniform were crawling all over the place, taking fingerprints and measuring stuff, like the distance Junipero Serra's head had traveled from his body, and the velocity it had to have traveled to make that many holes in a door that was made of three-inch-thick wood, and that kind of thing. I saw a guy in a dark blue windbreaker with the letters CBTSPD—Carmel-by-the-Sea Police Department?—on the back, conferring with Father Dominic, who looked really, really tired. I couldn't catch his eye, and supposed I'd have to wait until after Assembly to sneak away and apologize to him.

At Assembly, Sister Ernestine, the vice principal, told us vandals had done it. Vandals had broken in through Mr. Walden's classroom, and wreaked havoc all over the school. What was fortunate, we were told, was that the solid gold chalice and salver used for the sacramental wine and hosts had not been stolen, but were left sitting in their little cupboard behind the church altar. The vandals had rudely beheaded our school founder, but left the really valuable stuff alone. We were told that if any of us knew anything about this horrible violation, we were to come forward immediately. And that if we were uncomfortable coming forward personally, we could do it anonymously—Monsignor Constantine would be hearing confessions all morning.

As if! Hey, it hadn't been *my* fault Heather had gone berserk. Well, not really, anyway. If anybody should be going to confession, it was *her*.

As I stood in line—behind CeeCee, who couldn't hide her delight over what had happened; you could practically see the headline forming in her mind: *Father Serra Loses His Head Over Vandals*—I craned my neck, trying to see over to the seniors. Was Bryce there? I couldn't see him. Maybe Father Dom had gotten to him already, and sent him home. He had to have recognized that the mess in the courtyard was the result of spiritual, not human, agitation, and had acted accordingly. I hoped, for Bryce's sake, that Father Dom hadn't resorted to the head lice.

Okay, I hoped it for my sake, I admit it. I really wanted our date on Saturday to go well, and not be canceled due to head lice. Is that such a crime? A girl can't spend *all* her time battling psychic disturbances. She needs a little romance, too.

But of course, the minute Assembly was over and I tried to ditch homeroom and hightail it to Father Dom's office, Sister Ernestine caught me and said, just as I was about to duck under some of the yellow caution tape, "Excuse me, Miss Simon. Perhaps back in New York it is perfectly all right to ignore police warnings, but here in California it is considered highly ill-advised."

I straightened. I had nearly made it, too. I thought some uncharitable things about Sister Ernestine, but managed to say, civilly enough, "Oh, Sister, I'm so sorry. You see, I just need to get to Father Dominic's office."

"Father Dominic," Sister Ernestine said coldly, "is extremely busy this morning. He happens to be consulting with the police over last night's unfortunate incident. He won't be available until after lunch at the earliest."

I know it's probably wrong to fantasize about giving a nun a karate chop in the neck, but I couldn't help it. She was making me mad.

"Listen, Sister," I said. "Father Dominic asked me to come see him this morning. I've got some, um, transcripts from my old school that he wanted to see. I had to have them FedExed all the way from New York, and they just got here, so—"

I thought that was pretty quick thinking on my part, about the transcripts and the FedEx and all, but then Sister Ernestine held out her hand and went, "Give them to me, and I'll be happy to deliver them to the Father."

Damn!

"Uh," I said, backing away. "Never mind. I guess I'll just . . . I'll see him after lunch, then."

Sister Ernestine gave me a kind of aha-I-thought-so look, then turned her attention to some innocent kid who'd made the mistake of coming to school in a pair of Levi's, a blatant violation of the dress code. The kid wailed, "They were my only clean pants!" but Sister Ernestine didn't care. She stood there—unfortunately still guarding the only route to the principal's office—and wrote the kid up on the spot.

I had no choice but to go to class. I mean, what was there to tell Father Dominic, anyway, that he didn't already know? I'm sure he knew it was Heather who'd wrecked the school, and me who'd broken Mr. Walden's window. He probably wasn't going to be all that happy with me anyway, so why was I even bothering? What I ought to have been doing was trying as much as possible to stay out of his way.

Except . . . except what about Heather?

As near as I could tell, she was still recuperating from her explosive rage the night before. I saw no sign of her as I made my way to Mr. Walden's classroom for first period, which was good: It meant Father D. and I would have time to draw up some kind of plan before she struck again.

As I sat there in class trying to convince myself that everything was going to be all right, I couldn't help feeling kind of bad for poor Mr. Walden. He was taking having the door to his classroom obliterated pretty well. He didn't even seem to mind the broken window so much. Of course, everybody in school was buzzing about what had happened. People were saying that it had been a prank, the severing of Junipero Serra's head. A senior prank. One year, CeeCee told me, the seniors had strapped pillows to the clappers of the church bells, so that when they rang, all that came out was a muffled sort of splatting sound. I guess people suspected this was the same sort of thing.

If only they had known the truth. Heather's seat, next to Kelly Prescott, remained conspicuously vacant, while her locker—now assigned to me—was still unopenable thanks to the dent her body had made when I'd thrown her against it.

It was sort of ironic that as I was sitting there thinking this, Kelly Prescott raised her hand and, when Mr. Walden called on her, asked if he didn't think it was unfair, Monsignor Constantine declaring that no memorial service would be held for Heather.

Mr. Walden leaned back in his seat and put both his feet up on his desk. Then he said, "Don't look at me. I just work here."

"Well," Kelly said, "don't you think it's unfair?" She turned to the rest of the class, her big, mascara-rimmed eyes appealing. "Heather Chambers went here for ten years. It's inexcusable that she shouldn't be memorialized in her own school. And, frankly, I think what happened yesterday was a sign."

Mr. Walden looked vastly amused. "A sign, Kelly?"

"That's right. I believe what happened here last night—and even that piece of the breezeway nearly killing Bryce—are all connected. I don't believe Father Serra's statue was desecrated by vandals at all, but by angels. Angels who are angry about Monsignor Constantine not allowing Heather's parents to have her funeral here."

This caused a good deal of buzzing in the class-room. People looked nervously at Heather's empty chair. Normally, I don't talk much in school, but I couldn't let this one go by. I said, "So you're saying you think it was an angel who broke this window behind me, Kelly?"

Kelly had to twist around in her seat to see me. "Well," she said. "It could have been. . . ."

"Right. And you think it was angels who broke down Mr. Walden's door, and cut off that statue's head, and wrecked the courtyard?"

Kelly stuck out her chin. "Yes," she said. "I do. Angels angered over Monsignor Constantine's decision not to allow us to memorialize Heather."

I shook my head. "Bull," I said.

Kelly raised her eyebrows. "I beg your pardon?"

"I said bull, Kelly. I think your theory is full of bull."

Kelly turned a very interesting shade of red. I think she was probably regretting inviting me to her pool party. "You don't know it wasn't angels, Suze," she said acidly.

"Actually, I do. Because to the best of my knowledge, angels don't bleed, and there was blood all over the carpeting back here from where the vandal hurt himself breaking in. That's why the police cut up chunks of the rug and took them away."

Kelly wasn't the only one who gasped. Everybody kind of freaked out. I probably shouldn't have pointed out the blood—especially since it was mine—but hey, I couldn't let her go around saying it was all because of angels. Angels, my butt. What did she think this was, anyway, *Highway to Heaven*?

"Okay," Mr. Walden said. "On that note, everybody, it's time for second period. Susannah, could I see you a minute?"

CeeCee turned around to waggle her white eyebrows at me. "You're in for it now, sucker," she hissed.

But she had no idea how true her words were. All anybody would have to do was take a look at the Band-Aids all over my wrist, and they'd know I had firsthand knowledge of where that blood had come from.

On the other hand, they had no reason to suspect me, did they?

I approached Mr. Walden's desk, my heart in my throat. *He's going to turn you in,* I thought, frantically. *You are so busted, Simon.*

But all Mr. Walden wanted to do was compliment me on my use of footnotes in my essay on the battle of Bladensburg, which he had noticed as I handed it in.

"Uh," I said. "It was really no big deal, Mr. Walden."

"Yes, but footnotes—" He sighed. "I haven't seen footnotes used correctly since I taught an adult education class over at the community college. Really, you did a great job."

I muttered a modest thank-you. I didn't want to admit that the reason I knew so much about the battle of Bladensburg was that I'd once helped a veteran of that battle direct a couple of his ancestors to a long-buried bag of money he'd dropped during it. It's funny the things that hold people back from getting on with their life . . . or their death, I should say.

I was about to tell Mr. Walden that while I'd have loved, under ordinary circumstances, to stick around and chat about famous American battles, I really had to go—I was going to see if Sister Ernestine was still guarding the way to Father Dom's office—when Mr. Walden stopped me cold with these few words: "It's funny about Kelly bringing up Heather Chambers that way, actually, Susannah."

I eyed him warily. "Oh? How so?"

"Well, I don't know if you're aware of this, but Heather was the sophomore class vice president, and now that she's gone, we've been collecting nominations for a new VP. Well, believe it or not, you've been nominated. Twelve times so far."

My eyes must have bugged out of my head. I forgot all about how I had to go and see Father Dominic. "*Twelve* times?"

"Yes, I know, it's unusual, isn't it?"

I couldn't believe it. "But I've only been going here one day!"

"Well, you've made quite an impression. I myself would guess that you didn't exactly make any enemies yesterday when you offered to break Debbie Mancuso's fingers after school. She is not one of the better-liked girls in the class."

I stared at him. So Mr. Walden *had* overheard my little threat. The fact that he had and not sent me straight to detention made me appreciate him in a way I'd never appreciated a teacher before.

"Oh, and I guess your pushing Bryce Martinson out of the way of that flying chunk of wood—that probably didn't hurt much, either," he added.

"Wow," I said. I guess I probably don't need to point out that at my old school, I wouldn't exactly have won any popularity contests. I never even bothered going out for cheerleading or running for homecoming queen. Besides the fact that at my old school cheerleading was considered a stupid waste of time and in Brooklyn it isn't exactly a compliment to be called a queen, I never would have made either one. And no one—*no one*—had ever nominated me before for anything.

I was way too flattered to follow my initial instinct, which was to say, "Thanks, but no thanks," and run.

"Well," I said instead, "what does the vice president of the sophomore class have to do?"

Mr. Walden shrugged. "Help the president determine how to spend the class budget, mostly. It's not much, just a little over three thousand dollars. Kelly and Heather were planning on using the money to hold a dance over at the Carmel Inn, but—"

"Three thousand dollars?" My mouth was probably hanging open, but I didn't care.

"Yes, I know it's not much—"

"And we can spend it any way we want?" My mind was spinning. "Like, if we wanted to have a bunch of cookouts down at the beach, we could do that?"

Mr. Walden looked down at me curiously. "Sure. You have to have the approval of the rest of the class, though. I have a feeling there might be some noises from the administration about using the class money to mend the statue of Father Serra, but—"

But whatever Mr. Walden had been about to say,

he didn't get a chance to finish. CeeCee came running back into the classroom, her purple eyes wide behind the tinted prescription lenses of her glasses.

"Come quick!" she yelled. "There's been an accident! Father Dominic and Bryce Martinson—"

I whirled around, fast. "What?" I demanded way more sharply than I needed to. "What about them?"

"I think they're dead!"

CHAPTER 14

I ran so fast that later, Sister Mary Claire, the track coach, asked me if I'd like to try out for the team.

But CeeCee was wrong on all three counts. Father Dominic wasn't dead. Neither was Bryce.

And there'd been nothing accidental about it.

As near as anyone could figure out, what happened was this: Bryce went into the principal's office for something—nobody knew what. A late pass, maybe, since he'd missed Assembly—but not, as I'd hoped, because Father Dom had got hold of him. Bryce had been standing in front of the secretary's desk beneath the giant crucifix Adam had told me would weep tears of blood if a virgin ever graduated from the Mission Academy (the secretary hadn't been there, she'd been out serving coffee to the cops who were still hanging around the courtyard) when the six-foot-tall cross suddenly came loose from the wall. Father Dominic opened his office door just in time to see it falling forward, where it surely would have crushed Bryce's skull. But because Father Dominic shoved him to safety, it succeeded only in delivering a glancing blow that crushed Bryce's collarbone.

Unfortunately, Father Dominic ended up taking the weight of the falling cross himself. It pinned him to the office floor, smashing most of his ribs and breaking one of his legs.

Mr. Walden and a bunch of the sisters tried to get us to go to class instead of crowding the breezeway, watching for Father Dom and Bryce to emerge from the principal's office. Some people went when Sister Ernestine threatened everyone with detention, but not me. I didn't care if I got detention. I had to make sure they were all right. Sister Ernestine said something very nasty about how maybe Miss Simon didn't realize how unpleasant detention at the Mission Academy could be. I assured Sister Ernestine that if she was threatening corporal punishment, I would tell my mother, who was a local news anchorwoman and would be over here with a TV camera so fast, nobody would have time to say so much as a single Hail Mary.

Sister Ernestine was pretty quiet after that.

It was shortly after this that I found Doc pressed

up pretty close to me. I looked down and said, "What are *you* doing here?" since the little kids are supposed to stay way on the other side of the school.

"I want to see if he's all right." Doc's freckles were standing out, he was so pale.

"You're going to get in trouble," I warned him. Sister Ernestine was busily writing people up.

"I don't care," Doc said. "I want to see."

I shrugged. He was a funny kid, that Doc. He wasn't anything like his big brothers, and it wasn't because of his red hair, either. I remembered Dopey's teasing comment about the car keys and "Dave's ghost," and wondered how much, if anything, Doc knew about what had been going on lately at his school.

Finally, after what seemed like hours, they came out. Bryce was first, strapped onto a stretcher and moaning, I'm sorry to say, like a bit of a baby. I've had plenty of broken and dislocated bones, and believe me it hurts, but not enough to lie there moaning. Usually when I get hurt, I don't even notice. Like last night, for instance. When I'm *really* hurt all I can do is laugh because it hurts so much that it's actually funny.

Okay, I have to admit I sort of stopped liking Bryce so much when I saw him acting like such a baby. . . .

Especially when I saw Father Dom, who the paramedics wheeled out next. He was unconscious, his white hair sort of flopped over in a sad way, a jagged cut, partially covered by gauze, over his right eye. I hadn't eaten any breakfast in my haste to get to school, and I have to admit the sight of poor Father Dominic with his eyes closed and his glasses gone made me feel a little woozy. In fact, I might have swayed a little on my feet, and probably would have fallen over if Doc hadn't grabbed my hand and said confidently, "I know. The sight of blood makes me sick, too."

But it wasn't the sight of Father Dom's blood seeping through the bandage on his head that had made me sick. It was the realization that I had failed. I had failed miserably. It was only dumb blind luck that Heather hadn't succeeded in killing them both. It was only because of Father Dom's quick thinking that he and Bryce were alive. It was no thanks to me. No thanks to me whatsoever.

Because if I had handled things better the night before it wouldn't have happened. It wouldn't have happened at all.

That's when I got mad. I mean *really* mad.

Suddenly, I knew what I had to do. I looked down at Doc. "Is there a computer here at school? One with Internet access?"

"Sure," Doc said, looking surprised. "In the library. Why?"

I dropped his hand. "Never mind. Go back to class."

"Suze—"

"Anyone who isn't in his or her classroom in one minute," Sister Ernestine said imperiously, "will be suspended indefinitely!"

Doc tugged on my sleeve.

"What's going on?" he wanted to know. "Why do you need a computer?"

"Nothing," I said. Behind the wrought-iron gate that led to the parking lot, the paramedics slammed the doors to the ambulances in which they'd loaded Father Dom and Bryce. A second later, they were pulling away in a whine of sirens and a flurry of flashing lights. "Just . . . it's stuff you wouldn't understand, David. It isn't scientific."

Doc said, with no small amount of indignation, "I can understand lots of stuff that isn't scientific. Music, for instance. I've taught myself to play Chopin on my electronic keyboard back home. That isn't scientific. The appreciation of music is purely emotional as is the appreciation of art. I can understand art and music. So come on, Suze," he said. "You can tell me. Does it have anything to do with . . . what we were talking about the other night?"

I turned to gaze down at him in surprise. He shrugged. "It was a logical conclusion. I made a cursory examination of the statue—cursory because I was unable to approach it as closely as I would have liked thanks to the crime scene tape and evidence team—and was unable to discern any saw marks or other indications of how the head was severed. There is no possible way bronze can be cut that cleanly without the use of some sort of heavy machinery, but such machinery would never fit through—"

"Mr. Ackerman!" Sister Ernestine sounded like she meant business. "Would you like to be written up?"

David looked irritated. "No," he said.

"No, what?"

"No, Sister." He looked back at me, apologetically. "I guess I better go. But can we talk more about this tonight at home? I found out some stuff about—well, what you asked me. You know." He widened his eyes meaningfully. "About the house."

"Oh," I said. "Great. Okay."

"Mr. Ackerman!"

David turned to look at the nun. "Hold on a minute, okay, Sister? I'm trying to have a conversation here."

All of the blood left the middle-aged woman's face. It was incredible.

She reacted as childishly as if she were the twelve-year-old, and not David.

"Come with me, young man," she said, seizing hold of David's ear. "I can see your new stepsister has put some pretty big-city ideas into your head about how a boy speaks to his elders—"

David let out a noise like a wounded animal, but went along with the woman, hunched up like a shrimp, he was in so much pain. I swear I wouldn't have done anything—anything at all—if I hadn't suddenly noticed Heather standing just inside the gate, laughing her head off.

"Oh, God," she cried, gasping a little, she was laughing so hard. "If you could have seen your face when you heard Bryce was dead! I swear! It was the funniest thing I've ever seen!" She stopped laughing long enough to toss her long hair and say, "You know what? I think I'm going to clobber a few more people with stuff today. Maybe I'll start with that little guy over there—"

I stepped toward her. "You lay one hand on my brother, and I'll stuff you right back into that grave you crawled out of."

Heather only laughed, but Sister Ernestine, who I realized belatedly thought I was talking to her, let go of David so fast you'd have thought the kid had suddenly caught on fire.

"What did you say?"

Sister Ernestine was turning sort of purple. Behind her, Heather laughed delightedly. "Oh, now you've done it. Detention for a week!"

And just like that, she disappeared, leaving behind yet another mess for me to clean up.

As much to my surprise as, I think, her own, Sister Ernestine could only stare at me. David stood there rubbing his ear and looking bewildered. I said as quickly as I could, "We'll go back to our classrooms now. We were only concerned about Father Dominic, and wanted to see him off. Thanks, Sister."

Sister Ernestine continued to stare at me. She didn't say anything. She was a big lady, not quite as tall as me in my two-inch heels—I was wearing black Batgirl boots—but much wider, with exceptionally large breasts. Between them dangled a silver cross. Sister Ernestine fingered this cross unconsciously as she stared at me. Later, Adam, who'd watched the entire event unfold, would say that Sister Ernestine was holding up the cross as if to protect herself from me. That is untrue. She merely touched the cross as if uncertain it was still there. Which it was. It most certainly was.

I guess that was when David stopped being Doc to me, and started being David.

"Don't worry," I told him, just before we parted ways, because he looked so worried and cute and all with his red hair and freckles and sticky-outy ears. I reached out and rumpled some of that red hair. "Everything will be all right."

David looked up at me. "How do you *know*?" he asked.

I took my hand away.

Because, of course, the truth was I didn't. Know everything was going to be all right, I mean. Far from it, as a matter of fact.

CHAPTER 15

Lunch was almost over by the time I cornered Adam. I had spent almost the entire period in the library staring into a computer monitor. I still hadn't eaten, but the truth was, I wasn't hungry at all.

"Hey," I said, sitting down next to him and crossing my legs so that my black skirt hiked up just the littlest bit. "Did you drive to school this morning?"

Adam pounded on his chest. He'd started choking on a Frito the minute I'd sat down. When he finally got it down, he said proudly, "I sure did. Now that I got my license, I am a driving machine. You should've come out with us last night, Suze. We had a blast. After we went to the Coffee Clutch, we took a spin along Seventeen Mile Drive. Have you ever done that? Man, with last night's moon, the ocean was so beautiful—"

"Would you mind taking me somewhere after school?"

Adam stood up fast, scaring two fat seagulls that had been sitting near the bench he was sharing with CeeCee. "Are you kidding me? Where do you want to go? You name it, Suze, I'll take you there. Vegas? You want to go to Vegas? No problem. I mean, I'm sixteen, you're sixteen. We can get married there easy. My parents'll let us live with them, no problem. You don't mind sharing my room, do you? I swear I'll pick up after myself from now on—"

"Adam," CeeCee said. "Don't be such a spaz. I highly doubt she wants to marry you."

"I don't think it's a good idea to marry anyone until my divorce from my first husband is finalized," I said gravely. "What I want to do is go to the hospital and see Bryce."

Adam's shoulders slumped. "Oh," he said. There was no missing the dejection in his voice. "Is that all?"

I realized I'd said the wrong thing. Still, I couldn't unsay it. Fortunately, CeeCee helped me out by saying thoughtfully, "You know, a story about Bryce and Father Dominic bravely battling back from their wounds wouldn't be a bad idea for the paper. Would you mind if I tagged along, Suze?"

"Not at all." A lie, of course. With CeeCee along, it might be difficult to accomplish what I wanted without a lot of explaining. . . .

But what choice did I have? None.

Once I'd secured my ride, I started looking for Sleepy. I found him dozing with his back to the monkey bars. I nudged him awake with the toe of my boot. When he squinted up at me through his sunglasses, I told him not to wait for me after school, that I'd found my own ride. He grunted, and went back to sleep.

Then I went and found a pay phone. It's weird when you don't know your own mother's phone number. I mean, I still knew our number back in Brooklyn, but I didn't have the slightest idea what my new phone number was. Good thing I'd written it in my date book. I consulted the A's—for Ackerman—and found my new number, and dialed it. I knew no one was home, but I wanted to cover all my bases. I told the answering machine that I might be late getting back from school since I was going out with a couple of new friends. My mother, I knew, would be delighted when she got back from the station and heard it. She'd always worried, back in Brooklyn, that I was antisocial. She'd always go, "Susie, you're such a pretty girl. I just don't understand why no boys ever call you. Maybe if you didn't look so . . . well, tough. How about giving the leather jacket a rest?"

She'd probably have died of joy if she could have been in the parking lot after school and heard Adam as I approached his car.

"Oh, Cee, here she is." Adam flung open the passenger door of his car—which turned out to be one of the new Volkswagen Bugs; I guess Adam's parents weren't hurting for money—and shooed CeeCee into the backseat. "Come on, Suze, you sit right up front with me."

I peered through my sunglasses—as usual, the morning fog had burned away, and now at 3:00 the sun beat down hard from a perfectly clear blue sky— at CeeCee squashed in the backseat. "Um, really," I said. "CeeCee was here first. I'll sit in the back. I don't mind at all."

"I won't hear of it." Adam stood by the door, holding it open for me. "You're the new girl. The new girl gets to sit in the front."

"Yeah," CeeCee said from the depths of the backseat, "until you refuse to sleep with him. Then he'll relegate you to the backseat, too."

Adam said, in a *Wizard of Oz* voice, "Ignore that man behind the curtain."

I slid into the front seat, and Adam politely closed the door for me.

"Are you serious?" I turned around to ask CeeCee as Adam made his way around the car to the driver's seat.

CeeCee blinked at me from behind her protective lenses. "Do you really think anybody would sleep with *him*?"

I digested that. "I take it," I said, "that's a no, then."

"Damned straight," CeeCee said just as Adam slid behind the wheel.

"Now," the driver said, flexing his fingers experimentally before switching on the ignition. "I'm thinking this whole thing with the statue and Father Dom and Bryce has really stressed us all out. My parents have a hot tub, you know, which is really ideal for stress like the kind we've all been through today, and I suggest that we all go to my place first for a soak. . . ."

"Tell you what," I said. "Let's skip the hot tub this time and just go straight to the hospital. Maybe, if there's time later—"

"*Yes.*" Adam looked heavenward. "There is a god."

CeeCee said, from the backseat, "She said *maybe*, numbskull. God, try to control yourself."

Adam glanced at me as he eased out of his parking space. "Am I coming on too strong?"

"Uh," I said. "Maybe . . ."

"The thing is, it's been so long since even a remotely interesting girl has shown up around here." Adam, I saw with some relief, was a very careful driver—not like Sleepy, who seemed to think stop signs actually said PAUSE. "I mean, I've been surrounded by Kelly Prescotts and Debbie Mancusos for sixteen years. It's such a relief to have a Susannah Simon around for a change. You *decimated* Kelly this morning when you went, 'Hmm, do angels leave blood stains? I don't *think* so.'"

Adam went on in this vein for the rest of the trip to the hospital. I wasn't quite sure how CeeCee could stomach it. Unless I was mistaken, she felt the same way about him that he evidently felt about me. Only I didn't think his crush on me was very serious—if it had been, he wouldn't have been able to joke about it. CeeCee's crush on him, however, looked to me like the real thing. Oh, she was able to tease him and even insult him, but I'd looked into the rearview mirror a couple times and caught her looking at the back of his head in a manner that could only be called besotted.

But just when she was sure he wasn't looking.

When Adam pulled up in front of the Carmel hospital, I thought he had stopped at a country club or a private house by mistake. Okay, a really big private house, but hey, you should have seen some of the places in the Valley.

But then I saw a discreet little sign that said HOSPITAL. We piled out of the car and wandered through an immaculately kept garden, where the flower beds were bursting with blossoms. Hummingbirds buzzed all around, and I spotted some more of those palm trees I'd been sure I'd never see so far north of the equator.

At the information desk, I asked for Bryce Martinson's room. I wasn't sure he'd been admitted actually, but I knew from experience—unfortunately firsthand—that any accident in which a head wound might have occurred generally required an overnight stay for observation—and I was right. Bryce was there, and so was Father Dominic, conveniently situated right across the hall from one another.

We weren't the only people visiting these particular patients—not by a long shot. Bryce's room was packed. There wasn't, apparently, any limit on just how many people could crowd into a patient's room, and Bryce's looked as if it contained most of the Junipero Serra Mission Academy's senior class. In the middle of the sunny, cheerful room—where on every flat surface rested vases filled with flowers—lay Bryce in a shoulder cast, his right arm hanging from a pulley over his bed. He looked a lot better than he had that morning, mostly, I suppose, because he was pumped full of painkillers. When he saw me in the doorway, this big goofy smile broke out over his face, and he went, "Suze!"

Only he pronounced it "Soo-oo-ooze," so it sounded like it had more than one syllable.

"Uh, hi, Bryce," I said, suddenly shy. Everybody in the room had turned around to see who Bryce was talking to. Most of them were girls. They all did that thing a lot of girls do—they looked me over from the top of my head—I hadn't showered that morning because I'd been running so late, so I was not exactly having a good hair day—to the soles of my feet.

Then they smirked.

Not so Bryce would have noticed. But they did.

And even though I could not have cared less what a bunch of girls I had never met before, and would probably never meet again, thought of me, I blushed.

"Everybody," Bryce said. He sounded drunk, but pleasantly so. "This is Suze. Suze, this is everybody."

"Uh," I said. "Hi."

One of the girls, who was sitting on the end of Bryce's bed in a very white, wrinkle-free linen dress, went, "Oh, you're that girl who saved his life yesterday. Jake's new stepsister."

"Yeah," I said. "That's me." There was no way—no way—I was going to be able to ask Bryce what I needed to ask him with all these people in the room. CeeCee had steered Adam off into Father Dom's room in order to give me some time alone with Bryce, but it looked as if she'd done so in vain. There was no way I was going to get a minute with this guy alone. Not unless . . .

Well, not unless I asked for it.

"Hey," I said. "I need to talk to Bryce for a second. Do you guys mind?"

The girl on the end of the bed looked taken aback. "So talk to him. *We're* not stopping you."

I looked her right in the eye and said in my firmest mediation voice, "I need to talk to him *alone*."

Somebody whistled low and long. Nobody else moved. At least until Bryce went, "Hey, you guys. You heard her. Get out."

Thank God for morphine, that's all I have to say.

Grudgingly, the senior class filed out, everybody casting me dirty looks but Bryce, who lifted a hand connected to what looked like an IV and went, "Hey, Suze. C'mere and look at this."

I approached the bed. Now that we were the only people in it, I was able to see that Bryce actually had a very large room. It was also very cheerful, painted yellow, with a window that looked out over the garden outside.

"See what I got?" Bryce showed me a palm-sized instrument with a button on top of it. "My own pain-killer pump. Anytime I feel pain, I just hit this button, and it releases codeine. Right into my bloodstream. Cool, huh?"

The guy was gone. That was obvious. Suddenly, I didn't think my mission was going to be so hard after all.

"That's great, Bryce," I said. "I was real sorry to hear about your accident."

"Yeah." He giggled fatuously. "Too bad you weren't there. You might've been able to save me like you did yesterday."

"Yes," I said, clearing my throat uncomfortably. "You certainly do seem accident-prone these days."

"Yeah." His eyelids drifted closed, and for one panicky minute, I thought he'd gone to sleep. Then he opened his eyes and looked at me kind of sadly. "Suze,

I don't think I'm going to be able to make it."

I stared at him. God, what a baby! "Of course you're going to make it. You've got a busted collarbone, is all. You'll be better in no time."

He giggled. "No, no. I mean, I don't think I'm going to be able to make it to our date on Saturday night."

"Oh," I said, blinking. "Oh, no, of course not. I didn't think so. Listen, Bryce, I need to ask you a favor. You're going to think it's weird"—actually, doped up as he was, I doubted he'd think it weird at all—"but I was wondering whether, back when you and Heather were going out, did she ever, um, give you anything?"

He blinked at me groggily. "Give me anything? You mean like a present?"

"Yes."

"Well, yeah. She got me a cashmere sweater vest for Christmas."

I nodded. A cashmere sweater vest wasn't going to do me any good. "Okay. Anything else? Maybe . . . a picture of herself?"

"Oh," he said. "Sure, sure. She gave me her school picture."

"She did?" I tried not to look too excited. "Any chance you've got it on you? In your wallet, maybe?" It was a gamble, I knew, but most people only clean out their wallets once a year or so. . . .

He screwed up his face. I guess thinking must have been painful for him since I saw him give himself a couple pumps of painkiller. Then his face relaxed. "Sure," he said. "I've still got her picture. My wallet's in that drawer there."

I opened the drawer to the table beside his bed. His wallet was indeed there, a slim black leather deal. I lifted it up and opened it. Heather's photo was jammed between a gold American Express card and a ski lift ticket. It showed her looking extremely glam, with all her long blonde hair flowing over one shoulder, staring coquettishly into the camera. In my school pictures, I always look like somebody just yelled, "Fire!" I couldn't believe this guy, who'd been dating a girl who looked like that, would bother asking a girl like me out.

"Can I borrow this picture?" I asked. "I just need it for a little while. I'll give it right back." This was a lie, but I didn't figure he'd give it to me otherwise.

"Sure, sure," he said, waving a hand.

"Thanks." I slipped the photo into my backpack just as a tall woman in her forties came striding in wearing a lot of gold jewelry and carrying a box of pastries.

"Bryce, darling," she said. "Where did all your little friends go? I went all the way to the patisserie to get some snacks."

"Oh, they'll be back in a minute, Mom," Bryce said sleepily. "This is Suze. She saved my life yesterday."

Mrs. Martinson held out a smooth, tanned right hand. "Lovely to meet you, Susan," she said, giving my fingers the slightest of squeezes. "Can you believe what happened to poor little Bryce? His father's furious. As if things hadn't been going badly enough, what with that wretched girl—well, you know. And now this. I swear, it's like that academy was cursed, or something."

I said, "Yes. Well, nice to meet you. I'd better be going."

Nobody protested against my departure—Mrs. Martinson because she couldn't have cared less, and Bryce because he'd fallen asleep.

I found Adam and CeeCee standing outside a room across the hall. As I walked up to them, CeeCee put a finger to her lips. "Listen," she said.

I did as she asked.

"It simply couldn't have come at a worse time," a familiar voice—male, older—was saying. "What with the archbishop's visit not two weeks away—"

"I'm so sorry, Constantine." Father Dominic's voice sounded weak. "I know what a strain this must all be to you."

"And Bryce Martinson, of all people! Do you know who his father is? Only one of the best trial lawyers in Salinas!"

"Father Dom's getting reamed," Adam whispered to me. "Poor old guy."

"I wish he'd tell Monsignor Constantine to just go and jump in a lake." CeeCee's purple eyes flashed.

"Dried-up, crusty old—"

I whispered, "Let's see if we can help him out. Maybe you guys could distract the monsignor. Then I'll just see if Father Dom needs anything. You know. Just real quick before we go."

CeeCee shrugged. "Fine with me."

"I'm game," Adam said.

So I called loudly, "Father Dominic?" and banged into the Father's hospital room.

The room wasn't as big as Bryce's or as cheerful. The walls were beige, not yellow, and there was only one vase with flowers in it. The window looked out, as near as I could tell, over the parking lot. And nobody had hooked Father Dominic up to any self-pumped painkiller machine. I don't know what kind of insurance priests have, but it was nowhere as good as it should have been.

To say that Father Dominic looked surprised to see me would have been an understatement. His mouth dropped open. He seemed perfectly incapable of saying anything. But that was okay because CeeCee came bustling in after me, and went, "Oh, Monsignor! Great. We've been looking all over for you. We'd like to do an exclusive, if that's okay, on how last night's act of vandalism is going to affect the upcoming visit of the archbishop. Adversely, right? Do you have any comments? Maybe you could step out here into the hallway where my associate and I can—"

Looking flustered, Monsignor Constantine followed CeeCee out the door with an irritated, "Now see here, young lady—"

I sauntered over to Father Dominic's side. I wasn't exactly excited to see him. I mean, I knew he probably wasn't too happy with me. I was the one whom Heather had thrown Father Serra's head at, and I figured he probably knew it and probably wasn't feeling too warmly toward me.

That's what I figured, anyway. But of course, I figured wrong. I'm pretty good at figuring out what dead people are thinking, but I haven't quite gotten the hang of the living yet.

"Susannah," Father Dominic said in his gentle voice. "What are you doing here? Is everything all right? I've been very concerned about you—"

I guess I should have expected it. Father Dominic wasn't sore at me at all. Just worried, that was all. But *he* was the one who needed worrying over. Aside from the nasty gash above one eye, his color was off. He looked gray, and much older than he actually was. Only his eyes, blue as the sky outside, looked like they always did, bright and filled with intelligent good humor.

Still, it made me mad all over again, seeing him like that. Heather didn't know it, but she was in for it, and how.

"Me?" I stared at him. "What are you worried

about *me* for? *I'm* not the one who got clobbered by a crucifix this morning."

Father Dom smiled ruefully. "No, but I believe you do have a little explaining to do. Why didn't you tell me, Susannah? Why didn't you tell me what you had in mind? If I had known you planned on showing up at the Mission alone in the middle of the night, I never would have allowed it."

"Exactly why I didn't tell you," I said. "Look, Father, I'm sorry about the statue and Mr. Walden's door and all that. But I had to try talking to her myself, don't you see? Woman to woman. I didn't know she was going to go postal on me."

"What did you expect? Susannah, you saw what she tried to do to that young man yesterday—"

"Yeah, but I could understand that. I mean, she loved him. She's really mad at him. I didn't think she'd try to go after *me*. I mean, *I* had nothing to do with it. I just tried to let her know her options—"

"Which is what I'd been doing ever since she first showed up at the Mission."

"Right. But Heather's not liking any of the options we've put before her. I'm telling you, the girl's gone loco. She's quiet now because she thinks she killed Bryce, and she's probably all tuckered out, but in a little while she's going to perk up again, and God only knows what she'll do next now that she knows what she's capable of."

Father Dominic looked at me curiously, his concern over the archbishop's impending visit forgotten. "What do you mean 'now that she knows what she's capable of'?"

"Well, last night was just a dress rehearsal. We can expect bigger and better things from Heather now that she knows what she can do."

Father Dominic shook his head, confused. "Have you seen her today? How do you know all this?"

I couldn't tell Father Dominic about Jesse. I really couldn't. It wasn't any of his business, for one thing. But I also had an idea it might kind of shock him, knowing there was this guy living in my bedroom. I mean, Father Dom was a priest and all.

"Look," I said. "I've been giving this a lot of thought, and I don't see any other way. You've tried to reason with her, and so have I. And look where it's gotten us. You're in the hospital, and I'm having to look over my shoulder everywhere I go. I think it's time to settle the matter once and for all."

Father Dom blinked at me. "What do you mean, Susannah? What are you talking about?"

I took a deep breath. "I'm talking about what we mediators do as a last resort."

He still looked confused. "Last resort? I'm afraid I don't know what you mean."

"I'm talking," I said, "about an exorcism."

CHAPTER 16

"Out of the question," said Father Dominic.

"Look," I said. "I don't see any other way. She won't go willingly, we both know that. And she's too dangerous to let hang around indefinitely. I think we're going to have to give her a push."

Father Dominic looked away from me, and started staring bleakly at a spot on the ceiling above our heads. "That isn't what we're here for, people like you and me, Susannah," he said in the saddest voice I had ever heard. "We are the sentries who guard the gates of the afterlife. We are the ones who help guide lost souls to their final destinations. And every single one of the spirits I've helped have passed my gate quite willingly. . . ."

Yeah. And if you clap hard enough, Tinkerbell won't die. It must, I thought, have been nice to see the world through Father Dom's eyes. It seemed like a nice place. A lot better than the world *I'd* lived in for the past sixteen years.

"Yes," I said. "Well, I don't see any other way."

"An exorcism," Father Dominic murmured. He said the word like it was distasteful, like mucus or something.

"Look," I said, beginning to regret I'd said anything. "Believe me, it's not a method I recommend. But I don't see that we have much choice. Heather's not just a danger to Bryce anymore." I didn't want to tell him what she'd said about David. I could just see him jumping out of bed and hollering for a pair of crutches. But since I had already let spill what I was planning, I had to let him know why I felt such an extreme was necessary. "She's a danger to the whole school," I said. "She's got to be stopped."

He nodded. "Yes. Yes, of course, you're right. But Susannah, you've got to promise me you won't try it until I've been released. I was talking to the doctor, and she says she might let me go as early as Friday. That will give us plenty of time to research the proper methodology—" He glanced at his bedside table. "Hand me that Bible there, would you, Susannah? If we can get the wording correctly, we just might—"

I handed him the Bible. "I'm pretty sure," I said,

"that I've got it down pat."

He lifted his gaze, pinning me with those baby blues of his. Too bad he was so old, and a priest, besides. I wondered how many hearts he'd broken back before he'd gotten his calling. "How could you possibly," he wondered, "have gotten anything as complicated as a Roman Catholic exorcism down pat?"

I fidgeted uncomfortably. "Well, I wasn't really planning on doing the Roman Catholic version."

"Is there another?"

"Oh, sure. Most religions have one. Personally, I prefer Mecumba. It's pretty much to the point. No long incantations or anything."

He looked pained. "Mecumba?"

"Sure. Brazilian voodoo. I got if off the Net. All you need is some chicken blood and a—"

"Mary, mother of God," Father Dominic interrupted. Then, when he'd recovered himself, he said, "Out of the question. Heather Chambers was baptized a Roman Catholic, and despite the cause of her death, she deserves a Roman Catholic exorcism, if not burial. Her chances of being admitted into heaven at this point aren't great, I'll admit, but I certainly intend to see that she gets every opportunity to greet St. Peter at the gates."

"Father Dom," I said. "I really don't think it matters whether she gets a Roman Catholic exorcism or a Brazilian one, or a Pygmy one, for that matter. The fact is, if there is a heaven, there's no way Heather Chambers is getting in there."

Father Dominic made a *tut-tutt*ing noise. "Susannah, how can you say such a thing? There is good in everyone. Surely even you can see that."

"Even me? What do you mean, even me?"

"Well, I mean even Susannah Simon, who can be very hard on others, must see that even in the cruelest human being there can exist a flower of good. Maybe just the tiniest blossom, in need of water and sunlight, but a flower just the same."

I wondered what kind of painkillers Father Dom was on.

I said, "Well, okay, Father. All I know is, wherever Heather's going, it ain't heaven. If there *is* a heaven."

He smiled at me sadly. "I wish," he said, "you had half as much faith in the good Lord, Susannah, as you have courage. Listen to me now for a moment. You mustn't—you *must not*—attempt to stop Heather on your own. It is extremely clear that she very nearly killed you last night. I could not believe my eyes when I walked out and saw the damage she caused. You were lucky to escape with your life. And it is clear from what happened this morning that, like you say, she is only growing stronger. It would be stupid—criminally stupid—of you to try to do anything on your own again."

I knew he was right. What's more, if I really did go through with the exorcism thing, I couldn't let Jesse help me . . . the exorcism might send him back to his maker, right along with Heather.

"Besides," Father Dominic said. "There isn't any reason to hurry, is there? Now that she's managed to hospitalize Bryce, she won't be up to any more mischief—at least not until he comes back to school. He seems to be the only person she entertains murderous feelings toward—"

I didn't say anything. How could I? I mean, the poor guy looked so pathetic lying there. I didn't want to give him more to worry about. But the truth was, I couldn't possibly wait for Father Dom to get out of the hospital. Heather meant business. With every day that passed, she would only get stronger and nastier, and more filled with hate. I had to get rid of her, and I had to get rid of her soon.

So I committed what I'm sure must be some kind of mortal sin. I lied to a priest.

Good thing I'm not Catholic.

"Don't worry, Father Dom," I said. "I'll wait till you're feeling better."

Father Dominic was no dummy, though. He went, "Promise me, Susannah."

I said, "I promise."

I had my fingers crossed, of course. I hoped that, if there was a God, this would cancel out the sin of lying to one of his most deserving servants.

"Let me see," Father Dominic was murmuring.

"We'll need holy water, of course. That's no problem. And, of course, a crucifix."

As he was muttering over his exorcism grocery list, Adam and CeeCee came into the room.

"Hey, Father Dom," Adam said. "Boy, do you look terrible."

CeeCee elbowed him. *"Adam,"* she hissed. Then, to the Father, she said brightly, "Don't listen to him, Father Dom. I think you look great. Well, for a guy with a bunch of broken bones, I mean."

"Children." Father Dominic looked really happy to see them. "What a delight! But why are you wasting a beautiful afternoon like this one visiting an old man in a hospital? You ought to be down at the beach enjoying the nice weather."

"We're actually here doing an article for the *Mission News* about the accident," CeeCee said. "We just got done interviewing the monsignor. It's really unfortunate, about the archbishop coming, and all, and the statue of Father Serra not having a head."

"Yeah," Adam said. "A real bummer."

"Well," Father Dominic said. "Never mind that. It's the caring spirit of you children that should most impress the archbishop."

"Amen," said Adam solemnly.

Before either of us had a chance to berate Adam for being sarcastic, a nurse came in and told CeeCee and me that we had to leave because she had to give

Father Dom his sponge bath.

"Sponge bath," Adam grumbled as we made our way back to the car. "Father Dom gets a sponge bath, but me, a guy who can actually appreciate something like that, what do *I* get?"

"A chance to play chauffeur to the two most beautiful girls in Carmel?" CeeCee offered helpfully.

"Yeah," Adam said. "Right." Then he glanced at me. "Not that you aren't the most beautiful girl in Carmel, Suze. . . . I just meant . . . Well, *you* know. . . ."

"I know," I said with a smile.

"I mean, a sponge bath. And did you get a look at that nurse?" Adam held the passenger seat forward so CeeCee could crawl into the backseat. "There must be something to this priest thing. Maybe I should enroll."

From the backseat CeeCee said, "You don't enroll, you receive a calling. And believe me, Adam, you wouldn't like it. They don't let priests play Nintendo."

Adam digested this. "Maybe I could form a new order," he said, thoughtfully. "Like the Franciscans, only we'd be the Joystick Order. Our motto would be High Score for One, Pizza for All."

CeeCee said, "Look out for that seagull."

We were on Carmel Beach Road. Just beyond the low stone wall to our right was the Pacific, lit up like a jewel by the enormous yellow ball of sun hovering above it. I guess I must have been looking at it a little longingly—I still hadn't gotten used to seeing it all the time—because Adam went, "Aw, hell," and zipped into a parking space that a BMW had just vacated. I looked at him questioningly as he threw the car into park, and he said, "What? You don't have time to sit and watch the sunset?"

I was out of the car in a flash.

How, I wondered a little while later, had I ever not looked forward to moving here? Sitting on a blanket Adam had extricated from the trunk of his car, watching the joggers and the evening surfers, the Frisbee-catching dogs and the tourists with their cameras, I felt better than I had in a long time. It might have been the fact that I was still operating on about four hours of sleep. It might have been that the heavy odor of brine was clouding my senses. But I really felt, for the first time in what seemed like forever, at peace.

Which was weird, considering the fact that in a few hours, I was going to be doing battle with the forces of evil.

But until then, I decided to enjoy myself. I turned my face toward the setting sun, feeling its warming rays on my cheeks, and listened to the roaring of the waves, the shrieking of the gulls, and the chatter of CeeCee and Adam.

"So I said to her, 'Claire, you're nearly forty. If you and Paul want to have another kid, you had better hurry. Time is not on your side.'" Adam sipped a latte he'd picked up from a coffee shop near where we'd parked. "And she was all, 'But your father and I don't want you to feel threatened by the new baby,' and I was like, 'Claire, babies don't threaten me.' You know what makes me feel threatened? Steroid-popping Neanderthals like Brad Ackerman. *They* threaten me."

CeeCee shot Adam a warning look, then looked at me. "How are you getting along with your new stepbrothers, Suze?"

I tore my eyes away from the setting sun. "All right, I guess. Does Do—I mean, Brad really take steroids?"

Adam said, "I shouldn't have mentioned that. I'm sorry. I'm sure he doesn't. All those guys on the wrestling team, though—they scare me. And they're so homophobic . . . well, you can't help wondering about their sexual orientation. I mean, they all think *I'm* gay, but you wouldn't catch *me* in a pair of tights grabbing at some other guy's inner thigh."

I felt a need to apologize for my stepbrother, and did so, adding, "I'm not so sure he's gay. He got very excited when Kelly Prescott called the other night and invited us to her pool party on Saturday."

Adam whistled, and CeeCee said unexpectedly, "Well, well, well. Are you sure this blanket is good enough for you? Maybe you would prefer a cashmere beach blanket. That's what Kelly and all her friends sit on."

I blinked at them, realizing I'd just committed a faux pas. "Oh, I'm sorry. Kelly didn't invite you guys?

But I just assumed she was inviting all the sophomores."

"Certainly not," CeeCee said with a sniff. "Just the sophomores with status, which Adam and I definitely lack."

"But you," I said, "are the editor of the school paper."

"Right," Adam said. "Translate that into *dork*, and you'll have an idea why we've never been invited to any of Princess Kelly's pool parties."

"Oh," I said. I was quiet for a minute, listening to the waves. Then I said, "Well, it's not like I was planning on going."

"You weren't?" CeeCee's eyes bugged out behind her glasses.

"No. At first because I had a date with Bryce, which is off now. But now because . . . well, if you guys aren't going, who would I talk to?"

CeeCee leaned back on the blanket. "Suze," she said. "Have you ever considered running for class VP?"

I laughed. "Oh, right. I'm the new kid, remember?"

"Yeah," Adam said. "But there's something about you. I saw real leadership potential in the way you trounced Debbie Mancuso yesterday. Guys always admire girls who look as if any minute they might punch another girl in the mouth. We just can't help it." He shrugged. "Maybe it's in the genes."

"Well," I said with a laugh. "I'll certainly take it

under advisement. I did hear a rumor Kelly was planning on blowing the entire class budget on some kind of dance—"

"Right." CeeCee nodded. "She does that every year. The stupid spring dance. It's so boring. I mean, if you don't have a boyfriend, what is the point? There's nothing to do there but dance."

"Wait," Adam said. "Remember that time we brought the water balloons?"

"Well," CeeCee amended. "Okay, *that* year was fun."

"I was kind of thinking," I heard myself saying, "that something like this might be better. You know. A cookout at the beach. Maybe a couple of them."

"Hey," Adam said. "Yeah! And a bonfire! The pyro in me has always wanted to do a bonfire on the beach."

CeeCee said, "Totally. That's totally what we should do. Suze, you've *got* to run for VP."

Holy smoke, what had I done? I didn't want to be sophomore class VP! I didn't want to get involved! I had no school spirit—I had no opinion on anything! What was I doing? Had I lost my mind?

"Oh, look," Adam said, pointing suddenly at the sun. "There it goes."

The great orange ball seemed to sink into the sea as it began its slow descent below the horizon. I didn't see any splashing or steam, but I could have sworn I heard it hit the water's surface.

"There goes the sun," CeeCee sang softly.

"Da da da da," Adam said.

"There goes the sun," I joined in.

Okay, I have to admit, it was kind of childish, sitting there singing, watching the sun go down. But it was also kind of fun. Back in New York, we used to sit in the park and watch the undercover cops arrest drug dealers. But that wasn't anywhere near as nice as this, singing happily on a beach as the sun went down.

Something strange was happening. I wasn't sure what it was.

"And I say," the three of us sang, "it's all right!"

And, strangely enough, at that moment, I actually believed it would be. All right, I mean.

And that's when I realized what was happening: I was fitting in. Me, Susannah Simon, mediator. I was fitting in somewhere for the first time in my life.

And I was happy about it. Really happy. I actually believed, just then, that everything was going to be all right.

Boy, was I ever in denial.

CHAPTER 17

My alarm went off at midnight. I didn't hit the snooze button. I turned it off, clapped my hands to turn on the bedside lamp, rolled over, and stared at the canopy over my bed.

This was it. D-day. Or E-day, I should have called it.

I'd been so tired after dinner, I knew I'd never make it without a nap. I told my mother I was going upstairs to do homework, and then I'd lain down with the intention of sacking out for a few hours. Back in our old place in Brooklyn, this wouldn't have been a problem. My mom would have left me alone like I asked. But in the Ackerman household, the words *I want to be alone* were apparently completely meaning-less. And not because the place is crawling with ghosts, either. No, it was the living who kept on bugging me for a change.

First it was Dopey. When I'd sat down to another gourmet dinner, immaculately prepared by my new stepfather, an interrogation of sorts had begun because I had ended up not getting home until after 6:00. There was the usual "Where were you?" from my mother (even though I'd so conscientiously left her that explanatory message). Then a "Did you have fun?" from Andy. And then there was a "Who'd you go with?" from, of all people, Doc. And when I said, "Adam McTavish and CeeCee Webb," Dopey actually snorted disgustedly and, chewing on a meatball, said, "Christ. The class freaks."

Andy said, "Hey. Watch it."

"Well, jeez, Dad," Dopey said. "One's a freakin' albino and the other's a fag."

This earned him a very hard wallop on the head from his father, who also grounded him for a week. Meaning, I couldn't help pointing out to Dopey later as we were clearing our plates from the table, that he would be unable to attend Kelly Prescott's pool party, which, by the way, I—Queen of the Freaks—had gotten him invited to.

"Too bad, bubby," I said, giving Dopey a sympathetic pat on the cheek.

He slapped my hand away. "Yeah?" he said. "Well, at least nobody'll be callin' *me* a fag hag tomorrow."

"Oh, sweetie," I said. I reached out and tweaked the cheek I'd just patted. "You'll never have to worry about people calling you that. They call you *much* worse things."

He hit my hand again, his fury apparently so great, it rendered him temporarily speechless.

"Promise me you'll never change," I begged him. "You're so adorable just the way you are."

Dopey called me a very bad name just as his father entered the kitchen with the remains of the salad.

Andy grounded him for another week, and then sent him to his room. To show his unhappiness with this turn of events, Dopey put on the Beastie Boys and played them at such high decibels that sleep was impossible for me . . . at least until Andy came up and took away Dopey's speakers. Then everything got very quiet, and I was just about to doze off when someone tapped at my door. It was Doc.

"Um," he said, glancing nervously past me, into the darkness of my room—the "haunted" room of the house. "Is this a good time to, um, talk about the things I found out? About the house, I mean? And the people who died here?"

"People? In the plural sense?"

"Oh, sure," Doc said. "I was able to find a surprising amount of documentation listing the crimes committed in this house, many of which involved murder of varying degrees. Because it was a boardinghouse, there were any number of transient residents, most of whom were on their way home after striking it rich in the Gold Rush farther upstate. Many of them were killed in their sleep and their gold absconded with, some thought by the owners of the establishment, but most likely it was by other residents—"

Fearing I was going to hear that Jesse had died this way—and suddenly not at all eager to know anymore what had caused his death, particularly not if he happened to be around to overhear—I said, "Listen, Doc—I mean, Dave. I don't think I've gotten over my jet lag yet, so I'm trying to catch up a little on my sleep just now. Can we talk about this tomorrow at school? Maybe we could have lunch together."

Doc's eyes widened. "Are you serious? You want to have lunch with me?"

I stared at him. "Well, yeah. Why? Is there some rule high schoolers can't eat with middle schoolers?"

"No," Doc said. "It's just that . . . they never do."

"Well," I said. "I will. Okay? You buy the drinks, and I'll buy dessert."

"Great!" Doc said, and went back to his own room looking like I'd just said tomorrow I'd present him with the throne of England.

I was just on the verge of dozing off again when there was another knock on the door. This time when I opened it, Sleepy was standing there looking more wide awake, for once, than I felt.

"Look," he said. "I don't care if you're gonna take the car out at night, just put the keys back on the hook, okay?"

I stared up at him. "I haven't been taking your car out at night, Slee—I mean, Jake."

He said, "Whatever. Just put the keys back where you found 'em. And it wouldn't hurt if you pitched in for gas now and then."

I said slowly, so he would understand, "I haven't been taking your car out at night, Jake."

"What you do on your own time is your business," Sleepy said. "I mean, I don't think gangs are cool or anything. But it's your life. Just put my keys back so I can find 'em."

I could see there was no point in arguing this, so I said, "Okay, I will," and shut the door.

After that, I got a good few hours of much needed sleep. I didn't exactly wake up feeling refreshed—I could have slept for maybe another year—but I felt a little better, at least.

Good enough to go kick some ghost butt, anyway.

Earlier in the evening, I'd gotten together all the things I was going to need. My backpack was crammed with candles, paintbrushes, a Tupperware container of chicken blood that I'd bought at the butcher counter in the Safeway I made Adam take me to before dropping me off at home, and various other assorted necessary components of a real Brazilian exorcism. I was completely ready to go. All I had to do was throw on my high tops, and I was out of there.

Except, of course, Jesse had to show up just as I was jumping off the porch roof.

"Okay," I said, straightening up, my feet smarting a little in spite of the soft ground I'd landed on. "Let's get one thing straight right now. You are not going to show up down at the Mission tonight. Got that? You show up down there, and you are going to be very, very sorry."

Jesse was leaning against one of the giant pine trees in our yard. Just leaning there, his arms folded across his chest, looking at me as if I were some sort of interesting sideshow attraction or something.

"I mean it," I said. "It's going to be a bad night for ghosts. Real bad. So I wouldn't show up down there if I were you."

Jesse, I noticed, was smiling. There wasn't as much moon as there'd been the night before, but there was enough so that I could see that the little curl at the corners of his lips was turning skyward, not down.

"Susannah," he said. "What are you up to?"

"Nothing." I marched over to the carport, and yanked out the ten-speed. "I've just got some things to settle."

Jesse strolled over toward me as I was strapping on the bike helmet. "With Heather?" he asked lightly.

"Right. With Heather. I know things got out of

hand last time, but this time, things are going to be different."

"How, precisely?"

I swung a leg over that stupid bar they put on boys' bikes, and stood at the top of the driveway, my fingers curled around the handlebars. "Okay," I said. "I'll level with you. I'm going to perform an exorcism."

His right hand shot out. It gripped the bar between my fingers. "A *what*?" he said in a voice completely devoid of the good humor that had been in it before.

I swallowed. Okay, I wasn't feeling quite as confident as I was acting. In fact, I was practically quaking in my Converse All Stars. But what else could I do? I had to stop Heather before she hurt anybody else. And it would have been really helpful if everybody could have just supported me in my efforts.

"You can't help me," I said woodenly. "You can't go down there tonight, Jesse, or you might get exorcised, too."

"You," Jesse said, speaking as tonelessly as I was, "are insane."

"Probably," I said miserably.

"She'll kill you," Jesse said. "Don't you understand? That's what she wants."

"No." I shook my head. "She doesn't want to kill me. She wants to kill everybody I care about first. *Then* she wants to kill me." I sniffled. For some reason, my nose was running. Probably because it was so cold out. I don't see how those palm trees could stay alive. It was like forty degrees or something outside.

"But I'm not going to let her, see?" I continued. "I'm going to stop her. Now let go of my bike."

Jesse shook his head. "No. No. Even you wouldn't do something so stupid."

"Even me?" I was hurt, in spite of myself. "Thanks."

He ignored me. "Does the priest know about this, Susannah? Did you tell the priest?"

"Um, sure. He knows. He's, uh, meeting me there."

"The priest is meeting you there?"

"Yeah, uh-huh." I gave a shaky laugh. "You don't think I'd try something like this on my own, do you? I mean, jeez, I'm not *that* stupid, no matter what you might think."

His grip on the bike relaxed a little. "Well, if the priest will be there . . ."

"Sure. Sure he will."

The grip tightened again. Jesse's other hand came around, and a long finger wagged in my face as he said, "You're lying, aren't you? The priest isn't going to be there at all. She hurt him, didn't she? This morning? I thought so. Did she kill him?"

I shook my head. I didn't feel so much like talking all of a sudden. It felt like there was something in my throat. Something that hurt.

"That's why you're so angry," Jesse said wonderingly. "I should have known. You're going down there to get even with her for what she did to the priest."

"So what if I am?" I exploded. "She deserves it!"

He put his finger down, gripping the handlebars of my bike with both hands. And let me tell you, he was pretty strong for a dead guy. I couldn't budge the stupid thing with him hanging on to it like that.

"Susannah," he said. "This isn't the way. This wasn't why you were given this extraordinary gift, not so you could do things like—"

"Gift!" I nearly burst out laughing. I had to grit my teeth to keep from doing so. "Yeah, that's right, Jesse. I've been given a precious gift. Well, you know what? I'm sick of it. I really am. I thought coming out here, I'd be able to make a new start. I thought things might be different. And you know what? They are. They're *worse*."

"Susannah—"

"What am I supposed to do, Jesse? Love Heather for what she did? Embrace her wounded spirit? I'm sorry, but that's impossible. Maybe Father Dom could do it, but not me, and he's out of commission, so we're going to do things *my* way. I'm going to get rid of her, and if you know what's good for you, Jesse, you'll stay away!"

I gave my kickstand a vicious kick, and at the same time, yanked on the handlebars. The move surprised Jesse so much, he let go of the bike involuntarily. A second later, I was off, spraying gravel out from beneath my back wheel, leaving Jesse in my dust. I heard him say a bunch of stuff in Spanish as I sped down the driveway. I think it was probably swear words. The word *querida* was definitely not mentioned.

I didn't see much of my trip down into the valley. The wind was so cold that tears streamed in a pretty constant flow down my cheeks and back into my hair. There wasn't much traffic out, thank God, so when I flew through the intersection, it didn't really matter that I couldn't see. The cars stopped for me, anyway.

I knew it was going to be trickier to break into the school this time. They'd have beefed up the security in response to what had happened the night before. Beefed up the security? All they had to do was actually get some.

And they had. A police cruiser sat in the parking lot, its lights off. Just sitting there, the moonlight reflecting off the closed windows. The driver—doubtlessly some luckless rookie to have pulled so boring an assignment—was probably listening to music, though I couldn't hear any from where I stood just outside the gate to the parking lot.

So I was going to have to find another way to get in. No biggie. I stashed the bike in some bushes, then took a leisurely stroll around the perimeter of the school.

There aren't many buildings you can keep a fairly slender sixteen-year-old girl out of. I mean, we're pretty flexible. I happen to be double-jointed in a lot of places, too. I won't tell you how I managed to break in, since I don't want the school authorities figuring it out—you never know, I might have to do it again someday—but let's just say if you're going to make a gate, make sure it reaches all the way to the ground. That gap between the cement and where the gate starts is exactly all the room a girl like me needs to wriggle through.

Inside the courtyard, things looked a lot different than they had the night before—and a whole lot creepier. All the floodlights were turned off—this didn't seem like a very good safety precaution to me, but it was possible, of course, that Heather had blown all the bulbs—so the courtyard was dark and eerily shadowed. The fountain was turned off. I couldn't hear anything this time except for crickets. Just crickets chirping in the hibiscus. Nothing wrong with crickets. Crickets are our friends.

There was no sign of Heather. There was no sign of anybody. This was good.

I crept as quietly as I could—which was pretty quietly in my sneakers—to the locker Heather and I shared. Then I knelt down on the cold flagstones and opened my backpack.

I lit the candles first. I needed their light to see by. Holding my lighter—okay, it wasn't really my lighter, it was the long-handled lighter from the barbecue—to the candle's bottom, I dripped some wax onto the ground, then shoved the candle's base into the gooey drippings to keep it in place. I did this to each candle until I'd formed a ring of them in front of me. Then I peeled back the lid of the container holding the chicken blood.

I'm not going to write down the shape that I was required to paint in the center of the ring of candles in order for the exorcism to work. Exorcisms aren't things people should try at home, I don't care how badly you might be haunted. And they should only be performed by a professional like myself. You wouldn't, after all, want to hurt any innocent ghosts who happen to be hanging around. I mean, exorcising Grandma—that won't make you *too* unpopular, or anything.

And Mecumba—Brazilian voodoo—isn't something people should mess with, either, so I won't write down the incantation I had to say. It was all in Portuguese, anyway. But let's just say that I dipped my brush into the chicken blood and made the appropriate shapes, uttering the appropriate words as I did so. It wasn't until I reached into the backpack and pulled out Heather's photograph that I noticed the crickets had stopped chirping.

"What," she said in an irritated voice from just behind my right shoulder, "in the hell do you think you're doing?"

I didn't answer her. I put the photo in the center of the shape I had painted. The light from the candles illuminated it fairly well.

Heather came closer. "Hey," she said. "That's a picture of me. Where'd you get it?"

I didn't say anything except the Portuguese words I was supposed to say. This seemed to upset Heather.

Well, let's face it. Everything seemed to upset Heather.

"What are you doing?" Heather demanded again. "What's that language you're talking in? And what's that red paint for?" When I didn't answer her, Heather became—as seemed to be her nature—abusive. "Hey, bitch," she said, laying a hand upon my shoulder and pulling on it, not very gently. "Are you listening to me?"

I broke off the incantation. "Could you do me a favor, Heather," I said, "and stand right there next to your picture?"

Heather shook her head. Her long blonde hair shimmered in the candlelight. "What are you?" she demanded rudely. "High or something? I'm not standing anywhere. Is that . . . is that blood?"

I shrugged. Her hand was still on my shoulder. "Yes," I said. "Don't worry, though. It's just chicken blood."

"Chicken blood?" Heather made a face. "Gross. Are you kidding me? What's it for?"

"To help you," I said. "To help you go back."

Heather's jaw tightened. The doors to the lockers in front of me began to rattle. Not a lot. Just enough to let me know Heather was unhappy. "I thought," she said, "that I made it pretty clear to you last night that I'm not going anywhere."

"You said you wanted to go back."

"Yeah," Heather said. The dials on the combination locks began to spin noisily. "To my old life."

"Well," I said. "I found a way you can do it."

The doors began to hum, they were shaking so hard.

"No way," Heather said.

"Way. All you have to do is stand right here, between those candles, next to your picture."

Heather needed no further urging. In a second, she was exactly where I wanted her.

"Are you sure this will work?" Heather asked excitedly.

"It better," I said. "Otherwise, I've blown my allowance on candles and chicken blood for nothing."

"And things will be just like they were? Before I died, I mean?"

"Sure," I said. Should I have felt guilty for lying to her? I didn't. Feel guilty, I mean. All I felt was relieved. It had all been too easy. "Now shut up a minute while I say the words."

She was only too eager to oblige. I said the words.

And said the words.

And said the words.

I was just starting to be worried nothing was going to happen when the candle flames flickered. And it wasn't because there was any wind.

"Nothing's happening," Heather complained, but I shushed her.

The candle flames flickered again. And then, above Heather's head, where the roof of the breezeway should have been, appeared a hole filled with red, swirling gases. I stared at the hole.

"Uh, Heather," I said. "You might want to close your eyes."

She did so happily enough. "Why? Is it working?"

"Oh," I said. "It's working, all right."

Heather said something that might have been "goodie," but I wasn't sure. I couldn't hear her too well since the swirling red gas—it was more like smoke really—had started spiraling down from the hole, making a low sort of thundering noise as it did so. Soon long tendrils of the stuff were wrapping around Heather, lightly as fog. Only she didn't know it since her eyes were closed.

"I hear something," she said. "Is this it?"

Above her head, the hole had widened. I could see lightning flashing in it. It didn't look like the most pleasant place to go. I'm not saying I'd opened a gate to hell or anything—at least, I hope not—but it was definitely a dimension other than our own, and frankly, it didn't look like a nice place to visit, let alone live in for all eternity.

"Just one more minute," I said, as more and more

snaky red limbs wrapped around her slender cheer-leader's body. "And you'll be there."

Heather tossed her long hair. "Oh, God," she said. "I can't wait. First thing I'm going to do, I'm going to go down to the hospital and apologize to Bryce. Don't you think that's a good idea, Susie?"

I said, "Sure." The thunder was getting louder, the lightning more frequent. "That's a great idea."

"I hope my mom hasn't gotten rid of my clothes," Heather said. "Just because I was dead. You don't think my mom would have gotten rid of my clothes, do you, Susie?" She opened her eyes. "Do you?"

I shouted, "Keep your eyes closed!"

But it was too late. She had seen. Oh, boy, had she seen. She took one look at the red wisps wrapped around her and started shrieking.

And not with fear, either. Oh, no. Heather wasn't scared. She was mad. Really mad.

"You bitch!" she shrieked. "You aren't sending me back! You aren't sending me back at all! You're sending me *away*!"

And then, just when the thunder was getting loud-est, Heather stepped out of the circle.

Just like that. She just stepped out of it. Like it was no big deal. Like it was a hopscotch square. Those red wisps of smoke that had been wrapped all around her just fell away. Fell away like nothing. And the hole above Heather's head closed up.

Okay. I admit it. I got mad. Hey, I'd put a lot of work into this thing.

"Oh, no you don't," I growled. I strode up to Heather and grabbed her. Around the neck, I'm afraid.

"Get back in there," I said, from between gritted teeth. "Get back in there right now."

Heather only laughed. I had the girl by the throat, and she only laughed.

Behind her, though, the locker doors started humming again. More loudly than ever.

"You," she said, "are so dead. You are so dead, Simon. And you know what? I'm going to make sure that the rest of them go with you. All of your little freaky friends. And that stepbrother of yours, too."

I tightened my grip on her throat. "I don't think so. I think you're going to get back where you were and go away like a good little ghost."

She laughed again. "Make me," she said, her blue eyes glittering like crazy.

Well. If you put it that way.

I hit her hard with my right fist. Then, before she had a chance to recover, I hit her the other way with my left. If she felt the blows, she made no sign. No, that's not true. I know she felt the blows because the locker doors suddenly started opening and closing. Not closing, exactly. Slamming. Hard. Hard enough to shake the whole breezeway.

I mean it. The whole breezeway was pitching back

and forth, as if the ground beneath it was really ocean waves. The thick wooden support pillars that held up the arched roof shook in ground that had held them steady for close to three hundred years. Three hundred years of earthquakes, fires, and floods, and the ghost of a cheerleader sends them tumbling down.

I tell you, this mediation stuff is no damned fun.

And then *her* fingers were around *my* throat. I don't know how. I guess I got distracted by all the shaking. This was no good. I grabbed her by the arms, and started trying to push her back toward the circle of candles. As I did so, I muttered the Portuguese incantation under my breath, staring at the swaying rafters overhead, hoping that the hole to that shadowy land would open up again.

"Shut up," Heather said, when she heard what I was saying. "Shut your mouth! You are not sending me away. I belong here! A lot more than you!"

I kept saying the words. I kept pushing.

"Who the hell do you think you are?" Heather's face was red with rage. Out of the corner of my eye, I saw a planter packed with geraniums levitate a few inches off the stone balustrade on which it had been resting. "You're *no one*. You've only been at this school two days. Two days! You think you can just come in here and change everything? You think you can just *take my place*? Who do you think you are?"

I kicked out a leg and, pulling on the arms I held

at the same time as I swept her feet out from under her, sent us both crashing to the hard stone floor. The planter followed, not because we'd knocked it over, but because Heather sent it hurling through the air at me. I ducked at the last minute, and the heavy clay pot smashed against the locker doors in an explosion of mulch and geranium and pottery shards. I grabbed fistfuls of Heather's long, glossy, blonde hair. This was not very sporting of me, but hey, throwing the geraniums hadn't been very sporting of her.

She shrieked, kicking and writhing like an eel while I half dragged, half shoved her toward the circle of candles. She'd started levitating other objects. The combination locks spun out of their cores in the locker doors, and careened through the air at me like tiny little flying saucers. Then a tornado rolled in, sucking the contents of those lockers out into the breezeway, so that textbooks and three-ring binders were flying at me from four directions. I kept my head down, but didn't lose my hold on her even when somebody's trig book hit me hard in the shoulder. I kept saying the words I knew would open the hole again.

"Why are you doing this?" Heather shrieked. "Why can't you just leave me alone?"

"Because." I was bruised, I was out of breath, I was dripping with sweat, and all I wanted to do was let go of her, turn around and go home, crawl into my bed, and sleep for a million years.

But I couldn't.

So instead, I kicked her in the center of the chest and sent her staggering back to the center of the circle of candles. And the minute she stumbled over that photograph of herself she'd given to Bryce, the hole that had opened up above her head reappeared. And this time, the red smoke closed around her as suffocatingly as a thick wool blanket. She wasn't breaking out again. Not that easily.

The red fog had encased her so thickly, I couldn't see her anymore, but I could sure hear her. Her shrieks ought to have waked the dead—except, of course, she was the only dead around. Thunder clapped over her head. Inside the black hole that had opened above her, I thought I saw stars twinkling.

"*Why?*" Heather screamed. "Why are you doing this to me?"

"Because," I said. "I'm the mediator."

And then two things happened almost simultaneously.

The red smoke surrounding Heather began to be sucked back up into the spinning hole, taking Heather with it.

And the sturdy pillars that supported the breezeway over my head suddenly snapped in two as cleanly as if they'd been two inches, and not two feet, thick.

And then the breezeway collapsed on top of me.

CHAPTER 18

I have no idea how long I lay beneath the planks of wood and heavy clay tiles of the crumpled breezeway. Looking back, I realize I must have lost consciousness, if only for a few minutes.

All I can remember is something sharp hitting me on the head, and the next thing I knew, I'd opened my eyes to consummate blackness, and a feeling that I was being smothered.

A favorite trick of some poltergeists is to sit on their victim's chest while he or she is just waking, so that the poor soul feels he or she is being smothered, but can't see why. I couldn't see why, and for a second or two I thought I'd failed and that Heather was still in this world, sitting on my chest, torturing me, getting her revenge for what I'd tried to do.

Then I thought, *Maybe I'm dead.*

I don't know why. But it occurred to me. Maybe this was how being dead felt. At first, anyway. This must have been how it was for Heather when she woke up in her coffin. She must have felt the same way I did: trapped, suffocated, frightened witless. God, no wonder she'd been in such a bad mood all the time. No wonder she'd wanted so desperately to get back to the world she'd known pre-death. This was horrible. It was worse than horrible. It was hell.

But then I moved my hand—the only part of me I *could* move—and felt something rough and cool resting over me. That's when I knew what had happened. The breezeway had collapsed. Heather had used her last little bit of kinetic power to hurt me for sending her away. And she'd done a splendid job because here I was unable to move, trapped underneath who knew how many pounds of wood and Spanish tile.

Thanks, Heather. Thanks a lot.

I should have been scared. I mean, there I was pinned down, completely unable to move, in utter darkness. But before I had time to start panicking, I heard someone call my name. I thought at first I might be going crazy. Nobody knew, after all, that I'd gone down to the school except for Jesse, of course, and I'd told him what would happen if he showed up. He wasn't stupid. He knew I was performing an exorcism. Could he have decided to come down, anyway? Was it safe yet? I didn't know. If he happened to step into the circle of candles and chicken blood, would he be sucked into that same dark shadowland that took Heather?

Now I started to panic.

"Jesse!" I yelled, pounding on the wood above my head, causing dirt and bits of wood to fall down onto my face. "Don't!" I shrieked. All the dust was making me choke, but I didn't care. "Go back! It isn't safe!"

Then a great weight was lifted off my chest, and suddenly I could see. Above me stretched the night sky, velvet blue and spotted with a dusting of stars. And framed by those stars hung a face hovering over me worriedly.

"Here she is," Doc called, his voice wobbling in both pitch and volume. "Jake, I found her!"

A second face joined the first one, this one framed by a curtain of over-long blond hair. "Jesus Christ," Sleepy drawled, when he got a look at me. "Are you all right, Suze?"

I nodded dazedly. "Help me up," I said.

The two of them managed to get most of the bigger pieces of timber off me. Then Sleepy instructed me to wrap my arms around his neck, which I did, while David grabbed my waist. And with the two of them pulling, and me pushing with my feet, I finally managed to get clear of the rubble.

We sat for a minute in the darkness of the court-yard, leaning against the edge of the dais on which the headless statue of Junipero Serra stood. We just sat there, panting and staring at the ruin which had once been our school. Well, that's a bit dramatic, I guess. Most of the school was still standing. Even most of the breezeway was still up. Just the section in front of Heather's locker and Mr. Walden's classroom had come down. The twisted pile of wood neatly hid the evidence of my evening's activities, including the candles, which had evidently gone out. There was no sign of Heather. The night was perfectly quiet except for the sound of our breathing. And the crickets.

That's how I knew Heather was really gone. The crickets had started up again.

"Jesus," Sleepy said again, still panting pretty heavily, "are you sure you're all right, Suze?"

I turned to look at him. All he had on was a pair of jeans and an Army jacket, thrown hastily over a bare chest. Sleepy, I noticed, had almost as defined a six-pack as Jesse.

How is it that I'd nearly been smothered to death, and yet I could sit there and notice things like my step-brother's abdominal muscles a few minutes later?

"Yeah," I said, pushing some hair out of my eyes. "I'm fine. A little banged up, maybe. But nothing broken."

"She should probably go to the hospital and get

checked out." David's voice was still pretty wobbly. "Don't you think she should go to the hospital and get checked out, Jake?"

"No," I said. "No hospitals."

"You could have a concussion," David said. "Or a fractured skull. You might slip into a coma in your sleep and never wake up. You should at least get an X-ray. Or an MRI, maybe. A CAT scan wouldn't hurt, either—"

"No." I brushed my hands off on my leggings and stood up. My body felt pretty creaky, but whole. "Come on. Let's get out of here before somebody comes. They were bound to have heard all that." I nodded toward the part of the building where the priests and nuns lived. Lights had come on in some of the windows. "I don't want to get you guys in trouble."

"Yeah," Sleepy said, getting up. "Well, you might have thought of that before you snuck out, huh?"

We left the way we'd come in. Like me, David had wriggled in beneath the front gate, then unlocked it from the inside and let Sleepy in. We slipped out as quietly as we could, and hurried to the Rambler, which Sleepy had parked in some shadows, out of sight of the police car. The black-and-white was still sitting there, its occupant perfectly oblivious to what had gone on just a few dozen yards away. Still, I didn't want to risk anything by trying to sneak past him, and retrieve my bike. We just left it there, and hoped no one would notice it.

The whole way home, my new big brother Jake lectured me. Apparently, he thought I'd been at the school in the middle of the night as part of some sort of gang initiation. I kid you not. He was really very indignant about the whole thing. He wanted to know what kind of friends I thought these people were, leaving me to die under a pile of roofing tiles. He suggested that if I were bored or in need of a thrill, I should take up surfing because, and I quote, "If you're gonna have your head split open, it might as well be while you're riding a wave, dude."

I took his lecture as gracefully as I could. After all, I couldn't very well tell him the real reason I'd been down at the school after hours. I only interrupted Jake once during his little antigang speech, and that was to ask him just how he and David had known to come after me.

"I don't know," Jake said, as we pulled up the driveway. "All I know is, I was catching some pretty heavy-duty Z's, when all of a sudden Dave is all over me, telling me we have to go down to the school and find you. How'd you know she was down there, anyway, Dave?"

David's face was unnaturally white even in the moonlight. "I don't know," he said quietly. "I just had a feeling."

I turned to look at him, hard. But he wouldn't meet my eye.

That kid, I thought. *That kid knows.*

But I was too tired to talk about it just then. We snuck into the house, relieved that the only occupant who woke upon our entrance was Max, who wagged his tail and tried to lick us as we made our way to our rooms. Before I slipped into mine, I looked over at David just once, to see if he wanted—or needed—to say anything to me. But he didn't. He just went into his room and shut his door, a scared little boy. My heart swelled for him.

But only for a second. I was too tired to think of anything much but bed—not even Jesse. *In the morning,* I told myself, as I peeled off my dusty clothes. *I'll talk to him in the morning.*

I didn't, though. When I woke up, the light outside my windows looked funny. When I lifted my head and saw the clock, I realized why. It was two o'clock in the afternoon. All the morning fog had burned away, and the sun was beating down as hard as if it were July and not January.

"Well, hey there, sleepyhead."

I squinted in the direction of my bedroom door. Andy stood there, leaning against the doorframe with his arms folded across his chest. He was grinning, which meant I probably wasn't in trouble. What was I doing in bed at two o'clock in the afternoon on a school day, then?

"Feeling better?" Andy wanted to know.

I pushed the bedcovers down a little. Was I supposed to be sick? Well, that wouldn't be hard to fake. I felt as if someone had dropped a ton of bricks on my head.

Which, in a way, I suppose they had.

"Uh," I said. "Not really."

"I'll get you some aspirin. I guess it all caught up with you, huh? The jet lag, I mean. When we couldn't wake you up this morning, we decided just to let you sleep. Your mom said to tell you she's sorry, but she had to go to work. She put me in charge. Hope you don't mind."

I tried to sit up. It was really hard. Every muscle in my body felt as if it had been pounded on. I pushed some hair out of my eyes and blinked at him. "You didn't have to," I said. "Stay home on my account, I mean."

Andy shrugged. "It's no big deal. I've barely had a chance to talk to you since you got here, so I thought we could catch up. You want some lunch?"

The minute he said it, my stomach growled. I was starving.

He heard it and grinned. "No problem. Get dressed and come on downstairs. We'll have lunch on the deck. It's really beautiful out today."

I dragged myself out of bed with an effort. I had my pj's on. I didn't feel very much like getting dressed. So I just pulled on some socks and a bathrobe, brushed my teeth, and stood for a minute by the bay windows, looking out as I tried to work the snarls out of my hair. The red dome of the Mission church glowed in the sunlight. I could see the ocean winking behind it. You couldn't tell from up here that it had been the scene last night of so much destruction.

It wasn't long before an extremely appetizing aroma rose up from the kitchen and lured me down the stairs. Andy was making Reuben sandwiches. He waved me out of the kitchen, though, toward the huge deck he'd built onto the back of the house. The sun was pouring down there, and I stretched out on one of the padded chaise longues, and pretended like I was a movie star for a while. Then Andy came out with the sandwiches and a pitcher of lemonade, and I moved to the table with the big green umbrella over it, and dug in. For a non–New Yorker, Andy grilled a mean Reuben.

And that wasn't all he grilled. He spent a half hour grilling me pretty thoroughly . . . but not about what had happened the night before. To my astonishment, Sleepy and Doc had kept their mouths shut. Andy was perfectly in the dark about what had happened. All he wanted to know was whether I liked my new school, if I was happy, blah, blah, blah . . . .

Except for one thing. He did say to me, as he was asking me how I liked California, and was it really so very different from New York—uh, duh—"So, I guess you slept straight through your first earthquake."

I nearly choked on a chip. "What?"

"Your first quake. There was one last night, around two in the morning. Not a big one, really—round about a four pointer—but it woke *me* up. No damage, except down at the Mission, evidently. Breezeway collapsed. But then, that should come as no surprise to them. I've been warning them for years about that timber. It's nearly as old as the Mission itself. Can't be expected to last forever."

I chewed more carefully. Wow. Heather's goodbye bang must have really packed a wallop if people all over the Valley, and even up in the hills, had felt it.

But that still didn't explain how David had known to look for me down at the school.

I'd moved upstairs and was sitting on the window seat in my room flipping through a mindless fashion magazine, wondering where Jesse had gone off to, and how long I was going to have to wait before he showed up to give me another one of his lectures, and if there was any chance he might call me *querida* again, when the boys got home from school. Dopey stomped right past my room—he still blamed me for getting him grounded—but Sleepy poked his head in, looked at me, saw that I was all right, then went away, shaking his head. Only David knocked, and when I called for him to come in, did so, shyly.

"Um," he said. "I brought you your homework. Mr.

Walden gave it to me to give to you. He said he hoped you were feeling better."

"Oh," I said. "Thanks, David. Just put it down there on the bed."

David did so, but he didn't go. He just stood there staring at the bedpost. I figured he needed to talk, so I decided to let him by not saying anything myself.

"CeeCee says hi," he said. "And that other kid. Adam McTavish."

"That's nice of them," I said.

I waited. David did not disappoint.

"Everybody's talking about it, you know," he said.

"Talking about what?"

"You know. The quake. That the Mission must be over some fault no one ever knew about before, since the epicenter seemed to be . . . seemed to be right next to Mr. Walden's classroom."

I said, "Huh," and turned the page of my magazine.

"So," David said. "You're never going to tell me, are you?"

I didn't look at him. "Tell you what?"

"What's going on. Why you were down at the school in the middle of the night. How that breezeway came down. Any of it."

"It's better that you don't know," I said, flipping the page. "Trust me."

"But it doesn't have to do with . . . with what Jake said. With a gang. Does it?"

"No," I said.

I looked at him then. The sun, pouring through my windows, brought out the pink highlights in his skin. This boy—this redheaded boy with the sticky-outy ears—had saved my life. I owed him an explanation, at the very least.

"I saw it, you know," David said.

"Saw what?"

"It. The ghost."

He was staring at me, white-faced and intent. He looked way too serious for a twelve-year-old.

"What ghost?" I asked.

"The one who lives here. In this room." He glanced around, as if expecting to see Jesse looming in one of the corners of my bright, sunny room. "It came to me, last night," he said. "I swear it. It woke me up. It told me about you. That's how I knew. That's how I knew you were in trouble."

I stared at him with my mouth hanging open. *Jesse? Jesse* had told him? *Jesse* had woken him up?

"It wouldn't let me alone," David said, his voice trembling. "It kept on . . . touching me. My shoulder. It was cold and it glowed. It was just a cold, glowing thing, and inside my head there was this voice telling me I had to get down to the school and help you. I'm not lying, Suze. I swear it really happened."

"I know it did, David," I said, closing the magazine. "I believe you."

He'd opened his mouth to swear it was true some more, but when I told him I believed him, his jaw clicked shut. He only opened it again to say wonderingly, "You *do*?"

"I do," I said. "I didn't get a chance last night to say it, so I'll say it now. Thank you, David. You and Jake saved my life."

He was shaking. He had to sit down on my bed, or he probably would have fallen down.

"So . . ." he said. "So it's true. It really was . . . the ghost?"

"It really was."

He digested that. "And why were you down at the school?"

"It's a long story," I said. "But I promise you, it doesn't have anything to do with gangs."

He blinked at me. "Does it have to do with . . . the ghost?"

"Not the one who visited you. But yes, it had to do with a ghost."

David's lips moved, but I don't think he was really aware he was speaking. What came out of his mouth was an astonished, "There's more than one?"

"Oh, there's *way* more than one," I said.

He stared at me some more. "And you . . . you can see them?"

"David," I said. "This isn't really something I'm all that comfortable discussing—"

"Have you seen the one from last night? The one who woke me up?"

"Yes, David. I've seen him."

"Do you know who he is? How he died, I mean?"

I shook my head. "No. Remember? You were going to look it up for me."

David brightened. "Oh, yeah! I forgot. I checked some books out yesterday—stay here a minute. Don't go anywhere."

He ran from the room, all of his recent shock forgotten. I stayed where I was, exactly as he'd told me to. I wondered if Jesse was somewhere nearby, listening. I figured it would serve him right if he were.

David was back in a flash, bringing with him a large pile of dusty, oversize books. They looked really ancient, and when he sat down beside me and eagerly began leafing through them, I saw that they were every bit as old as they looked. None of them had been published after 1910. The oldest had been published in 1849.

"Look," David said, flipping through a large, leather-bound volume entitled *My Monterey*. *My Monterey* had been written by one Colonel Harold Clemmings. The colonel had a rather dry narrative style, but there were pictures to look at, which helped, even if they were in black and white.

"Look," David said again, turning to a reproduction of a photograph of the house we were sitting in.

Only the house looked a good deal different, having no porch and no carport. Also, the trees around it were much smaller. "Look, see, here's the house when it was a hotel. Or a boardinghouse, as they called it back then. It says here the house had a pretty bad reputation. A lot of people were murdered here. Colonel Clemmings goes into detail about all of them. Do you suppose the ghost who came to me last night is one of them? One of the people who died here, I mean?"

"Well," I said. "Most likely."

David began reading out loud—quickly and intelligently, and without stumbling over the big, old-fashioned words—the different stories of people who had died in what Colonel Clemmings referred to as the House in the Hills.

None of those people, however, was named Jesse. None of them sounded even remotely like him. When David was through, he looked up at me hopefully.

"Maybe the ghost belongs to that Chinese launderer," he said. "The one who was shot because he didn't wash that dandy's shirts fine enough."

I shook my head. "No. Our ghost isn't Chinese."

"Oh." David consulted the book again. "How about this guy? The guy who was killed by his slaves?"

"I don't think so," I said. "He was only five feet tall."

"Well, what about this guy? This Dane who they caught cheating at cards, and blew away?"

"He's not Danish," I said with a sigh.

David pursed his lips. "Well, what was he, then? This ghost?'

I shook my head. "I don't know. At least part Spanish. And . . ." I didn't want to go into it right there in my room, where Jesse might overhear. You know, about his liquid eyes and long brown fingers and all that.

I mean, I didn't want him to think that I *liked* him or anything.

Then I remembered the handkerchief. It had been gone when I'd woken up the next morning, after I'd washed my blood out of it, but I still remembered the initials. MDS. I told them to David. "Do those letters mean anything to you?"

He looked thoughtful for a minute. Then he closed Colonel Clemmings's book and picked up another one. This one was even older and dustier. It was so old, the title had rubbed off the spine. But when David opened it, I saw by the title page that it was called *Life in Northern California, 1800–1850*.

David scanned the index in the back, and then went, "Aha."

"Aha what?" I asked.

"Aha, I thought so," David said. He flipped to a page toward the end. "Here," he said. "I knew it. There's a picture of her." He handed me the book, and I saw a page with a layer of tissue over it.

"What's this?" I said. "There's Kleenex in this book."

"It isn't Kleenex. It's tissue. They used to put that over pictures in books to protect them. Lift it up."

I lifted up the tissue. Underneath it was a black-and-white copy on glossy paper of a painting. The painting was a portrait of a woman. Underneath the woman's portrait were the words MARIA DE SILVA DIEGO, 1830–1916.

My jaw dropped. *MDS!* Maria de Silva!

She looked like the type that would have a handkerchief like that tucked up her sleeve. She was dressed in a frilly white thing—at least, it looked white in the black-and-white picture—with her shiny black hair all ringleted on either side of her head, and a big old expensive-looking jewel hanging from a gold chain around her long neck. A beautiful, proud-looking woman, she stared out of the frame of the portrait with an expression you just had to call . . . well, contemptuous.

I looked at David. "Who was she?" I asked.

"Oh, just the most popular girl in California at around the time this house was built." David took the book away from me, and flipped through it. "Her father, Ricardo de Silva, owned most of Salinas back then. She was his only daughter, and he settled a pretty hefty dowry on her. That's not why people wanted to marry her, though. Well, not the only reason. Back then, people actually considered girls who looked like that beautiful."

I said, "She's *very* beautiful."

David glanced at me with a funny little smile. "Yeah," he said. "Right."

"No. She really is."

David saw I was serious, and shrugged. "Well, whatever. Her dad wanted her to marry this rich rancher—some cousin of hers who was madly in love with her—but she was all into this other guy, this guy named Diego." He consulted the book. "Felix Diego. This guy was bad news. He was a slave runner. At least, that's what he'd done for a living before he came out to California to strike it rich in the gold mines. And Maria's dad, he didn't approve of slavery, any more than he approved of gold diggers. So Maria and her dad, they had this big fight about it—who she was going to marry, I mean, the cousin or the slave runner—until finally, her dad said he was going to cut her off if she didn't marry the cousin. That shut Maria up pretty quick because she was a girl who liked money a lot. She had something like sixty dresses back when most women had two, one for work and one for church—"

"So what happened?" I interrupted. I didn't care how many dresses the woman owned. I wanted to know where Jesse came in.

"Oh." David consulted the book. "Well, the funny thing is, after all that, Maria won out in the end."

"How?"

"The cousin never showed up for the wedding."

I blinked at him. "Never showed up? What do you

mean, he never showed up?"

"That's just it. He never showed up. Nobody knows what happened to him. He left his ranch a few days before the wedding, you know, so he'd get there on time or whatever, but then nobody heard from him again. Ever. The end."

"And . . ." I knew the answer, but I had to ask, anyway. "And what happened to Maria?"

"Oh, she married the gold-digging slave runner. I mean, after they'd waited a decent interval and all. There were all these rules back then about that kind of thing. Her dad was so disappointed, you know, that the cousin had turned out to be so unreliable, that he finally just told Maria she could do whatever she wanted, and be damned. So she did. But she wasn't damned. She and the slave runner had eleven kids and took over her father's properties after he died and did a pretty good job running them—"

I held up my hand. "Wait. What was the cousin's name?"

David consulted the book. "Hector."

"Hector?"

"Yes." David looked back down at the book. "Hector de Silva. His mom called him Jesse, though."

When he looked back up, he must have seen something in my face since he went, in a small voice, "Is that our ghost?"

"That," I said softly, "is our ghost."

CHAPTER 19

The phone rang a little while later. Dopey yelled down the hall that it was for me. I picked up, and heard CeeCee squealing on the other end of the line.

"Ms. Vice President," she said. "Ms. Vice President, do you have any comment?"

I said, "No, and why are you calling me Ms. Vice President?"

"Because you won the election." In the background, I heard Adam shout, "Congratulations!"

"What election?" I asked, baffled.

"For vice president!" CeeCee sounded annoyed. "Duh!"

"How could I have won it?" I said. "I wasn't even there."

"That's okay. You still won two-thirds of the sopho-more class's vote."

"*Two-thirds?*" I'll admit it. That shocked me. "But, CeeCee—I mean, why did people vote for *me*? They don't even *know* me. I'm the new kid."

CeeCee said, "What can I say? You exude the con-fidence of a born leader."

"But—"

"And it probably doesn't hurt that you're from New York, and around here, people are fascinated by any-thing to do with New York."

"But—"

"And, of course, you talk really fast."

"I do?"

"Sure you do. And that makes you seem smart. I mean, *I* think you *are* smart, but you also *seem* smart because you talk really fast. And you wear a lot of black, and black is, you know, cool."

"But—"

"Oh, and the fact that you saved Bryce from that falling chunk of wood. People like that kind of thing."

Two-thirds of the sophomore class at Mission High School, I thought, would probably have voted for the Easter Bunny if someone could have gotten him to run for office. But I didn't say so. Instead, I said, "Well. Neat. I guess."

"*Neat?*" CeeCee sounded stunned. "*Neat?* That's all you have to say, *neat*? Do you have any idea how much fun we're going to have now that we've managed to get our hands on all that money? The cool things we'll be able to do?"

I said, "I guess that's really . . . great."

"Great? Suze, it's *awesome*! We are going to have an awesome, awesome semester! I'm so proud of you! And to think, I knew you when!"

I hung up the phone feeling a little overwhelmed. It isn't every day a girl gets elected vice president of a class she's been in for less than a week.

I hadn't even put the phone back into its cradle before it rang again. This time it was a girl's voice I didn't recognize, asking to speak to Suze Simon.

"This is she," I said, and Kelly Prescott shrieked in my ear.

"Omigod!" she cried. "Have you heard? Aren't you psyched? We are going to have a *bitching* year."

Bitching. All right. I said calmly, "I look forward to working with you."

"Look," Kelly said, suddenly all business. "We have to get together soon and choose the music."

"The music for what?"

"For the dance, of course." I could hear her flipping through an organizer. "I've got a DJ all lined up. He sent me a playlist, and we have to choose what songs for him to play. How's tomorrow night? What's wrong with you, anyway? You weren't in school today. You're not contagious, are you?"

I said, "Um, no. Listen, Kelly, about this dance. I don't know about it. I was thinking it might be more fun to spend the money on . . . well, something like a beach cookout."

She said in a perfectly flat tone of voice, "A beach cookout."

"Yeah. With volleyball and a bonfire and stuff." I twisted the phone cord around my finger. "After we have Heather's memorial, of course."

"Heather's what?"

"Her memorial service. See, I figure you already booked the room at the Carmel Inn, right, for the dance? But instead of having a dance there, I think we should have a memorial service for Heather. I really think, you know, she'd have wanted it that way."

Kelly's tone was flat. "You never even met Heather."

"Well," I said. "That may be. But I have a pretty good feeling I know what type of girl she was. And I think a memorial service at the Carmel Inn would be exactly what she'd want."

Kelly didn't say anything for a minute. Well, it had occurred to me she might not like my suggestions, but she couldn't really do anything about it now, could she? After all, I was the vice president. And I don't think, short of expulsion from the Mission Academy, I could be impeached.

"Kelly?" When she didn't answer, I said, "Well, look, Kell, don't worry about it now. We'll talk. Oh, and about your pool party on Saturday. I hope you don't mind, but I asked CeeCee and Adam to come. You know, it's funny, but they say they didn't get invited. But in a class as small as ours, it really isn't fair not to invite everybody, you know what I mean? Otherwise, the people who didn't get invited might think you don't like them. But I'm sure in CeeCee's and Adam's cases, you just forgot, right?"

Kelly went, "Are you mental?"

I chose not to dignify that with a response. "See you tomorrow, Kell," was all I said.

A few minutes later, the phone rang again. I picked up, since it appeared I was on a winning streak. And I wasn't wrong. It was Father Dominic.

"Susannah," he said in his pleasantly deep voice. "I do hope you don't mind my bothering you at home. But I just called to congratulate you on winning the sophomore class—"

"Don't worry, Father Dom," I said. "No one's on the other extension. It's only me."

"What," he said, in a completely different tone of voice, "could you have been thinking? You promised me! You promised me you wouldn't go back to the school grounds alone!"

"I'm sorry," I said. "But she was threatening to hurt David, and I—"

"I don't care if she was threatening your mother, young lady. Next time, you are to wait for me. Do you understand? Never again are you to attempt something so foolhardy and dangerous as an exorcism without a soul to help you!"

I said, "Well, okay. But I was kind of hoping there wasn't going to be a next time."

"Not be a next time? Are you daft? We're mediators, remember. So long as there are spirits, there will be a next time for us, young lady, and don't you forget it."

As if I could. All I had to do was look around my bedroom just about any time of day, and there was my very own reminder, in the form of a murdered cowboy.

But I didn't see any point in telling Father Dominic this. Instead, I said, "Sorry about your breezeway, Father Dominic. Your poor birds."

"Never mind my birds. You're all right, and that's all that matters. When I get out of this hospital, you and I are going to sit down and have a very long chat, Susannah, about proper mediation techniques. I don't know about this habit of yours of just walking up and punching the poor souls in the face."

I said, laughing, "Okay. I guess your ribs must be hurting you, huh?"

He said in a gentler tone, "They are, some. How did you know?"

"Because you're so pleasant."

"I'm sorry." Father Dominic actually sounded it, too. "I—yes, my ribs *are* hurting me. Oh, Susannah.

Did you hear the news?"

"Which? That I was voted sophomore class vice president, or that I wrecked the school last night?"

"Neither. A space has been found at Robert Louis Stevenson High School for Bryce. He'll be transferring there just as soon as he can walk again."

"But—" It was ridiculous, I know, but I actually felt dismayed. "But Heather's gone now. He doesn't have to transfer."

"Heather may be gone," Father Dominic said gently, "but her memory still exists very much in the minds of those who were . . . affected by her death. Surely you can't blame the boy for wanting a chance to start over at a new school where people won't be whispering about him?"

I said, not very graciously, thinking of Bryce's soft blond hair, "I guess."

"They say I should be well enough to return to work Monday. Shall I see you in my office then?"

"I guess," I said, just as enthusiastically as before. Father Dominic didn't appear to notice. He said, "I shall see you then." Right before I hung up, I heard him say, "Oh, and Susannah. Do try, in the interim, not to destroy what's left of the school."

"Ha-ha," I said, and hung up.

Sitting on the window seat, I rested my chin on my knees and gazed down across the valley toward the curve of the bay. The sun was starting to sink low in the west. It hadn't hit the water yet, but it would in a few minutes. My room was ablaze with reds and golds, and the sky around the sun looked as if it were striped. The clouds were so many different colors—blue and purple and red and orange—like the ribbons I once saw waving from the top of a maypole at a Renaissance fair. I could smell the sea, too, through my open window. The breeze carried the briny scent toward me, even as high up in the hills as I was.

Had Jesse, I wondered, sat in this window and smelled the ocean like I was doing, before he died? Before—as I was sure had happened—Maria de Silva's lover, Felix Diego, slipped into the room and killed him?

As if he'd read my thoughts, Jesse suddenly materialized a few feet away from me.

"Jeez!" I said, pressing a hand over my heart, which was beating so hard I thought it might explode. "Do you have to keep on *doing* that?"

He was leaning, sort of nonchalantly, against one of my bedposts, his arms folded across his chest. "I'm sorry," he said. But he didn't look it.

"Look," I said. "If you and I are going to be living together—so to speak—we need to come up with some rules. And rule number one is that you have got to stop sneaking up on me like that."

"And how do you suggest I make my presence known?" Jesse asked, his eyes pretty bright for a ghost.

"I don't know," I said. "Can't you rattle some chains or something?"

He shook his head. "I don't think so. What would rule number two be?"

"Rule number two . . ." My voice trailed off as I stared at him. It wasn't fair. It really wasn't. Dead guys should not look anywhere near as good as Jesse looked, leaning there against my bedpost with the sun slanting in and catching the perfectly sculpted planes of his face. . . .

He lifted that eyebrow, the one with the scar in it. "Something wrong, *querida*?" he asked.

I stared at him. It was clear he didn't know that I knew. About MDS, I mean. I wanted to ask him about it, but in another way, I sort of didn't want to know. Something was keeping Jesse in this world and out of the one he belonged to, and I had a feeling that something was directly related to the manner in which he'd lost his life. But since he didn't seem all that anxious to talk about it, I figured it was none of my business.

This was a first. Most times, ghosts were all over me to help them. But not Jesse.

At least, not for now.

"Let me ask you something," Jesse said so suddenly that I thought, for a minute, maybe he'd read my mind.

"What?" I asked cautiously, throwing down my magazine and standing up.

"Last night, when you warned me not to go near the school because you were doing an exorcism . . ."

I eyed him. "Yes?"

"Why did you warn me?"

I laughed with relief. Was that all? "I warned you because if you'd gone down there you would have been sucked away just like Heather."

"But wouldn't that have been a perfect way to get rid of me? You'd have this room to yourself, just the way you want it."

I stared at him in horror. "But that—that would have been completely unfair!"

He was smiling now. "I see. Against the rules?"

"Yeah," I said. "Big time."

"Then you didn't warn me"—he took a step toward me—"because you're starting to like me or anything like that?"

Much to my dismay, I felt my face start to heat up. "No," I said stubbornly. "Nothing like that. I'm just trying to play by the rules. Which you violated, by the way, when you woke up David."

Jesse took another step toward me. "I had to. You'd warned me not to go down to the school myself. What choice did I have? If I hadn't sent your brother in my place to help you," he pointed out, "you'd be a bit dead now."

I was uncomfortably aware that this was true. However, I wasn't about to let on that I agreed with him. "No way," I said. "I had things perfectly under control. I—"

"You had nothing under control." Jesse laughed. "You went barreling in there without any sort of plan, without any sort of—"

"I had a plan." I took a single furious step toward him, and suddenly we were standing practically nose to nose. "Who do you think you are, telling me I had no plan? I've been doing this for years, get it? Years. And I never needed help, not from anyone. And certainly not from someone like *you*."

He stopped laughing suddenly. Now he looked mad. "Someone like me? You mean—what was it you called me? A cowboy?"

"No," I said. "I mean from somebody who's *dead*."

Jesse flinched, almost as violently as if I'd hit him.

"Let's make rule number two be that from now on, you stay out of my business, and I'll stay out of yours," I said.

"Fine," Jesse said shortly.

"Fine," I said. "And thank you."

He was still mad. He asked sullenly, "For what?"

"For saving my life."

He stopped looking mad all of a sudden. His eyebrows, which had been all knit together, relaxed.

Next thing I knew, he'd reached out, and laid his hands on my shoulders.

If he'd stuck a fork in me, I don't think I'd have been

so surprised. I mean, I'm used to punching ghosts in the face. I am not used to them looking down at me as if . . . as if . . .

Well, as if they were about to kiss me.

But before I had time to figure out what I was going to do—close my eyes and let him do it, or invoke rule number three: absolutely no touching—my mother's voice drifted up from downstairs. "Susannah?" she called. "Susie, it's Mom. I'm home."

I looked at Jesse. He jerked his hands away from me. A second later, my mom opened my bedroom door, and Jesse disappeared.

"Susie," she said. She walked over and put her arms around me. "How are you? I hope you're not upset that we let you sleep in. You just seemed so tired."

"No," I said. I was still sort of dazed by what had happened with Jesse. "I don't mind."

"I guess it all finally caught up with you. I thought it might. Were you all right here with Andy? He said he made you lunch."

"He made me a fine lunch," I said automatically.

"And David brought you your homework, I hear." She let go of me and walked toward the window seat. "We were thinking about spaghetti for dinner. What do you think?"

"Sounds good." I came around long enough to notice that she was staring out of the windows. Then I noticed that I couldn't remember my mother ever looking so . . . well, serene.

Maybe it was the fact that since we'd moved out west, she'd given up coffee.

More likely, though, it was love.

"What are you looking at, Mom?" I asked her.

"Oh, nothing, honey," she said with a little smile. "Just the sunset. It's so beautiful." She turned to put her arm around me, and together we stood there and watched the sun sinking into the Pacific in a blaze of violent reds and purples and golds. "You sure wouldn't see a sunset like that back in New York," my mother said. "Now would you?"

"No," I said. "You wouldn't."

"So," she said, giving me a squeeze. "What do you think? You think we should stick around here awhile?"

She was joking, of course. But in a way, she wasn't.

"Sure," I said. "We should stick around."

She smiled at me, then turned back toward the sunset. The last of the bright orange ball was disappearing beneath the horizon. "There goes the sun," she said.

"And," I said, "it's all right."

Ninth Key

To Vic and Jack—
Cut it out already

CHAPTER 1

Nobody told me about the poison oak.

Oh, they told me about the palm trees. Yeah, they told me plenty about the palm trees, all right. But nobody ever said a word about this poison oak business.

"The thing is, Susannah—"

Father Dominic was talking to me. I was trying to pay attention, but let me tell you something: poison oak *itches*.

"As mediators—which is what we are, you and I, Susannah—we have a responsibility. We have a responsibility to give aid and solace to those unfortunate souls who are suffering in the void between the living and the dead."

I mean, yeah, the palm trees are nice and everything. It had been cool to step off the plane and see those palm trees everywhere, especially since I'd heard how cold it can get at night in northern California.

But what is the deal with this poison oak? How come nobody ever warned me about *that*?

"You see, as mediators, Susannah, it is our duty to help lost souls get to where they are supposed to be going. We are their guides, as it were. Their spiritual liaisons between this world and the next." Father Dominic fingered an unopened pack of cigarettes that was sitting on his desk, and regarded me with those big old baby blues of his. "But when one's spiritual liaison takes one's head and slams it into a locker door . . . well, you can see how that kind of behavior might not build the sort of trust we'd like to establish with our troubled brothers and sisters."

I looked up from the rash on my hands. Rash. That wasn't even the word for it. It was like a fungus. Worse than a fungus, even. It was a *growth*. An insidious growth that, given time, would consume every inch of my once smooth, unblemished skin, covering it with red, scaly bumps. That oozed, by the way.

"Yeah," I said, "but if our troubled brothers and sisters are giving us a hard time, I don't see why it's such a crime if I just haul off and slug them in the—"

"But don't you see, Susannah?" Father Dominic clenched the pack of cigarettes. I'd only known him a couple of weeks, but whenever he started fondling his cigarettes—which he never, by the way, actually smoked—it meant he was upset about something.

That something, at this particular moment, appeared to be me.

"That is why," he explained, "you're called a mediator. You are supposed to be helping to bring these troubled souls to spiritual fulfillment—"

"Look, Father Dom," I said. I tucked my oozing hands out of sight. "I don't know what kind of ghosts you've been dealing with lately, but the ones I've been running into are about as likely to find spiritual fulfillment as I'm going to find a decent New York City–style slice of pizza in this town. It ain't gonna happen. These folks are going to hell or they're going to heaven or they're going on to their next life as a caterpillar in Kathmandu, but any way you slice it, sometimes they're gonna need a little kick in the butt to get them there. . . ."

"No, no, no." Father Dominic leaned forward. He couldn't lean forward too much because a week or so before, one of those troubled souls of his had decided to forgo spiritual enlightenment and tried to snap his leg off instead. She also broke a couple of his ribs, gave him a pretty nifty concussion, tore up the school real good, and, let's see, what else?

Oh, yeah. *She tried to kill me.*

Father Dominic was back at school, but he was

wearing a cast that went all the way down to his toes, and disappeared up his long black robe, who knew how far? Personally, I didn't like to think about it.

He was getting pretty handy with those crutches, though. He could chase the late kids up and down the halls if he had to. But since he was the principal, and it was up to the novices to hand out late slips, he didn't have to. Besides, Father Dom was pretty cool, and wouldn't do something like that even if he could.

Though he takes the whole ghost thing a little too seriously, if you ask me.

"Susannah," he said, tiredly. "You and I, for better or for worse, were born with an incredible gift—an ability to see and speak to the dead."

"There you go again," I said, rolling my eyes, "with that *gift* stuff. Frankly, Father, I don't see it that way."

How could I? Since the age of two—*two years old*—I've been pestered with, pounded on, *plagued* by restless spirits. For fourteen years, I've put up with their abuse, helping them when I could, punching them when I could not, always fearful of somebody finding out my secret and revealing me to be the biological freak I've always known I am, but have tried so desperately to hide from my sweet, long-suffering mother.

And then Mom remarried and moved me out to California—in the middle of my sophomore year, thanks very much—where, wonder of wonders, I'd

264

actually met someone cursed with the same horrible affliction: Father Dominic.

Only Father Dominic refuses to view our "gift" in the same light as me. To him, it's a marvelous opportunity to help others in need.

Yeah, okay. That's fine for him. He's a *priest*. He's not a sixteen-year-old girl who, *hello*, would like to have a social life.

If you ask me, a "gift" would have some plus side to it. Like superhuman strength or the ability to read minds, or something. But I don't have any of that cool stuff. I'm just an ordinary sixteen-year-old girl—well, okay, with above ordinary looks, if I do say so myself—who happens to be able to converse with the dead.

Big deal.

"Susannah," he said now, very seriously. "We are mediators. We aren't . . . well, *terminators*. Our duty is to intervene on the spirits' behalf, and lead them to their ultimate destination. We do that by gentle guidance and counseling, not by punching them in the face or by performing Brazilian voodoo exorcisms."

He raised his voice on the word *exorcisms*, even though he knew perfectly well I'd only done the exorcism as a last resort. It's not my fault half the school fell down during it. I mean, technically, that was the ghost's fault, not mine.

"Okay, okay, already," I said, holding up both hands in an I-surrender sort of gesture. "I'll try it your way from now on. I'll do the touchy-feely stuff. Jeez. You West Coasters. It's all backrubs and avocado sandwiches with you guys, isn't it?"

Father Dominic shook his head. "And what would you call your mediation technique, Susannah? Headbutts and chokeholds?"

"That's very funny, Father Dom," I said. "Can I go back to class now?"

"Not yet." He puttered around with the cigarettes, tapping the pack like he was actually going to open it. That'll be the day. "How was your weekend?"

"Swell," I said. I held up my hands, knuckles turned toward him. "See?"

He squinted. "Good heavens, Susannah," he said. "What is *that*?"

"Poison oak. Good thing nobody told me it grows all over the place around here."

"It doesn't grow all over the place," Father Dominic said. "Only in wooded areas. Were you in a wooded area this weekend?" Then his eyes widened behind the lenses of his glasses. "Susannah! You didn't go to the cemetery, did you? Not alone. I know you believe yourself to be indomitable, but it isn't at all safe for a young girl like yourself to go sneaking around cemeteries even if you *are* a mediator."

I put down my hands and said, disgustedly, "I didn't catch this in any cemetery. I wasn't *working*. I got it at Kelly Prescott's pool party Saturday night."

"Kelly Prescott's pool party?" Father Dominic looked confused. "How would you have encountered poison oak there?"

Too late, I realized I probably should have kept my mouth shut. Now I was going to have to explain—to the principal of my school, who also happened to be a *priest*, no less—about how a rumor had gone around midway through the party that my stepbrother Dopey and this girl named Debbie Mancuso were going at it in the pool house.

I had of course denied the possibility since I knew Dopey was grounded. Dopey's dad—my new stepfather, who, for a mostly laid-back, California kind of guy, had turned out to be a pretty stern disciplinarian—had grounded Dopey for calling a friend of mine a fag.

So when the rumor went around at the party that Dopey and Debbie Mancuso were doing the nasty in the pool house, I was pretty sure everyone was mistaken. Brad, I kept insisting—everyone but me calls Dopey Brad, which is his real name, but believe me, Dopey fits him much better—was back home listening to Marilyn Manson through headphones, since his father had also confiscated his stereo speakers.

But then someone said, "Go take a look for yourself," and I made the mistake of doing so, tiptoeing up to the small window they'd indicated, and peering through it.

I had never particularly cared to see any of my step-brothers in the buff. Not that they are bad looking or anything. Sleepy, the oldest one, is actually considered something of a stud by most of the girls at Junipero Serra Mission Academy, where he is a senior and I am a sophomore. But that doesn't mean I have any desire to see him strutting around the house without his box-ers. And of course Doc, the youngest, is only twelve, totally adorable with his red hair and sticky-outy ears, but not what you'd call a babe.

And as for Dopey . . . well, I *particularly* never wanted to see Dopey in his altogether. In fact, Dopey is just about the *last* person on earth I'd ever wish to see naked.

Fortunately, when I looked through that window I saw that reports of my stepbrother's state of undress—as well as his sexual prowess—had been greatly exaggerated. He and Debbie were only making out. This is not to say that I wasn't completely repulsed. I mean, I wasn't exactly proud that my stepbrother was in there tongue wrestling with the second stupidest person in our class, after himself.

I looked away immediately, of course. I mean, we've got Showtime at home, for God's sake. I've seen plenty of French kissing before. I wasn't about to stand there gawking while my stepbrother engaged in it. And as for Debbie Mancuso, well, all I can say is, she ought to lay off the sauce. She can't afford to lose any more brain cells than she already has, what with all the hair spray she slathers on in the girls' room between classes.

It was as I was staggering away in disgust from the pool house window, which was situated above a small gravel path, that I believe I stumbled into some poison oak. I don't remember coming into contact with plant life at any other time this past weekend, being a generally indoors kind of girl.

And let me tell you, I *really* stumbled into those plants. I was feeling light-headed from the horror of what I'd just seen—you know, the tongues and all—plus I had on my platform mules, and I sort of lost my balance. The plants I grabbed on to were all that saved me from the ignominy of collapsing on Kelly Prescott's redwood pool deck.

What I told Father Dominic, however, was an abridged version. I said I must have staggered into some poison oak as I was getting out of the Prescotts' hot tub.

Father Dominic seemed to accept this, and said, "Well, some hydrocortisone ought to clear that up. You should see the nurse after this. Be sure not to scratch it or it will spread."

"Yeah, thanks. I'll be sure not to breathe, either. That'll probably be just about as easy."

Father Dominic ignored my sarcasm. It's funny about us two both being mediators. I've never met anybody else who happened to be one—in fact, until a couple of weeks ago, I thought I was the only mediator in the whole wide world.

But Father Dom says there are others. He's not sure how many, or even how, exactly, we precious few happened to be picked for our illustrious—have I mentioned unpaid?—careers. I'm thinking we should maybe start a newsletter or something. *The Mediator News.* And have conferences. I could give a seminar on five easy ways to kick a ghost's butt and not mess up your hair.

Anyway, about me and Father Dom. For two people who have the same weird ability to talk to the dead, we are about as different as can be. Besides the age thing, Father Dom being sixty and me being sixteen, he's Mister Nice himself, whereas I'm . . .

Well, not.

Not that I don't try to be. It's just that one thing I've learned from all of this is that we don't have very much time here on Earth. So why waste it putting up with other people's crap? Particularly people who are already dead, anyway.

"Besides the poison oak," Father Dominic said. "Is there anything else going on in your life you think I should know about?"

Anything else going on in my life that I thought he should know about. Let me see. . . .

How about the fact that I'm sixteen, and so far, unlike my stepbrother Dopey, I still haven't been kissed, much less asked out?

Not a major big deal—especially to Father Dom, a guy who took a vow of chastity about thirty years before I was even born—but humiliating just the same. There'd been a lot of kissing going on at Kelly Prescott's pool party—and some heavier stuff, even— but no one had tried to lock lips with me.

A boy I didn't know *did* ask me to slow dance at one point, though. And I said yes, but only because Kelly yelled at me after I turned him down the first time he asked. Apparently this boy was someone she'd had a crush on for a while. How my slow dancing with him was supposed to get him to like Kelly, I don't know, but after I turned him down the first time, she cornered me in her bedroom, where I'd gone to check my hair, and, with actual tears in her eyes, informed me that I had ruined her party.

"Ruined your party?" I was genuinely astonished. I'd lived in California for all of two weeks by then, so it amazed me that I had managed to make myself a social pariah in such a short period of time. Kelly was already mad at me, I knew, because I had invited my friends CeeCee and Adam, whom she and just about everyone else in the sophomore class at the Mission Academy consider freaks, to her party. Now I had apparently added insult to injury by not agreeing to dance with some boy I didn't even know.

"Jesus," Kelly said, when she heard this. "He's a

junior at Robert Louis Stevenson, okay? He's the star forward on their basketball team. He won last year's regatta at Pebble Beach, and he's the hottest guy in the Valley, after Bryce Martinson. Suze, if you don't dance with him, I swear I'll never speak to you again."

I said, "All right already. What is your glitch, anyway?"

"I just," Kelly said, wiping her eyes with a manicured finger, "want everything to go really well. I've had my eye on this guy for a while now, and—"

"Oh, yeah, Kel," I said. "Getting me to dance with him is sure to make him like you."

When I pointed out this fallacy in her thought process, however, all she said was, *Just do it,* only not the way they say it in Nike ads. She said it the way the Wicked Witch of the West said it to the winged monkeys when she sent them out to kill Dorothy and her little dog, too.

I'm not scared of Kelly or anything, but really, who needs the grief?

So I went back outside and stood there in my Calvin Klein one-piece—with a sarong tied ever-so-casually around my waist—totally not knowing I had just stumbled into a bunch of poison oak, while Kelly went over to her dream date and asked him to ask me to dance again.

As I stood there, I tried not to think that the only reason he wanted to dance with me in the first place was that I was the only girl at the party in a swimsuit. Having never been invited to a pool party before in my life, I had erroneously believed people actually swam at them, and had dressed accordingly.

Not so, apparently. Aside from my stepbrother, who'd apparently become overwarm while in Debbie Mancuso's impassioned embrace and had stripped off his shirt, I was wearing the least clothes of anybody there.

Including Kelly's dream date. He sauntered up a few minutes later, wearing a serious expression, a pair of white chinos, and a black silk shirt. Very Jersey, but then, this was the West Coast, so how was he to know?

"Do you want to dance?" he asked me in this really soft voice. I could barely hear him above the strains of Sheryl Crow, booming out from the pool deck's speakers.

"Look," I said, putting down my Diet Coke. "I don't even know your name."

"It's Tad," he said.

And then without another word, he put his arms around my waist, pulled me up to him, and started swaying in time to the music.

With the exception of the time I threw myself at Bryce Martinson in order to knock him out of the way when a ghost was trying to crush his skull with a large chunk of wood, this was as close to the body of a boy—a *live* boy, one who was still breathing—I had ever been.

And let me tell you, black silk shirt notwithstanding, I *liked* it. This guy felt *good*. He was all warm—it was kind of chilly in my bathing suit; being January, of course, it was supposed to be too chilly for bathing suits, but this *was* California, after all—and smelled like some kind of really nice, expensive soap. Plus he was just taller enough than me for his breath to kind of brush against my cheek in this provocative, romance-novel sort of way.

Let me tell you, I closed my eyes, put my arms around this guy's neck, and swayed with him for two of the longest, most blissful minutes of my life.

Then the song ended.

Tad said, "Thank you," in the same soft voice he'd used before, and let go of me.

And that was it. He turned around and walked back over to this group of guys who were hanging out by the keg Kelly's dad had bought for her on the condition she didn't let anybody drive home drunk, a condition Kelly was sticking strictly to by not drinking herself and carrying around a cell phone with the number of Carmel Cab on redial.

And then for the rest of the party, Tad avoided me. He didn't dance with anybody else. But he didn't speak to me again.

Game over, as Dopey would say.

But I didn't think Father Dominic wanted to hear about my dating travails. So I said, "Nope. Nada. Nothing."

"Strange," Father Dominic said, looking thoughtful. "I would have thought there'd be *some* paranormal activity—"

"Oh," I said. "You mean has any *ghost* stuff been going on?"

Now he didn't look thoughtful. He looked kind of annoyed. "Well, yes, Susannah," he said, taking off his glasses, and pinching the bridge of his nose between his thumb and forefinger like he had a headache all of a sudden. "Of course, that's what I mean." He put his glasses back on. "Why? Has something happened? Have you encountered anyone? I mean, since that unfortunate incident that resulted in the destruction of the school?"

I said, slowly, "Well . . ."

CHAPTER 2

The first time she showed up, it was about an hour after I'd come home from the pool party. Around three in the morning, I guess. And what she did was, she stood by my bed and started screaming.

Really screaming. *Really* loud. She woke me out of a dead sleep. I'd been lying there dreaming about Bryce Martinson. In my dream, he and I were cruising along Seventeen Mile Drive in this red convertible. I don't know whose convertible it was. His, I guess, since I don't even have my driver's license yet. Bryce's soft sandy-blond hair was blowing in the wind, and the sun was sinking into the sea, making the sky all red and orange and purple. We were going around these curves, you know, on the cliffs above the Pacific, and I wasn't even carsick or anything. It was one really terrific dream.

And then this woman starts wailing, practically in my ear.

I ask you: Who needs that?

Of course I sat up right away, completely wide awake. Having a walking dead woman show up in your bedroom screaming her head off can do that to you. Wake you up right away, I mean.

I sat there blinking because my room was really dark—well, it was nighttime. You know, nighttime, when normal people are asleep.

But not us mediators. Oh, no.

She was standing in this skinny patch of moonlight coming in from the bay windows on the far side of my room. She had on a gray hooded sweatshirt, hood down, a T-shirt, capri pants, and Keds. Her hair was short, sort of mousy brown. It was hard to tell if she was young or old, what with all the screaming and everything, but I kind of figured her for my mom's age.

Which was why I didn't get out of bed and punch her right then and there.

I probably should have. I mean, it wasn't like I could exactly yell back at her, not without waking the whole house. I was the only one in the house who could hear her.

Well, the only one who was alive, anyway.

After a while, I guess she noticed I was awake

because she stopped screaming and reached up to wipe her eyes. She was crying pretty hard.

"I'm sorry," she said.

I said, "Yeah, well, you got my attention. Now what do you want?"

"I need you," she said. She was sniffling. "I need you to tell someone something."

I said, "Okay. What?"

"Tell him . . ." She wiped her face with her hands. "Tell him it wasn't his fault. He didn't kill me."

This was sort of a new one. I raised my eyebrows. "Tell him he *didn't* kill you?" I asked, just to be sure I'd heard her right.

She nodded. She was kind of pretty, I guess, in a waifish sort of way. Although it probably wouldn't have hurt if she'd eaten a muffin or two back when she'd been alive.

"You'll tell him?" she asked me, eagerly. "Promise?"

"Sure," I said. "I'll tell him. Only who am I telling?"

She looked at me funny. "Red, of course."

Red? Was she *kidding*?

But it was too late. She was gone.

Just like that.

Red. I turned around and beat on my pillow to get it fluffy again. Red.

Why me? I mean, really. To be interrupted while having a dream about Bryce Martinson just because some woman wants a guy named *Red* to know he *didn't* kill her. . . . I swear, sometimes I am convinced my life is just a series of sketches for *America's Funniest Home Videos*, minus all that pants-dropping business.

Except my life really isn't all that funny if you think about it.

I especially wasn't laughing when, the minute I finally found a comfy spot on my pillow and was just about to close my eyes and go back to sleep, somebody else showed up in the sliver of moonlight in the middle of my room.

This time there wasn't any screaming. That was about the only thing I had to be grateful for.

"*What?*" I asked in a pretty rude voice.

He said, shaking his head, "You didn't even ask her name."

I leaned up on both elbows. It was because of this guy that I'd taken to wearing a T-shirt and boxer shorts to bed. Not that I had been going around in floaty negligees before he'd come along, but I sure wasn't going to take them up now that I had a male roommate.

Yeah, you read that right.

"Like she gave me the chance," I said.

"You could have asked." Jesse folded his arms across his chest. "But you didn't bother."

"Excuse me," I said, sitting up. "This is *my* bedroom. I will treat spectral visitors to it any way I want to, thank you."

He said, "Susannah."

He had the softest voice imaginable. Softer, even, than that guy Tad's. It was like silk or something, his voice. It was really hard to be mean to a guy with a voice like that.

But the thing was, I *had* to be mean. Because even in the moonlight, I could make out the breadth of his strong shoulders, the vee where his old-fashioned white shirt fell open, revealing dark, olive-complected skin, some chest hair, and just about the best-defined abs you've ever seen. I could also see the strong planes of his face, the tiny scar in one of his ink-black eyebrows, where something—or someone—had cut him once.

Kelly Prescott was wrong. Bryce Martinson was not the cutest guy in Carmel.

Jesse was.

And if I wasn't mean to him, I knew I'd find myself falling in love with him.

And the problem with that, you see, is that he's dead.

"If you're going to do this, Susannah," he said, in that silky voice, "don't do it halfway."

"Look, Jesse," I said. My voice wasn't a bit silky. It was hard as rock. Or that's what I told myself, anyway. "I've been doing this a long time without any help from you, okay?"

He said, "She was obviously in great emotional need, and you—"

"What about you?" I demanded. "You two live on the same astral plane, if I'm not mistaken. Why didn't *you* get her rank and serial number?"

He looked confused. On him, let me tell you, confused looks good. *Everything* looks good on Jesse.

"Rank and what?" he asked.

Sometimes I forget that Jesse died a hundred and fifty or so years ago. He's not exactly up on the lingo of the twenty-first century, if you know what I mean.

"Her *name*," I translated. "Why didn't *you* get her name?"

He shook his head. "It doesn't work that way."

Jesse's always saying stuff like that. Cryptic stuff about the spirit world that I, not being a spirit, am still somehow expected to understand. I tell you, it burns me up. Between that and the Spanish—which I don't speak, and which he spouts occasionally, especially when he's mad—I have no idea what Jesse's saying about a third of the time.

Which is way irritating. I mean, I have to share my bedroom with the guy because it was in this room that he got shot, or whatever, in like 1850, back when the house had been a kind of hotel for prospectors and cowboys—or, as in Jesse's case, rich ranchers' sons who were supposed to be marrying their beautiful, rich cousins, but were tragically murdered on the way to the ceremony.

At least, that's what had happened to Jesse. Not

that he's *told* me that, or anything. No, I had to figure that out on my own . . . though my stepbrother
Doc helped. It isn't something, it turns out, that Jesse
seems much interested in discussing. Which is sort
of weird because in my experience, all the dead ever
want to talk about is how they got that way.

Not Jesse, though. All he ever wants to talk about is
how much I suck at being a mediator.

Maybe he had a point, though. I mean, according
to Father Dominic, I was supposed to be serving as a
spiritual conductor between the land of the living and
the land of the dead. But mostly all I was doing was
complaining because nobody was letting me get any
sleep.

"Look," I said. "I fully intend to help that woman.
Just not now, okay? Now, I need to get some sleep. I'm
totally wrecked."

"Wrecked?" he echoed.

"Yeah. Wrecked." Sometimes I suspect Jesse
doesn't understand a third of what I'm saying, either,
though at least I'm speaking in English.

"Whacked," I translated. "Beat. All tuckered out.
Tired."

"Oh," he said. He stood there for a minute, looking
at me with those dark, sad eyes. Jesse has those kind
of eyes some guys have, the kind of sad eyes that make
you think you might want to try and make them not
so sad.

That's why I have to make a point of being so mean to him. I'm pretty sure there's a rule against that. I mean, in Father Dom's mediation guidelines. About mediators and ghosts getting together, and trying to, um, cheer each other up.

If you know what I mean.

"Good night, then, Susannah," Jesse said, in that deep, silky voice of his.

"Good night," I said. My voice isn't deep or silky. Right then, in fact, it sounded kind of squeaky. It usually does that when I'm talking to Jesse. Nobody else. Just Jesse.

Which is great. The only time I want to sound sexy and sophisticated, and I come out sounding squeaky. Swell.

I rolled over, bringing the covers up over my face, which I could tell was blushing. When I peeked out from underneath them a minute or so later, I saw that he was gone.

That's Jesse's M.O. He shows up when I least expect him to, and disappears when I least want him to. That's how ghosts operate.

Take my dad. He's been paying these totally random social calls on me since he died a decade ago. Does he show up when I really need him? Like when my mom moved me out here to a totally different coast and I didn't know anyone at first and I was totally lonely? Heck, no. No sign of good old Dad. He was always pretty irresponsible, but I'd really thought that the one time I needed him . . .

I couldn't really accuse Jesse of being irresponsible, though. If anything, he was a little *too* responsible. He had even saved my life, not once, but twice. And I'd only known him a couple of weeks. I guess you could say I kind of owed him one.

So when Father Dominic asked me, back in his office, whether or not any ghost stuff had been going on, I sort of lied and said no. I guess it's a sin to lie, especially to a priest, but here's the thing:

I've never exactly told Father Dom about Jesse.

I just thought he might get upset, you know, being a priest and all, to hear there was this dead guy hanging out in my bedroom. And the fact is, Jesse had obviously been hanging around the place for as long as he had for a reason. Part of the mediator's job is to help ghosts figure out what that reason is. Usually, once the ghost knows, he can take care of whatever it is that's keeping him stuck in that midway point between life and death, and move on.

But sometimes—and I suspected it was this way in Jesse's case—the dead guy doesn't *know* why he's still sticking around. He doesn't have the slightest idea. That's when I have to use what Father Dom calls my intuitive skills.

The thing is, I think I got sort of shortchanged in this department because I'm not very good at intuiting.

What I'm a lot better at is when they—the dead—know perfectly well why they are sticking around but they just don't want to get to where they're supposed to go because what they've got in store there probably isn't that great. These are the worst kinds of ghosts, the ones whose butts I have no choice but to kick.

They happen to be my specialty.

Father Dominic, of course, thinks we should treat all ghosts with dignity and respect, without the use of fists.

I disagree. Some ghosts just deserve to have the snot knocked out of them. And I don't mind doing it a bit.

Not the lady who'd showed up in my room, though. She seemed like a decent sort, just sort of messed up. The reason I didn't tell Father Dom about her was that, truthfully, I was kind of ashamed of how I'd treated her. Jesse had been right to yell at me. I'd been a bitch to her, and knowing that he was right, I'd been a bitch to him, too.

So you see, I couldn't tell Father Dom about either Jesse or the lady Red hadn't killed. I figured the lady I'd take care of soon, anyway. And Jesse . . .

Well, Jesse, I didn't know what to do about. I was pretty much convinced there wasn't anything I could do about Jesse.

I was also kind of scared I felt this way because I didn't really *want* to do anything about Jesse. Much as it sucked having to change clothes in the bathroom instead of in my room—Jesse seemed to have an aversion to the bathroom, which was a new addition to the house since he'd lived there—and not being able to wear floaty negligees to bed, I sort of liked having Jesse around. And if I told Father Dom about him, Father Dom would get all hot and bothered and want to help him get to the other side.

But what good would that do me? Then I'd never get to see him again.

Was this selfish of me? I mean, I kind of figured if Jesse wanted to go to the other side, then he would have done something about it. He wasn't one of those help-me-I'm-lost kind of ghosts like the one who'd shown up with the message for Red. No way. Jesse was more one of those don't-mess-with-me-I'm-so-mysterious kind of ghosts. You know the ones. With the accent and the killer abs.

So I admit it. I lied. So what? So sue me.

"Nope," I said. "Nothing to report, Father Dom. Supernatural or otherwise."

Was it my imagination or did Father Dominic look a little disappointed? To tell you the truth, I think he sort of liked that I'd wrecked the school. Seriously. Much as he complained about it, I don't think he minded my mediation techniques so much. It certainly gave him something to get on a soapbox about, and as the principal of a tiny private school in Carmel, California, I can't imagine he really had all that much to complain about. Other than me, I mean.

"Well," he said, trying not to let me see how let down he was by my lack of anything to report. "All right, then." He brightened. "I understand there was a three-car pileup out in Sunnyvale. Maybe we should drive out there and see if any of those poor lost souls need our aid."

I looked at him like he was out of his mind. "Father Dom," I said, shocked.

He fiddled with his glasses. "Yes, well . . . I mean, I just thought . . ."

"Look, *padre*," I said, getting up. "You gotta remember something. I don't feel the same way about this *gift* of ours that you do. I never asked for it and I've never liked it. I just want to be normal, you know?"

Father Dom looked taken aback. *"Normal?"* he echoed. As in, who would ever want to be *that*?

"Yes, *normal*," I said. "I want to spend my time worrying about the *normal* things sixteen-year-old girls worry about. Like homework and how come no boy wants to go out with me and why do my stepbrothers have to be such losers. I don't exactly relish the ghost-busting stuff, okay? So if they need me, let them find me. But I'm sure as heck not going looking for them."

Father Dominic didn't get out of his chair. He couldn't really, with that cast. Not without help. "No boy wants to go out with you?" he asked, looking perplexed.

"I know," I said. "It's one of the wonders of the modern world. Me being so good looking, and all. Especially with these." I raised my oozing hands.

Father Dominic was still confused, though.

"But you're terribly popular, Susannah," he said. "I mean, after all, you were voted vice president of the sophomore class your first week at the Mission Academy. And I thought Bryce Martinson was quite fond of you."

"Yeah," I said. "He was." Until the ghost of his ex-girlfriend—whom I was forced to exorcise—broke his collarbone, and he had to change schools, and then promptly forgot all about me.

"Well, then," Father Dominic said, as if that settled it. "You haven't anything to worry about in that category. The boy category, I mean."

I just looked at him. The poor old guy. It was almost enough to make me feel sorry for him.

"Gotta get back to class," I said, gathering my books. "I've been spending so much time in the principal's office lately, people are gonna think I've got ties with the establishment and ask me to resign from office."

"Certainly," Father Dominic said. "Of course. Here's your hall pass. And try to remember what we discussed, Susannah. A mediator is someone who *helps* others resolve conflicts. Not someone who, er, kicks them in the face."

I smiled at him. "I'll keep that in mind," I said.

And I would, too. Right after I'd kicked Red's butt. Whoever he was.

CHAPTER 3

I found out who he was easily enough, it turned out. All I had to do was ask at lunch if anybody knew of a guy named Red.

Generally it's not that easy. I won't even tell you about the number of phone books I've scoured, the hours I've spent on the Internet. Not to mention the lame excuses I've had to make to my mother, trying to explain the phone bills I've racked up calling Information. "I'm sorry, Mom. I just really had to find out if there was a store within a fifty-mile radius that carries Manolo Blahnik loafers. . . ."

This one was so easy, though, it almost made me think, Hey, maybe this mediator stuff's not so bad.

That, of course, was then. I hadn't actually *found*

Red at that point.

"Anybody know of a guy named Red?" I asked the crowd I had started eating lunch with, on what I guess was going to be a regular basis.

"Sure," Adam said. He was eating Cheetos out of a family-size bag. "Last name Tide, right? Enjoys killing harmless sea otters and other aquatic creatures?"

"Not that Red," I said. "This one is a human being. Probably adult. Probably local."

"Beaumont," CeeCee said. She was eating pudding from a plastic cup. A big fat seagull was sitting not even a foot away from her, eyeing the spoon each time CeeCee dipped it back into the cup, then raised it again to her lips. The Mission Academy has no cafeteria. We eat outside every day, even, apparently, in January. But this, of course, was no New York January. Here in Carmel, it was a balmy seventy degrees and sunny outside. Back home, according to the Weather Channel, it had just snowed six inches.

I'd been in California almost three weeks, but so far it hadn't rained once. I was still waiting to find out where we were supposed to eat if it was raining during lunch.

I had already learned the hard way what happens if you feed the seagulls.

"Thaddeus Beaumont is a real estate developer." CeeCee finished up the pudding, and started on a banana she pulled from a paper bag at her hip. CeeCee never buys school lunches. She has a thing about corn dogs.

CeeCee went on, peeling her banana, "His friends call him Red. Don't ask me why, since he doesn't have red hair. Why do you want to know, anyway?"

This was always the tricky part. You know, the why-do-you-want-to-know? part. Because the fact is, except for Father Dom, no one knows about me. About the mediator thing, I mean. Not CeeCee, not Adam. Not even my mother. Doc, my youngest stepbrother, suspects, but he doesn't *know*. Not all of it.

My best friend, Gina, back in Brooklyn, is probably the closest to having figured it out of anyone I know, and that's only because she happened to be there when Madame Zara, this tarot-card reader Gina had made me go to, looked at me with shock on her face and said, "You talk to the dead."

Gina had thought it was cool. Only she never knew—not really—what it meant. Because what it means, of course, is that I never get enough sleep, have bruises I can't explain given to me by people no one else can see, and, oh, yeah, I can't change clothes in my bedroom because the hundred-and-fifty-year-old ghost of this dead cowboy might see me naked.

Any questions?

To CeeCee I just said, "Oh, it's just something I heard on TV." It wasn't so hard, lying to friends. Lying to my mother, though, now *that* got a little sticky.

"Wasn't that the name of that guy you danced with at Kelly's?" Adam asked. "You remember, Suze. Tad, the hunchback with the missing teeth and the terrible body odor? You came up to me afterward and threw your arms around me and begged me to marry you so you'd be protected from him for the rest of your life."

"Oh, yeah," I said. "Him."

"That's his father," CeeCee said. CeeCee knows everything in the world because she is editor—and publisher, chief writer, and photographer—for the *Mission News*, the school paper. "Tad Beaumont is Red Beaumont's only child."

"Aha," I said. It made a little more sense then. I mean, why the dead woman had come to me. Obviously, she felt a connection to Red through his son.

"What aha?" CeeCee looked interested. Then again, CeeCee always looks interested. She's like a sponge, only instead of water, she absorbed facts. "Don't tell me," she said, "you've got it bad for that tool of a kid of his. I mean, what was that guy's problem? He never even asked your name."

This was true. I hadn't noticed it, either. But CeeCee was right. Tad hadn't even asked my name.

Good thing I wasn't interested in him.

"I've heard bad things about Tad Beaumont," Adam said, shaking his head. "I mean, besides the fact that he's carrying around his undigested twin in his bowels, well, there's that embarrassing facial tic, controlled only by strong doses of Prozac. And you know what Prozac does to a guy's libido—"

"What's Mrs. Beaumont like?" I asked.

"There's no Mrs. Beaumont," CeeCee said.

Adam sighed. "Product of divorce," he said. "Poor Tad. No wonder he has such issues about commitment. I've heard he usually sees three, four girls at a time. But that might be on account of the sexual addiction. I heard there's a twelve-step group for that."

CeeCee ignored him. "I think she died a few years ago."

"Oh," I said. Could the ghost who'd shown up in my bedroom have been Mr. Beaumont's deceased wife? It seemed worth a try. "Anybody got a quarter?"

"Why?" Adam wanted to know.

"I need to make a call," I said.

Four people in our lunch crowd handed me a cell phone. Seriously. I selected the one with the least intimidating number of buttons, then dialed Information, and asked for a listing for Thaddeus Beaumont. The operator told me the only listing they had was for a Beaumont Industries. I said, "Go for it."

Strolling over to the monkey bars—the Mission Academy holds grades K through twelve, and the playground where we eat lunch comes complete with a sandbox, though I wouldn't touch it, what with the seagulls and everything—so I could have a little privacy, I told the receptionist who picked up with a cheerful, "Beaumont Industries. How may I help you?" that I needed to speak to Mr. Beaumont.

"Who may I say is calling please?"

I thought about it. I could have said, "Someone who knows what really happened to his wife." But the thing is, I didn't, really. I didn't even know why it was, exactly, that I suspected his wife—if the woman even was his wife—of lying, and that Red really had killed her. It's kind of depressing, if you think about it. I mean, me being so young, and yet so cynical and suspicious.

So I said, "Susannah Simon," and then I felt lame. Because why would an important man like Red Beaumont take a call from Susannah Simon? He didn't know me.

Sure enough, the receptionist took me off hold a second later, and said, "Mr. Beaumont is on another call at the moment. May I take a message?"

"Uh," I said, thinking fast. "Yeah. Tell him . . . tell him I'm calling from the Junipero Serra Mission Academy newspaper. I'm a reporter, and we're doing a story on the . . . the ten most influential people in Salinas County." I gave her my home number. "And can you tell him not to call until after three? Because I don't get out of school till then."

Once the receptionist knew I was a kid, she got even nicer. "Sure thing, sweetheart," she said to me in this sugary voice. "I'll let Mr. Beaumont know. Buh-bye."

I hung up. Buh-bye bite me. Mr. Beaumont was going to be plenty surprised when he called me back, and got the Queen of the Night People, instead of Lois Lane.

But the thing was, Thaddeus "Red" Beaumont never even bothered calling back. I guess when you're a gazillionaire, being named one of the ten most influential people in Salinas County by a dinky school paper wasn't such a big deal. I hung around the house all day after school and nobody called. At least, not for me.

I don't know why I'd thought it would be so easy. I guess I'd been lulled into a false sense of security by the fact that I'd managed to get his name so easily.

I was sitting in my room, admiring my poison oak in the dying rays of the setting sun, when my mom called me down to dinner.

Dinner is this very big deal in the Ackerman household. Basically, my mom had already informed me that she'd kill me if I did not show up for dinner every night unless I had arranged my absence in advance with her. Her new husband, Andy, aside from being a master carpenter, is this really good cook and had been making these big dinners every night for his kids since they grew teeth, or something. Sunday pancake breakfasts, too. What is wrong, I ask you, with a simple bagel with cream cheese, and maybe a little lox on the side with a wedge of lemon and a couple of capers?

"There she is," my mom said, when I came shuffling into the kitchen in my after-school clothes: ripped-up jeans, black silk tee, and motorcycle boots. It is outfits like this that have caused my stepbrothers to suspect that I am in a gang, in spite of my strenuous denials.

My mom made this big production out of coming over to me and kissing me on top of the head. This is because ever since my mom met Andy Ackerman— or Handy Andy as he's known on the cable home improvement show he hosts—married him, and then forced me to move to California with her to live with him and his three sons, she's been incredibly, disgustingly happy.

I tell you, between that and the pancakes, I don't know which is more revolting.

"Hello, honey," my mom said, smushing my hair all around. "How did your day go?"

"Oh," I said. "Great."

She didn't hear the sarcasm in my voice. Sarcasm has been completely wasted on my mother ever since she met Andy.

"And how," she asked, "was the student government meeting?"

"Bitchin'."

That was Dopey, trying to be funny by imitating my voice.

"What do you mean, bitching?" Andy, over at the stove, was flipping quesadillas that were sizzling on this griddle thing he'd set out over the burners. "What was bitching about it?"

"Yeah, Brad," I said. "What was bitching about it? Were you and Debbie Mancuso playing footsie underneath your desks, or something?"

Dopey got all red in the face. He is a wrestler. His neck is as thick as my thigh. When his face gets red, his neck gets even redder. It's a joy to see.

"What are you talking about?" Dopey demanded. "I don't even like Debbie Mancuso."

"Sure, you don't," I said. "That's why you sat next to her at lunch today."

Dopey's neck turned the color of blood.

"David!" Andy, over by the stove, suddenly started yelling his head off. "Jake! Get a move on, you two. Soup's on."

Andy's two other sons, Sleepy and Doc, came shuffling in. Well, Sleepy shuffled. Doc bounded. Doc was the only one of Andy's kids who I could ever remember to call by his real name. That's because with red hair and these ears that stick out really far from his head, he looked like a cartoon character. Plus he was really smart, and in him I saw a lot of potential help with my homework, even if I was three grades ahead of him.

Sleepy, on the other hand, is of no use whatsoever to me, except as a guy I could bum rides to and from school with. At eighteen, Sleepy was in full possession of both his license and a vehicle, a beat-up old Rambler with an iffy starter, but you were taking your life into your hands riding with him since he was hardly ever fully awake due to his night job as a pizza delivery boy. He was saving up, as he was fond of reminding us on the few occasions when he actually spoke, for a Camaro, and as near as I could tell, that Camaro was all he ever thought about.

"*She* sat by *me*," Dopey bellowed. "I do not like Debbie Mancuso."

"Surrender the fantasy," I advised him as I sidled past him. My mom had given me a bowl of salsa to take to the table. "I just hope," I whispered into his ear as I went by, "that you two practiced safe sex that night at Kelly's pool party. I'm not ready to be a step-aunt yet."

"Shut up," Dopey yelled at me. "You . . . you . . . Fungus Hands!"

I put one of my fungus hands over my heart, and pretended like he'd stabbed me there.

"Gosh," I said. "That really hurts. Making fun of people's allergic reactions is so incredibly incisive and witty."

"Yeah, dork," Sleepy said to Dopey, as he walked by. "What about you and cat dander, huh?"

Dopey, in out of his depth, began to look desperate.

"Debbie Mancuso," he yelled, "and I are not having sex!"

I saw my mom and Andy exchange a quick, bewildered glance.

"I should certainly hope not," Doc, Dopey's little brother, said as he breezed past us. "But if you are, Brad, I hope you're using condoms. While a good-quality latex condom has a failure rate of about two percent when used as directed, typically the failure rate averages closer to twelve percent. That makes them only about eighty-five percent effective against preventing pregnancy. If used with a spermicide, the effectiveness improves dramatically. And condoms are our best defense—though not as good, of course, as abstention—against some STDs, including HIV."

Everyone in the kitchen—my mother, Andy, Dopey, Sleepy, and I—stared at Doc, who is, as I think I mentioned before, twelve.

"You," I finally said, "have way too much time on your hands."

Doc shrugged. "It helps to be informed. While I myself am not sexually active at the current time, I hope to become so in the near future." He nodded toward the stove. "Dad, your chimichangas, or whatever they are, are on fire."

While Andy jumped to put out his cheese fire, my mother stood there, apparently, for once in her life, at a loss for words.

"I—" she said. "I . . . oh. My."

Dopey wasn't about to let Doc have the last word. "I

am not," he said, again, "having sex with—"

"Aw, Brad," Sleepy said. "Put a sock in it, will ya?"

Dopey, of course, wasn't lying. I'd seen for myself that they'd only been playing tonsil hockey. Dopey and Debbie's fiery passion was the reason I had to keep slathering my hands with cortisone cream. But what was the fun of having stepbrothers if you couldn't torture them? Not that I was going to tell anyone what I'd seen, of course. I am many things, but not a snitch. But don't get me wrong: I would have liked Dopey to have gotten caught sneaking out while he was grounded. I mean, I don't think he'd exactly learned anything from his "punishment." He would still probably refer to my friend Adam as a fag the next time he saw him.

Only he wouldn't do it in my presence. Because, wrestler or not, I could kick Dopey's butt from here to Clinton Avenue, my street back in Brooklyn.

But I wasn't going to be the one to turn him in. It just wasn't classy, you know?

"And did you," my mother asked me, with a smile, "feel that the student government meeting was as bitching as Brad seems to think it was, Suze?"

I sat down at my place at the dining table. As soon as I did so, Max, the Ackerman family dog, came snuffling along and put his head in my lap. I pushed it off my lap. He put it right back. Although I'd lived there less than a month, Max had already figured out that

I am the person in the household most likely to have leftovers on my plate.

Mealtime was, of course, the only time Max paid attention to me. The rest of the time, he avoided me like the plague. He especially avoided my bedroom. Animals, unlike humans, are very perceptive about paranormal phenomena, and Max sensed Jesse, and accordingly stayed far away from the parts of the house where he normally hung out.

"Sure," I said, taking a sip of ice water. "It was bitching."

"And what," my mother wanted to know, "was decided at this meeting?"

"I made a motion to cancel the spring dance," I said. "Sorry, Brad. I know how much you were counting on escorting Debbie to it."

Dopey shot me a dirty look from across the table.

"Why on earth," my mother said, "would you want to cancel the spring dance, Susie?"

"Because it's a stupid waste of our very limited funds," I said.

"But a dance," my mother protested. "I always loved going to school dances when I was your age."

That, I wanted to say, is because you always had a *date*, Mom. Because you were pretty and nice and boys *liked* you. You weren't a pathological freak, like I am, with fungus hands and a secret ability to talk to the dead.

Instead, I said, "Well, you'd have been in the minority in our class. My motion was seconded and passed by twenty-seven votes."

"Well," my mother said. "What are you going to do with the money instead?"

"Kegger," I said, shooting a look at Dopey.

"Don't even joke about that," my mother said, sternly. "I'm very concerned about the amount of teen drinking that goes on around here." My mother is a television news reporter. She does the morning news on a local station out of Monterey. Her best thing is looking grave while reading off a TelePrompTer about grisly auto accidents. "I don't like it. It isn't like back in New York. There, none of your friends drove, so it didn't matter so much. But here . . . well, everyone drives."

"Except Suze," Dopey said. He seemed to feel it was his duty to rub in the fact that although I am sixteen, I don't have a license yet. Or even, for that matter, a learner's permit. As if driving were the most important thing in the world. As if my time was not already fully occupied with school, my recent appointment as vice president of the Mission Academy's sophomore class, and saving the lost souls of the undead.

"What are you *really* going to do with the money?" my mother asked.

I shrugged. "We have to raise money to replace that statue of our founding father, Junipero Serra, before the Archbishop's visit next month."

"Oh," my mother said. "Of course. The statue that was vandalized."

Vandalized. Yeah, right. That's what everyone was going around saying, of course. But that statue hadn't been vandalized. What had happened to it was, this ghost who was trying to kill me severed the statue's head and tried to use it as a bowling ball.

And I was supposed to be the pin.

"Quesadillas," Andy said, coming over to the table with a bunch of them on a tray. "Get 'em while they're hot."

What ensued was such chaos that I could only sit, Max's head still on my lap, and watch in horror. When it was over every single quesadilla was gone, but my plate and my mom's plate were still empty. After a while, Andy noticed this, put his fork down and said, in an angry way, "Hey, guys! Did it ever occur to you to wait to take seconds until everyone at the table had had their first serving?"

Apparently, it had not. Sleepy, Dopey, and Doc looked sheepishly down at their plates.

"I'm sorry," Doc said, holding his plate, cheese and salsa dripping from it, toward my mother. "You can have some of mine."

My mother looked a little queasy. "No, thank you, David," she said. "I'll just stick with salad, I think."

"Suze," Andy said, putting his napkin on the table.

"I'm gonna make you the cheesiest quesadilla you ever—"

I shoved Max's head out of the way and was up before Andy could get out of his seat. "You know what," I said. "Don't bother. I really think I'll just have some cereal, if that's okay."

Andy looked hurt. "Suze," he said, "it's no trouble—"

"No, really," I said. "I was gonna do my kickboxing tape later, anyway, and a lot of cheese'll just weigh me down."

"But," Andy said, "I'm making more, anyway. . . ."

He looked so pathetic, I had no choice but to say, "Well, I'll try one. But for right now, finish what's on your plate, and I'll just go and get some cereal."

As I was talking, I'd been backing out of the room. Once I was safely in the kitchen, Max at my heels— he was no dummy, he knew he wasn't going to get a crumb out of those guys in there: I was Max's ticket to people food—I got out a box of cereal and a bowl, then opened the fridge to get some milk. That was when I heard a soft voice behind me whisper, "Suze."

I whipped around. I didn't need to see Max slinking from the kitchen with his tail between his legs to know that I was in the presence of another member of that exclusive club known as the Undead.

CHAPTER 4

I nearly jumped out of my skin.

"Jeez, Dad." I slammed the fridge door closed. "I told you not to do that."

My father—or the ghost of my father, I should say—was leaning against the kitchen counter, his arms folded across his chest. He looked smug. He always looks smug when he manages to materialize behind my back and scare the living daylights out of me.

"So," he said, as casually as if we were talking over lattes in a coffee shop. "How's it going, kiddo?"

I glared at him. My dad looked exactly like he always had back when he used to make his surprise visits to our apartment in Brooklyn. He was wearing the outfit he'd been in when he died, a pair of gray sweatpants and a blue shirt that had HOMEPORT, MEN-EMSHA, FRESH SEAFOOD ALL YEAR ROUND written on it.

"Dad," I said. "Where have you been? And what are you doing here? Shouldn't you be haunting the new tenants back in our apartment in Brooklyn?"

"They're boring," my dad said. "Coupla yuppies. Goat cheese and cabernet sauvignon, that's all they ever talk about. Thought I'd see how you and your mom were getting on." He was peering out of the pass-through Andy had put in when he was trying to update the kitchen from the 1850s-style decor that had existed when he and my mom bought it.

"That him?" my dad wanted to know. "Guy with the—what is that, anyway?"

"It's a quesadilla," I said. "And yeah, that's him." I grabbed my dad's arm, and dragged him to the center island so he couldn't see them anymore. I had to talk in a whisper to make sure no one overheard me. "Is that why you're here? To spy on Mom and her new husband?"

"No," my dad said, looking indignant. "I've got a message for you. But I'll admit, I did want to drop by and check out the lay of the land, make sure he's good enough for her. This Andy guy, I mean."

I narrowed my eyes at him. "Dad, I thought we'd been through all this. You were supposed to move on, remember?"

He shook his head, trying for his sad puppy-dog

face, thinking it might make me back down. "I tried, Suze," he said, woefully. "I really did. But I can't."

I eyed him skeptically. Did I mention that in life, my dad had been a criminal lawyer like his mother? He was about as good an actor as Lassie. He could do sad puppy-dog like nobody's business.

"Why, Dad?" I asked, pointedly. "What's holding you back? Mom's happy. I swear she is. It's enough to make you want to puke, she's so happy. And I'm doing fine, I really am. So what's keeping you here?"

He sighed sadly. "You *say* you're fine, Suze," he said. "But you aren't *happy*."

"Oh, for Pete's sake. Not that again. You know what would make me happy, Dad? If you'd move on. That's what would make me happy. You can't spend your afterlife following me around worrying about me."

"Why not?"

"Because," I hissed, through gritted teeth. "You're going to drive me crazy."

He blinked sadly. "You don't love me anymore, is that it, kiddo? All right. I can take a hint. Maybe I'll go haunt Grandma for a while. She's not as much fun because she can't see me, but maybe if I rattle a few doors—"

"Dad!" I glanced over my shoulder to make sure no one was listening. "Look. What's the message?"

"Message?" He blinked, and then went, "Oh, yeah. The message." Suddenly, he looked serious. "I understand you tried to contact a man today."

I narrowed my eyes at him suspiciously. "Red Beaumont," I said. "Yeah, I did. So?"

"This is not a guy you want to be messing around with, Susie," my dad said.

"Uh-huh. And why not?"

"I can't tell you why not," my dad said. "Just be careful."

I stared at him. I mean, really. How annoying can you get? "Thanks for the enigmatic warning, Dad," I said. "That really helps."

"I'm sorry, Suze," my dad said. "Really, I am. But you know how this stuff works. I don't get the whole story, just . . . feelings. And my feeling on this Beaumont guy is that you should stay away. Far, far away."

"Well, I can't do that," I said. "Sorry."

"Suze," my dad said. "This isn't one you should take on alone."

"But I'm not alone, Dad," I said. "I've got—"

I hesitated. Jesse, I'd almost said.

You would think my dad already knew about him. I mean, if he knew about Red Beaumont, why didn't he know about Jesse?

But apparently he didn't. Know about Jesse, I mean. Because if he had, you could bet I would have heard about it. I mean, come on, a guy who wouldn't get out of my bedroom? Dads hate that.

So I said, "Look, I've got Father Dominic."

"No," my dad said. "This one's not for him, either."

I glared at him. "Hey," I said. "How do *you* know about Father Dom? Dad, have you been spying on me?"

My dad looked sheepish. "The word *spying* has such negative connotations," he said. "I was just checking up on you, is all. Can you blame a guy for wanting to check up on his little girl?"

"Check up on me? Dad, how much checking up on me have you done?"

"Well," he said, "I'll tell you something. I'm not thrilled about this Jesse character."

"Dad!"

"Well, whaddya want me to say?" My dad held out his arms in a so-sue-me gesture. "The guy's practically living with you. It's not right. I mean, you're a very young girl."

"He's deceased, Dad, remember? It's not like my virtue's in any danger here." Unfortunately.

"But how're you supposed to change clothes and stuff with a *boy* in the room?" My dad, as usual, had cut to the chase. "I don't like it. And I'm gonna have a word with him. You, in the meantime, are gonna stay away from this Mr. Red. You got that?"

I shook my head. "Dad, you don't understand. Jesse and I have it all worked out. I don't—"

"I mean it, Susannah."

When my dad called me Susannah, he meant business.

I rolled my eyes. "All right, Dad. But about Jesse. Please don't say anything to him. He's had it kind of tough, you know? I mean, he pretty much died before he ever really got a chance to live."

"Hey," my dad said, giving me one of his big, innocent smiles. "Have I ever let you down before, sweetheart?"

Yes, I wanted to say. Plenty of times. Where had he been, for instance, last month when I'd been so nervous about moving to a new state, starting at a new school, living with a bunch of people I barely knew? Where had he been just last week when one of his cohorts had been trying to kill me? And where had he been Saturday night when I'd stumbled into all that poison oak?

But I didn't say what I wanted to. Instead, I said what I felt like I had to. This is what you do with family members.

"No, Dad," I said. "You never let me down."

He gave me a big hug, then disappeared as abruptly as he'd shown up. I was calmly pouring cereal into a bowl when my mom came into the kitchen and switched on the overhead light.

"Honey?" she said, looking concerned. "Are you all right?"

"Sure, Mom," I said. I shoveled some cereal—dry—into my mouth. "Why?"

"I thought—" My mother was peering at me curiously. "Honey, I thought I heard you say, um. Well. I thought I heard you talking to . . . Did you say the word *dad*?"

I chewed. I was totally used to this kind of thing. "I said bad. The milk in the fridge. I think it's gone bad."

My mother looked immensely relieved. The thing is, she's caught me talking to Dad more times than I can count. She probably thinks I'm a mental case. Back in New York she used to send me to her therapist, who told her I wasn't a mental case, just a teenager. Boy, did I pull one over on old Doc Mendelsohn, let me tell you.

But I had to feel sorry for my mom, in a way. I mean, she's a nice lady and doesn't deserve to have a mediator for a daughter. I know I've always been a bit of a disappointment to her. When I turned fourteen, she got me my own phone line, thinking so many boys would be calling me, her friends would never be able to get through. You can imagine how disappointed she was when nobody except my best friend, Gina, ever called me on my private line, and then it was usually only to tell me about the dates *she'd* been on. The boys in my old neighborhood were never much interested in asking *me* out.

"Well," my mom said, brightly. "If the milk's bad, I guess you have no choice but to try one of Andy's quesadillas."

"Great," I groaned. "Mom, you do understand that

around here, it's swimsuit season all year round? We can't just pig out in the winter like we used to back home."

My mom sighed sort of sadly. "Do you really hate it here that much, honey?"

I looked at her like she was the crazy one, for a change. "What do you mean? What makes you think I hate it here?"

"You. You just referred to Brooklyn as 'back home.'"

"Well," I said, embarrassed. "That doesn't mean I hate it here. It just isn't home yet."

"What do you need to make it feel that way?" My mom pushed some of my hair from my eyes. "What can I do to make this feel like home to you?"

"God, Mom," I said, ducking out from beneath her fingers. "Nothing, okay? I'll get used to it. Just give me a chance."

My mom wasn't buying it, though. "You miss Gina, don't you? You haven't made any really close friends here, I've noticed. Not like Gina. Would you like it if she came for a visit?"

I couldn't imagine Gina, with her leather pants, pierced tongue, and extension braids, in Carmel, California, where wearing khakis and a sweater set is practically enforced by law.

I said, "I guess that would be nice."

It didn't seem very likely, though. Gina's parents don't have very much money, so it wasn't as if they could just send her off to California like it was nothing. I would have liked to see Gina taking on Kelly Prescott, though. Hair extensions, I was quite certain, were going to fly.

Later, after dinner, kickboxing, and homework, a quesadilla congealing in my stomach, I decided, despite my dad's warning, to try to tackle the Red problem one last time before bed. I had gotten Tad Beaumont's home phone number—which was unlisted, of course—in the most devious way possible: from Kelly Prescott's cell phone, which I had borrowed during our student council meeting on the pretense of calling for an update on the repairs of Father Serra's statue. Kelly's cell phone, I'd noticed at the time, had an address book function, and I'd snagged Tad's phone number from it before handing it back to her.

Hey, it's a dirty job, but somebody's got to do it.

I had forgotten to take into account, of course, the fact that Tad, and not his father, might be the one to pick up the phone. Which he did after the second ring.

"Hello?" he said.

I recognized his voice instantly. It was the same soft voice that had stroked my cheek at the pool party.

Okay, I'll admit it. I panicked. I did what any red-blooded American girl would do under similar circumstances.

I hung up.

Of course, I didn't realize he had caller ID. So

when the phone rang a few seconds later, I assumed it was CeeCee, who'd promised to call with the answers to our geometry homework—I'd fallen a little behind, what with all the mediating I'd been doing . . . not that that was the excuse I'd given CeeCee, of course—so I picked up.

"Hello?" that same, soft voice said into my ear. "Did you just call me?"

I said a bunch of swear words real fast in my head. Aloud, I only said, "Uh. Maybe. By mistake, though. Sorry."

"Wait." I don't know how he'd known I'd been about to hang up. "You sound familiar. Do I know you? My name is Tad. Tad Beaumont."

"Nope," I said. "Doesn't ring a bell. Gotta go, sorry."

I hung up and said a bunch more swear words, this time out loud. Why, when I'd had him on the phone, hadn't I asked to speak to his father? Why was I such a loser? Father Dom was right. I was a failure as a mediator. A big-time failure. I could exorcise evil spirits, no problem. But when it came to dealing with the living, I was the world's biggest flop.

This fact was drilled into my head even harder when, about four hours later, I was wakened once again by a blood-curdling shriek.

CHAPTER 5

I sat up, fully awake at once.

She was back.

She was even more upset than she'd been the night before. I had to wait a really long time before she calmed down enough to talk to me.

"*Why?*" she asked, when she'd stopped screaming. "Why didn't you *tell* him?"

"Look," I said, trying to use a soothing voice, the way Father Dom would have wanted me to. "I tried, okay? The guy's not the easiest person to get hold of. I'll get him tomorrow, I promise."

She had kind of slumped down onto her knees. "He blames himself," she said. "He blames himself for my death. But it wasn't his fault. You've got to tell him. *Please.*"

Her voice cracked horribly on the word *please*. She was a wreck. I mean, I've seen some messed-up ghosts in my time, but this one took the cake, let me tell you. I swear, it was like having Meryl Streep put on that big crying scene from *Sophie's Choice* live on your bedroom carpet.

"Look, lady . . ." I said. Soothing, I reminded myself. Soothing.

There isn't anything real soothing about calling somebody *lady*, though. So, remembering how Jesse had been kind of mad at me before for not getting her name, I went, "Hey. What's your name, anyway?"

Sniffling, she just went, "Please. You've got to tell him."

"I said I'd do it." Jeez, what'd she think I was running here? Some kind of amateur operation? "Give me a chance, will you? These things are kind of delicate, you know. I can't just go blurting it out. Do you want that?"

"Oh, God, no," she said, lifting a knuckle to her mouth, and chewing on it. "No, please."

"Okay, then. Chill out a little. Now tell me—"

But she was already gone.

A split second later, though, Jesse showed up. He was applauding softly as if he were at the theater.

"Now that," he said, putting his hands down, "was your finest performance yet. You seemed caring, yet disgusted."

I glared at him. "Don't you," I asked, grumpily, "have some chains you're supposed to be rattling somewhere?"

He sauntered over to my bed and sat down on it. I had to jerk my feet over to keep him from squashing them.

"Don't you," he countered, "have something you want to tell me?"

I shook my head. "No. It's two o'clock in the morning, Jesse. The only thing I've got on my mind right now is sleep. You remember sleep, right?"

Jesse ignored me. He does that a lot. "I had a visitor of my own not too long ago. I believe you know him. A Mr. Peter Simon."

"Oh," I said.

And then—I don't know why—I flopped back down and pulled a pillow over my head.

"I don't want to hear about it," I said, my voice muffled beneath the pillow.

The next thing I knew, the pillow had flown out of my hands—even though I'd been clenching it pretty tightly—and slammed down to the floor. As hard as a pillow can slam, anyway, which isn't very hard.

I lay where I was, blinking in the darkness. Jesse hadn't moved an inch. That's the thing about ghosts, see. They can move stuff—pretty much anything they want—without lifting a finger. They do it with their minds. It's pretty creepy.

"What?" I demanded, my voice squeakier than ever.

"I want to know why you told your father that there's a man living in your bedroom."

Jesse looked mad. For a ghost, he's actually pretty even-tempered, so when he gets mad, it's really obvious. For one thing, things around him start shaking. For another, the scar in his right eyebrow turns white.

Things weren't shaking right then, but the scar was practically glowing in the dark.

"Uh," I said. "Actually, Jesse, there *is* a guy living in my bedroom, remember?"

"Yes, but—" Jesse got up off the bed and started pacing around. "But I'm not really *living* here."

"Well," I said. "Only because technically, Jesse, you're dead."

"I *know* that." Jesse ran a hand through his hair in a frustrated sort of way. Have I mentioned that Jesse has really nice hair? It's black and short and looks sort of crisp, if you know what I mean. "What I don't understand is why you told him about me. I didn't know it bothered you that much, my being here."

The truth is, it doesn't. Bother me, I mean. It used to, but that was before Jesse had saved my life a couple of times. After that, I sort of got over it.

Except it does bother me when he borrows my CDs and doesn't put them back in the right order when he's done with them.

"It doesn't," I said.

"It doesn't what?"

"It doesn't bother me that you live here." I winced. Poor choice of words. "Well, not that you *live* here, since . . . I mean, it doesn't bother me that you *stay* here. It's just that—"

"It's just that what?"

I said, all in a rush, before I could chicken out, "It's just that I can't help wondering *why*."

"Why what?"

"Why you've stayed here so long."

He just looked at me. Jesse has never told me anything about his death. He's never told me anything, really, about his life before his death, either. Jesse isn't what you'd call really communicative, even for a guy. I mean, if you take into consideration that he was born a hundred and fifty years before *Oprah*, and doesn't know squat about the advantages of sharing his feelings, how not keeping things bottled up inside is actually good for you, this sort of makes sense.

On the other hand, I couldn't help suspecting that Jesse was perfectly in touch with his emotions, and that he just didn't feel like letting me in on them. What little I had found out about him—like his full name, for instance—had been from an old book Doc had scrounged up on the history of northern California. I had never really had the guts to ask Jesse about it. You know, about how he was supposed to marry his cousin, who it turned out loved someone else, and how Jesse had mysteriously disappeared on the way to their wedding ceremony. . . .

It's just not the kind of thing you can really bring up.

"Of course," I said, after a short silence, during which it became clear that Jesse wasn't going to tell me jack, "if you don't want to discuss it, that's okay. I would have hoped that we could have, you know, an open and honest relationship, but if that's too much to ask—"

"What about you, Susannah?" he fired back at me. "Have you been open and honest with me? I don't think so. Otherwise, why would your father come after me like he did?"

Shocked, I sat up a little straighter. "My dad came *after* you?"

Jesse said, sounding irritated, *"Nombre de Dios*, Susannah, what did you expect him to do? What kind of father would he be if he didn't try to get rid of me?"

"Oh my God," I said, completely mortified. "Jesse, I never said a word to him about you. I swear. He's the one who brought you up. I guess he's been spying on me or something." This was a humiliating thing to have to admit. "So . . . what'd you do? When he came after you?"

Jesse shrugged. "What could I do? I tried to explain myself as best I could. After all, it's not as if my intentions are dishonorable."

Damn! Wait a minute, though—"You have *intentions*?"

I know it's pathetic, but at this point in my life, even hearing that the *ghost* of a guy might have intentions—even of the not dishonorable sort—was kind of cool. Well, what do you expect? I'm sixteen and no one's ever asked me out. Give me a break, okay?

Besides, Jesse's way hot, for a dead guy.

But unfortunately, his intentions toward me appeared to be nothing but platonic, if the fact that he picked up the pillow that he'd slammed onto the floor—with his hands this time—and smashed it in my face was any indication.

This did not seem like the kind of thing a guy who was madly in love with me would do.

"So what did my dad say?" I asked him when I'd pushed the pillow away. "I mean, after you reassured him that your intentions weren't dishonorable?"

"Oh," Jesse said, sitting back down on the bed. "After a while he calmed down. I like him, Susannah."

I snorted. "Everybody does. Or did, back when he was alive."

"He worries about you, you know," Jesse said.

"He's got way bigger things to worry about," I muttered, "than me."

Jesse blinked at me curiously. "Like what?"

"Gee, I don't know. How about why he's still here instead of wherever it is people are supposed to go after they die? That might be one suggestion, don't you think?"

Jesse said, quietly, "How are you so sure this isn't where he's supposed to be, Susannah? Or me, for that matter?"

I glared at him. "Because it doesn't work that way, Jesse. I may not know much about this mediation thing, but I do know that. This is the land of the living. You and my dad and that lady who was here a minute ago—you don't belong here. The reason you're stuck here is because something is wrong."

"Ah," he said. "I see."

But he didn't see. I knew he didn't see.

"You can't tell me you're happy here," I said. "You can't tell me you've *liked* being trapped in this room for a hundred and fifty years."

"It hasn't been all bad," he said with a smile. "Things have picked up recently."

I wasn't sure what he meant by that. And since I was afraid my voice might get all squeaky again if I asked, I settled for saying, "Well, I'm sorry about my dad coming after you. I swear I didn't tell him to."

Jesse said softly, "It's all right, Susannah. I like your father. And he only does it because he cares about you."

"You think so?" I picked at the bedspread. "I wonder. I think he does it because he knows it annoys me."

Jesse, who'd been watching me pull on a chenille

ball, suddenly reached out and seized my fingers.

He's not supposed to do that. Well, at least I'd been meaning to tell him he's not supposed to do that. Maybe it had slipped my mind. But anyway, he's not supposed to do that. Touch me, I mean.

See, even though Jesse's a ghost, and can walk through walls and disappear and reappear at will, he's still . . . well, *there*. To me, anyway. That's what makes me—and Father Dom—different from everybody else. We not only can see and talk to ghosts, but we can feel them, too—just as if they were anybody else. Anybody alive, I mean. Because to me and Father Dom, ghosts *are* just like anyone else, with blood and guts and sweat and bad breath and whatever. The only real difference is that they kind of have this glow around them—an aura, I think it's called.

Oh, and did I mention that a lot of them have superhuman strength? I usually forget to mention that. That's how come, in my line of work, I frequently get the you-know-what knocked out of me. That's also why it kind of freaks me out when one of them—like Jesse was doing just then—touches me, even in a non-aggressive way.

And I mean, seriously, just because, to me, ghosts are as real as, say, Tad Beaumont, that doesn't mean I want to go around slow dancing with them or anything.

Well, okay, in Jesse's case, I would, except how

weird would that be to slow dance with a ghost? Come on. Nobody but me'd ever be able to see him. I'd be like, "Oh, let me introduce you to my boyfriend," and there wouldn't be anybody there. How embarrassing. Everyone would think I was making him up like that lady on that movie I saw once on the Lifetime channel who made up an extra kid.

Besides, I'm pretty sure Jesse doesn't like me that way. You know, in the slow dancing way.

Which he unfortunately proved by flipping my hands over and holding them up to the moonlight.

"What's wrong with your fingers?" he wanted to know.

I looked up at them. The rash was worse than ever. In the moonlight I looked deformed, like I had monster hands.

"Poison oak," I said, bitterly. "You're lucky you're dead and can't get it. It bites. Nobody warned me about it, you know. About poison oak, I mean. Palm trees, sure, everybody said there'd be palm trees, but—"

"You should try putting a poultice of gum flower leaves on them," he interrupted.

"Oh, okay," I said, managing not to sound too sarcastic.

He frowned at me. "Little yellow flowers," he said. "They grow wild. They have healing properties, you know. There are some growing on that hill out behind the house."

"Oh," I said. "You mean that hill where all the poison oak is?"

"They say gunpowder works, too."

"Oh," I said. "You know, Jesse, you might be surprised to learn that medicine has advanced beyond flower poultices and gunpowder in the past century and a half."

"Fine," he said, dropping my hands. "It was only a suggestion."

"Well," I said. "Thanks. But I'll put my faith in hydrocortisone."

He looked at me for a little while. I guess he was probably thinking what a freak I am. *I* was thinking how weird it was, the fact that this guy had held my scaly, poison-oaky hands. Nobody else would touch them, not even my mother. But Jesse hadn't minded.

Then again, it wasn't as if he could catch it from me.

"Susannah," he said, finally.

"What?"

"Go carefully," he said, "with this woman. The woman who was here."

I shrugged. "Okay."

"I mean it," Jesse said. "She isn't—she isn't who you think she is."

"I know who she is," I said.

He looked surprised. So surprised it was kind of insulting, actually. "You *know*? She *told* you?"

"Well, not exactly," I said. "But you don't have to

worry. I've got things under control."

"No," he said. He got up off the bed. "You don't, Susannah. You should be careful. You should listen to your father this time."

"Oh, okay," I said, very sarcastically. "Thanks. Do you think maybe you could be creepier about it? Like, could you drool blood, or something, too?"

I guess maybe I'd been a little *too* sarcastic, though, because instead of replying he just disappeared.

Ghosts. They just can't take a joke.

CHAPTER 6

"You want me to *what*?"

"Just drop me off," I said. "On your way to work. It's not out of your way."

Sleepy eyed me as if I'd suggested he eat glass or something. "I don't know," he said slowly as he stood in the doorway, the keys to the Rambler in his hand. "How are you going to get home?"

"A friend is coming to pick me up," I said, brightly.

A total lie, of course. I had no way of getting home.

But I figured in a pinch, I could always call Adam. He'd just gotten his license as well as a new VW Bug. He was so hot to drive, he'd have picked me up from Albuquerque if I'd called him from there. I didn't think he'd mind too much if I called him from Thaddeus

Beaumont's mansion on Seventeen Mile Drive.

Sleepy still looked uncertain. "I don't know. . . ." he said, slowly.

I could tell he thought I was headed for a gang meeting, or something. Sleepy has never seemed all that thrilled about me, especially after our parents' wedding when he caught me smoking outside the reception hall. Which is so totally unfair since I've never touched a cigarette since.

But I guess the fact that he'd recently been forced to rescue me in the middle of the night when this ghost made a building collapse on me didn't exactly help form any warm bond of trust between us. Especially since I couldn't tell him the ghost part. I think he believes I'm just the type of girl buildings fall on top of all the time.

No wonder he doesn't want me in his car.

"Come on," I said, opening up my camel-colored calf-length coat. "How much trouble could I get up to in this outfit?"

Sleepy looked me over. Even he had to admit I was the epitome of innocence in my white cable-knit sweater, red plaid skirt, and penny loafers. I had even put on this gold cross necklace I had been awarded as a prize for winning an essay contest on the War of 1812 in Mr. Walden's class. I figured this was the kind of outfit an old guy like Mr. Beaumont would appreciate: you know, the sassy schoolgirl thing.

"Besides," I said. "It's for school."

"All right," Sleepy said at last, looking like he really wished he were someplace else. "Get in the car."

I hightailed it out to the Rambler before he had a chance to change his mind.

Sleepy got in a minute later, looking drowsy, as usual. His job, for a pizza stint, seemed awfully demanding. Either that or he just put in a lot of extra shifts. You would think by now he'd have saved enough for that Camaro. I mentioned that as we pulled out of the driveway.

"Yeah," Sleepy said. "But I want to really cherry her out, you know? Alpine stereo, Bose speakers. The works."

I have this thing about boys who refer to their cars as "she," but I didn't figure it would pay to alienate my ride. Instead, I said, "Wow. Neat."

We live in the hills of Carmel, overlooking the valley and the bay. It's a beautiful place, but since it was dark out all I could see were the insides of the houses we were driving by. People in California have these really big windows to let in all the sun, and at nighttime, when their lights are on, you can see practically everything they're doing, just like in Brooklyn, where nobody ever pulled down their blinds. It's kind of homey, actually.

"What class is this for, anyway?" Sleepy asked, making me jump. He so rarely spoke, especially when he was doing something he liked, like eating or driving, that I had sort of forgotten he was there.

"What do you mean?" I asked.

"This paper you're doing." He took his eyes off the road a second and looked at me. "You did say this was for school, didn't you?"

"Oh," I said. "Sure. Uh-huh. It's, um, a story I'm doing for the school paper. My friend CeeCee, she's the editor. She assigned it to me."

Oh my God, I am such a liar. And I can't leave at just one lie, either. Oh, no. I have to pile it on. I am sick, I tell you. Sick.

"CeeCee," Sleepy said. "That's that albino chick you hang out with at lunch, right?"

CeeCee would have had an embolism if she'd heard anyone refer to her as a chick, but since, technically, the rest of his sentence was correct, I said, "Uh-huh."

Sleepy grunted and didn't say anything else for a while. We drove in silence, the big houses with their light-filled windows flashing by. Seventeen Mile Drive is this stretch of highway that's supposed to be like the most beautiful road in the world, or something. The famous Pebble Beach Golf Course is on Seventeen Mile Drive, along with about five other golf courses and a bunch of scenic points, like the Lone Cypress, which is some kind of tree growing out of a boulder, and Seal Rock, on which there are, you guessed it, a lot of seals.

Seventeen Mile Drive is also where you can check

out the colliding currents of what they call the Restless Sea, the ocean along this part of the coast that's too filled with riptides and undertows for anyone to swim in. It's all giant crashing waves and tiny stretches of sand between great big boulders on which seagulls are always dropping mussels and stuff, hoping to split the shells open. Sometimes surfers get split open there, too, if they're stupid enough to think they can ride the waves.

And if you want, you can buy a really big mansion on a cliff overlooking all this natural beauty, for a mere, oh, zillion dollars or so.

Which was apparently what Thaddeus "Red" Beaumont had done. He had snatched up one of those mansions, a really, really big one, I saw, when Sleepy finally pulled up in front of it. Such a big one, in fact, that it had a little guardhouse by the enormous spiky gate in front of its long, long driveway, with a guard in it watching TV.

Sleepy, looking at the gate, went, "Are you sure this is the place?"

I swallowed. I knew from what CeeCee had said that Mr. Beaumont was rich. But I hadn't thought he was *this* rich.

And just think, his kid had asked me to slow dance!

"Um," I said. "Maybe I should just see if he's home before you take off."

Sleepy said, "Yeah, I guess."

I got out of the car and went up to the little guard-house. I don't mind telling you, I felt like a tool. I had been trying all day to get through to Mr. Beaumont, only to be told he was in a meeting, or on another line. For some reason, I'd imagined a personal touch might work. I don't know what I'd been thinking, but I believe it had involved ringing the doorbell and then looking winsomely up into his face when he came to the door.

That, I could see now, wasn't going to happen.

"Um, excuse me," I said, into the little microphone at the guard's house. Bulletproof glass, I noticed. Either Tad's dad had some people who didn't like him, or he was just a little paranoid.

The guard looked up from his TV. He checked me out. I saw him check me out. I had kept my coat open so he'd be sure to see my plaid skirt and loafers. Then he looked past me, at the Rambler. This was no good. I did not want to be judged by my stepbrother and his crappy car.

I tapped on the glass again to direct the guard's attention back to me.

"Hello," I said, into the microphone. "My name's Susannah Simon, and I'm a sophomore at the Mission Academy. I'm doing a story for our school paper on the ten most influential people in Carmel, and I was hoping to be able to interview Mr. Beaumont, but unfortunately, he hasn't returned any of my calls, and the story is due tomorrow, so I was wondering if he might be home and if he'd see me."

The guard looked at me with a stunned expression on his face.

"I'm a friend," I said, "of Tad, Tad Beaumont, Mr. Beaumont's son? He knows me, so if you want him, you know, to check me out on the security camera or whatever, I'm sure he could, you know, ID me. If my ID needs verifying, I mean."

The guard continued to stare at me. You would think a guy as rich as Mr. Beaumont could afford smarter guards.

"But if this is a bad time," I said, starting to back away, "I guess I could come back."

Then the guard did an extraordinary thing. He leaned forward, pressed a button, and said, into the speaker, "Honey, you talk faster than anyone I ever heard in my life. Would you care to repeat all that? Slowly, this time?"

So I said my little speech again, more slowly this time, while behind me, Sleepy sat at the wheel with the motor running. I could hear the radio blaring inside the car, and Sleepy singing along. He must have thought that his car was soundproof with the windows rolled up.

Boy, was he ever wrong.

After I was done giving my speech the second time, the guard, with a kind of smile on his face, said, "Hold on, miss," and got on this white phone, and started saying a bunch of stuff into it that I couldn't hear. I stood there wishing I'd worn tights instead of pantyhose since my legs were freezing in the cold wind that was coming in off the ocean, and wondering how I could ever have possibly thought this was a good idea.

Then the microphone crackled.

"Okay, miss," the guard said. "Mr. Beaumont'll see you."

And then, to my astonishment, the big spiky gates began to ease open.

"Oh," I said. "Oh my God! Thank you! Thanks—"

Then I realized the guard couldn't hear me since I wasn't talking into the microphone. So I ran back to the car and tore open the door.

Sleepy, in the middle of a pretty involved air guitar session, broke off and looked embarrassed.

"So?" he said.

"So," I said back to him, slamming the passenger door behind me. "We're in. Just drop me off at the house, will you?"

"Sure thing, Cinderella."

It took like five minutes to get down that driveway. I am not even kidding. It was *that* long. On either side of it were these big trees that formed sort of an alley. A tree alley. It was kind of cool. I figured in the daytime it was probably really beautiful. Was there anything Tad Beaumont didn't have? Looks, money, a beautiful place to live . . .

All he needed was cute little old me.

Sleepy pulled the car to a stop in front of this paved entranceway, which was flanked on either side by these enormous palm trees, kind of like the Polynesian Resort at Disney World. In fact, the whole place had kind of a Disney feel to it. You know, really big, and kind of modern and fake. There were all these lights on, and at the end of all the paved stones I could see this giant glass door with somebody hovering behind it.

I turned to Sleepy and said, "Okay, I'm good. Thanks for the ride."

Sleepy looked out at all the lights and palm trees and stuff. "You sure you got a way home?"

"I'm sure," I said.

"Okay." As I got out of the car, I heard him mutter, "Never delivered a pie *here* before."

I hurried up the paved walkway, conscious, as Sleepy drove away, that I could hear the ocean somewhere, though in the darkness beyond the house, I couldn't see it. When I got to the door, it swung open before I could look for a bell, and a Japanese man in black pants and a white housecoat-looking thing bowed to me and said, "This way, miss."

I had never been in a house where a servant answered the door before—let alone been called miss—so I didn't know how to act. I followed him into this huge room where the walls were made out of actual rocks from which actual water was dripping in these little rivulets, which I guess were supposed to be waterfalls.

"May I take your coat?" the Japanese man said, and so I shrugged out of it, though I kept my bag from which my writing tablet was peeking out. I wanted to look the part, you know.

Then the Japanese man bowed to me again and said, "This way, miss."

He led me toward a set of sliding glass doors, which opened out onto a long, open-air courtyard in which there was a huge pool lit up turquoise in the dark. Steam rose from its surface. I guess it was heated. There was a fountain in the middle of it and a rock formation from which water gushed, and all around it were plants and trees and hibiscus bushes. A very nice place, I thought, for me to hang out in after school in my Calvin Klein one-piece and my sarong.

Then we were inside again in a surprisingly ordinary-looking hallway. It was at this point that my guide bowed to me for a third time and said, "Wait here, please," then disappeared through one of three doors off the corridor.

So I did as he said, though I couldn't help wondering what time it was. I don't wear a watch since every one I ever owned has ended up getting smashed by some evil spirit. But I hadn't planned on spending more than a few minutes of my time with this guy. My plan was to get in, deliver the dead lady's message, and then get out. I'd told my mom I'd be home by nine, and it had to be nearly eight by now.

Rich people. They just don't care about other people's curfews.

Then the Japanese man reappeared, bowed, and said, "He will see you now."

Whoa. I wondered if I should genuflect.

I restrained myself. Instead, I went through the door—and found myself in an elevator. A tiny little elevator with a chair and an end table in it. There was even a plant on the end table. The Japanese man had shut the door behind me, and now I was alone in a tiny room that was definitely moving. Whether it was going up or down, I had no way of knowing. There were no numbers over the door to indicate the direction the thing was taking. And there was only one button . . .

The room stopped moving. When I reached for the doorknob, it turned. And when I stepped out of the elevator, I found myself in a darkened room with big velvet curtains pulled over the windows, containing only a massive desk, an even more massive aquarium, and a single visitor's chair, evidently for me, in front of that desk. Behind the desk sat a man. The man, when he saw me, smiled.

"Ah," he said. "You must be Miss Simon."

CHAPTER 7

"Um," I said. "Yes."

It was hard to tell, because it was so dark in the room, but the man behind the desk appeared to be about my stepfather's age. Forty-five or so. He was wearing a sweater over a button-down collared shirt, sort of like Bill Gates always does. He had brown hair that was obviously thinning. CeeCee was right: It certainly wasn't red.

And he wasn't anywhere near as good-looking as his son.

"Sit down," Mr. Beaumont said. "Sit down. I'm so delighted to see you. Tad's told me so much about you."

Yeah, right. I wondered what he'd say if I pointed out that Tad didn't even know my name. But since I was still playing the part of the eager girl reporter, I smiled as I settled into the comfortable leather chair in front of his desk.

"Would you like anything?" Mr. Beaumont asked. "Tea? Lemonade?"

"Oh, no thank you," I said. It was hard not to stare at the aquarium behind him. It was built into the wall, almost filling it up, and was stocked with every color fish imaginable. There were lights built into the sand at the bottom of the tank that cast this weird, watery glow around the room. Mr. Beaumont's face, with this wavy light on it, looked kind of Grand Moff Tarkin-ish. You know, in the final Death Star battle scene.

"I don't want to put you to any trouble," I said in response to his question about liquid refreshment.

"Oh, it's no trouble at all. Yoshi can get it for you." Mr. Beaumont reached for the phone in the center of his giant, Victorian-looking desk. "Shall I ask him to get you anything?"

"Really," I said. "I'm fine." And then I crossed my legs because I was still freezing from when I'd stood outside by the guard's house.

"Oh, but you're cold," Mr. Beaumont said. "Here, let me light a fire."

"No," I said. "Really. It's all . . . right. . . ."

My voice trailed off. Mr. Beaumont had not, as Andy would have done, stood up, gone to the fireplace, stuffed wadded-up pieces of newspaper under some logs, lit the thing, and then spent the next half hour blowing on it and cursing.

Instead, he lifted a remote control, hit a button, and all of a sudden this cheerful fire was going in the black marble fireplace. I felt its heat at once.

"Wow," I said. "That sure is . . . convenient."

"Isn't it?" Mr. Beaumont smiled at me. He kept looking, for some reason, at the cross around my neck. "I never was one for building fires. So messy. I was never a very good Boy Scout."

"Ha ha," I said. The only way, I thought to myself, that this could get any weirder would be if it turned out he had that dead lady's head on ice somewhere in the basement, ready for transplantation onto Cindy Crawford's body as soon as it becomes available.

"Well, if I could get straight to the point, Mr. Beaumont—"

"Of course. Ten most influential people in Carmel, is it? And what number am I? One, I hope."

He smiled even harder at me. I smiled back at him. I hate to admit it, but this is always my favorite part. There is definitely something wrong with me.

"Actually, Mr. Beaumont," I said, "I'm not really here to do a story on you for my school paper. I'm here because someone asked me to get a message to you, and this is the only way I could think of to do it. You are a very hard person to get a hold of, you know."

His smile had not faltered as I'd told him that I

was there under false pretenses. He may have hit some secret alarm button under his desk, calling for security, but if he did, I didn't see it. He folded his fingers beneath his chin and, still staring at my gold cross, said, "Yes?" in this expectant way.

"The message," I said, sitting up straight, "is from a woman—sorry, I didn't get her name—who happens to be dead."

There was absolutely no change in his expression. Obviously, I decided, a master at hiding his emotions.

"She said for me to tell you," I went on, "that you did not kill her. She doesn't blame you. And she wants you to stop blaming yourself."

That triggered a reaction. He quickly unfolded his fingers, then flattened his hands out across his desk, and stared at me with a look of utter fascination.

"She said that?" he asked me, eagerly. "A dead woman?"

I eyed him uneasily. That wasn't quite the reaction I was used to getting when I delivered messages like the one I'd just given him. Some tears would have been good. A gasp of astonishment. But not this—let's face it—sick kind of interest.

"Yeah," I said, standing up.

It wasn't just that Mr. Beaumont and his creepy staring was freaking me out. And it wasn't that my dad's warning was ringing in my ears. My mediator instincts were telling me to get out, now. And when my instincts tell me to do something, I usually obey. I have often found it beneficial to my health.

"Okay," I said. "Buh-bye."

I turned around and headed back for the elevator. But when I tugged on the doorknob, it didn't budge.

"Where did you see this woman?" Mr. Beaumont's voice, behind me, was filled with curiosity. "This dead person?"

"I had a dream about her, okay?" I said, continuing to tug lamely on the door. "She came to me in a dream. It was really important to her that you knew that she doesn't hold you responsible for anything. And now I've done my duty, so would you mind if I go now? I told my mom I'd be home by nine."

But Mr. Beaumont didn't release the elevator door. Instead, he said in a wondering voice, "You *dreamed* of her? The dead speak to you in your dreams? Are you a *psychic*?"

Damn, I said to myself. I should have known.

This guy was one of those New Agers. He probably had a sensory deprivation tank in his bedroom and burned aromatherapy candles in his bathroom and had a secret little room dedicated to the study of extraterrestrials somewhere in his house.

"Yeah," I said, since I'd already dug the hole. I figured I might just as well climb in now. "Yeah, I'm psychic."

Keep him talking, I said to myself. Keep him talking while you find another way out. I began to edge toward one of the windows hidden behind the sweeping velvet curtains.

"But look, I can't tell you anything else, okay?" I said. "I just had this one dream. About someone who seems like she might have been a very nice lady. It's a shame about her being dead, and all. Who was she, anyway? Your, um, wife?"

On the word *wife*, I pulled the curtains apart, expecting to find a window I could neatly put my foot through, then jump to safety. No biggie. I'd done it a hundred times before.

And there was a window there, all right. A ten-foot one with lots of individual panes, set back a foot, at least, in a nicely paneled casement.

But someone had pulled the shutters—you know, the ones that go on the outside of the house and are mostly just decorative—closed. Tightly closed. Not a ray of sunshine could have penetrated those things.

"It must be terribly exciting," Mr. Beaumont was saying behind me as I stared at the shutters, wondering if they'd open if I kicked them hard enough. But then who was to say what kind of drop lay below them? I could be fifty feet up for all I knew. I've made some serious leaps in my life, but I usually like to know what I'm leaping into before I go for it. "Being psychic, I mean," Tad's dad went on. "I wonder if you would mind getting in touch with other deceased individuals

I might know. There are a few people I've been longing to talk to."

"It doesn't"—I let go of those curtains and moved to the next window—"work that way."

Same thing. The window was completely shuttered up. Not even a chink where sunlight might spill through. In fact, they looked almost nailed shut.

But that was ridiculous. Who would nail shutters over their windows? Especially with the kind of sea view I was sure Mr. Beaumont's house afforded.

"Oh, but surely, if you really concentrated"—Mr. Beaumont's pleasant voice followed me as I moved to the next window—"you could communicate with just a few others. I mean, you've already succeeded with one. What's a few more? I'd pay you, of course."

I couldn't believe it. Every single one of the windows was shuttered.

"Um," I said as I got to the last window and found it similarly shuttered. "Agoraphobic much?"

Mr. Beaumont must have finally noticed what I was doing since he said, casually, "Oh, that. Yes. I'm sensitive to sunlight. So bad for the skin."

Oh, okay. This guy was certifiable.

There was only one other door in the room, and that one was behind Mr. Beaumont, next to the aquarium. I didn't exactly relish the idea of going anywhere near that guy, so I headed back for the door to the elevator.

"Look, can you please unlock this so I can go

home?" I tugged on the knob, trying not to let my fear show. "My mom is really strict, and if I miss my curfew, she . . . she might *beat* me."

I know this was shoveling it on a bit thick—especially if he ever happened to watch the local news and saw my mother doing one of her reports. She is so not the abusive type. But the thing was, there was something so creepy about him, I really just wanted to get out, and I didn't care how. I'd have said anything to get out of there.

"Do you think," Mr. Beaumont wanted to know, "that if I were very quiet, you might be able to summon this woman's spirit again so that I could have a word with her?"

"No," I said. "Could you please open this door?"

"Don't you wonder what she could have meant?" Mr. Beaumont asked me. "I mean, she told you to tell me not to blame myself for her death. As if I, in some way, were responsible for killing her. Didn't that make you wonder a little, Miss Simon? I mean, about whether or not I might be a—"

Right then, to my utter relief, the knob to the elevator door turned in my hand. But not, it turned out, because Mr. Beaumont had released it. No, it turned out somebody was getting off the elevator.

"Hello," said a blond man, much younger than Mr. Beaumont, dressed in a suit and tie. "What have we here?"

"This is Miss Simon, Marcus," Mr. Beaumont said, happily. "She's a psychic."

Marcus, for some reason, kept looking at my necklace, too. Not just my necklace, either, but my whole throat area.

"Psychic, eh?" he said, his gaze sweeping the neckline of my sweater. "Is that what you two were discussing down here? Yoshi told me something about a newspaper article. . . ."

"Oh, no." Mr. Beaumont waved a hand as if to dismiss the whole newspaper thing. "That was just something she made up to get me to see her so she could tell me about the dream. Really quite an extraordinary dream, Marcus. She says she had a dream that a woman told her I didn't kill her. *Didn't* kill her, Marcus. Isn't that interesting?"

"It certainly is," Marcus said. He took hold of my arm. "Well, I'm glad you two had a nice little visit. Now I'm afraid Miss Simon has to go."

"Oh, no." Mr. Beaumont, for the first time, stood up behind his desk. He was very tall, I noticed. He also had on green corduroy pants. Green!

Really, if you ask me, that was the weirdest thing of all.

"We were just getting to know each other," Mr. Beaumont said mournfully.

"I told my mom I'd be home by nine," I told Marcus really fast.

Marcus was no dummy. He steered me right into that elevator, saying to Mr. Beaumont, "We'll have Miss Simon back sometime soon."

"Wait." Mr. Beaumont started to come around from behind his desk. "I haven't had a chance to—"

But Marcus jumped into the elevator with me and, letting go of me, slammed the door behind him.

CHAPTER 8

A second later we were moving. Whether we were going up or down, I still couldn't tell. But it didn't really matter. The fact was, we were moving, and away from Mr. Beaumont, which was all I cared about.

"Jeez," I couldn't help bursting out as soon as I knew I was safe. "What is *with* that guy?"

Marcus looked down at me.

"Did Mr. Beaumont hurt you in any way, Miss Simon?"

I blinked at him. "No."

"I'm very glad to hear that." Marcus looked a little relieved, but he tried to cover it up by being business-like. "Mr. Beaumont," he said, "is a little tired this evening. He is a very important, very busy man."

"I hate to be the one to tell you this, but that guy's more than just tired."

"Be that as it may," Marcus said, "Mr. Beaumont does not have time for little girls who enjoy playing pranks."

"*Prank?*" I echoed, mightily offended. "Listen, mister, I really did . . ." What was I *saying*? "I really did, um, have that dream, and I resent—"

Marcus looked down at me tiredly. "Miss Simon," he said, in a bored voice. "I really don't want to have to call your parents. And if you promise me you won't bother Mr. Beaumont ever again with any more of this psychic dream business, I won't."

I almost laughed out loud at that. My *parents*? I'd been worried he was set to call the *police*. My parents I could handle. The police were another matter entirely.

"Oh," I said when the elevator stopped and Marcus opened the door to let me back out into the little corridor off the courtyard where the pool was. "All right." I tried to put a lot of petulant disappointment in my voice. "I promise."

"Thank you," Marcus said.

He nodded, and then started walking me toward the front door.

He probably would have kicked me out without another thought if it hadn't been for the fact that as we were heading past the pool I happened to notice that someone was swimming laps in it. I couldn't tell who it was at first. It was really dark out, the night sky both moonless and starless because of a thick layer of clouds, and the only lights were the big round ones under the water. They made the person in it look all distorted—kind of like Mr. Beaumont's face with the light from the aquarium all over it.

But then the swimmer reached the end of the pool and, his exercise regimen apparently complete, lifted himself out of it, and reached for a towel he'd thrown across a deck chair.

I froze.

And not just because I recognized him. I froze because really, it's not every day you see a *Greek god* right here on earth.

I mean it. Tad Beaumont in a bathing suit was a beautiful sight to see. In the blue light from the pool, he looked like an Adonis, with water sparkling all over the dark hair that coated his chest and legs. And if his abs weren't quite as impressive as Jesse's, well, at least he had a really buff set of biceps to make up for it.

"Hi, Tad," I said.

Tad looked up. He'd been drying himself with the towel. Now he paused and looked me over.

"Oh, hey," he said, recognizing me. A big smile broke out across his face. "It's you."

CeeCee had been right. He didn't even know my name.

"Yeah," I said. "Suze Simon. From Kelly Prescott's party."

"Sure, I remember." Tad sauntered over to us, the towel slung casually over his shoulders. "How you doin'?"

His smile was something to see, let me tell you. His dad had probably paid some orthodontist a pretty penny for it, but it was worth it, every cent.

"You know this young lady, Tad?" Marcus said, his disbelief evident in his tone.

"Oh, sure," Tad said. He stood next to me, water still dripping from his dark hair like diamonds. "We go way back."

"Well," Marcus said. And then he evidently couldn't think of anything to add to that, since he said it again. "*Well.*"

And then, after an awkward silence, he said it a third time, but then added, "I guess I'll leave you two alone then. Tad, you'll show Miss Simon the way out?"

"Sure," Tad said. Then, when Marcus had disappeared back through the sliding glass doors into the house, he whispered, "Sorry about that. Marcus is a great guy, but he's kind of a worrier."

Having met his boss, I didn't exactly blame Marcus for worrying. But since I couldn't say that to Tad, I just went, "I'm sure he's very nice."

And then I told him about the story I was doing for the school paper. I figured even if they discussed it later, his dad wasn't going to go, "Oh, no, *that's* not why she was here. She was here to tell me about this dream she had."

And even if he did, he was so weird I doubt even his own son would believe him.

"Huh," Tad said when I was through describing my article on the ten most influential people in Carmel. "That's cool."

"Yeah," I babbled on. "I didn't even know he was your dad." God, I can lay it on when I try. "I mean, I never did get your last name. So this is a real surprise. Hey, listen, can I borrow a phone? I've got to see about engineering a ride home."

Tad looked down at me in surprise. "You need a ride? No sweat. I'll take you."

I couldn't help looking him up and down. I mean, he was practically naked, and all. Okay, well, not naked, since he was wearing a pair of swimming trunks that did reach practically to his knees. But he was naked enough for me not to be able to look away.

"Um," I said. "Thanks."

He followed my gaze, and looked down at his dripping shorts.

"Oh," he said, the beautiful smile going gorgeously sheepish. "Let me just throw something on first. Wait here for me?"

And he took the towel from around his neck and started toward the back of his house—

—but froze when I gasped and said, "Oh my God! What's wrong with your *neck*?"

Instantly, he hunched his shoulders, and spun around to face me again. "Nothing," he said too fast.

"There most certainly is *not* nothing wrong with it," I said, taking a step toward him. "You've got some kind of horrible—"

And then, my voice trailing off, I dropped my gaze down toward my hands.

"Look," Tad said, uncomfortably. "It's just poison oak. I know it's gross. I've had it for a couple of days. It looks worse than it is. I don't know how I got it, especially on the back of my neck, but—"

"I do."

I held up both my hands. In the blue glow from the pool lights, the rash on them looked particularly grotesque—just like the rash on the back of his neck.

"I tripped and fell into some plants the night of Kelly's party," I explained. "And right after that, you asked me to dance. . . ."

Tad looked down at my hands. Then he started to laugh.

"I'm so sorry," I said. I really felt bad. I mean, I had disfigured the guy. This incredibly sexy, fabulous-looking guy. "Really, you don't know—"

But Tad just kept laughing. And after a while, I started laughing with him.

CHAPTER 9

"Shuttered," Father Dominic repeated. "The windows were shuttered?"

"Well, not all of them," I said. I was sitting in the chair across from his desk, picking at my poison oak. The hydrocortisone was drying it out. Now, instead of oozy, it was just plain scaly. "Just the ones in his office, or whatever it was. He said he's sensitive to light."

"And you say he kept staring at your neck?"

"At my necklace. It was his assistant who checked out my throat like he expected to see a giant hickey there, or something. But you're missing the point, Father Dom."

I had decided to come clean with the good father. Well, at least about the dead woman who'd been waking me up in the middle of the night lately. I still wasn't ready to tell him about Jesse—especially considering what had happened when Tad had dropped me off the night before—but I figured if Thaddeus Beaumont Senior was actually the creepy killer I couldn't help suspecting he might be, I was going to need Father D.'s help to bring him to justice.

"The point," I said, "is that he was surprised for the wrong reason. He was surprised this woman had said he *hadn't* killed her. Which implies—to me, anyway—that he really had. Killed her, I mean."

Father Dom had been working a straightened-out coat hanger underneath his cast when I'd walked in. Apparently he had an itch. He'd stopped scratching, but he couldn't let go of the piece of wire. He kept fingering it thoughtfully. But at least he hadn't gotten the cigarettes out yet.

"Sensitive to light," he kept murmuring. "Looking at your neck."

"The point," I said again, "is that it seems like he really did kill this lady. I mean, he practically admitted it. The problem is, how can we prove it? We don't even know her name, let alone where she's buried—if anybody bothered burying her at all. We don't even have a body to point to. Even if we went to the cops, what would we say?"

Father D., however, was deeply absorbed in his own thoughts, turning the wire over and over in his hands.

I figured if he was going to slip off into la-la land, well, then I would, too. I sat back in my chair, scratching my poison oak, and thought about what had happened after Tad and I were done laughing at each other's disfiguring rashes—the only part of my evening I hadn't described to Father Dom.

Tad had gone and changed clothes. I had waited out by the pool, the steam rising from it warming my pantyhose-clad legs. Nobody bothered me, and it had actually been kind of restful listening to the waterfall. After a while, Tad reappeared, his hair still wet, but fully dressed in jeans and, unfortunately, another black silk shirt. He was even wearing a gold necklace, though I doubt he won his by writing a scintillating essay on James Madison.

It was all I could do not to point out that the gold was probably irritating his rash, and that black silk with jeans on a man is hopelessly Staten Island.

I managed to restrain myself, however, and Tad took me back inside, where Yoshi reappeared like magic with my coat. Then we went out to Tad's car, which I saw to my complete horror was some kind of sleek black thing that I swear to God David Hasselhoff drove on that show he did before *Baywatch*. It had these deep leather seats and the kind of stereo system that Sleepy would have killed for, and as I put my seat belt on, I prayed Tad was a good driver since I would die of embarrassment if anyone ever had to use the jaws of life to pry me from a car like that.

Tad, however, seemed to think the car was cool, and that in it, he was, too. And I'm sure that in Poland, or somewhere, it is considered cool to drive a Porsche and wear necklaces and black silk, but at least back in Brooklyn if you did those things you were either a drug dealer or from New Jersey.

But Tad apparently didn't know that. He put the car in gear and an instant later, we were on the Drive, taking the hairpin curves along the coast as easily as if we were on a magic carpet. As he drove, Tad asked if I wanted to go somewhere, maybe get a cup of coffee. I guess now that we shared the common bond of poison oak, he wanted to hang.

I said sure, even though I hate coffee, and he let me use his cell phone to call my mother and tell her I'd be late. My mom was so thrilled to hear I was going somewhere with a boy, she didn't even do the usual things mothers do when their daughters are out with a boy they don't know, like demand his mother's name and home phone number.

I hung up, and we went to the Coffee Clutch, a particularly favorite haunt of kids from the Mission Academy. CeeCee and Adam, it turned out, were there, but when they saw me come in with a boy, they tactfully pretended not to know me. At least, CeeCee did. Adam kept looking over and making rude faces whenever Tad's back was turned. I don't know if the faces were due to the fact that Tad's rash was plainly evident even in the Coffee Clutch's dim lighting, or if Adam was just expressing his personal feelings for Tad Beaumont in general.

In any case, after two cappuccinos—for him—and two hot ciders for me, we left, and Tad drove me home. He wasn't, I'd discovered, an especially bright guy. He talked an awful lot about basketball. When he wasn't talking about basketball, he was talking about sailing, and when he wasn't talking about sailing, he was talking about jet-skiing.

And suffice to say, I know nothing about basketball, sailing, or jet-skiing.

But he seemed like a decent enough guy. And unlike his father, he was clearly not nuts, always a positive. And he was, of course, devastatingly good-looking, so all in all, I would have rated the evening around a seven or eight, on a one to ten scale, one being lousy, ten being sublime.

And then, as I was undoing my seat belt after having said good night, Tad suddenly leaned over, took my chin in his hand, turned my face toward him, and kissed me.

My first kiss. Ever.

I know it's hard to believe. I'm so vibrant and bubbly and all, you would think boys had been flocking to me like bees to honey all my life.

Let's just say that's not exactly what happened. I

like to blame the fact that I am a biological freak—being able to communicate with the dead, and all—for the fact that I have never once been on a date, but I know that's not really it. I'm just not the kind of girl guys think about asking out. Well, maybe they think about it, but they always seem to manage to talk themselves out of it. I don't know if it's because they think I might ram a fist down their throats if they try anything, or if it's just because they are intimidated by my superior intelligence and good looks (ha ha). In the end, they just aren't interested.

Until Tad, that is. Tad was interested. Tad was *very* interested.

Tad was expressing his interest by deepening our kiss from just a little good-night one to a full fledged French—which I was enjoying immensely, by the way, in spite of the necklace and the silk shirt—when I happened to notice—yeah, okay. I'll admit it. My eyes were open. Hey, it was my first kiss, I wasn't going to miss anything, okay?—that there was somebody sitting in the Porsche's tiny little backseat.

I pulled my head away and let out a little scream.

Tad blinked at me in confusion.

"What's wrong?" he asked.

"Oh, please," said the person in the backseat, pleasantly. "Don't stop on my account."

I looked at Tad. "I gotta go," I said. "Sorry."

And I practically flew out of that car.

I was barreling up the driveway to my house, my cheeks on fire with embarrassment, when Jesse caught up to me. He wasn't even walking fast. He was just strolling along.

And he actually had the nerve to say, "It's your own fault."

"How is it *my* fault?" I demanded, as Tad, after hesitating a moment, started backing out of our driveway.

"You shouldn't," Jesse said, calmly, "have let him get so forward."

"*Forward?* What are you *talking* about? *Forward?* What does that even *mean?*"

"You hardly know him," Jesse said. "And you were letting him—"

I whirled around to face him. Fortunately, by that time, Tad was gone. Otherwise, he would have seen me, in the glow of his headlights, twirling around in my driveway, yelling at the moon, which had finally broken through the clouds.

"Oh, no," I said, loudly. "Don't even *go* there, Jesse."

"Well," Jesse said. In the moonlight, I could see that his expression was one of stubborn determination. The stubbornness was no mystery—Jesse was just about the stubbornest person I had ever met—but what he was so determined about, except maybe ruining my life, I couldn't figure out. "You were."

"*We were just saying good night,*" I hissed at him.

"I may have been dead for the past hundred and

fifty years, Susannah," Jesse said, "but that doesn't mean I don't know how people say good night. And generally, when people say good night, they keep their tongues to themselves."

"Oh my God," I said. I turned away from him, and started heading back toward the house. "Oh my God. He did *not* just say that."

"Yes, I did just say that." Jesse followed me. "I know what I saw, Susannah."

"You know what you sound like?" I asked him, turning around at the bottom of the steps to the front porch to face him. "You sound like a jealous boyfriend."

"*Nombre de Dios.* I am not," Jesse said with a laugh, "jealous of that—"

"Oh, yeah? Then where's all this hostility coming from? Tad never did anything to you."

"Tad," Jesse said, "is a . . ."

And then he said a word I couldn't understand, because it was in Spanish.

I stared at him. "A what?"

He said the word again.

"Look," I said. "Speak English."

"There is no English translation," Jesse said, setting his jaw, "for that word."

"Well," I said. "Keep it to yourself, then."

"He's no good for you," Jesse said, as if that settled the matter.

"You don't even *know* him."

"I know enough. I know you didn't listen to me or to your father when you went off tonight by yourself to that man's house."

"Right," I said. "And I'll admit, it was very, very creepy. But Tad brought me home. Tad's not the problem there. His dad's the one who is a freak, not Tad."

"The problem here," Jesse said, shaking his head, "is you, Susannah. You think you don't need anyone, that you can handle everything on your own."

"I hate to break it to you, Jesse," I said, "but I *can* handle everything on my own." Then I remembered Heather, the ghost of the girl who'd almost killed me the week before. "Well, most everything," I corrected myself.

"Ah," Jesse said. "See? You admit it. Susannah, this one—you need to ask the priest for help."

"*Fine,*" I said. "I will."

"*Fine,*" he said. "You had better."

We were so mad at each other, and had been standing there yelling so hard, our faces ended up only a few inches apart. For a split second, I stared up at Jesse, and even though I was totally mad at him, I wasn't thinking about what a self-righteous jerk he was.

Instead, I was thinking about this movie I saw once where the hero caught the heroine kissing another man, and so he grabbed her and looked down at her all passionately and said, "If kisses were what you were looking for, little fool, why didn't you come to me?"

And then he laughed this evil laugh and started kissing her.

Maybe, I couldn't help thinking, Jesse would do that, only he'd call me *querida*, like he does sometimes when he's not all mad at me for Frenching guys in cars.

And so I sort of closed my eyes, and let my mouth get all relaxed, you know, in case he decided to stick his tongue in there.

But all that happened was that the screen door slammed, and when I opened my eyes, Jesse was gone.

Instead, Doc was there standing on the front porch looking down at me, eating an ice-cream sandwich.

"Hey," Doc said, between licks. "What are you doing out here? And who were you yelling at? I could hear you all the way inside. I'm trying to watch *Nova*, you know."

Furious—but at myself more than anybody—I said, "Nobody," and stalked up the stairs and into the house.

Which was why the next day, I went to Father Dom's office first thing, and spilled my guts. No way was Jesse getting away with accusing me of thinking I don't need anyone. I need a lot of people.

And a boyfriend would be number one on that list, thank you very much.

"Sensitive to light," Father Dominic said, coming out of his thoughtful reverie. "His nickname is Red, but he doesn't have red hair. He was looking at your neck." Father Dom opened the top drawer of his desk and took out his crumpled, unopened pack of cigarettes. "Don't you see, Susannah?" he asked me.

"Sure," I said. "He's a whacko."

"I don't think so," Father Dom said. "I think he's a vampire."

CHAPTER 10

I gaped at him.

"Uh, Father D.?" I said after a while. "No offense, but have you taken too many of your pain pills, or something? Because I hate to be the one to break it to you, but there's no such thing as vampires."

Father Dom looked closer than I'd ever seen him to ripping that pack open and popping one of those cigarettes into his mouth. He restrained himself, however.

"How," he asked, "do you know?"

"How do I know what?" I demanded. "That there's no such thing as vampires? Um, the same way I know there's no Easter Bunny or Tooth Fairy."

Father Dominic said, "Ah, but people say that about ghosts. And you and I both know that that's not true."

"Yeah," I said, "but I've *seen* ghosts. I've never seen a vampire. And I've hung out in a lot of cemeteries."

Father Dominic said, "Well, not to state the obvious, Susannah, but I've been around a good deal longer than you have and while I myself have never before encountered a vampire, I am at least willing to concede the possibility of such a creature existing."

"Yeah," I said. "Okay, Father D. Let's just go out on a limb here and say the guy's a vampire. Red Beaumont is a very high-profile guy. If he was going to go running around after dark biting people on the neck, somebody would notice, don't you think?"

"Not," Father Dominic said, "if he has, like you said, employees who are eager to protect him."

This was too much. I said, "Okay. This has gotten a little too Stephen King for me. I gotta get back to class or Mr. Walden's going to think I'm AWOL. But if I get a note from you later saying I'm gonna have to stake this guy in the heart, all bets are off. Tad Beaumont will so totally not ask me to the prom if I kill his dad."

Father Dominic put the cigarettes aside. "This," he said, "is going to take some research. . . ."

I left Father Dominic doing what he loved best, which was surfing the Net. The Mission's administrative offices had only recently gotten computers, and no one there really knew how to use them very well. Father Dominic in particular had no idea how a mouse worked, and was constantly sweeping it from one side of his desk to the other, no matter how many times I told him all he had to do was keep it on the mouse pad. It would have been cute if it hadn't been so frustrating.

I decided, as I walked down the breezeway, that I would have to get CeeCee on the job. She was a little more adept at surfing the Web than Father Dominic.

As I approached Mr. Walden's classroom—which last week had unfortunately received the brunt of the damage from what everyone had assumed was a freak earthquake, but which had actually been an exorcism gone awry—I noticed, standing to one side of the pile of rubble that had once been a decorative arch, a little boy.

It wasn't unusual to see very little kids hanging around the halls of the Mission Academy since the school had classes from kindergarten all the way up to twelfth grade. What was unusual about this kid, however, was that he was glowing a little.

And also, the construction workers who were swarming around trying to put the breezeway back up occasionally walked right through him.

He looked up at me as I approached, as if he'd been waiting for me. Which, in fact, he had been.

"Hey," he said.

"Hi," I said. The workmen were playing the radio pretty loud, so fortunately none of them noticed the weird girl standing there talking to herself.

"You the mediator?" the kid wanted to know.

"One of them," I said.

"Good. I got a problem."

I looked down at him. He couldn't have been more than nine or ten years old. Then I remembered that the other day at lunch, the Mission's bells had rung out nine times, and CeeCee had explained it was because one of the third graders had died after a long bout with cancer. You couldn't tell it to look at the kid—the dead I encounter never wear outward signs of the cause of their death, assuming instead the form in which they'd lived before whatever illness or accident had taken their lives—but this little guy had apparently had a wicked case of leukemia. Timothy, I thought CeeCee had said his name was.

"You're Timothy Mahern," I said.

"Tim," he corrected me, making a face.

"Sorry. What can I do for you?"

Timothy, all business, said, "It's about my cat."

I nodded. "Of course. What about your cat?"

"My mom doesn't want him around," Timothy said. For a dead kid, he was surprisingly straightforward. "Every time she sees him, he reminds her of me so she starts crying."

"I see," I said. "Would you like me to find your cat another home?"

"That's the basic idea," Timothy said.

I was thinking that about the last thing I wanted to

deal with right then was finding some mangy cat a new home, but I smiled gamely and said, "No problem."

"Great," Timothy said. "There's just one catch. . . ."

Which was how, after school that day, I found myself standing in a field behind the Carmel Valley mall, yelling, "Here, kitty, kitty, kitty!"

Adam, whose help—and car—I'd enlisted, was the one beating the tall yellow grass since I'd shown him my poison-oaky hands and explained that I could not possibly be expected to venture anywhere near vegetation. He straightened, lifted a hand to wipe the sweat from his forehead—the sun was beaming down hard enough to make me long for the beach with its cool ocean breezes and, more importantly, totally hot lifeguards—and said, "Okay. I get that it's important that we find this dead kid's cat. But why are we looking for it in a field? Wouldn't it be smarter to look for it at the kid's house?"

"No," I said. "Timothy's father couldn't stand listening to his wife cry every time she saw the cat, so he just packed it up in the car and dumped it out here."

"Nice of him," Adam said. "A real animal lover. I suppose it would have been too much trouble to take the cat to the animal shelter where someone might have adopted it."

"Apparently," I said, "there isn't a whole lot of chance of anybody adopting this cat." I cleared my throat. "It might be a good idea for us to call him by his name. Maybe he'd come then."

"Okay." Adam pulled up his chinos. "What's his name?"

"Um," I said. "Spike."

"Spike." Adam looked heavenward. "A cat called Spike. This I can't wait to see. Here, Spike. Here, Spikey, Spikey, Spikey . . ."

"Hey, you guys." CeeCee came toward us waving her laptop in the air.

I'd enlisted CeeCee's help as well as Adam's, only with a project of a different nature. All of my new friends, I'd discovered, had different talents and abilities. Adam's lay primarily in the fact that he owned a car, but CeeCee's strengths lay in her superlative research skills . . . and what's more, in the fact that she actually *liked* looking stuff up. I'd asked her to look up what she could on Thaddeus Beaumont Senior, and she'd obliged. She'd been sitting in the car cruising the Net with the help of the remote modem she'd gotten for her birthday—have I mentioned that everyone in Carmel, with the exception of myself, is way rich?— while Adam and I looked for Tim's cat.

"Hey," CeeCee said. "Get a load of this." She skimmed something she'd downloaded. "I ran the name Thaddeus Beaumont through a search engine, and came up with dozens of hits. Thaddeus Beaumont is listed as CEO, partner, or investor in over thirty land development projects—most of which, by the way, are commercial ventures, like cineplexes, strip malls, or health clubs—on the Monterey peninsula alone."

"What does that mean?" Adam asked.

"It means that if you add up the number of acres owned by companies that list Thaddeus Beaumont as either an investor or a partner, he becomes roughly the largest land owner in northern California."

"Wow," I said. I was thinking about the prom. I bet a guy who owned that much land could afford to rent his son a stretch limo for the night. Dorky, I know, but I'd always wanted to ride in one.

"But he doesn't really own all that land," Adam pointed out. "The companies do."

"Exactly," CeeCee said.

"Exactly what do you mean by 'exactly'?"

"Well," CeeCee said, "just that it might explain why it is that the guy hasn't been hauled into court for suspicion of murder."

"Murder?" Suddenly, I forgot all about the prom. "What about a murder?"

"A murder?" CeeCee spun her laptop around so that we could see the screen. "We're talking multiple murders. Although technically, the victims have all been listed only as missing."

"What are you *talking* about?"

"Well, after I made a list of all of the companies affiliated with Thaddeus Beaumont, I entered each company name into that same search engine and came up with a couple of pretty disturbing things. Look here." CeeCee had pulled up a map of the Carmel Valley. She highlighted the areas she was talking about as she mentioned them. "See this property here? Hotel and spa. See how close it is to the water? That was a no-building zone. Too much erosion. But RedCo—that's the name of the corporation that bought the land, RedCo, get it?—used some pull down at city hall and got a permit anyway. Still, this one environmentalist warned RedCo that any building they put up there would not only be dangerously unstable, but would endanger the seal population that hangs out on the beach below it. Well, check this out."

CeeCee's fingers flew over her keyboard. A second later, a picture of a weird-looking guy with a goatee filled the screen, along with what looked like a news-paper story. "The environmentalist who was making such a fuss over the seals disappeared four years ago, and no one has seen him since."

I squinted at the computer screen. It was hard to see in the strong sunlight. "What do you mean, disap-peared?" I asked. "Like, he died?"

"Maybe. Nobody knows. His body was never found if he was killed," CeeCee said. "But check this out." Her fingers did some quick rat-tat-tatting. "Another project, this strip mall here, was endangering the habitat of this rare kind of mouse, found only in this area. And this lady here—" Another photo came up on screen. "She tried to stop it to save the mouse, and poof. She disappeared, too."

"Disappeared," I echoed. "Just disappeared?"

"Just disappeared. Problem solved for Mount Beau—that was the name of that project's sponsor. Mount Beau. Beaumont. Get it?"

"We get it," Adam said. "But if all these environmentalists connected with Red Beaumont's companies are disappearing, how come nobody has looked into it?"

"Well, for one thing," CeeCee said, "Beaumont Industries made one of the biggest campaign donations in the state to our recently elected governor. They also made considerable contributions to the guy who was voted sheriff."

"A cover-up?" Adam made a face. "Come *on*."

"You're assuming anyone even suspects anything. These people aren't dead, remember. Just gone. Near as I can tell, the attitude seems to be, well, environmentalists are kind of flighty anyway, so who's to say these folks didn't just take off for some bigger, more menacing disaster? All except this one." CeeCee hit another button, and a third photo filled the page. "This lady didn't belong to any kooky save-the-seals group. She owned some land Beaumont Industries had its eye on. They wanted to expand one of their cineplexes. Only she wouldn't sell."

"Don't tell me," I said. "She disappeared."

"Sure did. And seven years later to the day—seven years being the time after which you can legally declare a missing person dead—Beaumont Industries made an offer to her kids, who jumped on it."

"Finks," I said, meaning the lady's kids. I leaned forward so I could get a better look at her picture.

And had quite a little shock: I was looking at a picture of the ghost who'd been paying me those charming social calls.

Okay, well, maybe she didn't look *exactly* the same. But she was white and skinny and had the same hair-cut. There was certainly enough of a resemblance to make me go, "That's her!" and point.

Which was, of course, the worst thing I could have done. Because both CeeCee and Adam turned to look at me.

"That's her who?" Adam wanted to know.

And CeeCee said, "Suze, you can't possibly know her. She disappeared over seven years ago, and you just moved here last month."

I am such a loser.

I couldn't even think of a good excuse, either. I just repeated the one I'd stammered to Tad's father: "Oh, um, I had this dream and she was in it."

What was *wrong* with me?

I had not, of course, explained to CeeCee the reason why I'd wanted her to look up stuff on Red Beaumont, any more than I had told Adam how it was that I knew so much about little Timothy Mahern's cat. I had merely mentioned that Mr. Beaumont had said something odd during my brief meeting with him the night before. And that Father Dom had sent me to look for the cat, presumably because Timothy's dad had admitted abandoning it during his weekly confession—only Father Dom, being sworn to secrecy, couldn't actually *tell* me that. I was only, I assured Adam, *surmising.* . . .

"A dream?" Adam echoed. "About some lady who's been dead for seven years? That's weird."

"It probably wasn't her," I said quickly, backpedaling for all I was worth. "In fact, I'm sure it wasn't her. The woman I saw was much . . . taller." Like I could even tell how tall this woman was by looking at her picture somebody had posted on the Internet.

Adam said, "You know, CeeCee has an aunt who dreams about dead people all the time. They visit her, she says."

I threw CeeCee a startled glance. Could we, I wondered, be talking about *another* mediator? What, was there some kind of glut of us in the greater peninsula area? I knew Carmel was a popular retirement spot, but this was getting ridiculous.

"She doesn't have dreams about them," CeeCee said, and I didn't think I was imagining the level of disgust in her voice. "Aunt Pru summons the spirits of the dead and she'll tell you what they said. For a small fee."

"Aunt *Pru*?" I grinned. "Wow, CeeCee. I didn't know you had a psychic in the family."

"She isn't a psychic." CeeCee's disgust deepened. "She's a complete flake. I'm embarrassed to be related to her. Talk to the dead. Right!"

"Don't hold back, CeeCee," I said. "Let us know how you really feel."

"Well," CeeCee said. "I'm sorry. But—"

"Hey," Adam interrupted brightly. "Maybe Aunt Pru could help tell us why"—he bent down for a closer look at the dead woman's photo on CeeCee's computer screen—"Mrs. Deirdre Fiske here is popping up in Suze's dreams."

Horrified, I leaned forward and slammed CeeCee's laptop closed. "No thanks," I said.

CeeCee, opening her computer back up again, said irritably, "Nobody fondles the electronics but me, Simon."

"Aw, come on," Adam said. "It'll be fun. Suze's never met Pru. She'll get a big kick out of her. She's a riot."

CeeCee muttered, "Yeah, you know how funny the mentally ill can be."

I said, hoping to get the subject back on track, "Um, maybe some other time. Anything else, CeeCee, that you were able to dig up on Mr. Beaumont?"

"You mean other than the fact that he might possibly be killing anyone who stands in the way of his amassing a fortune by raping our forests and beaches?" CeeCee, who was wearing a khaki rainhat to protect her sensitive skin from the sun, as well as her violet-lensed sunglasses, looked up at me. "You're not satisfied yet, Simon? Haven't we thoroughly vetted your paramour's closest relations?"

"Yeah," Adam said. "It must be reassuring to know that last night you hooked up with a guy who comes from such a nice, stable family, Suze."

"Hey," I said with an indignation I was far from actually feeling. "There's no *proof* Tad's dad is the one who's responsible for those environmentalists' disappearances. And besides, we just had coffee, okay? We did not hook up."

CeeCee blinked at me. "You went out with him, Suze. That's all Adam meant by hooking up."

"Oh." Where I come from, hooking up means something else entirely. "Sorry. I—"

At that moment, Adam let out a shout. "Spike!"

I whirled around, following his pointing finger. There, peering out from the dry underbrush, sat the biggest, meanest-looking cat I'd ever seen. He was the same color yellow as the grass, which was probably how we'd missed him. He had orange stripes, one chewed-off ear, and an extremely nasty look on his face.

"Spike?" I asked, softly.

The cat turned his head in my direction and glared

at me malevolently.

"Oh my God," I said. "No wonder Tim's dad didn't take him to the animal shelter."

It took some doing—and the ultimate sacrifice of my Kate Spade book bag, which I'd managed to purchase only at great physical risk at a sample sale back in SoHo—but we finally managed to capture Spike. Once he was zipped up inside my bag, he seemed to resign himself to captivity, although throughout the ride to Safeway, where we went to stock up on litter and food for him, I could hear him working industriously on the bag's lining with his claws. Timothy, I decided, owed me big time.

Especially when Adam, instead of turning up the street to my house, turned in the opposite direction, heading farther up the Carmel hills until the big red dome covering the basilica of the Mission below us was the size of my thumbnail.

"No," CeeCee immediately said as firmly as I've ever heard her say anything. "Absolutely not. Turn the car around. Turn the car around *now*."

Only Adam, chuckling diabolically, just sped up.

Holding my Kate Spade bag on my lap, I said, "Uh, Adam. I don't know where, exactly, you think you're going, but I'd really like to at least get rid of this, um, animal first—"

"Just for a minute," Adam said. "The cat'll be all right. Come *on*, Cee. Stop being such a spoilsport."

CeeCee was madder than I'd ever seen her. "I said *no*!" she shouted.

But it was too late. Adam pulled up in front of a little stucco bungalow that had wind chimes hanging all over the place tinkling in the breeze from the bay, and giant hibiscus blossoms turned up toward the late afternoon sun. He put his VW in park and switched off the ignition.

"We'll just pop in to say hi," he said to CeeCee. And then he unfastened his seat belt and hopped out of the car.

CeeCee and I didn't move. She was in the backseat. I was in the front with the cat. From my bag came an ominous rumbling.

"I hesitate to ask," I said, after a while of sitting there listening to the wind chimes and Spike's steady growling. "But where are we?"

That question was answered when, a second later, the door to the bungalow burst open and a woman whose hair was the same whitish yellow as CeeCee's— only so long that she could sit on it—yoo-hooed at us.

"Come in," CeeCee's aunt Pru called. "Please come in! I've been expecting you!"

CeeCee, not even glancing in her aunt's direction, muttered, "I just bet you have, you psychic freak."

Remind me never to tell CeeCee about the whole mediator thing.

CHAPTER 11

"Oh, goodness," CeeCee's aunt Pru said. "There it is again. The ninth key. This is just so strange."

CeeCee and I exchanged glances. Strange wasn't quite the word for it.

Not that it was unpleasant. Far from it. At least, in my opinion, anyway. Pru Webb, CeeCee's aunt, was a little odd. That was certainly true.

But her house was very aromatic what with all the scented candles she kept lit everywhere. And she'd been quite the attentive hostess, giving us each a glass of homemade lemonade. It was too bad, of course, that she'd forgotten to put sugar in it, but that kind of forgetfulness apparently wasn't unusual for someone so in touch with the spirit world. Aunt Pru had informed us that her mentor, the most powerful psychic on the West Coast, often couldn't remember his own name because he was channeling so many other souls.

Still, our little visit hadn't been particularly enlightening so far. I had learned, for instance, that according to the lines in my palm, I am going to grow up to have a challenging job in the field of medical research (Yeah! That'll be the day). CeeCee, meanwhile, is going to be a movie star, and Adam an astronaut.

Seriously. An *astronaut*.

I was, I admit, a little jealous of their future careers, which were clearly a great deal more exciting than my own, but I tried hard to control my envy.

What I'd given up trying to control—and CeeCee apparently had as well—was Adam. He had told Aunt Pru, before I could stop him, about my "dream," and now the poor woman was trying—pro bono, mind you—to summon Deirdre Fiske's spirit using tarot cards and a lot of humming.

Only it did not appear to be working because every time she started to turn the cards over, she kept coming up with the same one.

The ninth key.

This was, apparently, upsetting to her. Shaking her head, Aunt Pru—that's what she'd told me to call her—scooped all the cards back into a pile, shuffled them, and then, closing her eyes, pulled one from the middle of the deck, and laid it, face up, for us to see.

Then she opened her eyes, looked down at it, and went, "Again! This doesn't make any sense."

She wasn't kidding. The idea of anyone summoning a ghost with a deck of cards made no sense whatsoever . . . to me, at least. I couldn't even summon them by standing there screaming their names—something I'd tried, believe me—and I'm a mediator. My *job* is to communicate with the undead.

But ghosts aren't dogs. They don't come if you call them. Take my dad, for instance. How many times had I wanted—even needed—him? He'd shown up, all right: three, four weeks later. Ghosts are way irresponsible for the most part.

But I couldn't exactly explain to CeeCee's aunt that what she was doing was a huge waste of time . . . and that while she was sitting there doing it, there was a cat trying to eat his way out of my book bag in Adam's car.

Oh, and that a guy who might or might not have been a vampire—but was certainly responsible for the disappearances of quite a number of people—was running around loose. I could only just sit there with this big stupid smile on my face, pretending to be enjoying myself, while really I was itching to get home and on the phone with Father D., so we could figure out what we were going to do about Red Beaumont.

"Oh, dear," Aunt Pru said. She was very pretty, CeeCee's aunt Pru. An albino like her niece, her eyes were the color of violets. She wore a flowing sundress of the same shade. The contrast her long white hair made against the purple of her dress was startling—and cool. CeeCee, I knew, was probably going to look just like her aunt Pru someday, once she got rid of the braces and puppy fat, that is.

Which was probably why CeeCee couldn't stand her.

"What can this mean?" Aunt Pru muttered to herself. "The hermit. The hermit."

There appeared, from what I could see, to be a hermit on the card Aunt Pru kept turning over and over. Not of the crab variety, either, but the old-man-living-in-a-cave type. I didn't know what a hermit had to do with Mrs. Fiske, either, but one thing I did know: I was bored stupid.

"One more time," Aunt Pru said, sending a cautious glance in CeeCee's direction. CeeCee had made it clear that we didn't have all day. I was the one who needed to get home most, of course. I had an Ackerman dinner to contend with. Kung pao chicken night. If I was late, my mom was going to kill me.

"Um," I said. "Ms. Webb?"

"Aunt Pru, darling,"

"Right. Aunt Pru. May I use your phone?"

"Of course." Aunt Pru didn't even glance at me. She was too busy channeling.

I wandered out of the darkened room and went out

into the hallway. There was an old-fashioned rotary phone on a little table there. I dialed my own number—after a brief struggle to remember it since I'd only had it for a few weeks—and when Dopey picked up, I asked him to tell my mother that I hadn't forgotten about dinner and was on my way home.

Dopey not very graciously informed me that he was on the other line and that because he was not my social secretary, and had no intention of taking any messages for me, I should call back later.

"Who are you talking to?" I asked. "Debbie, your love slave?"

Dopey responded by hanging up on me. Some people have no sense of humor.

I put down the receiver and was standing there looking at this zodiac calendar and wondering if I was in some kind of celestial good-luck zone—considering what had happened with Tad and all—when someone standing right beside me said, in an irritated voice, "Well? What do you want?"

I jumped nearly a foot. I swear, I've been doing this all my life, but I just can't get used to it. I would so rather have some other secret power—like the ability to do long division in my head—than this mediator crap, I swear.

I spun around, and there she was, standing in Aunt Pru's entranceway, looking cranky in a gardening hat and gloves.

She was not the same woman who'd been waking me up at night. They were similar body types, little and slender, with the same pixieish haircut, but this woman was easily in her sixties.

"Well?" She eyed me. "I don't have all day. What did you call me for?"

I stared at the woman in wonder. The truth was, I hadn't called her. I hadn't done anything, except stand there and wonder if Tad was still going to like me when Mercury retrograded into Aquarius.

"Mrs. Fiske?" I whispered.

"Yes, that's me." The old lady looked me up and down. "You *are* the one who called me, aren't you?"

"Um." I glanced back toward the room where I could still hear Aunt Pru saying, apparently to herself, since neither CeeCee nor Adam could have understood what she was talking about, "But the ninth key has no *bearing* . . ."

I turned back to Mrs. Fiske. "I guess so," I said.

Mrs. Fiske looked me up and down. It was clear she didn't much like what she was seeing. "Well?" she said. "What is it?"

Where to begin? Here was a woman who'd disappeared, and been presumed dead, for almost half as long as I'd been alive. I glanced back at Aunt Pru and the others, just to make sure they weren't looking in my direction, and then whispered, "I just need to know, Mrs. Fiske . . . Mr. Beaumont. He killed you, didn't he?"

Mrs. Fiske suddenly stopped looking so crabby. Her eyes, which were very blue, fixed on mine. She said, in a shocked voice, "My God. My God, finally . . . someone knows. Someone finally knows."

I reached out to lay a reassuring hand upon her arm. "Yes, Mrs. Fiske," I said. "I know. And I'm going to stop him from hurting anybody else."

Mrs. Fiske shrugged my hand off and blinked at me. "*You?*" She still looked stunned, but now in a different way.

I realized how when she burst out laughing.

"*You're* going to stop him?" she cackled. "You're . . . you're a baby!"

"I'm no baby," I assured her. "I'm a mediator."

"A mediator?" To my surprise, Mrs. Fiske threw back her head and laughed harder. "A mediator. Oh, well, that makes it all better, doesn't it?"

I wanted to tell her I didn't really care for her tone, but Mrs. Fiske didn't give me a chance.

"And you think you can stop Beaumont?" she demanded. "Honey, you've got a lot to learn."

I didn't think this was very polite. I said, "Look, lady, I may be young, but I know what I'm doing. Now, just tell me where he hid your body, and—"

"Are you insane?" Mrs. Fiske finally stopped laughing. Now she shook her head. "There's nothing left of me. Beaumont's no amateur, you know. He made sure there weren't any mistakes. And there weren't.

You won't find a scrap of evidence to implicate him. Believe me. The guy's a monster. A real bloodsucker." Then her mouth hardened. "Though no worse, I suppose, than my own kids. Selling my land to that leech! Listen, you. You're a mediator. Give my kids this message for me: tell them I hope they burn in—"

"Hey, Suze." CeeCee suddenly appeared in the hallway. "The witch has given up. She has to consult her guru, 'cause she keeps coming up bust."

I threw a frantic look at Mrs. Fiske. Wait! I still hadn't had a chance to ask her how she'd died! Was Red Beaumont really a vampire? Had he sucked all the life out of her? Did she mean he was *literally* a bloodsucking leech?

But it was too late. CeeCee, still coming toward me, walked right through what looked—and felt—to me like a little old lady in a gardening hat and gloves. And the little old lady shimmered indignantly.

Don't, I wanted to scream. *Don't go!*

"Ew," CeeCee said with a little shudder as she threw off the last of Mrs. Fiske's clinging aura. "Come on. Let's get out of here. This place gives me the creeps."

I never did find out what Mrs. Fiske's message to her kids was—though I had a bit of an idea. The old lady, with a last, disgusted look at me, disappeared.

Just as Aunt Pru came into the hallway, looking apologetic.

"I'm so sorry, Susie," she said. "I really tried, but

the Santa Anas have been particularly strong this year, and so there's been a lot of interference in the spiritual pathways I normally utilize."

Maybe that explained how I had managed to summon the spirit of Mrs. Fiske. Could I do it again, I wondered, and this time remember to ask exactly how Red Beaumont had killed her?

Adam, as we headed back toward his car, looked immensely pleased with himself.

"Well, Suze?" he said, as he held open the passenger side door for CeeCee and me. "You ever in your life met anybody like that?"

I had, of course. Being a magnet for the souls of the unhappily dead, I'd met people from all walks of life, including an Incan priestess, several witch doctors, and even a Pilgrim who'd been burned at the stake as a witch.

But since it seemed so important to him, I smiled and said, "Not exactly," which was the truth, in a way.

CeeCee didn't look too thrilled with the fact that one of her family members had managed to provide the boy she—let's face it—had a huge crush on with so much entertainment. She crawled into the backseat and glowered there. CeeCee was a straight-A student who didn't believe in anything that couldn't be proved scientifically, especially anything to do with the hereafter . . . which made the fact that her parents had stuck her in Catholic school a bit problematic.

More problematic to me, however, than CeeCee's lack of faith or my newfound ability to summon spirits at will was what I was going to do with this cat. While we'd been inside Aunt Pru's house, he'd managed to chew a hole through one corner of my bag, and now he kept poking one paw through it, swiping blindly with claws fully outstretched at whatever came his way—primarily me, since I was the one holding the bag. Adam, no matter how hard I wheedled, wouldn't take the cat home with him, and CeeCee just laughed when I asked her. I knew there was no way I was going to talk Father Dominic into taking Spike to live in the rectory: Sister Ernestine would never allow it.

Which left me only one alternative. And I really, really wasn't happy about it. Besides what the cat had done to the inside of my bag—God only knew what he'd do to my room—there was the fact that I was pretty sure felines were verboten in the Ackerman household due to Dopey's delicate sensitivity to their dander.

So I still had the stupid cat, plus a Safeway bag containing a litter box, the litter itself, and about twenty cans of Fancy Feast, when Adam pulled up to my house to drop me off.

"Hey," he said, appreciatively, as I struggled to get out of the car. "Who's visiting you guys? The Pope?"

I looked where he was pointing . . . and then my jaw dropped.

Parked in our driveway was a big, black stretch limo, just like the kind I'd fantasized about going to prom with Tad in!

"Uh," I said, slamming the door to Adam's VW shut. "I'll see you guys."

I hurried up the driveway with Spike, determined not to be forgotten just because he'd been zipped into a book bag, growling and spitting the whole way. As I was coming up the front steps to the porch, I heard the rumble of voices coming from the living room.

And when I stepped through the front door, and I saw who those voices belonged to . . . well, Spike came pretty close to becoming a kitty pancake, I squeezed that bag so tight to my chest.

Because sitting there chatting amiably with my mother and holding a cup of tea was none other than Thaddeus "Red" Beaumont.

CHAPTER 12

"Oh, Susie," my mom said, turning around as I came into the house. "Hello, honey. Look who stopped by to see you. Mr. Beaumont and his son."

It was only then that I noticed Tad was there, too. He was standing by the wall that had all of our family photos on it—which weren't many since we'd only been a family for a few weeks. Mostly they were just school photos of me and my stepbrothers, and pictures from Andy and my mom's wedding.

Tad grinned at me, then pointed at a photo of me at the age of ten—in which I was missing both my front teeth—and said, "Nice smile."

I managed to give him a reasonable facsimile of that smile, minus the missing teeth. "Hi," I said.

"Tad and Mr. Beaumont were on their way home," my mom said, "and they thought they'd stop by and see if you'd have dinner with them tonight. I told them I didn't think you had any other plans. You don't, do you, Suze?"

My mom, I could tell, was practically frothing at the mouth at the idea of me having dinner with this guy and his kid. My mom would have frothed at the mouth at the idea of me having dinner with Darth Vader and his kid, that's how hot she was to get me a boyfriend. All my mom has ever wanted is for me to be a normal teenage girl.

But if she thought Red Beaumont was prime in-law material, boy, was she barking up the wrong tree.

And speaking of barking, I had suddenly become an object of considerable interest to Max, who had started sniffing around my book bag and whining.

"Um," I said. "Would you mind if I just ran upstairs and, um, dumped my stuff off?"

"Not at all," Mr. Beaumont said. "Not at all. Take your time. I was just telling your mother about your article. The one you're doing for the school paper."

"Yes, Susie," my mom said, turning around in her seat with this huge smile. "You never told me you were working for the school paper. How exciting!"

I looked at Mr. Beaumont. He smiled blandly back at me.

And suddenly, I had a very bad feeling.

Oh, not that Mr. Beaumont was going to get up, come over, and bite me on the neck. Not that.

But all of a sudden, I got this very bad feeling that he was going to tell my mother the real reason I'd gone to visit him the night before. Not the newspaper article thing, but the thing about my dream.

Which my mom would instantly suspect was you-know-what. If she heard I'd been going around feeding wealthy real estate tycoons lines about psychic dreams, I'd be grounded from now until graduation.

And the worst part of it was, considering how much trouble I used to be in all the time back in New York, I wasn't at all eager to let my mom in on the fact that I was actually up to even *more* stuff on *this* side of the country. I mean, she really had no clue. She thought all of it—the fact that I'd constantly missed my curfew, my run-ins with the police, my suspensions, the bad grades—were behind us, over, kaput, the end. We were on a new coast, making a new start.

And my mom was just so *happy* about it.

So I said, "Oh, yeah, the *article* I'm doing," and gave Mr. Beaumont a meaningful look. At least, I hoped it would be meaningful. And I hoped what it meant to him was: Don't spill the beans, buster, or you'll pay for it big time.

Though I'm not certain how scared a guy like Red Beaumont would actually be of a sixteen-year-old girl.

He wasn't. He sent a look right back at me. A look

394

that said, if I wasn't mistaken: I won't spill the beans, sister, if you play along like a good little girl.

I nodded to let him know I'd gotten the message, whirled around, and hurried up the stairs.

Well, I figured as I went, Max loping at my heels, still trying to get a gander into my bag, at least Tad was with him. Mr. Beaumont certainly wasn't going to be able to bite me on the neck with his own kid in the room. Tad, I was pretty sure, wasn't a vampire. And he didn't seem like the kind of guy who'd just stand by and let his dad kill his date.

And with any luck, that guy Marcus would be there. Marcus certainly wouldn't allow his employer to sink his fangs into me.

I wasn't too surprised when, as we reached the door to my bedroom, Max suddenly turned tail and, with a yelp, ran in the opposite direction. He wasn't too thrilled by Jesse's presence.

Neither, I figured, was Spike going to be. But Spike didn't have any other choice.

I went into my room and took the litter box out of my giant Safeway bag and shoved it under the sink in my bathroom, then filled it with litter. From the center of my room where I'd left my book bag came some pretty unearthly howling. That paw kept shooting out of the hole Spike had chewed, feeling around for something to claw.

"I'm going as fast as I can," I grumbled as I poured

some water into a bowl then opened a can of food and left it on a plate on the floor along with the water.

Then, making sure I unzipped it away from me, I opened the bag.

Spike came tearing out like . . . well, more like the Tasmanian Devil than any cat I'd ever seen. He was completely out of control. He tore around the room three times before he spotted the food, skidded suddenly to a halt, and began to suck it down.

"What," I heard Jesse say, "is *that*?"

I looked up. I hadn't seen Jesse since our fight the night before. He was leaning against one of my bedposts—my mom had gone whole hog when she'd decorated my room, going for the frilly dressing table, canopy bed, the works—looking down at the cat like it was some kind of alien life form.

"It's a cat," I said. "I didn't have any choice. It's just until I find a home for it."

Jesse eyed Spike dubiously. "Are you sure it's a cat? It doesn't look like any cat I've ever seen. It looks more like . . . what do they call them? Those small horses. Oh yes, a pony."

"I'm sure it's a cat," I said. "Listen, Jesse, I'm kind of in a jam here."

He nodded at Spike. "I can see that."

"Not about the cat," I said, quickly. "It's about Tad."

Jesse's expression, which had been a fairly pleasant, teasing one, suddenly darkened. If I hadn't been sure he didn't give a hang about me aside from as a friend, I'd have sworn he was jealous.

"He's downstairs," I said quickly, before Jesse could start yelling at me again for being too easy on a first date. "With his father. They want me to come over for dinner. And I'm not going to be able to get out of it."

Jesse muttered some stuff in Spanish. Judging from the look on his face, whatever he said hadn't exactly been an expression of regret that he, too, had not been invited.

"The thing is," I went on, "I've found out some things about Mr. Beaumont, things that kind of make me . . . well, nervous. So could you, um, do me a favor?"

Jesse straightened. He seemed pretty surprised. I don't really ask him to do me favors all that often.

"Of course, *querida*," he said, and my heart gave a little flip-flop inside my chest at the caressing tone he always gave that word. I didn't even know what it meant.

Why am I so *pathetic*?

"Look," I said, my voice squeakier than ever, unfortunately, "if I'm not back by midnight, can you just let Father Dominic know that he should probably call the police?"

As I'd been speaking, I'd taken out a new bag, a Kate Spade knockoff, and I was slipping the stuff I normally use for ghost-busting into it. You know, my flashlight, pliers, gloves, the roll of dimes I keep in my fist ever since my mom found and confiscated my brass knuckles, pepper spray, bowie knife, and, oh yeah, a pencil. It was the best I could come up with in lieu of a wooden stake. I don't believe in vampires, but I do believe in being prepared.

"You want *me* to speak to the priest?"

Jesse sounded shocked. I guess I couldn't blame him. While I'd never exactly forbidden him from speaking to Father Dom, I'd never actually encouraged him, either. I certainly hadn't told him why I was so reluctant for the two of them to meet—Father D. was sure to have an embolism over the living arrangements—but I hadn't exactly given him the all clear to go strolling into Father Dominic's office.

"Yes," I said. "I do."

Jesse looked confused. "But Susannah," he said. "If he's this dangerous, this man, why are you—"

Someone tapped on my bedroom door. "Susie?" my mom called. "You decent?"

I grabbed my bag. "Yeah, Mom," I said. I threw Jesse one last, pleading look, and then I hurried from the room, careful not to let out Spike, who'd finished his meal and was doing some pretty serious nosing around for more food.

In the hallway, my mother looked at me curiously. "Is everything all right, Susie?" she asked me. "You were up here for so long. . . ."

"Uh, yeah," I said. "Listen, Mom—"

"Susie, I didn't know things were so serious with this boy." My mom took my arm and started steering me back down the stairs. "He's so handsome! And so sweet! It's just so adorable, his wanting you to have dinner with him and his father."

I wondered how sweet she'd have thought it if she'd known about Mrs. Fiske. My mom had been a television news journalist for over twenty years. She'd won a couple of national awards for some of her investigations, and when she'd first started looking for a job on the West Coast, she'd pretty much had her pick of news stations.

And a sixteen-year-old albino with a laptop and a modem knew a heck of a lot more about Red Beaumont than she did.

It just goes to show that people only know what they want to.

"Yeah," I said. "About Mr. Beaumont, Mom. I don't think I really—"

"And what's all this about you writing a story for the school paper? Suze, I didn't know you were interested in journalism."

My mom looked almost as happy as she had the day she and Andy had finally tied the knot. And considering that that was about as happy as I'd ever seen her—since my dad had died, anyway—that was pretty happy.

"Susie, I'm just so proud of you," she gushed. "You

really are finding yourself out here. You know how I used to worry, back in New York. You always seemed to be getting into trouble. But it looks as if things are really turning around . . . for the both of us."

This was when I should have said, "Listen, Mom. About Red Beaumont? Okay, definitely up to no good, possibly a *vampire*. Enough said. Now could you tell him I've got a migraine and that I can't go to dinner?"

But I didn't. I couldn't. I just kept remembering that look Mr. Beaumont had given me. He was going to tell my mother. He was going to tell my mother the truth. About how I'd busted into his place under false pretenses, about that dream I'd said I'd had.

About how I can talk to the dead.

No. No, that was not going to happen. I had finally gotten to a point in my life where my mom was beginning to be proud of me, to trust me, even. It was kind of like New York had been this really bad nightmare from which she and I had finally woken up. Here in California I was popular. I was normal. I was cool. I was the kind of daughter my mom had always wanted instead of the social reject who'd constantly been dragged home by the police for trespassing and creating a public nuisance. I was no longer forced to lie to a therapist twice a week. I wasn't serving permanent detention. I didn't have to listen to my mother cry into her pillow at night, or notice her surreptitiously starting a Valium regimen whenever parent-teacher conferences rolled around.

Hey, with the exception of the poison oak, even my skin had cleared up. I was a completely different kid.

I took a deep breath.

"Sure, Mom," I said. "Sure, things are really turning around for us."

CHAPTER 13

He didn't eat.

He'd invited me to dinner, but he didn't eat.

Tad did. Tad ate a lot.

Well, boys always do. I mean, look at mealtime in the Ackerman household. It was like something out of a Jack London novel. Only instead of White Fang and the rest of the sled dogs, you have Sleepy, Dopey, and even Doc, chowing down like it might be their last meal.

At least Tad had good manners. He'd held my chair for me as I'd sat down. He actually employed a napkin, instead of simply wiping his hands on his pants, one of Dopey's favorite tricks. And he made sure I was served first, so there was plenty to go around.

Especially since his father wasn't eating.

But he did sit with us. He sat at the head of the table with a glass of red wine—at least, it *looked* like wine—and beamed at me as each course was presented. You read that right: courses. I'd never had a meal with courses before. I mean, Andy was a good cook and all, but he usually served everything all at once—you know, entree, salad, rolls, the whole thing at the same time.

At Red Beaumont's house, the courses all came individually, served by waiters with this big flourish; two waiters, so that each of our plates—Tad's and mine, I mean—were put down at the same time, and nobody's food got cold while he or she was waiting for everyone else to be served.

The first course was a consommé, which turned out to have bits of lobster floating in it. That was pretty good. Then came some kind of fancy sea scallops in this tangy green sauce. Then came lamb with garlic mashed potatoes, then salad, a mess of weeds with balsamic vinegar all over them, followed by a tray on which there were all these different kinds of stinky cheeses.

And Mr. Beaumont didn't touch a thing. He said he was on a special diet and had already had his dinner.

And even though I don't believe in vampires, I just kept sitting there wondering what his special diet consisted of, and if Mrs. Fiske and those missing environmentalists had provided any part of it.

I know. I *know*. But I couldn't help it. It was creeping me out the way he just sat there drinking his wine and smiling as Tad chatted about basketball. From what I could gather—I was having trouble concentrating, what with wondering why Father D. hadn't given me a bottle of holy water when he'd first realized there might be a chance we were dealing with a vampire— Tad was Robert Louis Stevenson's star player.

As I sat there listening to Tad go on about all the three-pointers he'd scored, I realized with a sinking heart that not only was he possibly the descendant of a vampire, but also that, except for kissing, he and I really had no mutual interests. I mean, I don't have a whole lot of time for hobbies, what with homework and the mediating stuff, but I was pretty sure if I'd had an interest, it wouldn't be chasing a ball up and down a wooden court.

But maybe kissing was enough. Maybe kissing was the only thing that mattered, anyway. Maybe kissing could overcome the whole vampire/basketball thing.

Because as we got up from the table to go to the living room, where dessert, I was told, would be served, Tad picked up my hand—which was, by the way, still a bit poison oaky, but he evidently didn't care; there was still a healthy amount of it on the back of his neck, after all—and gave it a squeeze.

And all of a sudden I was convinced that I had

probably way overreacted back home when I'd asked Jesse to have Father Dominic call the cops if I wasn't home by midnight. I mean, yeah, there were people who might think Red Beaumont was a vampire, and he certainly may have made his fortune in a creepy way.

But that didn't necessarily make him a bad guy. And we didn't have any actual *proof* he really had killed all those people. And what about that dead woman who kept showing up in my bedroom? She was convinced Red *hadn't* killed her. She'd gone to great lengths to assure me that he was innocent of her death, at least. Maybe Mr. Beaumont wasn't that bad.

"I thought you were mad at me," Tad whispered as we followed Yoshi, who was carrying a tray of coffee—herbal tea for me—into the living room ahead of us.

"Why should I be mad at you?" I asked, curiously.

"Well, last night," Tad whispered, "when I was kissing you—"

All at once I remembered how I'd seen Jesse sitting there, and how I'd screamed bloody murder over it. Blushing, I said, unable to look Tad in the eye, "Oh, that. That was just . . . I thought . . . I saw a spider."

"A spider?" Tad pulled me down onto this black leather couch next to him. In front of the couch there was a big coffee table that looked like it was made out of Plexiglas. "In my *car*?"

"I've got a thing about spiders," I said.

"Oh." Tad looked at me with his sleepy brown eyes. "I thought maybe you thought I was—well, a little forward. Kissing you like that, I mean."

"Oh, no," I said with a laugh that I hoped sounded all sophisticated, as if guys were going around sticking their tongues in my mouth all the time.

"Good," Tad said, and he put his arm around my neck and started pulling me toward him—

But then his dad walked in, and went, "Now, where were we? Oh, yes. Susannah, you were going to tell us all about how your class is trying to raise money to restore the statue of Father Serra that was so unfortunately vandalized last week. . . ."

Tad and I pulled quickly apart.

"Uh, sure," I said. And I started telling the long, boring tale, which actually involved a bake sale, of all things. As I was telling it, Tad reached over to the massive glass coffee table in front of him and picked up a cup of coffee. He put cream and sugar into it, and then took a sip.

"And then," I said, really convinced now that the whole thing had been a giant misunderstanding— the thing about Tad's dad, I mean—"we found out it's actually cheaper to get a whole new statue cast than to repair the old one, but then it wouldn't be an authentic . . . well, whoever the artist is, I forget. So we're still trying to figure it out. If we repair the old one, there'll be a seam that will show where the neck was reattached, but we could hide the seam if we raise the collar of Father Serra's cassock. So there's some wrangling going on about the historical accuracy of a high-collared cassock, and—"

It was at this point in my narration that Tad suddenly pitched forward and plowed face-first into my lap.

I blinked down at him. Was I really *that* boring? God, no wonder no one had ever asked me out before.

Then I realized Tad wasn't asleep at all. He was *unconscious*.

I looked over at Mr. Beaumont, who was gazing sadly at his son from the leather couch opposite mine.

"Oh my God," I said.

Mr. Beaumont sighed. "Fast-acting, isn't it?" he said.

Horrified, I exclaimed, "God, poison your kid, why don't you?"

"He hasn't been poisoned," Mr. Beaumont said, looking appalled. "Do you think I would do something like that to my own boy? He's merely drugged, of course. In a few hours he'll wake up and not remember a thing. He'll just feel extremely well rested."

I was struggling to push Tad off me. The guy wasn't huge or anything, but he was dead weight, and it was no easy task getting his face out of my lap.

"Listen," I said to Mr. Beaumont as I struggled to squirm out from under his son, "you better not try anything."

With one hand I pushed Tad, while with the other I surreptitiously unzipped my bag. I hadn't let it out of my sight since I'd entered the house, in spite of the fact that Yoshi had tried to take it and put it with my coat. A few squirts of pepper spray, I decided, would suit Mr. Beaumont very nicely in the event that he tried anything physical.

"I mean it," I assured him, as I slipped a hand inside my bag and fumbled around inside it for the pepper spray. "It would be a really bad idea for you to mess with me, Mr. Beaumont. I'm not who you think I am."

Mr. Beaumont just looked more sad when he heard that. He said, with another big sigh, "Neither am I."

"No," I said. I had found the pepper spray, and now, one-handed, I worked the little plastic safety cap off it. "You think I'm just some stupid girl your son's brought home for dinner. But I'm not."

"Of course you're not," Mr. Beaumont said. "That's why it was so important that I speak with you again. You talk to the dead, and I, you see . . ."

I eyed him suspiciously. "You what?"

"Well." He looked embarrassed. "I make them that way."

What had that dopey lady in my bedroom meant when she insisted he hadn't tried to kill her? Of course he had! Just like he'd killed Mrs. Fiske!

Just like he was getting ready to kill me.

"Don't think I don't appreciate your sense of humor, Mr. Beaumont," I said. "Because I do. I really do. I think you're a very funny guy. So I hope you won't take this personally—"

And I sprayed him, full in the face.

Or at least I meant to. I held the nozzle in his direction and I pressed down on it. Only all that came out was sort of a *spliff* noise.

No paralyzing pepper spray, though. None at all.

And then I remembered that bottle of Paul Mitchell styling spritz that had leaked all over the bottom of my bag the last time I was at the beach. That stuff, mixed with sand, had gunked up nearly everything I owned. And now, it seemed, it had coated the hole my pepper spray was supposed to squirt out of.

"Oh," Mr. Beaumont said. He looked very disappointed in me. "Mace? Now is that fair, Susannah?"

I knew what I had to do. I threw down the useless bottle and started to make a run for it—

Too late, however. He lashed out—so suddenly, I didn't even have time to move—and seized my wrist in a grip that, let me tell you, hurt quite a bit.

"You better let go of me," I advised him. "I mean it. You'll regret it—"

But he ignored me, and spoke without the least bit of animosity, almost as if I hadn't just tried to paralyze his mucous membranes.

"I'm sorry if I seemed flippant before," he said,

apologetically. "But I really mean it. I have, unfortunately, made some very serious errors in judgment that have resulted in several persons losing their lives, and at my own hands. . . . It is imperative that you help me speak to them, to assure them that I am very, very sorry for what I've done."

I blinked at him. "Okay," I said. "That's it. I'm out of here."

But no matter how hard I pulled on my arm, I couldn't break free of his viselike grip. The guy was surprisingly strong for someone's dad.

"I know that to you I seem horrible," he went on. "A monster, even. But I'm not. I'm really not."

"Tell that to Mrs. Fiske," I grunted as I tugged on my arm.

Mr. Beaumont didn't seem to have heard me. "You can't imagine what it's like. The hours I've spent torturing myself over what I've done . . ."

With my free hand, I was rooting through my bag again. "Well, a real good prescriptive for guilt, I've always found, is confessing." My fingers closed over the roll of dimes. No. No good. He had my best punching arm. "Why don't you let me make a phone call, and we can get the police over here, and you can tell them all about it. How does that sound?"

"No," Mr. Beaumont said, solemnly. "That's no good. I highly doubt the police would have any respect whatsoever for my somewhat, well, *special* needs. . . ."

And then Mr. Beaumont did something totally unexpected. He smiled at me. Ruefully, but still, a smile.

He had smiled at me before, of course, but I had always been across the room, or at least the width of a coffee table away. Now I was right there, right in his face.

And when he smiled, I was given a very special glimpse of something I certainly never expected to see in my lifetime:

The pointiest incisors ever.

Okay, I'll admit it. I freaked. I may have been battling ghosts all of my life, but that didn't mean I was at all prepared for my first encounter with a real live vampire. I mean, ghosts, I knew from experience, were real.

But vampires? Vampires were the stuff of nightmares, mythological creatures like Bigfoot and the Loch Ness monster. I mean, come on.

But here, right in front of me, smiling this completely sickening my-kid-is-an-honor-student kind of smile at me, was an actual, real-life vampire in the flesh.

Now I knew why, when Marcus had shown up that day in Mr. Beaumont's office, he'd kept looking at my neck. He'd been checking to make sure his boss hadn't tried to go for my jugular.

I guess that's why, considering that my free hand

was still inside my shoulder bag, I did what I did next.

Which was grasp the pencil I'd put in there at the last minute, pull it out, and plunge it, with all my might, into the center of Mr. Beaumont's sweater.

For a second, both of us froze. Both Mr. Beaumont and I stared at the pencil sticking out of his chest.

Then Mr. Beaumont said, in a very surprised voice, "Oh, my."

To which I replied, "Eat lead."

And then he pitched forward, missing the glass coffee table by only a few inches, and ended up on the floor between the couch and the fireplace.

Where he lay unmoving for several long moments, during which all I could do was massage the wrist he'd been clutching so hard.

He didn't, I noticed after a while, crumble into dust the way vampires on TV did. Nor did he burst into flame as vampires in the movies often do. Instead, he just lay there.

And then, little by little, the reality of what I had just done sank in:

I had just killed my boyfriend's dad.

CHAPTER 14

Well, okay, Tad wasn't exactly my boyfriend, and I had honestly believed that his dad was a vampire.

But guess what? He wasn't. And I had killed him.

How unpopular was *that* going to make me?

And this little bubble of hysteria started rising up into my throat. I could tell I was going to scream. I really didn't want to. But there I was in a room with an unconscious kid and his psycho dad, whom I had just staked through the heart with a Number Two pencil. How could I help thinking, You know, they are so totally going to kick me off the student council. . . .

Come on. You'd have started screaming, too.

But no sooner had I sucked in a lungful of air and was getting ready to let it out in a shriek guaranteed to bring Yoshi and all those waiters who'd served me dinner come running, than someone standing behind me asked, sharply, "What happened here?"

I spun around. And there, looking stunned, stood Marcus, Red Beaumont's secretary.

I said the first thing that came into my head, which was, "I didn't mean to, I swear it. Only he was scaring me, so I stabbed him."

Marcus, dressed much like the last time I'd seen him, in a suit and tie, rushed toward me. Not toward his boss, who was sprawled out on the floor. But toward me.

"Are you all right?" he demanded, grabbing me by the shoulders and looking all up and down my body . . . but mostly at my neck. "Did he hurt you?"

Marcus's face was white with anxiety.

"*I'm* fine," I said. I was starting to feel a lump in my throat. "It's your boss you ought to be worried about. . . ." My gaze flitted toward Tad, still face-down on the couch. "Oh, and his kid. He poisoned his kid."

Marcus went over to Tad and pried open one of his eyelids. Then he bent and listened to his breathing. "No," he said, almost to himself. "Not poisoned. Just drugged."

"Oh," I said, with a nervous laugh. "Oh, then that's okay."

What the hell was going on here? Was this guy for real?

He seemed like it. He was obviously very concerned. He shoved the coffee table out of the way, then bent and turned his boss over.

I had to look away. I didn't think I could bear to see that pencil sticking out of Mr. Beaumont's chest. I mean, I had rammed ghosts in the chest with all sorts of stuff—pickaxes, butcher's knives, tent poles, whatever was handy. But the thing about ghosts is . . . well, they're already dead. Tad's father had been alive when I'd jabbed that pencil into him.

Oh, God, *why* had I let Father Dom put that stupid vampire idea into my head? What kind of idiot believes in vampires? I must have been out of my mind.

"Is he . . ." I could barely choke the question out. I had to keep my gaze on Tad because if I looked down at his dad, I had a feeling I'd hurl all that lamb and mesclun salad. Even in my anxiety I couldn't help noticing that, unconscious, Tad still looked pretty hot. He certainly wasn't drooling or anything. "Is he dead?"

And I thought my mother was going to be mad if she found out about the mediator thing. Could you imagine how mad she'd be if she found out I'm a teenage killer?

Marcus's voice sounded surprised. "Of course he's not dead," he said. "Just fainted. You must have given him quite a little scare."

I snuck a peek in his direction. He had straightened up, and was standing there with my pencil in his hands. I looked hastily away, my stomach lurching.

"Is this what you used on him?" Marcus asked, in a wry voice. When I nodded silently, still not willing to glance in his direction in case I caught a glimpse of Mr. Beaumont's blood, he said, "Don't worry. It didn't go in very far. You hit his sternum."

Jeesh. Good thing Red Beaumont hadn't turned out to be the real thing or I'd have been in serious trouble. I couldn't even stake a guy properly. I really must be losing my touch.

As it was, all I had succeeded in doing was making a complete ass of myself. I said, still feeling that little bubble of hysteria in my chest, which I blamed for causing me to babble a little incoherently, "He poisoned Tad, and then he grabbed me, and I just freaked out . . ."

Marcus left his boss's unconscious body and laid a comforting hand on my arm. He said, "Shhh, I know, I know," in a soothing voice.

"I'm really sorry," I jabbered on. "But he has that thing about sunlight, and then he wouldn't eat, and then when he smiled, he had those pointy teeth, and I really thought—"

"—he was a vampire." Marcus, to my surprise, finished my sentence for me. "I know, Miss Simon."

I'm embarrassed to admit it, but the truth is, I was pretty close to bursting into tears. Marcus's admission, however, made me forget all about my urge to

416

break down into big weepy sobs.

"You *know*?" I echoed, staring up at him incredulously.

He nodded. His expression was grim. "It's what his doctors call a fixation. He's on medication for it, and most days, he does all right. But sometimes, when we aren't careful, he skips a dose, and . . . well, you can see the results for yourself. He becomes convinced that he is a dangerous vampire who has killed dozens of people—"

"Yeah," I said. "He mentioned that, too." And had looked very upset about it, too.

"But I assure you, Miss Simon, that he isn't in any way a menace to society. He's actually quite harmless—he's never hurt a soul."

My gaze strayed over toward Tad. Marcus must have noticed because he added quickly, "Well, let's just say he's never caused any *permanent* damage."

Permanent damage? Your own dad slipping you a mickey wasn't considered permanent damage around here? And how did that explain Mrs. Fiske and those missing environmentalists?

"I can't apologize enough to you, Miss Simon," Marcus was saying. He had put his arm around me, and was walking me away from the couch, and toward, of all things, the front entranceway. "I'm very sorry you had to witness this disturbing scene."

I glanced over my shoulder. Behind me, Yoshi

had appeared. He turned Tad over so his face wasn't squashed into the seat cushion, then draped a blanket over him while a couple of other guys hauled Mr. Beaumont to his feet. He murmured something and rolled his head around.

Not dead. Definitely not dead.

"Of course, I needn't point out to you that none of this would have happened"—Marcus didn't sound quite so apologetic as he had before—"if you hadn't played that little prank on him last night. Mr. Beaumont is not a well man. He is very easily agitated. And one thing that gets him particularly excited is any mention whatsoever of the occult. The so-called dream that you described to him only served to trigger another one of his episodes."

I felt that I had to try, at least, to defend myself. And so I said, "Well, how was I supposed to know that? I mean, if he's so prone to episodes, why don't you keep him locked up?"

"Because this isn't the Middle Ages, young lady."

Marcus removed his arm from around my shoulders and stood looking down at me very severely.

"Today, physicians prefer to treat persons suffering from disorders like the one Mr. Beaumont has with medication and therapy rather than keeping him in isolation from his family," Marcus informed me. "Tad's father can function normally, and even well, so long as little girls who don't know what's good for them keep their noses out of his business."

Ouch! That was harsh. I had to remind myself that I wasn't the bad guy here. I mean, *I* wasn't the one running around insisting I was a vampire.

And I hadn't caused a bunch of people to disappear just because they'd stood in the way of my building another strip mall.

But even as I thought it, I wondered if it were true. I mean, it didn't seem as if Tad's father had enough marbles rolling around in his head to organize something as sophisticated as a kidnapping and murder. Either my weirdo meter was out of whack or there was something seriously wrong here . . . and a mere "fixation" just didn't explain it. What, I wondered, about Mrs. Fiske? She was dead and Mr. Beaumont had killed her—she'd said so herself. Marcus was obviously trying to downplay the severity of his employer's psychosis.

Or was he? A man who fainted just because a girl poked him with a pencil didn't exactly seem the sort to successfully carry out a murder. Was it possible he hadn't been suffering from his current "disorder" when he'd offed Mrs. Fiske and those other people?

I was still trying to puzzle all of this out when Marcus, who'd shepherded me to the front door, produced my coat. He helped me into it, then said, "Aikiku will drive you home, Miss Simon."

I looked around and saw another Japanese guy,

this one all in black, standing by the front door. He bowed politely to me.

"And let's get one thing straight."

Marcus was still speaking to me in fatherly tones. He seemed irritated, but not really mad.

"What happened here tonight," he went on, "was very strange, it's true. But no one was injured. . . ."

He must have noticed my gaze skitter toward Tad still passed out on the couch, since he added, "Not seriously hurt, anyway. And so I think it would behoove you to keep your mouth shut about what you've seen here. Because if you should take it into your head to tell anyone about what you've seen here," Marcus went on in a manner one might almost call friendly, "I will, of course, have to tell your parents about that unfortunate prank you played on Mr. Beaumont . . . and press formal assault charges against you, of course."

My mouth dropped open. I realized it, after a second, and snapped it shut again.

"But he—" I began.

Marcus cut me off. "Did he?" He looked down at me meaningfully. "Did he really? There are no witnesses to that fact, save yourself. And do you really believe anyone is going to take the word of a little juvenile delinquent like yourself over the word of a respectable businessman?"

The jerk had me, and he knew it.

He smiled down at me, a little triumphant twinkle in his eye.

"Good night, Miss Simon," he said.

Proving once again that the life of a mediator just ain't all it's cracked up to be: I didn't even get to stay for dessert.

CHAPTER 15

Dropped off with about as much ceremony as a rolled-up newspaper on a Monday morning, I trudged up the driveway. I'd been a little scared Marcus had changed his mind about not pressing charges and that our house might have been surrounded by cops there to haul me in for assaulting Mr. B.

But no one jumped out at me, gun drawn, from behind the bushes, which was a good sign.

As soon as I walked in, my mother was all over me, wanting to know what it had been like at the Beaumonts—What had we had for dinner? What had the decor been like? Had Tad asked me to the prom?

I declared myself too sleepy to talk and, instead, went straight up to my room. All I could think about was how on earth I was going to prove to the world that Red Beaumont was a cold-blooded killer.

Well, okay, maybe not a cold-blooded one, since he evidently felt remorse for what he'd done. But a killer, just the same.

I had forgotten, of course, about my new roommate. As I approached my bedroom door, I saw Max sitting in front of it, his huge tongue lolling. There were scratch marks all up and down the door where he'd tried clawing his way in. I guess the fact that there was a cat in there was more overpowering than the fact that there was also a ghost in there.

"Bad dog," I said when I saw the scratch marks.

Instantly, Doc's bedroom door across the hall opened.

"Have you got a cat in there?" he demanded, but not in an accusing way. More like he was really interested, from a scientific point of view.

"Um," I said. "Maybe."

"Oh. I wondered. Because usually Max, you know, he stays away from your room. You know why."

Doc widened his eyes meaningfully. When I'd first moved in, Doc had very chivalrously offered to trade rooms with me, since mine, he'd noted, had a distinct cold spot in it, a clear indication that it was a center for paranormal activity. While I'd chosen to keep the room, I'd been impressed by Doc's self-sacrifice. His two elder brothers certainly hadn't been as generous.

"It's just for one night," I assured him. "The cat, I mean."

"Oh," Doc said. "Well, that's good. Because you know that Brad does suffer from an adverse reaction to feline dander. Allergens, or allergy-producing substances, cause the release of histamines, organic compounds responsible for allergic symptoms. There are a variety of allergens, such as contactants—like poison oak—and airborne, like Brad's sensitivity to cat dander. The standard treatment is, of course, avoidance, if at all possible, of the allergen."

I blinked at him. "I'll keep that in mind," I said.

Doc smiled. "Great. Well, good night. Come on, Max."

He hauled the dog away, and I went into my room.

To find that my new roommate had flown the coop. Spike was gone, and the open window told me how he'd escaped.

"Jesse," I muttered.

Jesse was always opening and closing my windows. I hauled them open at night, only to find them securely closed come morning. Usually I appreciated this since the morning fog that rolled in from the bay was often freezing.

But now his good intentions had resulted in Spike escaping.

Well, I wasn't going looking for the stupid cat. If he wanted to come back, he knew the way. If not, I figured I'd done my duty, at least so far as Timothy was concerned. I'd found his wretched pet and brought it to safety. If the stupid thing refused to stay, that wasn't my problem.

I was just getting ready to climb into the hot, steaming bath I'd run for myself—I think best when submerged in soapy water—when the phone rang. I didn't answer it, of course, because the phone is hardly ever for me. It's usually either Debbie Mancuso—despite Dopey's protests that they were not seeing each other—or one of the multitudes of giggly young women who called for Sleepy . . . who was never home due to his grueling pizza-delivery schedule.

This time, however, I heard my mother holler up the stairs that it was Father Dominic for me. My mother, in spite of what you might think, doesn't consider it the least bit weird that I am constantly getting phone calls from the principal of my school. Thanks to my being vice president of my class, and chairwoman of the Restore Junipero Serra's Head committee, there are actually quite a few completely innocuous reasons why the principal might need to call me.

But Father D. never calls me at home to discuss anything remotely school-related. He only calls when he wants to ream me out for something to do with mediating.

Before I picked up the extension in my room, I wondered—irritably, since I was wearing nothing but a towel and suspected my bath water would be cold by the time I finally got into it—what I had done this time.

And then, as if I'd already slid into that bath, and found it freezing, chills went up my spine.

Jesse. My hasty discussion with Jesse before I'd left for Tad's. Jesse had gone to Father Dominic.

No, he wouldn't have. I'd told him not to. Not unless I wasn't back by midnight. And I'd gotten home by ten. Earlier, even. Nine forty-five.

That couldn't be it, I told myself. That couldn't possibly be it. Father Dominic did not know about Jesse. He did not know a thing.

Still, when I said hello, I said it tentatively.

Father Dominic's voice was warm. "Oh, hello, Susannah," he gushed. "So sorry to call so late, only I needed to discuss yesterday's student council meeting with you—"

"It's okay, Father D.," I said, "My mom hung up the downstairs phone."

Father Dominic's voice changed completely. It was no longer warm. Instead, it was very indignant.

"Susannah," he said. "Delighted as I am to find that you are all right, I would just like to know when, if ever, you were going to tell me about this Jesse person."

Oops.

"He tells me he has been living in your bedroom since you moved to California several weeks ago, and that you have been perfectly aware, all this time, of that fact."

I had to hold the phone away from my ear. I'd always known, of course, that Father Dominic would be mad when he found out about Jesse. But I never guessed he'd go ballistic.

"This is the most outrageous thing I've ever heard." Father D. was really warming to the subject. "What would your poor mother say if she knew? I simply don't know what I'm going to do with you, Susannah. I thought you and I had established a certain amount of trust in our relationship, but all this time, you've been keeping this Jesse fellow secret—"

Fortunately, at that moment, the call-waiting went off. I said, "Oh, hold on a minute, would you, Father D.?"

As I hit the receiver, I heard him say, "Do not put me on hold while I am speaking to you, young lady—"

I'd been expecting Debbie Mancuso to be on the other line, but to my surprise, it was CeeCee.

"Hey, Suze," she said. "I was doing a little more research on your boyfriend's dad—"

"He's not my boyfriend," I said, automatically. Especially not now.

"Yeah, okay, your would-be boyfriend, then. Anyway, I thought you might be interested to know that after his wife—Tad's mom—died ten years ago, things really started going downhill for Mr. B."

I raised my eyebrows. "Downhill? Like how? Not financially. I mean, if you ever saw where they live . . ."

"No, not financially. I mean that after she died—breast cancer, diagnosed too late to treat; don't worry, nobody killed her—Mr. B. sort of lost interest in all of his many companies, and started keeping to himself."

Aha. This was probably when the first onset of his "disorder" began.

"Here's the really interesting part, though," CeeCee said. I could hear her tapping on her keyboard. "It was around this time that Red Beaumont handed over almost all of his responsibilities to his brother."

"Brother?"

"Yeah. Marcus Beaumont."

I was genuinely surprised. Marcus was *related* to Mr. Beaumont? I'd thought him a mere flunky. But he wasn't. He was Tad's *uncle*.

"That's what it says. Mr. Beaumont—Tad's dad—is still the figurehead, but this other Mr. Beaumont is the one who's really been running things for the past ten years."

I froze.

Oh my God. Had I gotten it wrong?

Maybe it hadn't been Red Beaumont at all who'd killed Mrs. Fiske. Maybe it had been Marcus. The *other* Mr. Beaumont.

Did Mr. Beaumont kill you? That's what I'd asked Mrs. Fiske. And she'd said yes. But Mr. Beaumont to her might have been Marcus, not poor, vampire-wannabe Red Beaumont.

No, wait, Tad's father had told me straight out that he felt sorry for having killed all those people. That had been his motivation for inviting me over all along: He'd been hoping I'd help him communicate with his victims.

But Tad's father was clearly a couple of fries short of a Happy Meal. I don't think he could have killed a cockroach, let alone another human being.

No, whoever had killed Mrs. Fiske and those other people had been smart enough to cover his tracks . . . and Tad's dad was no Daniel Boone, let me tell you.

His brother, on the other hand . . .

"I'm getting a really bad feeling about all this," CeeCee was saying. "I mean, I know we can't prove anything—and despite what Adam thinks, it's highly unlikely anything my aunt Pru would have to contribute would be permissible in court—but I think we have a moral obligation—"

The call-waiting went off again. Father D. I'd forgotten all about Father D. He'd hung up in a rage and was calling back.

"Look, CeeCee," I said, still feeling sort of numb. "We'll talk about it tomorrow at school, okay?"

"Okay," CeeCee said. "But I'm just letting you know, Suze, I think we've stumbled onto something big here."

Big? Try gargantuan.

But it wasn't Father Dominic on the other line, I found out, after I pressed down on the receiver: It was Tad.

"Sue?" he said. He still sounded a little groggy.

And he still seemed to have only a slight clue what my name was.

"Um, hi, Tad," I said.

"Sue, I am so sorry," he said. Grogginess aside, he sounded as if he meant it. "I don't know what happened. I guess I was more tired than I thought. You know, at practice they run us pretty hard, and some nights I just conk out sooner than others. . . ."

Yeah, I said to myself. *I bet.*

"Don't worry about it," I said. Tad had way bigger things to concern himself with than falling asleep during a date.

"But I want to make it up to you," Tad insisted. "Please let me. What are you doing Saturday night?"

Saturday night? I forgot all about how this kid was related to a possible serial killer. What did *that* matter? He was asking me out. On a date. A *real* date. On Saturday night. Visions of candlelight and French kissing danced in my head. I could hardly speak, I was so flattered.

"I have a game," Tad went on, "but I figured you could come watch me play, and then afterward we could maybe get a pizza with the rest of the guys or something."

My excitement died a rapid little death.

Was he kidding? He wanted me to come watch him play *basketball*? Then go out with him and *the rest of the team*? For *pizza*? I wasn't even *burger* material? I mean, at this point, I'd settle for Sizzler, for crying out loud.

"Sue," Tad said when I didn't say anything right away. "You aren't mad at me, are you? I mean, I really didn't mean to fall asleep on you."

What was I thinking, anyway? It would never work out between the two of us. I mean, I'm a mediator. His dad's a vampire. His uncle's a killer. What if we got married? Think how our kids would turn out. . . .

Confused. Way confused.

Kind of like Tad.

"It wasn't that you were boring me, or anything," he went on. "Really. Well, I mean, that thing you were talking about *was* kind of boring—the thing about that statue with the head that needed gluing back on. That story, I mean. But not *you*. *You're* not boring, Susan. That's not why I fell asleep, I swear it."

"Tad," I said, annoyed by how many times he'd felt it necessary to assure me I hadn't been boring him—a sure sign I'd been boring him senseless—and of course by the fact that he could not seem to remember my name. "Grow up."

He said, "Whaddya mean?"

"I mean you didn't fall asleep, okay? You passed

out because your dad slipped some Seconal or something into your coffee."

Okay, maybe that wasn't the most diplomatic way to tell the guy his father needed to up his meds. But hey, nobody's going to go around accusing me of being boring. *Nobody.*

Besides, don't you think he had a right to know?

"Sue," he said, after a moment's pause. Pain throbbed in his voice. "Why would you *say* something like that? I mean, how could you even *think* something like that?"

I guess I couldn't blame the poor guy. It was pretty hard to believe. Unless you'd seen it up close and personal the way I had.

"Tad," I said. "I mean it. Your old man . . . his phaser seems set on permanent stun, if you get my drift."

"No," Tad said, a little sullenly, I thought. "I don't know what you're talking about."

"Tad," I said. "Come on. The guy thinks he's a vampire."

"He does not!" Tad, I realized, was up to his armpits in some major denial. "You're full of it!"

I decided to show Tad just how full of it I was.

"No offense, buddy," I said, "but next time you're putting on one of those gold chains of yours, you might ask yourself where the money to pay for it came from. Or better yet, why don't you ask your uncle Marcus?"

"Maybe I will," Tad said.

"Maybe you should," I said.

"I will, then," Tad said.

"Fine, then do it."

I slammed down the phone. Then I sat there staring down at it.

What on earth had I just done?

CHAPTER 16

In spite of the fact that I'd nearly killed a man that night, I didn't have too many problems falling asleep.

Seriously.

Okay, so I was tired, all right? I mean, let's face it: I'd had a trying day.

And it wasn't like those phone calls I'd gotten just before I'd gone to bed had helped. Father Dominic was totally mad at me for not having told him sooner about Jesse, and Tad seemed to pretty much hate me now, too.

Oh, and his uncle Marcus? Yeah, possible serial killer. Almost forgot that part.

But seriously, what was I supposed to do? I mean, I'd known perfectly well Father D. wasn't going to be thrilled about Jesse. And as for Tad, well, if my dad had ever drugged me stupid, I would totally want to know.

I'd done the right thing telling Tad.

Except I did sort of wonder what was going to happen if Tad really did go ask his uncle Marcus what I'd meant about where his money came from. Marcus would probably think it was some obscure reference to Tad's father's mental illness.

I hoped.

Because if he figured out that I suspected the truth—you know, that whole thing about his killing anyone who stood in the way of Beaumont Industries gobbling up as much of the available property in northern California that it possibly could—I had a feeling he wasn't going to take too kindly to it.

But how scared would a big-time player like Marcus Beaumont be of a sixteen-year-old schoolgirl? I mean, really. He had no idea about the whole mediator thing, how I'd actually spoken to one of his victims and confirmed the whole thing.

Well, more or less.

Still, in spite of all that, I did finally get to sleep. I was dreaming that Kelly Prescott had heard about Tad and me being at the Coffee Clutch together, and that she was threatening to veto the decision not to have a spring dance in revenge when a soft *thud* woke me. I raised my head and squinted in the direction of the window seat.

Spike was back. And he had company.

Jesse, I saw, was sitting next to Spike. To my utter amazement the cat was letting him pet him. That stupid cat who had tried to bite me every time I'd come near him was letting a ghost—his natural enemy—pet him.

And what's more, Spike seemed to *like* it. He was purring so loud I could hear him all the way across the room.

"Whoa," I said, leaning up on my elbows. *"That* is one for *Ripley's Believe It or Not."*

Jesse grinned at me. "I think he likes me," he said.

"Don't get too attached. He can't stay here, you know."

I could have sworn Jesse looked crestfallen. "Why not?"

"Because Dopey's allergic, for one thing," I said. "And because I didn't even ask anyone if it was okay for me to have a cat."

"It is your house now, as well as your brothers'," Jesse said with a shrug.

"Stepbrothers," I corrected him. I thought about what he said, then added, "And I guess I still feel like more of a guest here than an actual occupant."

"Give yourself a century or so." He grinned some more. "And you'll get over it."

"Very funny," I said. "Besides, that cat hates me."

"I'm sure he doesn't hate you," Jesse said.

"Yes, he does. Every time I come near him, he tries to bite me."

"He just doesn't know you," Jesse said. "I will introduce you." He picked up the cat and pointed him in my direction. "Cat," he said. "This is Susannah. Susannah, meet the cat."

"Spike," I said.

"I beg your pardon?"

"Spike. That cat's name is Spike."

Jesse put the cat down and looked at him in horror. "That is a terrible name for a cat."

"Yeah," I said. Then I added—strictly conversationally, if you know what I mean—"So I hear you met Father Dominic."

Jesse raised his gaze and let it rest expressionlessly on me. "Why didn't you tell him about me, Susannah?"

I swallowed. What do they do, teach guys that reproachful look at birth, or something? I mean, they all seem to have it so down pat. Except Dopey, that is.

"Look," I said. "I *wanted* to. Only I knew he was going to freak out. I mean, he's a priest. I didn't figure he'd be too thrilled to hear that I've got a guy—even a dead guy—living in my bedroom." I tried to sound as concerned as I felt. "So, um, I take it you two didn't hit it off?"

"Between your father and the priest," Jesse said, wryly, "I would take your father any time."

"Well," I said. "Don't worry about it. Tomorrow I'll

437

just tell Father Dom about all the times you saved my life, and then he'll just have to deal."

He clearly didn't believe it was going to be that simple if the scowl that appeared on his face was any indication. The sad thing was, he was right. Father D. wasn't going to be mollified that easily, and we both knew it.

"Look." I threw back the covers and got up out of bed, padding over to the window seat in my boxers and T-shirt. "I'm sorry. I'm really sorry, Jesse. I should have told him sooner and introduced the two of you properly. It's my fault."

"It isn't your fault," Jesse said.

"Yes, it is." I sat down next to him, making sure Jesse was between me and the cat. "I mean, you may be dead, but I haven't got any right to treat you as if you were. That's just plain rude. Maybe what we can do is, you and me and Father Dom can all sit down and have lunch together or something, and then he can see what a nice guy you really are."

Jesse looked at me like I was a mental case. "Susannah," he said. "I don't eat, remember?"

"Oh, yeah. I forgot."

Spike butted Jesse in the arm, and he lifted his hand and began scratching the cat's ears. I felt so bad for Jesse—I mean, think about it: He had been hanging around in that house for a *hundred and fifty years* before I'd gotten there, with no one to talk to, no one at all—that I suddenly blurted out, "Jesse, if there was any way I could make you not dead, I'd do it."

He smiled, but at the cat, not at me. "Would you?"

"In a minute," I said, and then went on, with complete recklessness, "Except that if you weren't dead, you probably wouldn't want to hang out with me."

That made him look at me. He said, "Of course I would."

"No," I said, examining one of my bare knees in the moonlight. "You wouldn't. If you weren't dead, you'd be in college or something, and you'd want to hang around with college girls, and not boring high school girls like me."

Jesse said, "You aren't boring."

"Oh, yes, I am," I assured him. "You've just been dead so long, you don't know it."

"Susannah," he said. "I know it, all right?"

I shrugged. "You don't have to try to make me feel better. It's okay. I've come to accept it. There are some things you just can't change."

"Like being dead," Jesse said, quietly.

Well, *that* certainly put a damper on things. I was feeling kind of depressed about everything—the fact that Jesse was dead, and that in spite of this, Spike still liked him better than me, and stuff like that—when all of a sudden Jesse reached out and took hold of my chin—almost exactly the way Tad had that night in his car—between his index finger and thumb and turned my face toward his.

And things suddenly started looking up.

Instead of collapsing in shock—my first instinct—I lifted my gaze to his face. The moonlight that had been filtering into my room through the bay windows was reflected in Jesse's soft dark eyes, and I could feel the heat from his fingers coursing through me.

That's when I realized that in spite of how hard I'd been trying to not fall in love with Jesse, I wasn't doing a very good job. I could tell this by the way my heart started thudding very hard against my T-shirt when he touched me. It hadn't done that when Tad had touched me in the exact same way.

And I could also tell by the way I instantly started worrying about the fact that he had chosen this particular moment to kiss me, the middle of the night, when it had been hours since I'd brushed my teeth and I was sure I probably had morning breath. How appetizing was that?

But I never discovered whether or not Jesse would have been grossed out by my morning breath—or even if he'd really been going to kiss me at all—because at that moment, that crazy woman who kept insisting Red hadn't killed her suddenly showed up again, shrieking her head off.

I swear I nearly jumped a foot. She was the last person I'd been expecting to see.

"Oh my God," I cried, slapping my hands over my

ears as she let loose like some kind of smoke detector. "What's the matter?"

The woman had been wearing the hood of her gray sweatshirt. Now she pushed it back, and in the moonlight, I could see the tears that had made tracks down her thin, pale cheeks. I couldn't believe I had mistaken her for Mrs. Fiske. This woman was years and years younger, and a heck of a lot prettier.

"You didn't tell him," she said, between sobbing wails.

I blinked. "Yes, I did."

"You didn't!"

"No, I did, I really did." I was shocked by this unfair accusation. "I told him a couple of days ago. Jesse, tell her."

"She told him," Jesse assured the dead woman.

You would think one ghost would take the word of another. But she wasn't having any of it. She cried, "You *didn't*! And you've *got* to tell him. You've just *got* to. It's tearing him up inside."

"Wait a minute," I said. "Red Beaumont is the Red you're talking about, right? Isn't he the one who killed you?"

She shook her head so hard, her hair smacked her cheeks and then stuck there, glued to her skin by her tears. "No," she said. "No! I told you Red *didn't* do it."

"Marcus, I mean," I amended, quickly. "I know Red didn't do it. He just blames himself for it, right? That's what you want me to tell him. That it wasn't his fault. It was his brother, Marcus Beaumont, who killed you, wasn't it?"

"No!" She looked at me like I was a moron. And I was starting to feel like one. "Not Red *Beaumont*. Red. *Red! You know him.*"

I know him? I know someone named Red? Not in this life.

"Look," I said. "I need a little more info than that. Why don't we start with introductions. I'm Susannah Simon, okay? And you are . . . ?"

The look she gave me would have broken the heart of even the coldest mediator.

"You *know*," she said, with an expression so wounded, I had to look away. "You *know*. . . ."

And then, when I risked another glance in her direction, she was gone again.

"Um," I said, uncomfortably, to Jesse. "I guess I got the wrong Red."

CHAPTER 17

Okay, I admit it: I wasn't happy.

I mean, seriously. I had invested all that time and effort in Red Beaumont, and he hadn't even been the right guy.

Okay, yeah, so he—or his brother; my money was on his brother—had apparently killed a bunch of people, but I'd stumbled over this fact completely by accident. The ghost who'd originally come to me for help didn't have anything to do with Red Beaumont or even with his brother, Marcus. Her message remained undelivered because I couldn't figure out who she was, even though, apparently, I knew her.

And meanwhile, Mrs. Fiske's killer was still walking around free.

And as if all of that weren't enough, my midnight caller showing up the way she did had completely killed the mood between Jesse and me. He so totally did not kiss me after that. In fact, he acted like he'd never intended to kiss me in the first place, which, considering my luck, is probably the truth. Instead, he asked how my poison oak was progressing.

My poison oak! Yeah, thanks, it's great.

God, I am such a loser.

But you know, I pretended like I didn't care. I got up the next morning and acted like nothing had happened. I put on my best butt-kicking outfit—my black Betsey Johnson miniskirt with black ribbed tights, sidezip Batgirl boots, and purple Armani sweater set—and strutted around my room like all I was thinking about was how I was going to bring Marcus Beaumont to justice. The last thing on my mind, I pretended, was Jesse.

Not like he noticed. He wasn't even around.

But all my strutting around had made me late, and Sleepy was standing at the bottom of the stairs bellowing my name, so even if he'd wanted to, it wouldn't have been such a good thing for Jesse to materialize just then, anyway.

I grabbed my leather jacket and came pounding down the stairs to where Andy was standing shelling out lunch money to each of us as we came by.

"My goodness, Suze," he said when he saw me.

"*What*?" I demanded, defensively.

"Nothing," he said, quickly. "Here."

I plucked the five-dollar bill from his hand and, casting him one last, curious glance, followed Doc down to the car. When I got there, Dopey took one look at me and let out a howl.

"Oh my God," he cried, pointing at me. "Run for your lives!"

I narrowed my eyes at him.

"Do you have a problem?" I asked him, coldly.

"Yeah, I do," he sneered at me. "I didn't know it was Halloween."

Doc said, knowingly, "It isn't Halloween, Brad. Halloween isn't for another two hundred and seventy-nine days."

"Tell that to the Queen of the Undead," Dopey said.

I don't know what made me do it. I was in a bad mood, I guess. Everything that had happened the night before, from stabbing Mr. Beaumont to finding out I'd had the wrong man all along—not to mention my discovery that my feelings about Jesse weren't exactly what I'd have liked them to be—came back to me.

And the next thing I knew, I'd turned around and sunk my fist into Dopey's stomach.

He let out a groan and pitched forward, then sprawled out into the grass, gasping for air.

Okay, I admit it. I felt bad. I shouldn't have done it.

But still. What a baby. I mean, seriously. He's on

the wrestling team. What are they teaching these wrestlers, anyway? Clearly not how to take a punch.

"Whoa," Sleepy said when he noticed that Dopey was on the ground. "What the hell happened to you?"

Dopey pointed at me, trying to say my name. But all that came out were gasps.

"Aw, Jesus," Sleepy said, looking at me disgustedly.

"He called me," I said, with all the dignity I could muster, "the Queen of the Undead."

Sleepy said, "Well, what do you expect him to say? You look like a hooker. Sister Ernestine's going to send you home if she sees you in that skirt."

I sucked in my breath, outraged. "This skirt," I said, "happens to be by Betsey Johnson."

"I don't care if it's by Betsy Ross. And neither will Sister Ernestine. Come on, Brad, get up. We're going to be late."

Brad got up with elaborate care, as if every movement was causing him excruciating pain. Sleepy didn't look as if he felt too sorry for him. "I told you not to mess with her, sport," was all he said as he slid behind the wheel.

"She sucker-punched me, man," Brad whined. "She can't get away with that."

"Actually," Doc said pleasantly, as he climbed into the backseat and fastened his seatbelt, "she can. While statistics concerning domestic violence are always difficult to obtain due to low reportage, incidents in which females batter male family members are reported even less, as the victims are almost always too embarrassed to tell members of law enforcement that they have, in fact, been beaten by a woman."

"Well, I'm not embarrassed," Dopey declared. "I'm telling Dad as soon as we get home."

"Go ahead," I said, acidly. I was in a really bad mood. "He's just going to ground you again when I tell him you went ahead and snuck out the night of Kelly Prescott's pool party."

"I did not," he practically screamed in my face.

"Then how is it," I inquired, "that I saw you in her pool house giving Debbie Mancuso's tongue a Jiffy Lube?"

Even Sleepy hooted at that one.

Dopey, completely red with embarrassment, looked as if he might start crying. I licked my finger and made a little slashing motion in the air as if I were writing on a scoreboard. Suze, one. Dopey, zero.

But Dopey, unfortunately, was the one who had the last laugh.

We were approaching our lines for Assembly—they seriously make every single grade stand outside the school in these lines separated by sex, boys on one side, girls on the other, for fifteen minutes before class officially starts, so they can take attendance and read announcements—when Sister Ernestine blew her whistle at me, and signaled for me to come over to her, where she was standing by the flagpole.

Fortunately, she did this in front of the entire soph-omore class—not to mention the freshmen—so that every single one of my peers had the privilege of seeing me get bawled out by a nun for wearing a miniskirt to school.

The upshot of it all was that Sister Ernestine said I had to go home and change.

Oh, I argued. I insisted that a society that valued its members solely for their outward appearance was a society destined for destruction, which was a line I'd heard Doc use a few days earlier when she'd busted him for wearing Levi's—there's a strict anti-jeans rule at the Academy.

But Sister Ernestine didn't go for it. She informed me that I could go home and change, or I could sit in her office and help grade the second graders' math quiz-zes until my mother arrived with a pair of slacks for me.

Oh, that wouldn't be *too* embarrassing.

Given the alternative, I elected to go home and change—although I argued strenuously on behalf of Ms. Johnson and her designs. A skirt however, with a hem higher than three inches above the knee, is not considered appropriate Academy attire. And my skirt, unfortunately, was more than four inches above my knees. I know because Sister Ernestine took out a ruler and showed me. And the rest of the sophomore class, as well.

And so it was that, with a wave to CeeCee and Adam, who were leading the class's shouts of encouragement to me—which fortunately drowned out the catcalls Dopey and his friends were making—I shouldered my backpack and left the school grounds. I had, of course, to walk home, since I could not face the indignity of calling Andy for a ride, and I still hadn't figured out whether or not there was such a thing as public transportation in Carmel.

I wasn't too deeply bummed. After all, what had I had to look forward to? Oh, just Father Dominic reaming me out for not telling him about Jesse. I could, I suppose, have distracted him by telling him how wrong he'd been about Tad's dad being a vampire—he just *thinks* he's one—and what CeeCee had discovered about his brother, Marcus. That certainly would have gotten him off my back . . . for a little while, anyway.

But then what? So a couple of environmentalists were missing? That didn't prove anything. So a dead lady had told me a Mr. Beaumont had killed her? Oh, yeah, that'd stand up in court, all right.

Not a lot to go on. We had, in fact, nothing. Nada. Zilch.

Which was what I was feeling like as I strolled along. A big miniskirted zero.

As if whoever was in charge of the weather agreed with me about my loser status, it was sort of raining. It was foggy every morning along the coast in northern California. The fog rolled in from the sea and sat in the bay until the sun burned it all off.

But this morning, on top of the fog, there was this light drizzle coming down. It wasn't so bad at first, but I hadn't gotten farther than the school gates before my hair started curling up. After all the time I'd spent that morning straightening it. I didn't, of course, have an umbrella. Nor, it seemed, did I have much of a choice. I was going to be a drenched, curly-haired freak by the time I walked the two miles—mostly uphill—to the house, and that was the end of it.

Or so I thought. Because as I was passing the school gates, a car pulling in between them slowed.

It was a nice car. It was an expensive car. It was a black car with smoked windows. As I looked at it one of those windows lowered and a familiar face peered out at me from the backseat.

"Miss Simon," Marcus Beaumont said pleasantly. "Just the person I was looking for. May I have a word?"

And he opened the passenger door invitingly, beckoning for me to come in out of the rain.

Every single one of my mediator neurons fired at once. *Danger,* they screamed. *Run for it,* they shrieked.

I couldn't believe it. Tad had done it. Tad had asked his uncle what I'd meant.

And Marcus, instead of shrugging it off, had come here to my school in a car with smoked windows to "have a word" with me.

I was dead meat.

But before I had a chance to spin around and high-tail back into the school, where I knew I'd be safe, the passenger doors of Marcus Beaumont's sedan sprang open and these two guys came at me.

Let me just say in my defense that deep down, I never thought Tad would have the guts to do it. I mean, Tad seemed like a nice enough guy, and God knew he was a great kisser, but he didn't seem to be the sharpest knife in the drawer, if you know what I mean. This, I imagine, is why a girl like Kelly Prescott would find him so appealing: Kelly's used to being the Wüsthof. She doesn't welcome competition in that capacity.

But I had obviously underestimated Tad. Not only had he gone to his uncle as I'd suggested, but he'd evidently managed to raise Marcus's suspicions that I knew more than I'd let on.

Way more if the two thugs who were circling me, cutting off any possible chance at escape, were any indication.

My option for flight pretty much voided by these two clowns, I saw that I was going to have to fight. I do not consider myself a slouch in the fighting department. I actually kind of like it, if you haven't figured that out already. Of course, usually I'm fighting ghosts, and not live human beings. But if you think about it, there's not really that much of a difference. I mean, nasal cartilage is nasal cartilage. I was willing to give it a go.

This seemed to come as something of a surprise to Marcus's flunkies. A couple of thickset frat boys who looked as if they were more used to pounding brewskies than people, they were out to impress the boss in a big way.

At least until I threw down my book bag, hooked my foot behind the knee of one them, and brought him down with a ground-shaking thud to the wet asphalt.

While Thug #1 lay there staring up at the overcast sky with a surprised look on his face, I got in an excellent kick to Thug #2. He was too tall for me to get him in the nose, but I knocked the wind out of him by applying my three-inch heel to his rib cage. That had to have hurt, let me tell you. He went spinning around, lost his balance, and hit the ground.

Amateur.

Marcus got out of the car then. He stood with the rain beating down on his fluffy blond hair and went, "You idiot," to Thug #2.

He was right to be upset, if you think about it. I mean, here he'd hired these guys to roust me, and they were doing a thoroughly bad job of it. It just goes to show you can't get good help anymore.

You would think that, with all this going on in front of a pretty popular tourist destination like the Mission—not to mention a *school*—somebody would have noticed and phoned the cops. You would think that, wouldn't you?

But if you're thinking that, you obviously haven't been in California when it was raining out. I'm not kidding, it's like New York City on New Year's Eve: Only the tourists venture outside. Everyone else stays inside and waits until it's safe to come out.

Oh, a couple of cars whizzed by going fifty miles an hour in a twenty-mile-per-hour zone. I was hoping one of them would notice us and decide that two guys on one girl wasn't quite playing fair—even if the girl did look a bit like a hooker.

But our little tussle went on for a surprisingly long time before Marcus—who'd apparently realized what his thugs hadn't, that I wasn't exactly your typical Catholic schoolgirl—cut the whole thing short by laying me out with a totally unfair right to the chin.

I didn't even see him coming. What with the rain and all, my hair was getting plastered to my face, obscuring my peripheral vision. I'd been concentrating on applying a knee to Thug #1's groin—it had been a bad idea, his decision to get up again—while keeping my eye on Thug #2, who kept grabbing for handfuls of my hair—he had obviously gone to the Dopey school of fighting—and hadn't even noticed that Marcus was headed my way.

But suddenly, a heavy hand landed on my shoulder and spun me around. A second later, an explosion sounded in my head. The world tilted sickeningly, and I felt myself stumble. Next thing I knew, I was inside the car, and brakes were squealing.

"Ow," I said when the stars I'd been seeing had receded enough for me to speak. I reached up and touched my jaw. None of my teeth felt loose, but I was definitely going to have a bruise that there wasn't enough Clinique in the world to cover up. "What'd you have to hit me so hard for?"

Marcus just blinked at me expressionlessly from where he sat on the seat beside me. Thug #1 was driving and Thug #2 sat beside him in the front seat. Judging from the backs of their extremely thick necks, they were unhappy. It couldn't have been too pleasant sitting there with all those various body parts throbbing with pain in wet, muddy clothes. My leather jacket had fortunately protected me from the worst of the rain. My hair, however, was undoubtedly a lost cause.

We were going fast down the highway. Water sluiced on either side of us as we barreled through what had become a steady downpour. There wasn't a soul on the highway but us. I tell you, you've never seen people as scared of a little bit of rain as native Californians. Earthquakes? They're nothing. But a hint of drizzle and it's head-between-the-knees time.

"Look," I said. "I think you should know something. My mother is a reporter for WCAL in Monterey, and if anything happens to me, she is going to be all over you like ants on a Jolly Rancher."

Marcus, clearly bored by my posturing, pulled back his coat sleeve and looked at his Rolex. "She won't," he said, tonelessly. "No one knows where you are. It was quite fortuitous, your leaving the school at the very moment we were pulling up to it. Did another one of your *ghosts*"—he said the word with a sarcasm I suppose he found scathing—"warn you that we were coming?"

Scowling, I muttered, "Not exactly." No way was I going to tell him I'd been sent home for violating the school dress code. I'd been humiliated enough for one day.

"Just what were *you* doing there, anyway?" I demanded. "I mean, were you just going to stroll in and yank me out of class at gunpoint in front of everyone?"

"Certainly not," Marcus said, calmly.

What I was hoping was that somebody—anybody—had seen Marcus slug me and had taken down the license number of his expensive Eurotrash car. Any minute sirens might begin to wail behind us. The *cops* couldn't be afraid of a little rain—although to tell the truth, I don't remember *CHiPs* officers Ponch and Jon ever venturing out in a downpour. . . .

Keep him talking, I told myself. If he's talking, he won't be able to concentrate on killing you.

"So what was the plan, then?"

"If you must know, I was going to go to the principal and inform him that Beaumont Industries was interested in sponsoring a student's tuition for the year, and that you were one of our finalists." Marcus picked some invisible lint off his trouser leg. "We would, of course, require a personal interview, after which we intended to take you—the candidate—to a celebratory lunch."

I rolled my eyes. The idea of me winning any kind of scholarship was laughable. This guy obviously hadn't seen my latest geometry quiz scores.

"Father Dominic would never have let me go with you," I said. Especially, I thought, after I'd filled him in on what had gone on at chez Beaumont the night before.

"Oh, I think he might have. I was planning on making a sizable donation to his little mission."

I had to laugh at that one. This guy obviously didn't know Father D. at all.

"I don't think so," I said. "And even if he did, don't you think he would mention how the last time he saw me, I was going off in a car with you? If the cops should happen to question him, you know, after I disappeared, that is."

Marcus said, "Oh, you're not going to disappear, Miss Simon."

This surprised me. "I'm not?" Then what was all this about?

"Oh, no," Marcus assured me, confidently. "There won't be the slightest question about what's happened to you. Your corpse is going to be found rather quickly, I imagine."

CHAPTER 18

This was so not what I wanted to hear, I can't even tell you.

"Look," I said, quickly. "I think you should know that I left a letter with a friend of mine. If anything happens to me, she's supposed to go to the cops and give it to them."

I smiled sunnily at him. Of course, it was all a big fat lie, but he didn't know that.

Or maybe he did.

"I don't think so," he said, politely.

I shrugged, pretending I didn't care. "Your funeral."

"You really," Marcus said, as I was busy straining my ears for sirens, "oughtn't to have tipped off the boy. That was your first mistake, you know."

Didn't I know it.

"Well," I said. "I thought he had a right to know what his own father was up to."

Marcus looked a little disappointed in me. "I didn't mean that," he said, and there was just a hint of contempt in his voice.

"What, then?" I opened my eyes as wide as they would go. Little Miss Innocent.

"I wasn't certain you knew about me, of course," Marcus went on, almost amiably. "Not until you tried to run back there, in front of the school. That, of course, was your second mistake. Your evident fear of me was a dead giveaway. Because then there was no question that you knew more than was good for you."

"Yeah, but look," I said, in my most reasonable voice. "What was it you said last night? Who's going to believe the word of a sixteen-year-old juvenile delinquent like myself over a big important businessman like you? I mean, please. You're friends with the governor, for crying out loud."

"And your mother," Marcus reminded me, "is a reporter with WCAL, as you pointed out."

Me and my big mouth.

The car, which had showed no signs of slowing down up until that point, started rounding a curve in the road. We were, I realized suddenly, on Seventeen Mile Drive.

I didn't even think about what I was doing. I just

reached for the door handle, and the next thing I knew, a guardrail was looming at me, and rainwater and gravel were splashing up into my face.

But instead of rolling out of the car and up against that guardrail—below which I could see the roiling waves of the Restless Sea crashing against the boulders that rested at the bottom of the cliff we were on—I stayed where I was. That was because Marcus grabbed the back of my leather jacket and wouldn't let go.

"Not so fast," he said, trying to haul me back into the seat.

I wasn't giving up so easily, though. I twisted around—quite nimble in my Lycra skirt—and tried to slam my boot heel into his face. Unfortunately, Marcus's reflexes were as good as mine since he caught my foot and twisted it very painfully.

"Hey," I yelled. "That hurt!"

But Marcus just laughed and clocked me again.

Let me tell you, that didn't feel so swell. For a minute or so, I couldn't see too straight. It was during this moment that it took for my vision to adjust that Marcus closed the passenger door, which had continued to yawn open, stowed me back into my place, and buckled me safely in. When my eyeballs finally settled back into their sockets, I looked down, and saw that he was keeping a firm hold on me, primarily by clutching a handful of my sweater set.

"Hello," I said, feebly. "That's cashmere, you know."

Marcus said, "I will release you if you promise to be reasonable."

"I think it's perfectly reasonable," I said, "to try to escape from a guy like you."

Marcus didn't look very impressed by my sensible take on the matter.

"You can't possibly imagine that I'm going to let you go," he said. "I've got damage control to worry about. I mean, I can't have you going around telling people about my, er . . . unique problem-solving techniques."

"There's nothing very unique," I informed him, "about murder."

Marcus said, as if I hadn't spoken, "Historically, you understand, there have always been an ignorant few who have insisted upon standing in the way of progress. These are the people I was forced to . . . relo-cate."

"Yeah," I said. "To their graves."

Marcus shrugged. "Unfortunate, certainly, but nevertheless necessary. Still, in order for us to advance as a civilization, sacrifices must occasionally be made by a select few—"

"I doubt Mrs. Fiske agrees with who you selected to be sacrificed," I interrupted.

"What may appear to one party to be improvement may appear to another to be wanton destruction—"

"Like the annihilation of our natural coastline by money-grubbing parasites like yourself?"

Well, he'd already said he was going to kill me. I didn't figure it mattered whether or not I was polite to him.

"And so for progress—real progress," he went on, as if he hadn't even heard me, "to be made, some simply have to do without."

"Without their *lives*?" I glared at him. "Dude, let me tell you something. You know your brother, the wannabe-vampire? You are every bit as sick as he is."

The car, right at that moment, pulled into the driveway of Mr. Beaumont's house. The guard at the gate waved to us as we went by, though he couldn't see me through the tinted windows. He probably had no idea that inside his boss's car was a teenage girl who was about to be executed. No one—*no one*—I realized, knew where I was: not my mother, not Father Dominic, not Jesse—not even my dad. I had no idea what Marcus had planned for me, but whatever it was, I suspected I wasn't going to like it very much . . . especially if it got me where it had gotten Mrs. Fiske.

Which I was beginning to think it probably would.

The car pulled to a halt. Marcus's fingers bit into my upper arm.

"Come on," he said, and he started dragging me across the seat toward his side of the car and the open passenger door.

"Wait a minute," I said, in a last-ditch effort to convince him that I could be perfectly reasonable given the right incentive—for instance, being killed. "What if I promised not to tell anyone?"

"You already have told someone," Marcus reminded me. "My nephew, Tad, remember?"

"Tad won't tell anyone. He can't. He's related to you. He's not allowed to testify against his own relatives in court, or something." My head was still kind of wobbly from the smack Marcus had given me, so I wasn't at my most lucid. Nevertheless, I tried my best to reason with him. "Tad is a super secret keeper."

"The dead," Marcus reminded me, "usually are."

If I hadn't been scared before—and I most definitely had been—I was super scared now. What did he mean by that? Did he mean . . . did he mean Tad wouldn't talk because he'd be dead? This guy was going to kill his own nephew? Because of what *I'd* told him?

I couldn't let that happen. I had no idea what Marcus intended to do with me, but one thing I knew for sure:

He wasn't going to lay a finger on my boyfriend.

Although at that particular moment, I had no idea how I was going to prevent him from doing so.

As Marcus yanked on me, I said to his thugs, "I just want to thank you guys for helping me out. You know, considering I'm a defenseless young girl and this guy is a cold-blooded killer, and all. Really. You've been great—"

Marcus gave me a jerk and I came flying out of the car toward him.

"Whoa," I said, when I'd found my feet. "What's with the rough stuff?"

"I'm not taking any chances," Marcus said, keeping his iron grip on my arm as he dragged me toward the front door of the house. "You've proved a good deal more trouble than I ever anticipated."

Before I had time to digest this compliment, Marcus had hauled me into the house while behind us the thugs got out of the car and followed along . . . just in case, I suppose, I suddenly broke free and tried to pull a *La Femme Nikita*–type escape.

Inside the Beaumonts' house—from what I could see given the speed with which Marcus was dragging me around—things were much the same as they'd been the last time I'd visited. There was no sign of Mr. Beaumont—he was probably in bed recovering from my brutal attack on him the night before. Poor thing. If I'd known it was Marcus who was the bloodsucking parasite and not his brother, I'd have shown the old guy a little compassion.

Which reminded me.

"What about Tad?" I asked as Marcus steered me across the patio, where rain was pattering into the pool, making hundreds of little splashes and thousands of ripples. "Where've you got him locked up?"

"You'll see," Marcus assured me as he pulled

me into the little corridor where the elevator to Mr. Beaumont's office sat.

He threw open the elevator door and pushed me inside the little moving room, then joined me there. His thugs took up positions in the hallway since there was no room for them and their overmuscled girth in the elevator. I was glad because Thug #1's wool pea-coat had been starting to smell a little ripe.

Once again, I had a sensation of moving, but couldn't trace whether it was up or down. As we rode, I had a chance to study Marcus up close and personal. It was funny, but he really looked like an ordinary guy. He could have been anyone, a travel agent, a lawyer, a doctor.

But he wasn't. He was a murderer.

How proud his mom must be.

"You know," I remarked, "when my mom finds out about this, Beaumont Industries is going down. Way down."

"She's not going to connect your death with Beaumont Industries," Marcus informed me.

"Oh, yeah? Dude, let me tell you something. The minute my mutilated corpse is found, my mom's gonna turn into that creature from *Aliens*. You know the one where Sigourney Weaver gets into that forklift thing? And then—"

"You aren't going to be mutilated," Marcus snapped. He was obviously not a movie buff. He flung open the elevator door, and I saw that we were back where all of this had started, in Mr. Beaumont's spooky office.

"You're going," he said, with satisfaction, "to drown."

CHAPTER 19

"Here."

Marcus, by applying steady pressure to the small of my back, had steered me into the middle of the room. He went around the desk, reached into a drawer, and pulled out something red and silky. He threw it at me.

I, with my lightning quick reflexes, caught it, dropped it, then picked it up and squinted down at it. Except for the lights at the bottom of the aquarium, the room was in darkness.

"Put it on," Marcus said.

It was a bathing suit. A Speedo one-piece. I tossed it, as if it had burned my fingers, onto the top of Red Beaumont's desk.

"No thanks," I said. "Racerback straps don't really do it for me."

Marcus sighed. His gaze strayed toward the wall to my right. "Tad," he said, "wasn't nearly so difficult to persuade as you."

I spun around. Stretched out on a leather sofa I hadn't noticed before lay Tad. He was either asleep or unconscious. My vote was for unconscious, since most people don't nod off in their swimwear.

That's right: Tad was sans apparel, save for those swim trunks I'd been lucky enough to have seen him in once before.

I turned back toward his uncle Marcus.

"Nobody's going to believe it," I said. "I mean, it's raining outside. Nobody's going to believe we'd go swimming in weather like this."

"You aren't going swimming," Marcus said. He'd wandered over toward the aquarium. Now he tapped on the glass to get the attention of an angel fish. "You're taking out my brother's yacht, and then you're going jet-skiing."

"In the *rain*?"

Marcus looked at me pityingly. "You've never been jet-skiing before, have you?"

Actually, no. I prefer to keep my feet, whenever possible, on dry land. Preferably in Prada, but I'll settle for Nine West.

"The water is particularly choppy in weather like

this," Marcus explained patiently. "Seasoned jet-skiers—like my nephew—can't get enough of the whitecaps. On the whole, it's the perfect kind of activity for a couple of thrill-seeking teenagers who have cut school to enjoy one another's company . . . and who will, of course, never make it back to shore. Well, not alive, anyway."

Marcus sighed, and went on, "You see, regrettably, Tad refuses to wear a life vest when he goes out on the water—much too restricting—and I'm afraid he's going to convince you to go without, as well. The two of you will stray too far from the boat, a particularly strong swell will knock you over, and . . . well, the currents will probably toss your lifeless body to shore eventually—" He pulled up his sleeve and glanced at his watch again. "Most likely tomorrow morning. Now hurry and change. I have a lunch appointment with a gentleman who wants to sell me a piece of property that would be perfect for a Chuck E. Cheese."

"You can't kill your own *nephew*." My voice cracked. I was truly feeling . . . well, horrified. "I mean, I can't imagine something like that is going to make you too popular at Grandma's around the holidays."

Marcus's mouth set into a grim line. "Perhaps you didn't understand me. As I have just taken great pains to explain to you, Miss Simon, your death, as well as my nephew's, is going to look like a tragic accident."

"Is this how you got rid of Mrs. Fiske?" I demanded.

"Jet-ski accident?"

"Hardly," he said, rolling his eyes. "I wasn't interested in having her body found. Without a body there's no proof a murder has taken place, correct? Now, be a good girl and—"

This guy was a complete mental case. I mean, Red Beaumont, for all his believing he's from Transylvania, isn't anywhere near as cuckoo for Cocoa Puffs as his little brother.

"Is this how you get your kicks?" I glared at him. "You really are a sicko. And for your information, I am *not*," I declared, "taking a stitch off. Whoever finds this body is going to find it fully clothed, thank you very much."

"Oh, I *am* sorry," he said. He actually sounded apologetic. "Of course you'd like a little privacy while you change. You'll have to forgive me. It's been a long time since I've been in the company of such a *modest* young lady." His gaze flickered disparagingly down toward my miniskirt.

More than ever, I wanted to plunge one of my thumbs into his eyes. But I was getting the impression that there was a chance he might actually leave me alone for a minute. And that was too tempting to resist. So I just stood there, trying to summon up a blush.

"I suppose," he said with a sigh, "that I can spare you five minutes." He strolled back toward the elevator. "Just remember, Miss Simon, that I *will* get you into that bathing suit one way or another. You see, of course, what poor Tad chose." He nodded toward the couch. "It would be simpler—and less painful for you in the long run—if you'd put it on yourself and spare me the trouble."

He pulled the elevator door shut behind him.

There really *was* something wrong with him, I decided. I mean, he'd just given up a chance to see a babe like me in the buff. The guy clearly had a nacho platter where his brains should have been.

Well, that's what I told myself, anyway.

Alone in Mr. Beaumont's office—except for Tad and the fish, neither of whom were particularly communicative at the moment—I immediately began trying to figure out a way to escape. The windows, I knew, were hopeless. But there was a phone on Mr. Beaumont's desk. I picked it up and began dialing.

"Miss Simon." Marcus's voice, coming through the receiver, sounded amused. "It's a house phone. You don't imagine we'd let Tad's father make any outgoing calls in his condition, do you? Please hurry up and change. We haven't much time."

He hung up. So did I.

Half a minute wasted.

The door to the elevator was locked. So was the door on the opposite side of the room. I tried kicking it, but it was made of some kind of really thick, solid wood, and didn't budge.

I decided to turn my attention to the windows. Wrapping the end of one of the velvet curtains around my fist, I punched out a few panes of glass, then tried slamming my foot against the wooden shutters.

No good. They appeared to have been nailed permanently shut.

Three minutes left.

I looked around for a weapon. My plan, I decided, since escape appeared to be impossible, was to climb the bookshelf behind the back of the elevator door. When Marcus came through that door, I'd leap down upon him, and point a sharp object at his throat. Then I'd use him as a hostage to make my way past the two thugs.

Okay, so it was a little *Xena, Warrior Princess*. Hey, it was a plan, all right? I never said it was a good one. It was just the best one I could come up with under the circumstances. I mean, it wasn't as if anybody was going to come bursting in to rescue me. I didn't see how anybody could—except for maybe Jesse, who was pretty slick at walking through walls and stuff.

Only Jesse didn't know I needed him. He didn't know I was in trouble. He didn't even know where I was.

And I had no way of letting him know, either.

A shard of glass, I decided, would make an excellent, very threatening weapon, and so I looked for a particularly lethal-looking one amid the rubble I'd made of a few of Mr. Beaumont's windows.

Two minutes.

Holding my shard of glass in my hand—wishing I had my ghost-busting gloves with me so I'd be sure not to cut myself—I scrambled up the bookshelf, no easy feat in three-inch heels.

One and a half minutes.

I glanced over at Tad. He lay limp as a rag doll, his bare chest rising and falling in a gentle, rhythmic motion. It was quite a nice-looking chest, actually. Not as nice-looking, maybe, as Jesse's. But still, in spite of his uncle being a murderer, and his dad being fore-man at the cracker factory—not to mention the whole basketball thing—I wouldn't have minded resting my head against it. His chest, I mean. You know, under other circumstances, Tad actually in a conscious state being one of them.

But I'd never have the chance if I didn't get us out of this alive.

There was no sound in the room, save Tad's steady breathing and the burbling of the aquarium.

The aquarium.

I looked at the aquarium. It made up most of one whole wall of the office. How, I wondered, did those fish get fed? The tank was built into the wall. I could detect no convenient trapdoor through which some-one might sprinkle food. The tank had to be accessed through the room next door.

The room I couldn't get to because the door to it was locked.

Unless.

Thirty seconds.

I dropped down from the bookshelf and began striding toward the aquarium.

I could hear the elevator begin to hum. Marcus, right on time, was on his way back. Needless to say, I had not put on my swimsuit like a good little girl. Although I did grab it—along with the wheeled swivel chair that had been behind Mr. Beaumont's desk—as I walked toward the fish tank.

The humming of the elevator stopped. I heard the doorknob turn. I kept walking. The chair's wheels were noisy on the parquet floor.

The door to the elevator opened. Marcus, seeing that I had not done as he asked, shook his head.

"Miss Simon," he said, in a disappointed tone. "Are we being difficult?"

I positioned the swivel chair in front of the aquarium. Then I lifted a foot and balanced it on top of the seat. From one finger, I dangled the bathing suit.

"Sorry," I said, apologetically. "But dead's never been my color."

Then I grabbed that chair, and flung it with all my might at the glass of that giant fish tank.

CHAPTER 20

The next thing I knew there was a tremendous crash.

Then a wall of water, glass, and exotic marine life was coming at me.

It knocked me flat onto my back. A tidal wave hit me with the weight of a freight train, pushing me to the floor, then flattening me against the far wall of the room. The wind knocked out of me, I lay there a second, soaked, coughing up briny water, some of which I accidentally swallowed.

When I opened my eyes, all I could see were fish. Big fish, little fish, trying to swim through the three inches of water that lay upon the wood floor, opening and closing their mouths in a pathetic attempt to snatch a few more seconds of life. One fish in particular had washed up next to me, and it stared at me with eyes almost as glassy and lifeless as Marcus's had been when he'd been explaining how he intended to kill me.

Then a very familiar voice cut through my dazed musings on the paradoxes of life and death.

"Susannah?"

I lifted my head, and was extremely surprised to see Jesse standing over me, a very worried look on his face.

"Oh," I said. "Hi. How did you get here?"

"You called me," Jesse said.

How could I ever have thought, I wondered as I lay there gazing up at him, that any guy, even Tad, could ever be quite as hot as Jesse? Everything, from the tiny scar in his eyebrow, to the way his dark hair curled against the back of his neck, was perfect, as if Jesse were the original mold for the archetypal hottie.

He was polite, too. Old-world manners were the only ones he knew. He leaned down and offered me his hand . . . his lean, brown, completely poison oak–free hand.

I reached up. He helped me to my feet.

"Are you all right?" he asked, probably because I wasn't mouthing off as much as usual.

"I'm fine," I said. Drenched, and smelling of fish, but fine. "But I didn't call you."

From the opposite corner of the room came a very low snarl.

Marcus was struggling to get to his feet, but he kept slipping on all the water and fish. "What the *hell* did you do that for?" he wanted to know.

I couldn't actually remember. I think maybe when the water hit me, I'd banged my head against something. Wow, I thought. Amnesia. Cool. I'd get out of tomorrow's geometry quiz for sure.

Then my gaze fell on Tad—still sleeping peacefully on the couch, an exotic-looking fish flopping in death throes on his bare legs—and I remembered.

Oh, yeah. Tad's uncle Marcus was trying to kill us. *Would* kill us, too, if I didn't stop him.

I'm not sure I was really thinking straight. All I could remember from before the water hit was that it had been important, for some reason, for me to get to the other side of that fish tank.

And so I waded through all that water—thinking to myself, *My boots are so ruined*—and climbed up onto what was now just a raised platform, like a stage, looking out across a sea of slapping fishtails. The accent lights, still buried in the colored gravel at the bottom of the tank, shined up on me.

"Susannah," I heard Jesse say. He'd followed me, and now stood looking up at me curiously. "What are you doing?"

I ignored him—and Marcus, too, who was still swearing as he tried to get across the room without getting his Cole-Haans more wet than they already were.

I stood inside the ruined aquarium and looked up. As I'd suspected, the fish were fed from a room behind the tank . . . a room in which there was nothing except aquarium maintenance equipment. The locked door from Mr. Beaumont's office led into this room. There was no other form of egress.

Not that it mattered now, of course.

"Get down from there." Marcus sounded really mad. "Get down there from there, by God, or I'll climb in and fish you out—"

Fish me out. That struck me as kind of amusing under the circumstances. I started to laugh.

"Susannah," Jesse said. "I think—"

"We'll see how hard you're laughing," Marcus bellowed, "when I get through with you, you stupid bitch."

I stopped laughing all of a sudden.

"Susannah," Jesse said. Now he *really* sounded worried.

"Don't worry, Jesse," I said, in a perfectly calm voice. "I've got this one under control."

"Jesse?" Marcus looked around. Not seeing anyone else in the room, however, but Tad, he said, "It's Marcus. I'm Marcus, remember? Now, come on down here. We don't have any more time for these childish games. . . ."

I bent down and seized one of the accent lights that glowed, hidden in the sand at the bottom of the tank. Shaped like a small floodlight, it proved to be very hot in my hands when I touched it.

Marcus, realizing I wasn't going to come with him on my own accord, sighed, and reached into his suit coat, which was wet and smelly now. He'd have to change before his lunch meeting.

"Okay, you want to play games?" Marcus pulled something made of shiny metal from his breast pocket. It was, I realized, a tiny little gun. A .22, from the looks of it. I knew from having watched so many episodes of *Cops*.

"See this?" Marcus pointed the muzzle at me. "I don't want to have to shoot you. The coroner tends to be suspicious of drowning victims bearing gunshot wounds. But we can always let the propellers dismember you so no one will actually be able to tell. Maybe just your head will toss up onto shore. Wouldn't your mother love *that*? Now, put the light down and let's go."

I straightened, but I didn't put the light down. It came up with me, along with the black rubber-coated cord that had grounded it beneath the sand.

"That's right," Marcus said, looking pleased. "Put the light down, and let's go."

Jesse, standing in the water beside my would-be assassin, looked extremely interested in what was going on. "Susannah," he said. "That is a gun he is holding. Do you want me to—"

"Don't worry, Jesse," I said, approaching the edge of the tank, where there'd once been a wall of glass— before I'd broken it, that is. "Everything's under control."

"Who the hell is Jesse?" Marcus, I realized, was getting testy. "There is no Jesse here. Now put the light down and let's—"

I did what he said. Well, sort of. That is, I wrapped the cord that was attached to the light around my left hand. Then with my other hand, I pulled the bulb so that the cord came popping right out of the back of the socket.

Then I stood there holding the lamp in one hand, and the cord with frayed wires now sticking out of one end of it in the other.

"That's great," Marcus said. "You broke the light. You really showed me. Now"—his voice rose—"*get down here!*"

I stepped up to the edge of the tank.

"I am not," I informed Marcus, "stupid."

He gestured with the gun. "Whatever you say. Just—"

"Nor," I added, "am I a bitch."

Marcus's eyes widened. Suddenly, he realized what I was up to.

"No!" he shrieked.

But it was way too late. I had already thrown the cord into the murky water at Marcus's feet.

There was a brilliant blue flash and a lot of popping noises. Marcus screamed.

And then we were plunged into impenetrable darkness.

CHAPTER 21

Well, okay, not really impenetrable. I could still see Jesse, glowing the way he did.

"That," he said, looking down at the moaning Marcus, "was very impressive, Susannah."

"Thanks," I said, pleased to have won his approval. It happened so rarely. I was glad I'd listened to Doc during one of his recent electrical safety lectures.

"Now, do you think you want to tell me," Jesse asked, moving to offer me a steadying hand as I climbed down from the aquarium, "just what is going on here? Is that your friend Tad on the couch there?"

"Uh-huh." Before stepping down, I bent down, searching for the cord along the floor. "Step over here, will you, so I can—" Jesse's glow, subtle as it was, soon revealed what I was looking for. "Never mind." I pulled the cord back up into the aquarium. "Just in case," I said, straightening and climbing out of the aquarium, "they get the circuit breaker fixed before I'm out of here."

"Who is *they*? Susannah, what is going on here?"

"It's a long story," I said. "And I'm not sticking around to tell it. I want to be out of here when he"—I nodded toward Marcus, who was moaning more loudly now—"wakes up. He's got a couple of thick-necked compadres waiting for me, too, in case—" I broke off.

Jesse looked at me questioningly. "What is it?"

"Do you smell that?"

Stupid question. I mean, after all, the guy's dead. Can ghosts smell?

Apparently so, since he went, "Smoke."

A single syllable, but it sent a chill down my spine. Either that, or a fish had found its way inside my sweater.

I glanced at the aquarium. Beyond it, I could see a rosy glow emanating from the room next door. Just as I had suspected, by giving Marcus a giant electric shock, I had managed to spark a fire in the circuit panel. It appeared to have spread to the walls around it. I could see the first tiny licks of orange leaping out from behind the wood paneling.

"Great," I said. The elevator was useless without

electricity. And as I knew only too well, there was no other way out of that room.

Jesse wasn't quite the defeatist I was, however.

"The windows," he said, and hurried toward them.

"It's no good." I leaned against Mr. Beaumont's desk and picked up the house phone. Dead, just as I'd expected. "They're nailed shut."

Jesse glanced at me over his shoulder. He looked amused. "So?" he said.

"So." I slammed the receiver down. "*Nailed*, Jesse. As in impossible to budge."

"For you, maybe." Even as he said it, the wooden shutters over the window closest to me began to tremble ominously as if blown by some unseen gale. "But not for me."

I watched, impressed. "Golly gee, mister," I said. "I forgot all about your superpowers."

Jesse's look went from amused to confused. "My what?"

"Oh." I dropped the imitation I'd been doing of a kid from an episode of *Superman*.

"Never mind."

I heard, above the sound of nails screaming as if caught in the suck zone of an F5 tornado, people shouting. I glanced toward the elevator. The thugs, apparently concerned for their employer's welfare, were calling his name up the shaft.

I guess I didn't blame them. Smoke was steadily

filling the room. I could hear small eruptions now as chemicals—most likely of a hazardous nature—used in the upkeep of Mr. Beaumont's fish tank burst into flames next door. If we didn't get out of there soon, I had a feeling we'd all be inhaling some pretty toxic fumes.

Fortunately, at that moment the shutters burst off first one and then another of the windows, with all the force as if a hurricane had suddenly ripped them off. *Blam!* And then *blam* again. I'd never seen anything like it before, not even on the Discovery Channel.

Gray light rushed in. It was, I realized, still raining out.

I didn't care. I don't think I'd ever been so glad to see the sky, even as darkly overcast as it was. I rushed to the window closest to me and looked out, squinting against the rain.

We were, I saw, in the upper story of the house. Below us lay the patio. . . .

And the pool.

The shouting up the elevator shaft was growing louder. The thicker the smoke grew, apparently, the more frantic the thugs became. God forbid one of them should think to dial 911. Then again, considering the career choices they'd made, that number probably didn't hold much appeal for them.

I measured the distance between myself and the deep end of the pool.

"It can't be more than twenty feet." Jesse, observing my calculations, nodded to Marcus. "You go. I'll look after him." His dark-eyed gaze flicked toward the elevator shaft. "And them, if they make any progress."

I didn't ask what he meant by "looking after." I didn't have to. The dangerous light in his eyes said it all.

I glanced at Tad. Jesse followed my gaze, then rolled his eyes, the dangerous light extinguished. He muttered some stuff in Spanish.

"Well, I can't just leave him here," I said.

"No."

Which was how, a few seconds later, Tad, supported by me, but transported via the Jesse kinetic connection, ended up perched on the sill of one of those windows Jesse had blown open for me.

The only way to get Tad into the pool—and to safety—was to drop him into it out the window. This was a risky enough endeavor without having an inferno blazing next door, and hired assassins bearing down on you. I had to concentrate. I didn't want to do it wrong. What if I missed and he smacked onto the patio, instead? Tad could break his poison-oaky neck.

But I didn't have much choice in the matter. It was either turn him into a possible pancake, or let him be barbecued for sure. I went with the possible pancake, thinking that he was likelier to heal in time for the prom from a cracked skull than third-degree burns, and, after aiming as best I could, I let go. He fell backward, like a scuba diver off the side of a boat, tumbling once through the sky and doing what Dopey would call a pretty sick inverted spin. (Dopey is an avid, if untalented, snowboarder.)

Fortunately, Tad's sick inverted spin ended with him floating on his back in the deep end of his father's pool.

Of course, to guarantee he didn't drown—unconscious people aren't the best swimmers—I jumped in after him . . . but not before one last look around.

Marcus was finally starting to regain consciousness. He was coughing a little because of the smoke, and splashing around in the fishy water. Jesse stood over him, looking grim-faced.

"Go, Susannah," he said when he noticed I'd hesitated.

I nodded. But there was still one thing I had to know.

"You're not . . ." I didn't want to, but I had to ask. "You're not going to kill him, are you?"

Jesse looked as incredulous as if I'd asked him if he were going to serve Marcus a slice of cheesecake. He said, "Of course not. *Go*."

I went.

The water was warm. It was like jumping into a giant bathtub. When I'd swum up to the surface—not exactly easy in boots, by the way—I hurried to Tad's side. . . .

Only to find that the water had revived him. He was splashing around, looking confused and taking in great lungfuls of water. I smacked him on the back a couple of times, and steered him to the side of the pool, which he clung to gratefully.

"S-Sue," he sputtered, bewilderedly. "What are *you* doing here?" Then he noticed my leather jacket. "And why aren't you wearing a bathing suit?"

"It's a long story," I said.

He looked even more confused after that, but that was all right. I figured that, with as much stuff as he was going to have to deal with—his dad being a Prozac candidate, his uncle a serial killer—he didn't need to have all the gory details spelled out for him right away. Instead, I guided him over toward the shallow end. We'd only been standing there a minute before Mr. Beaumont opened the sliding glass door and stepped outside.

"Children," he said. He was wearing a silk dressing gown and his bedroom slippers. He looked very excited. "What are you doing in that pool? There's a fire! Get away from the house at once."

Even as he said it, I could hear, off in the distance, the whine of a siren. The fire department was on its way. Someone, anyway, had dialed 911.

"I warned Marcus," Mr. Beaumont said, as he held

out a big fluffy towel for Tad to step into, "about the wiring in my office. I had a feeling it was faulty. My telephone absolutely would not make outgoing calls."

Still standing in the waist-high water, I followed Mr. Beaumont's gaze, and found myself looking up at the window I'd just leaped from. Smoke was billowing out of it. The fire seemed to be contained in that section of the house, but still, it looked pretty bad. I wondered if Marcus and his thugs had gotten out in time.

And then someone stepped up to the window and looked down at me.

It wasn't Marcus. And it wasn't Jesse, either, though this person was giving off a telltale glow.

It was someone who waved cheerfully down at me. Mrs. Deirdre Fiske.

CHAPTER 22

I never saw Marcus Beaumont again.

Oh, stop worrying: He didn't croak. Of course, the firemen looked for him. I told them I thought there was at least one person trapped in that burning room, and they did their best to get in there in time to save him.

But they didn't find anyone. And no human remains were discovered by the investigators who went in after the fire was finally put out. They found an awful lot of burned fish, but no Marcus Beaumont.

Marcus Beaumont was officially missing.

Much in the same way, I realized, that his victims had gone missing. He simply vanished, as if into thin air.

A lot of people were puzzled by the disappearance

of this prominent businessman. In later weeks, there would be articles about it in the local papers, and even a mention on one cable news network. Interestingly, the person who knew the most about Marcus Beaumont's last moments before he vanished was never interviewed, much less questioned, about what might have led up to his bizarre disappearance.

Which is probably just as well, considering the fact that she had way more important things to worry about. For instance, being grounded.

That's right. Grounded.

If you think about it, the only thing I'd really done wrong on the day in question was dress a little less conservatively than I should have. Seriously. If I'd gone Banana Republic instead of Betsey Johnson, none of this might have happened. Because then I wouldn't have been sent home to change, and Marcus would never have gotten his mitts on me.

On the other hand, he'd still probably be going around, slipping environmentalists into cement booties and tossing them off the side of his brother's yacht . . . or however it was he got rid of all those people without ever being caught. I never really did get the full story on that one.

In any case, I got grounded, completely unjustly, although I wasn't exactly in a position to defend myself . . . not without telling the truth, and I couldn't, of course, do that.

I guess you could imagine how it must have looked to my mother and stepfather when the cop car pulled up in front of our house and Officer Green opened the back door to reveal . . . well, me.

I looked like something out of a movie about post-apocalyptic America. *Tank Girl,* but without the awful haircut. Sister Ernestine wasn't going to have to worry about me showing up to school in Betsey Johnson ever again, either. The skirt was completely ruined, as was my cashmere sweater set. My fabulous leather motorcycle jacket might be all right, someday, if I can ever figure out a way to get the fishy smell out of it. The boots, however, are a lost cause.

Boy, was my mom mad. And not because of my clothes, either.

Interestingly, Andy was even madder. Interestingly because, of course, he's not even my real parent.

But you should have seen the way he lit into me right there in the living room. Because of course I'd had to explain to them what it was I'd been doing at the Beaumonts' place when the fire broke out, instead of being where I was supposed to have been: school.

And the only lie I could think of that seemed the least bit believable was my newspaper article story.

So I told them that I'd skipped school in order to do some follow-up work on my interview with Mr. Beaumont.

They didn't believe me, of course. It turned out

they knew I'd been sent home from school to change clothes. Father Dominic, alarmed when I didn't return in a timely fashion, had immediately called my mother and stepfather at their respective places of work to alert them to the fact that I was missing.

"Well," I explained. "I was on my way home to change when Mr. Beaumont's brother drove by and offered me a ride, and so I took it, and then when I was sitting in Mr. B's office, I started to smell smoke, and so I jumped out the window. . . ."

Okay, even I have to admit that the whole thing sounded super suspicious. But it was better than the truth, right? I mean, were they really going to believe that Tad's uncle Marcus had been trying to kill me because I knew too much about a bunch of murders he'd committed for the sake of urban sprawl?

Not very likely. Even Tad didn't try that one on the cops who showed up along with the fire department, and demanded an explanation as to why he was hanging around the house in a swimsuit on a school day. I guess he didn't want to get his uncle in trouble since it would look bad for his dad, and all. He started lying like crazy about how he had a cold, and the doctor had recommended he try to clear his sinuses by sitting for long bouts in his hot tub (good one: I was definitely going to have to remember it for future reference— Andy was talking about building a hot tub onto our deck out back).

Tad's father, God bless him, denied both our stories completely, insisting he'd been in his room waiting for his lunch to be delivered when one of the servants had informed him that his office was in flames. No one had said anything about Tad having stayed home with a cold, or a girl waiting for an interview with him.

Fortunately, however, he also claimed that while waiting for his lunch to be delivered, he'd been taking a nap in his coffin.

That's right: his *coffin*.

This caused a number of raised eyebrows, and eventually, it was decided that Mr. Beaumont ought to be admitted to the local hospital's psychiatric floor for a few days' observation. This, as you might understand, necessarily cut off any conversation Tad and I might have had at the time, and while he went off with EMS and his father, I was unceremoniously led to a squad car and, eventually, when the cops remembered me, driven home.

Where, instead of being welcomed into the bosom of my family, I received the bawling out of a lifetime.

I'm not even kidding. Andy was enraged. He said I should have gone straight home, changed clothes, and gone straight back to school. I had no business accepting rides from anyone, particularly wealthy businessmen I hardly knew.

Furthermore, I had skipped school, and no matter how many times I pointed out that a) I'd actually been kicked *out* of school, and b) I'd been doing an assignment *for* school (at least according to the story I told him), I had, essentially, betrayed everyone's trust. I was grounded for one week.

I tell you, it was almost enough to make me consider telling the truth.

Almost. But not quite.

I was getting ready to slink upstairs to my room—in order to "think about what I'd done"—when Dopey strolled in and casually announced that, by the way, on top of all my other sins, I had also punched him very hard in the stomach that morning for no apparent reason.

This, of course, was an outright lie, and I was quick to remind him of this: I had been provoked, unnecessarily so. But Andy, who does not condone violence for any reason, promptly grounded me for another week. Since he also grounded Dopey for whatever it was he had said that had led to my punching him, I didn't mind too much, but still, it seemed a bit extreme. So extreme, in fact, that after Andy had left the room, I sort of had to sit down, exhausted in the wake of his rage, which I had never before seen unleashed—well, not in *my* direction, anyway.

"You really," my mother said, taking a seat opposite me, and looking a bit worriedly down at the slipcover on which I was slumped, "should have let us know where you were. Poor Father Dominic was frightened out of his mind for you."

"Sorry," I said woefully, fingering the remnants of my skirt. "I'll remember next time."

"Still," my mother said. "Officer Green told us that you were very helpful during the fire. So I guess . . ."

I looked at her. "You guess what?"

"Well," my mother said. "Andy doesn't want me to tell you now, but . . ."

She actually got up—my mother, who had once interviewed Yasir Arafat—and slunk out of the room, ostensibly to check whether or not Andy was within earshot.

I rolled my eyes. Love. It could make a pretty big sap out of you.

As I rolled my eyes, I noticed that my mother, who always gets a lot of nervous energy in a crisis, had spent the time that I'd been missing hanging up more pictures in the living room. There were some new ones, ones I hadn't seen before. I got up to inspect them more closely.

There was one of her and my dad on their wedding day. They were coming down the steps of the court-house where they'd been married, and their friends were throwing rice at them. They looked impossibly young and happy. I was surprised to see a picture of my mom and dad right alongside the pictures of my mom's wedding to Andy.

But then I noticed that beside the photo of my mom

and dad was a picture from what had to have been Andy's wedding to his first wife. This was more of a studio portrait than a candid shot. Andy was standing, looking stiff and a little embarrassed, next to a very skinny, hippyish-looking girl with long, straight hair.

A hippyish-looking girl who seemed a little familiar.

"Of course she does," a voice at my shoulder said.

"Jeez, Dad," I hissed, whirling around. "When are you going to stop doing that?"

"You are in a heap of trouble, young lady," my father said. He looked sore. Well, as sore as a guy in jogging pants could look. "Just what were you thinking?"

I whispered, "I was thinking of making it safe for people to protest the corporate destruction of northern California's natural resources without having to worry about being sealed up in an oil drum and buried ten feet under."

"Don't get smart with me, Susannah. You know what I'm talking about. You could have been killed."

"You sound like *him*." I rolled my eyes toward Andy's picture.

"He did the right thing, grounding you," my father said, severely. "He's trying to teach you a lesson. You behaved in a thoughtless and reckless manner. And you shouldn't have hit that kid of his."

"Dopey? Are you *joking*?"

But I could tell he was serious. I could also tell that this was one argument I wasn't going to win.

So instead, I looked at the picture of Andy and his first wife, and said, sullenly, "You could have told me about her, you know. It would have made my life a whole lot simpler."

"I didn't know, either," my dad said, with a shrug. "Not until I saw your mom hang up the photo this afternoon."

"What do you mean, you didn't know?" I glared at him. "What was with all the cryptic warnings, then?"

"Well, I knew Beaumont wasn't the Red you were looking for. I told you that."

"Oh, big help," I said.

"Look." My dad seemed annoyed. "I'm not all-knowing. Just dead."

I heard my mother's footsteps on the wood floor. "Mom's coming," I said. "Scat."

And Dad, for once, did as I asked, so that when my mother returned to the living room, I was standing in front of the wall of photos, looking very demure—well, for a girl who'd practically been burned alive, anyway.

"Listen," my mother whispered.

I looked away from the picture. My mother was holding an envelope. It was a bright pink envelope, covered with little hand-drawn hearts and rainbows. The kind of hearts and rainbows Gina always put on her letters to me from back home.

"Andy wanted me to wait to tell you about this," my mom said in a low voice, "until after your grounding was up. But I can't. I want you to know I've spoken with Gina's mom, and she's agreed to let us fly Gina out here for a visit during her school's Spring Break next month—"

My mother broke off as I flung both my arms around her neck.

"Thank you!" I cried.

"Oh, honey," my mom said, hugging me—although a little tentatively, I noticed, since I still smelled like a fish. "You're welcome. I know how much you miss her. And I know how tough it's been on you, adjusting to a whole new high school, and a whole new set of friends—and to having stepbrothers. We're so proud of how well you're doing." She pulled away from me. I could tell she'd wanted to go on hugging me, but I was just too gross even for my own mother. "Well, up until now, anyway."

I looked down at Gina's letter, which my mom had handed to me. Gina was a terrific letter writer. I couldn't wait to go upstairs and read it. Only . . . only something was still bothering me.

I looked back, over my shoulder, at the photo of Andy and his first wife.

"You hung up some new pictures, I see," I said.

My mom followed my gaze. "Oh, yes. Well, it kept my mind occupied while we were waiting to hear from you. Why don't you go upstairs and get yourself cleaned up? Andy's making individual pizzas for dinner."

"His first wife," I said, my eyes still glued to the photo. "Dopey's—I mean, Brad's—mom. She died, right?"

"Uh-huh," my mother said. "Several years ago."

"What of?"

"Ovarian cancer. Honey, be careful where you put those clothes when you take them off. They're covered with soot. Look, there's black gunk now all over my new Pottery Barn slipcovers."

I stared at the photo.

"Did she . . ." I struggled to formulate the correct question. "Did she go into a coma, or something?"

My mother looked up from the slipcover she'd been yanking from the armchair where I'd been lounging.

"I think so," she said. "Yes, toward the end. Why?"

"Did Andy have to . . ." I turned Gina's letter over and over in my hands. "Did they have to pull the plug?"

"Yes." My mother had forgotten about the slipcover. Now she was staring at me, obviously concerned. "Yes, as a matter of fact, they had to ask that she be taken off life support at a certain point since Andy believed she wouldn't have wanted to live like that. Why?"

"I don't know." I looked down at the hearts and rainbows on Gina's envelope. *Red*. I had been so stupid. *You know me,* Doc's mother had insisted. God, I should so have my mediator license revoked. If there were a license, which, of course, there isn't.

"What was her name?" I asked, nodding my head toward the photo. "Brad's mom, I mean?"

"Cynthia," my mother said.

Cynthia. God, what a loser I am.

"Honey, come help me, would you?" My mother was still futzing with the chair I'd been sitting in. "I can't get this one cushion loose—"

I tucked Gina's envelope into my pocket and went to help my mother. "Where's Doc?" I asked. "I mean, David."

My mother looked at me curiously. "Upstairs in his room, I think, doing his homework. Why?"

"Oh, I just have to tell him something."

Something I should have told him a long time ago.

CHAPTER 23

"So?" Jesse asked. "How did he take it?"

"I don't want to talk about it."

I was stretched out on my bed, totally without makeup, attired in my oldest jogging clothes. I had a new plan: I had decided I was going to treat Jesse exactly the way I would my stepbrothers. That way, I'd be guaranteed not to fall in love with him.

I was flipping through a copy of *Vogue* instead of doing my geometry homework like I was supposed to. Jesse was on the window seat—of course—petting Spike.

Jesse shook his head. "Come on," he said. It always sounded strange to me when Jesse said things like *Come on*. It seemed so strange coming out of a guy who was wearing a shirt with laces instead of buttons. "Tell me what he said."

I flipped a page of my magazine. "Tell me what you guys did to Marcus."

Jesse looked a little too surprised by the question. "We did nothing to him."

"Baloney. Where'd he go, then?"

Jesse shrugged and scratched Spike beneath the chin. The stupid cat was purring so loud, I could hear it all the way across the room.

"I think he decided to travel for a while." Jesse's tone was deceptively innocent.

"Without any money? Without his credit cards?" One of the things the firemen had found in the room was Marcus's wallet . . . and his gun.

"There is something to be said"—Jesse gave Spike a playful swat on the back of the head when the cat took a lazy swipe at him—"for seeing this great country of ours on foot. Maybe he will come to have a better appreciation for its natural beauty."

I snorted, and turned a page of my magazine. "He'll be back in a week."

"I think not."

He said it with such certainty that I instantly became suspicious.

"Why not?"

Jesse hesitated. He didn't want to tell me, I could tell.

"What?" I said. "Telling me, a mere living being, is going to violate some spectral code?"

"No," Jesse said with a smile. "He's not coming back, Susannah, because the souls of the people he killed won't let him."

I raised my eyebrows. "What do you mean?"

"In my day, it was called bedevilment. I don't know what they call it now. But your intervention had a rallying effect on Mrs. Fiske and the three others whose lives Marcus Beaumont took. They have banded together, and will not rest until he has been sufficiently punished for his crimes. He can run from one end of the earth to the other, but he will never escape them. Not until he dies himself. And when that happens"— Jesse's voice was hard—"he will be a broken man."

I didn't say anything. I couldn't. As a mediator, I knew I shouldn't approve of this sort of behavior. I mean, ghosts should not be allowed to take the law into their own hands any more than the living should.

But I had no particular fondness for Marcus, and no way of proving that he'd killed those people anyway. He'd never be punished, I knew, by inhabitants of this world. So was it so wrong that he be punished by those who lived in the next?

I glanced at Jesse out of the corner of my eyes, remembering that, from what I'd read, no one had ever been convicted of *his* murder, either.

"So," I said. "I guess you did the same thing, huh, to the, um, people who killed you, right?"

Jesse didn't fall for this sly question, though. He only smiled, and said, "Tell me what happened with your brother."

"Stepbrother," I reminded him.

And I wasn't going to tell Jesse about my interview with Doc, any more than Jesse was going to tell me diddly about how he'd died. Only in my case, it was because what had happened with Doc was just too excruciatingly embarrassing to go into. Jesse didn't want to talk about how he'd died because . . . well, I don't know. But I doubt it's because he's embarrassed about it.

I had found Doc exactly where my mother had told me he'd be, in his room doing his homework, a paper that wasn't due until the following month. But that was Doc for you: Why put off until tomorrow homework you could be doing today?

His "Come in," when I'd tapped at the door had been casual. He hadn't suspected it would be me. I never ventured into my stepbrothers' rooms if I could avoid it. The odor of dirty socks was simply too overwhelming.

Only since I wasn't smelling too daisy-fresh myself at that particular moment, I thought I could bear it.

He was shocked to see me, his face turning almost

as red as his hair. He jumped up and tried to hide his pile of dirty underwear beneath the comforter of his unmade bed. I told him to relax. And then I sat down on that unmade bed, and said I had something to tell him.

How did he take it? Well, for one thing, he didn't ask me a lot of stupid questions like *How do you know?* He knew how I knew. He knew a little about the mediation thing. Not a lot, but enough to know that I communicate, on a somewhat regular basis, with the undead.

I guess it was the fact that it was his own mother I'd been communicating with this time that brought tears to his blue eyes . . . which freaked me out a bit. I had never seen Doc cry before.

"Hey," I said, alarmed. "Hey, it's okay—"

"What—" Doc was choking back a sob. I could totally tell. "What did she l-look like?"

"What did she *look* like?" I echoed, not sure I'd heard him right. At his vigorous nod, however, I said, carefully, "Well, she looked . . . she looked very pretty."

Doc's tear-filled eyes widened. "She did?"

"Uh-huh," I said. "That's how I recognized her, you know. From the wedding photo of her and your dad, downstairs. She looked like that. Only her hair was shorter."

Doc said, the effort he was making not to cry causing his voice to shake, "I wish I could . . . I wish I could see her looking like that. The last time I saw her, she looked terrible. Not like in that picture. You wouldn't have recognized her. She was in a c-coma. Her eyes were sunken in. And there were all these tubes coming out of her—"

Even though I was sitting like a foot away from him, I felt the shudder that ran through him. I said, gently, "David, what you did, when you guys made the decision to let her go . . . it was the right thing. It was what she wanted. That's what she needs to make sure you understand. You know it was the right thing, don't you?"

His eyes were so deeply pooled in tears, I could hardly see his irises anymore. As I watched, one drop escaped, and trickled down his cheek, followed quickly by another on the opposite side of his face.

"I-intellectually," he said. "I guess. B-but—"

"It was the right thing," I repeated, firmly. "You've got to believe that. She does. So stop beating yourself up. She loves you very much—"

That did it. Now the tears were coming down in full force.

"She said that?" he asked, in a broken voice that reminded me that he was, after all, still a pretty young kid, and not the superhuman computer he sometimes acts like.

"Of course she did."

She hadn't, of course, but I'm sure she would have

if she hadn't been so disgusted by my gross incompe-
tency.

Then Doc did something that completely shocked
me: He flung both his arms around my neck.

This kind of impassioned display was so unlike
Doc, I didn't know what to do. I sat there for one awkward moment, not moving, afraid that if I did, I might
gouge his face with some of the rivets on my jacket.
Finally, however, when he didn't let go, I reached up
and patted him uncertainly on the shoulder.

"It's okay," I said, lamely. "Everything is going to
be okay."

He cried for about two minutes. His clinging to
me, crying like that, gave me a strange feeling. It was
kind of a protective feeling.

Then he finally leaned back, and, embarrassed,
wiped his eyes again and said, "Sorry."

I said, "It's no big deal," even though, of course, it
was.

"Suze," he said. "Can I ask you something?"

Expecting more questions about his mother, I said,
"Sure."

"Why do you smell like fish?"

I went back to my room a little while later, shaken
not just by Doc's emotional reaction to the message I'd
delivered but by something else, as well. Something I
had not told Doc, and which I had no intention of
mentioning to Jesse, either.

And it was that while I'd been hugging Doc, his mother had materialized on the opposite side of the bed and looked down at me.

"Thank you," she said. She was, I saw, crying about as hard as her kid. Only her tears, I was uncomfortably aware, were of gratitude and love.

With all these people crying around me, was it really any wonder that *my* eyes filled up, too? I mean, come on. I'm only human.

But I really hate it when I cry. I'd much rather bleed or throw up or something. Crying is just . . .

Well, it's the worst.

You can see why I couldn't tell any of this stuff to Jesse. It was just too . . . personal. It was between Doc and his mom and me, and wild horses—or excessively cute ghosts who happened to live in my bedroom—weren't going to get it out of me.

Jesse, I saw when I glanced up from the article I'd been staring at unseeingly—*How to Tell If He Secretly Loves You*. Yeah, right. A problem I so don't have—was grinning at me.

"Still," he said. "You must be feeling good. It's not every mediator who single-handedly stops a murderer."

I grunted, and flipped over another page. "It's an honor I could definitely have lived without," I said. "And I didn't do it single-handedly. You helped." Then I remembered that, really, I'd had the situation well in hand by the time Jesse had shown up. So I added, "Well, sort of."

But that sounded ungracious. So I said, grudgingly, "Thanks for showing up the way you did."

"How could I not? You called me." He had found a piece of string somewhere, and now he dragged it in front of Spike, who eyed it with an expression on his face that seemed to say, "Whaddya think, I'm stupid?"

"Um," I said. "I did not call you, all right? I don't know where you're getting this."

He looked at me, his eyes darker than ever in the rays of the setting sun, which poured unmercifully into my room every night at sundown. "I distinctly heard you, Susannah."

I frowned. This was all getting a little too weird for me. First Mrs. Fiske had shown up when all I'd been doing was thinking about her. And then Jesse did the same thing. Only I hadn't, to my knowledge, *called* either of them. I'd been *thinking* about them, true.

Jeez. There was way more stuff to this mediating thing than I'd ever even suspected.

"Well, while we're on the subject," I said, "how come you didn't just tell me that Red was Doc's mom's nickname for him?"

Jesse threw me a perplexed look. "How would I have known?"

True. I hadn't thought of that. Andy and my mother

had bought the house—Jesse's house—only last summer. Jesse couldn't have known who Cynthia was. And yet . . .

Well, he'd known *something* about her.

Ghosts. Would I *ever* figure them out?

"What did the priest say?" Jesse asked me, in an obvious attempt to change the subject. "When you told him about the Beaumonts, I mean?"

"Not a whole lot. He's pretty peeved at me for not having filled him in right away about Marcus and stuff." I was careful not to add that Father D. was also still ballistic over the whole Jesse issue. That, he'd promised me, was a topic we were going to discuss at length tomorrow morning at school. I could hardly wait. It was no wonder I wasn't doing so hot in geometry if you took into account all the time I was spending in the principal's office.

The phone rang. I snatched up the receiver, grateful for an excuse not to have to go on lying to Jesse.

"Hello?"

Jesse gave me a sour look. The telephone is one modern convenience Jesse insists he could live very happily without. TV is another. He doesn't seem to mind Madonna, though.

"Sue?"

I blinked. It was Tad.

"Oh, hi," I said.

"Um," Tad said. "It's me. Tad."

Don't ask me how this guy, and the guy who'd gotten away with so many murders, could be from the same gene pool. I really don't get it.

I rolled my eyes, and, throwing the copy of *Vogue* onto the floor, picked up Gina's letter and re-read it.

"I know it's you, Tad," I said. "How's your dad?"

"Um," Tad said. "Much better, actually. It looks as if someone was giving him something—something my dad seems to have thought was medicine—that may actually have been having some kind of hallucinatory effect on him. Turns out the doctors think that might be what's making him think he's . . . well, what he thinks he is."

"Really?"

Dude, Gina wrote, in her big, loopy cursive. *Looks like I'm headin' out West to see you! Your mom rocks! So does that new stepdad of yours. Can't wait to meet the new bros. They can't possibly be as bad as you say.*

Wanna bet?

"Yeah. So they're going to try to, you know, detox him for a while, and the hope is that once this stuff, whatever it is, is out of his system, he'll be back to his old self again."

"Wow, Tad," I said. "That's great."

"Yeah. It's going to take a while, though, since I guess he's been taking this stuff since right after my mom died. I think . . . well, I didn't tell anyone, but I'm wondering if my uncle Marcus might have been giving this stuff to my dad. Not to hurt him or anything—"

Yeah, right. He hadn't been trying to hurt him. He'd been trying to gain control of Beaumont Industries, that's all.

And he'd succeeded.

"I think he really must have thought he was helping my dad. Right after my mom died, Dad was way messed up. Uncle Marcus was only trying to help him, I'm sure."

Just like he was just trying to help you, Tad, when he pistol-whipped you and swapped your Levi's for swim trunks. Tad, I realized, had some major denial going on.

"Anyway," Tad went on. "I just want to say, um, thanks. I mean, for not saying anything to the cops about my uncle. I mean, we probably should have, right? But it seems like he's gone now, and it would have, you know, looked kind of bad for my dad's business—"

This conversation was getting way too weird for me. I returned to the comfort of Gina's letter.

So what should I bring? I mean, to wear. I got this totally hot pair of Miu Miu slacks, marked down to twenty bucks at Filene's, but isn't it Baywatch *weather there? The slacks are a wool blend. Also, you better get us invited to some rockin' parties while I'm there because I just got new extensions, and girlfriend, let me tell you, I look GOOD. Shauna did them, and she* only charged me a buck per. Of course I have to baby-sit her stinking brother this Saturday, but who cares? It's so worth it.

"Well, anyway, I just called to say thanks for being, you know, so cool about everything."

Also, Gina wrote, *I think you should know, I am very seriously thinking about getting a tattoo while I'm out there. I know, I know. Mom wasn't exactly thrilled by the tongue stud. But I'm thinking there's no reason she has to see the tattoo, if I get it where I'm thinking about getting it. If you know what I mean! XXXOOO—G*

"Also, I guess I should tell you, since my uncle's gone, and my dad's . . . you know, in the hospital . . . it looks like I have to go stay with my aunt for a while up in San Francisco. So I won't be around for a few weeks. Or at least until my dad gets better."

I was never, I realized, going to see Tad again. To him, I would eventually become just an awkward reminder of what had happened. And why would he want to hang around someone who reminds him of the painful time when his dad was running around pretending to be Count Dracula?

I found this a little sad, but I could understand it.

P.S. Check this out! I found it in a thrift shop. Remember that whacked-out psychic we went to see that one time? The one who called you—what was it again? Oh, yeah, a mediator. Conductor of souls?

Well, here you are! Nice robes. I mean it. Very Cynthia Rowley.

Tucked into the envelope with Gina's letter was a battered tarot card. It appeared to have been from a beginner's set since there was an explanation printed under the illustration, which was of an old man with a long white beard holding a lantern.

The Ninth Key, the explanation went. *Ninth card in the Tarot, the Hermit guides the souls of the dead past the temptation of illusory fires by the roadside, so that they may go straight to their higher goal.*

Gina had drawn a balloon coming from the hermit's mouth, in which she'd penned the words, *Hi, I'm Suze, I'll be your spiritual guide to the afterlife. All right, which one of you lousy spooks took my lip gloss?*

"Sue?" Tad sounded concerned. "Sue, are you still there?"

"Yeah," I said. "I'm here. That's really too bad, Tad. I'll miss you."

"Yeah," Tad said. "Me, too. I'm really sorry you never got to see me play."

"Yeah," I said. "That's a real shame."

Tad murmured a last good-bye in his sexy, silky voice, then hung up. I did the same, careful not to look in Jesse's direction.

"So," Jesse said without so much as an excuse-me-for-eavesdropping-on-your-private-conversation. "You and Tad? You are no more?"

I glared at him.

"Not," I said, stiffly, "that it's any of your business. But yes, it appears that Tad is moving to San Francisco."

Jesse didn't even have the decency to try to hide his grin.

Instead of letting him get to me, I picked up the tarot card Gina had sent me. It's funny, but it looked like the same one CeeCee's aunt Pru had kept turning over when we'd been at her house. Had *I* made that happen? I wondered. Had it been because of me?

But I was certainly no great shakes as a conductor of souls. I mean, look how badly I'd messed up the whole thing with Doc's mom.

On the other hand, I *had* figured it out eventually. And along the way, I'd helped stop a murderer. . . .

Maybe I wasn't quite as bad at this mediating thing as I thought.

I was sitting there in the middle of my bed, trying to figure out what I should do with the card—Pin it to my door? Or would that generate too many curious questions? Tape it up inside my locker?—when somebody banged on my bedroom door.

"Come in," I said.

The door swung open and Dopey stood there.

"Hey," he said. "Dinner's ready. Dad says for you to come downst—Hey." His normally idiotic expression turned into a grin of malicious delight. "Is that a *cat*?"

I glanced at Spike. And swallowed.

"Um," I said. "Yeah. But listen, Dope—I mean, Brad. Please don't tell your—"

"You," Dopey said, "are . . . so . . . *busted.*"

For a look at more books by

MEG CABOT

check out the following pages!

Still not enough?
For even more about Meg Cabot, go to

www.megcabot.com

You can read Meg's online diary,
find the latest info on her books,
watch her vidlit video, and win fabulous prizes!

Is it just bad luck . . .
Or could it be Witchcraft?

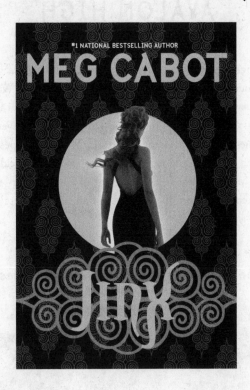

Is she just the unluckiest girl on the planet, or could Jean "Jinx" Honeychurch actually be . . . a witch?

Since the day she was born, Jinx has been a lightning rod for bad luck—everything just seems to go wrong when she's around. But she's sure her luck is going to change, now that she's moving to New York City to stay with her aunt, uncle, and super-sweet cousin Tory. Because things can only get better, right? Wrong! Not only is Tory not super-sweet anymore, she thinks she's a witch. She even has a coven of other pretty Upper East Side girls. Jinx is afraid they might hurt someone with their "magic," but she isn't sure how to stop them. Could Jinx's bad luck be the thing that saves the day?

1-800-WHERE-R-YOU

Ever since a freakish lightning strike, Jessica Mastriani has had the psychic ability to locate missing people. But her life of crime-solving is anything but easy. If you had the gift, would you use it?

Read them all!

WHEN LIGHTNING STRIKES
CODE NAME CASSANDRA
SAFE HOUSE
SANCTUARY
MISSING YOU

ALL-AMERICAN GIRL

What if you were going about your average life when all of a sudden, you accidentally saved the president's life? Oops! This is exactly what happens to Samantha Madison while she's busy eating cookies and rummaging through CDs. Suddenly her life as a sophomore in high school, usually spent pining after her older sister's boyfriend or living in the academic shadows of her younger sister's genius, is sent spinning. Now everyone at school—and in the country!—seems to think Sam is some kind of hero. Everyone, that is, except herself. But the number-one reason Samantha Madison's life has gone completely insane is that, on top of all this . . . the president's son just might be in love with her!

READY OR NOT

In this sequel to *All-American Girl*, everyone thinks Samantha Madison—who, yes, DID save the president's life—is ready: Her parents think she's ready to learn the value of a dollar by working part-time, her art teacher thinks she's ready for "life drawing" (who knew that would mean "naked people"?!), the president thinks she's ready to make a speech on live TV, and her boyfriend (who just happens to be David, the president's son) seems to think they're ready to take their relationship to the Next Level. . . .

The only person who's not sure Samantha Madison is ready for any of the above is Samantha herself!

*Girl-next-door Jenny Greenley goes stir-crazy
(or star-crazy?) in Meg Cabot's*

TEEN IDOL

Jenny Greenley's good at solving problems—so good she's the school paper's anonymous advice columnist. But when nineteen-year-old screen sensation Luke Striker comes to Jenny's small town to research a role, he creates havoc that even level-headed Jenny isn't sure she can repair . . . especially since she's right in the middle of all of it. Can Jenny, who always manages to be there for everybody else, learn to take her own advice, and find true love at last?

Meg Cabot is also the author of the Princess Diaries series, upon which the Disney movies are based. In the books, though, Princess Mia has yield-sign-shaped hair, lives in New York, and Fat Louie is orange. And those are the least of the differences. The following is a complete list of the Princess Diaries books:

The Princess Diaries

THE PRINCESS DIARIES, VOLUME II:
Princess in the Spotlight

THE PRINCESS DIARIES, VOLUME III:
Princess in Love

THE PRINCESS DIARIES, VOLUME IV:
Princess in Waiting

Valentine Princess
A PRINCESS DIARIES BOOK (VOLUME IV AND A QUARTER)

THE PRINCESS DIARIES, VOLUME IV AND A HALF:
Project Princess

THE PRINCESS DIARIES, VOLUME V:
Princess in Pink

A hilarious novel about getting in trouble,
getting caught, and getting the guy,
from #1 nationally bestselling author Meg Cabot

#1 NATIONAL BESTSELLING AUTHOR

MEG CABOT

Pants on Fire

Katie Ellison has everything going for her senior year—a great job, two boyfriends, and a good shot at being crowned Quahog Princess of her small coastal town in Connecticut. So why does Tommy Sullivan have to come back into her life? Sure, they used to be friends, but that was before the huge screwup that turned their whole town against him. Now he's back, and making Katie's perfect life a total disaster. Can the Quahog Princess and the *freak* have anything in common? Could they even be falling for each other?

HARPER TEEN
An Imprint of HarperCollins Publishers

But wait!
There's more by Meg:

NICOLA AND THE VISCOUNT

VICTORIA AND THE ROGUE

THE BOY NEXT DOOR
BOY MEETS GIRL
EVERY BOY'S GOT ONE
QUEEN OF BABBLE
QUEEN OF BABBLE IN THE BIG CITY
QUEEN OF BABBLE GETS HITCHED
SIZE 12 IS NOT FAT
SIZE 14 IS NOT FAT EITHER
BIG BONED
SHE WENT ALL THE WAY
RANSOM MY HEART
INSATIABLE